THE CALL OF ANCIENT LIGHT - BOOK ONE

THE CALL OF ANCIENT LIGHT

BEN WOLF

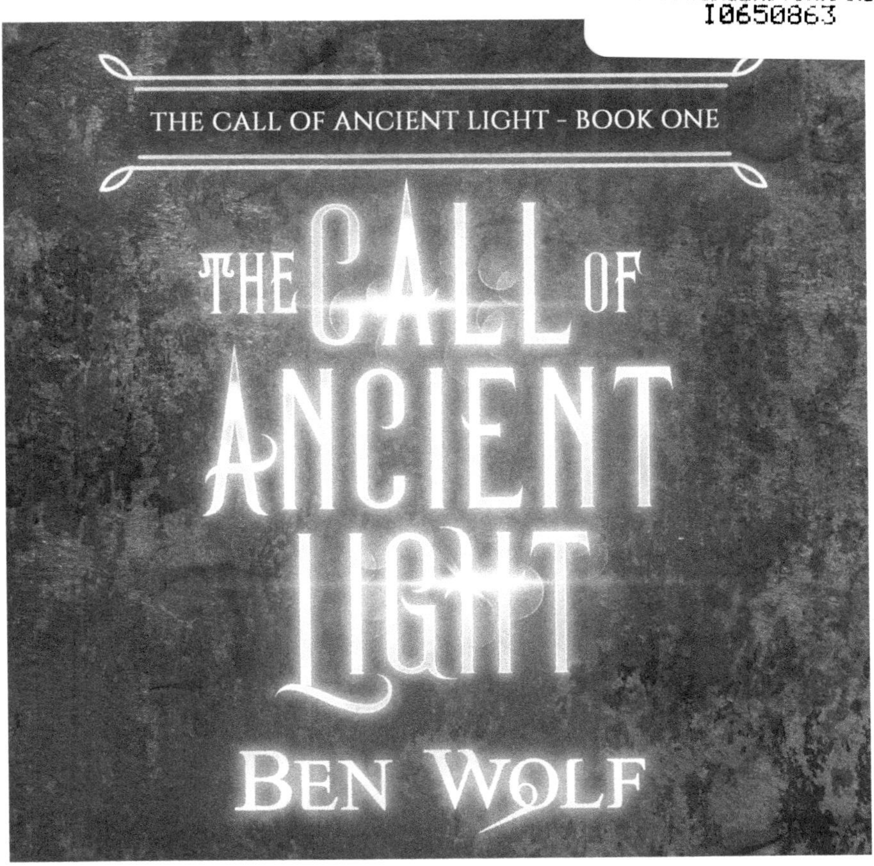

A COMING OF AGE FANTASY NOVEL

PUBLISHED BY

WWW.BENWOLF.COM

The Call of Ancient Light
Book One of The Call of Ancient Light Series

Published by
Splickety Publishing Group, Inc.
www.splickety.com

Ebook ISBN: 978-1-942462-45-3
Print ISBN: 978-1-942462-46-0

Cover design by Hannah Sternjakob
https://www.hannah-sternjakob-design.com

Contact Ben Wolf directly at ben@benwolf.com for signed copies
and to schedule author appearances and speaking events.

To Daniel Kuhnley, Paige Guido, and Luke Messa:

*Thank you for your boundless inspiration and support,
both as readers and as friends.*

CONTENTS

ORIGINAL MAP OF KANARAH

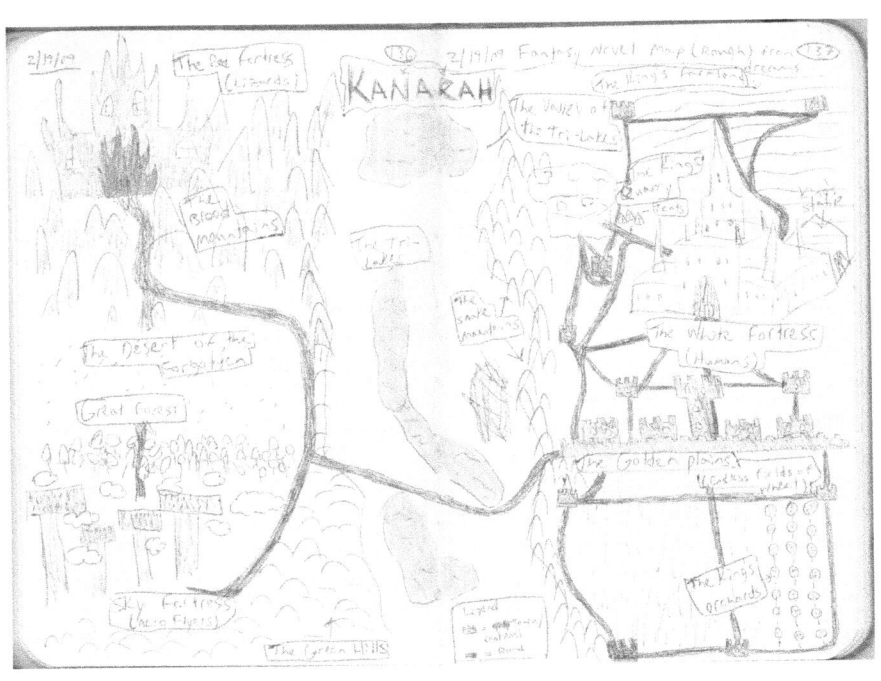

PROLOGUE

Lumen lay on a mound of ashes—all that remained of his once mighty army. After what seemed like millennia of fighting, he had lost the battle.

His sword, a silver-and-gold weapon of wondrous power, lay just beyond his reach. Close enough to tempt him, but not close enough to obtain.

Lumen's blurred vision focused on the tip of the spear that hovered over his chest. He traced its long bronze handle up to the stern face of its wielder.

The King.

"Your rebellion is finished, General of Light." The King stared at him with vibrant green eyes full of power. "And the people of Kanarah have paid the ultimate price for your betrayal."

Lumen returned the King's steely gaze. "I welcome death if it means freedom from your tyranny."

No discernible emotion crossed the King's face. "For your crimes, I banish you from Kanarah. You will descend to the deepest depths, to the Hidden Abyss itself. Your sentence shall last 1,000 years."

"You prove your foolishness once again," Lumen said. "If you spare me, I *will* return to finish this."

"Should you rekindle the fires of rebellion a second time, you will no longer face my mercy—" The King's eyes narrowed. "—but my judgment."

Lumen scoffed. "Mercy? A thousand years in the Hidden Abyss is *mercy* to you?"

"It is mercy for the people of Kanarah, not for you."

"The people of Kanarah are nothing but *slaves* to you," Lumen spat. "And when I return, I will free them from your oppression once and for all."

"*Enough.*" The King's jaw tightened with tension, and his green eyes narrowed. "Your sentence begins now."

The tip of the King's spear touched Lumen's breastplate, and fire spiraled through Lumen's veins. He screamed as his body disintegrated piece by piece, starting with his chest.

The sensation seared through his legs and arms to his fingers and toes, then crawled up his neck. Fiery grains of sand filled his vision before everything plunged into darkness and his screams finally silenced.

The 1,000 years had begun.

CHAPTER ONE

999 Years Later
Western Kanarah

A twig snapped in the darkness to Lilly's left.
She jerked upright, her eyes wide, and snatched up her bow. She nocked an arrow and held two other arrows in her shooting hand, ready to fire them in quick succession as she scanned the woods around her.

Her campfire had reduced to smoldering coals, and she breathed relief for it. No need to attract any extra attention.

Except for the hiss of tree branches swaying in the wind around her, the ubiquitous chirping of crickets, and the occasional hoot of a nearby owl, the woods remained silent. She glanced at the opening in the canopy above her. The half-moon shone brightly in the star-studded sky, and despite the wind blowing through the trees, the air seemed warmer than last night.

She'd chosen this spot on purpose. If she needed to, she could launch straight up into the night sky and away from danger. Being a Windgale had its benefits.

Lilly waited another few moments to reclaim her sense of calm and to confirm she was, in fact, alone. Satisfied, she lowered her bow and arrows, but she didn't put the other arrows back in the quiver on her hip. She wanted them in hand, just in case.

She shifted her cape, still hooked to her armor at her shoulders, into a ball under her head again, and she lay down on the rock she'd adopted as her pillow. She sighed. Not as comfortable as home by any means, but it would have to do.

Exhaustion wracked her body. Sleep encroached on Lilly's eyelids once again, and they drooped shut. A yawn stretched her lips, and she reached up to cover her mouth with her hand. Always proper, even in the wilderness.

A nearby rustle cracked her eyes open. She jerked upright.

Something moved in the trees directly in front of her. She was sure of it this time.

Enough of this. With a powerful leap, she bolted to the sky, her bow and arrows primed to fell whatever or whoever had been hounding her for the last two days.

"Come out and let's settle this!" she yelled, now hovering twenty feet off the ground.

The forest responded with another long windy hiss, but no figures emerged from the darkness. Why would they? If someone *was* following her, they would've seen her skill with her bow by now. They would know that stepping out meant death—or at the very least, an arrow lodged somewhere important.

Minutes passed, but still Lilly hovered.

Had she imagined it? Dreamed it?

Whether or not anyone had actually been following her, exhaustion continued to wear on her senses. After a week away from the comforts of home, she longed for a good night's sleep, but that wouldn't happen out here in such an unfamiliar, ever-changing setting.

And she couldn't go back. Not until her parents came to their senses.

She exhaled another long sigh and relaxed the tension on her bowstring. Unless other Windgales were chasing her, she could just as easily fly a few miles over to a different location above all of these trees.

But doing so without getting her pack, which still lay near the campfire below her, would complicate her time in the woods.

Maybe that's what they were waiting for—assuming "they" were even there to begin with. Paranoia was no way to live.

She remembered General Balena's words during her training: "Do not let fear rule you. Face it, overcome it, and become its master. Then you will be a true warrior."

A true warrior? Windgales under his charge remained soldiers for life. She wasn't one of them, and she never would be, but she took his meaning nonetheless: she wouldn't become a slave to fear.

Alright, Lilly. Enough stalling.

She'd need a free hand to grab her pack, so she tucked two of her arrows back into her hip quiver. She gripped her bow and the still-nocked arrow mid-shaft with her left hand, but with no tension on the bow's string. It freed her right hand to scoop up her pack. If needed, she could get her hand back in place in time to fire.

You're overthinking it, Lilly. Just go down, grab the pack, then fly away.

She exhaled another breath and swooped down with her right hand extended. Her fingers came within inches of the pack when a man's voice boomed from the woods.

"Now!"

Scratchy tendrils dropped over her and hauled her closer to the ground—a net, anchored by the strong arms of several men.

Lilly released the pack and shifted her right hand back to her arrow, then her right shoulder hit the ground. They had her pinned on her side, but if she could get one shot off, then maybe…

She drew the bowstring and pointed the arrow at one of the men holding the net, then released. The arrow knifed through the net's strands and plunged into his thigh. He screamed amid the other men's grunts and released his hold on the net to clutch his bleeding leg.

Good enough. Lilly clamped the arrows in her quiver to her leg so they wouldn't catch on the net and launched toward the new opening where the man had held it.

The man standing beside her victim cursed and shifted his hands over to close the gap in the net, but Lilly drove her shoulder into his chest. He fell back, and the net billowed open even wider. Lilly dug her boots into the ground and sprung out of the net's coverage, taking flight once again.

She'd ascended little more than a few feet when a pair of arms, strong and covered with dark armor, wrapped around her waist. The attacker's weight dropped them to the ground hard, stunning her. Dirt caked on Lilly's teeth, and pain from the impact sent shudders through her body.

"I've got her," a man's deep voice grunted next to her ear as his bear hug grasp adjusted to lock her arms against her sides. "Get her cape. Bring the shackles."

"No!" Lilly shrieked and tried to pull free. *Shackles?*

"Easy, Angel," the man whispered into her ear as if they were old friends. "I'm stronger than you'll ever be. No sense resisting."

Lilly strained all the more, but she might as well have been encased in steel. "Let me go!"

"Not gonna happen, Angel."

One of the other men, his eyes glistening with fiendish intent, reached for her neck. She snapped her teeth at his fingers, and he retracted his hand, then backhanded her cheek hard.

"*Hey!*" The armored man's arms released Lilly, but one of his hands still gripped her right wrist. His armored leg slammed into the chest of the man who'd slapped her and sent him skidding across the dirt until his body cracked against a tree. "No harm comes to her. *None*. Got it?"

Lilly sprang into the air again, but she couldn't free herself from the armored man's grip, and he pulled her back down. She whipped her boot at his jaw, but he yanked her to the side as if she weighed nothing before her kick could connect.

The abrupt motion wrenched her shoulder, and she yelped. The armored man pinned her to the ground facedown and held her there with his knee pressed into her back.

"Let me go!" she shouted to no avail.

"Any one of you so much as *touches* this girl and you'll deal with me, crystal?" The armored man unclasped her cape and her quiver and handed them to one of the others.

Lilly moaned. Without her cape, she couldn't fly away.

"This one's what we call a jackpot, boys. She'll fetch a pretty price, but only if she remains unspoiled."

The armored man flipped her onto her back and kept her pinned down with one hand on her sternum. He stared at her with devilish gray eyes. Spiky red hair jutted out from his head, and his square chin bobbed when he spoke.

"Oh, yes. I've got just the buyer in mind for you, Angel." To his men, he ordered, "Drug her, and remove her armor."

Lilly's stomach lurched. They were slave traders.

CHAPTER TWO

Eastern Kanarah

Aloud hiss stalled Calum's pickax mid-swing, and he jumped back. He scanned the patch of dried grass near his feet to find the serpent he'd just startled, but he didn't see anything.

The hiss sounded again, followed by deep grunts, this time behind him. Burtis, the quarry's fat foreman, led a group of armed men past him—the King's soldiers, by their black leather armor.

Among them walked a reptilian creature about seven feet tall with a long tail, a smooth green hide, and a dark-yellow underbelly. Thick steel chains and shackles bound its hands and feet, and a black leather muzzle encased its snout. As it walked past on its hind legs, it fixed its golden eyes on Calum.

He stepped back and bumped into something.

Hardink, a quarry worker in his mid-forties, shoved Calum away. "Watch where you're walkin', kid! Yous almost stepped on my bad foot."

"Sorry." Calum continued leaning on his pickax, grateful for the break, and kept staring at the creature. Its tail carved shallow streaks in the sandy dirt behind it as it walked. "What is *that*?"

Hardink scoffed. "What, never seens a Saurian?"

Calum shook his head in wonder. He'd never even heard the term before.

Hardink gingerly squatted to the ground and rocked back until he landed on his duff. There, he took to chiseling away at a stone loaded with shining gemstones embedded into it. With his bad foot, Hardink got relegated to do that kind of work rather than splitting rocks and hauling loads.

"He's a types of lizard," Hardink explained as he picked away at the stone. "But I isn't talkin' 'bout them little creepers that runs underfoot and clings to the outside of the tents at nights. I means an entire race of peoples, like that one. Walks on their hind legs. Skins get tougher the older they gets. Biggest ones gets to be eight or nine feets tall, so I hears."

"Never heard of such a thing." Through the morning sunlight, Calum squinted at the Saurian, which stood upright despite his chains.

"I seens 'em before. Not many 'round these parts. That's for sure." Hardink switched out his little chisel for a scrubbing cloth and wiped the dust from the stone in his hand. The gems caught even more morning sunlight, and they glinted with vibrant greens, blues, and reds.

The group of soldiers stopped, and their leader started talking to Burtis. Then they shook hands, and Burtis passed him a cloth bag that bulged to about the size of a child's head. In exchange, another soldier handed him a key.

Hardink squinted in the sunlight. "Looks like Burtis just boughts 'imself a new slave."

Calum frowned. "Slavery's illegal, isn't it?"

"*Ha.*" Hardink shook his head. "What do yous think *we* are?"

Calum's jaw tensed. "I'm *not* a slave."

"You're too young to knows the difference. Even so, not worth getting' upsets over it. We are what we are. Can't be helped, right?"

"No, I know the difference." Calum's eyes narrowed.

Hardink rolled his eyes and resumed his chiseling. "If yous say so."

The soldiers left the quarry behind with smiles on their faces, and Burtis approached the Saurian with one of his own. He reached to pat the Saurian on his shoulder, but the beast hissed at him.

Burtis grabbed the rope tied to the muzzle and jerked it down, and the Saurian's head went with it, finally breaking the beast's proud posture. Burtis leaned close and growled something at him, but Calum couldn't discern what it was.

"Probably shouldn't makes that Saurian mads, though." Hardink set the first gem, a ruby, in a rusted metal pan next to him. "Those things're 'bout ten times as strongs as any of us here in the quarry. He gets his hands free, he could kills Burtis or me or yous in no time. Probably could even *with* his hands bounds, for all I knows. Dangerous beasts, theys are."

Calum tilted his head. Out of all the other workers, he was both the youngest and the weakest. He'd always felt like the runt of the litter around the quarry, but the sight of the Saurian towering over everyone else made him feel even smaller, even more insignificant.

With creatures like the Saurian roaming Kanarah, what was Calum even worth?

"If they're so dangerous, why would Burtis bring one here?"

Hardink pushed himself up to his feet, leaning most of his weight on his good foot. He picked up the pan, and the gemstone rattled around in it. "Ten times as strongs means ten times the works, probably. Worth the risk. A boulder that takes seven or eight mens to moves? That Saurian can do that on his owns."

"If he's that strong, can't he break out of those shackles?"

"Now what're yous askin' me all these questions for?" Hardink shook his head and pointed at Calum's pile of rocks with the gem in his hand. "Get back to works. I gots this first gem near done, and you've made hardly any progress since thens. You wanna gets us all whipped?"

When Burtis looked over at them, Calum tightened his grip on his pickax. He raised it over his head and swung at a chunk of the boulder he'd already split once. It was a quick and careless swing that only glanced off the rock, but at least it would appear to Burtis that he'd been working the whole time.

After a few better-placed strikes, Calum stole a glance at the Saurian, whom Burtis had chained to a cart full of huge rocks.

As the Saurian pulled the cart behind him, a feat that even a trio of horses would struggle to accomplish, his golden eyes met Calum's again. Just as before, they contained nothing but disdain.

"Calum."

His head swiveled toward the call, and he almost dropped his pickax.

Burtis glared at him. One of his hands rested on his hip, and the other held a leather whip, all coiled up. For Calum and anyone else working in the quarry, that whip only meant one thing.

Pain.

He stood there, tan, hairy, and bare-chested with his belly lolling over the front of his belt. He wore his usual scowl and extended his pointer finger. "Get over here."

Calum swallowed the lump in his throat and glanced at Hardink, who didn't make eye contact with him. Hardink just kept chiseling and scrubbing the ruby in his pan.

"*Now.*"

When Calum got there, Burtis snatched the pickax from his hand and tossed it aside.

Calum braced himself for a blow, but it never came.

"You don't need that no more." Burtis held out his whip toward Calum, still coiled. "Take this. You're in charge of that thing over yonder."

Calum glanced over Burtis's shoulder at the Saurian. "You mean... *him?*"

"You deaf now? That's what I *just* said." Burtis grunted. "As it is, you're not good for much 'round here, so we're not losin' much by you not workin'."

Aside from his bald head and thick black beard, the only things that distinguished him from the other workers were a dirty purple foreman's sash he wore across his bare chest and the rusted sword hanging from his belt.

"Teach 'im all the jobs you've done here."

Calum couldn't believe his ears. Burtis wasn't known for his bright ideas, but this one was especially bad. "You trying to get me killed, boss? That thing's gonna eat me ali—"

The back of Burtis's hand stung Calum's cheek, and he staggered backward, woozy from the blow. He tasted the copper tang of blood in his mouth as he tried to regain his balance.

"What'd I say 'bout how you talk to me?" Burtis growled.

The wooziness faded, and Calum spat a red glob of saliva onto the ground. Then he clenched his teeth until Burtis grabbed him by the shoulders and shook him.

Burtis stood a few inches taller than Calum and was twice as wide, though aside from his gut, most of his bulk was muscle. And when he hit, he didn't hold back.

Before his promotion, Burtis had worked in the quarry along with the rest of the men, often doing the hardest work, including routine forays into the Gronyx's pit.

No wonder everyone feared him.

"I asked you a question, *boy*. You got an answer for me, or do I gotta beat one outta you again?"

Calum bit his lip. "You said I need to speak to you with the respect you deserve."

"Better start doin' it, then." Burtis shoved Calum to the ground and tossed the whip beside him. "You oughta count yourself lucky I picked you for this task. Make sure the Saurian learns every job, and I mean *every* job. I want 'im busy all daylight hours. He don't get no breaks. Doesn't need 'em. Crystal?"

Calum stared at the whip on the ground next to him. "If that's what you want."

"Don't be a'feared to use that thing. He's not movin' fast enough, you lash 'im once or twice. He's real sluggish, you give 'im a few more, just like I do with the men. You can't kill 'im with it, which means you can't use it too much."

"What do you mean?" Calum grabbed the whip and stood to his feet. It didn't happen often, but men in the quarry had died from excessive thrashing before, including a few by Burtis's hand.

"Saurians regenerate. They heal much faster 'an humans do. Least that's what the soldiers told me when I bought 'im." Burtis smirked, but Calum barely saw it through his thick beard. "So flay 'im as much as you like. It'll hurt 'im enough to keep 'im workin', but it won't do any lastin' harm."

Calum had already decided he wouldn't whip the Saurian unless he had to. No sense in making an enemy out of a giant—and probably carnivorous—creature. And if Hardink had been right about Saurians being another race of people, then whipping the Saurian just because he was a Saurian and could handle it was unnecessarily cruel.

Calum might've been a lot of things, but cruel wasn't one of them. He'd endured enough cruelty in his life to never wish it on anyone or anything else.

"You're done with your old job 'til I tell you otherwise." Burtis glanced over at another group of workers, all big, burly men like him. "I'll send Jidon over to help you keep 'im in line. When he's learned everything else, Jidon can show 'im how to work the Gronyx's pit. I want 'im down there this afternoon."

Calum raised his eyebrows. The Saurian had just gotten there, and Burtis already wanted him down in the Gronyx's pit?

"Don't act surprised. Just 'cause Markham died down there last week don't mean anyone else will. Asides, if we lose that Saurian, I'm only out a few hundred in gems anyway. Better 'im than one of us."

Markham had tried to run off, and when Burtis and the others had caught him and brought him back, the Gronyx pit had been his "reward." He'd gone down into the pit and never come back up.

Calum shuddered. *No one deserves that kind of fate. No one.*

Aloud, he said, "If you say so."

"Look, kid..." Burtis clapped a meaty hand on Calum's shoulder and leaned down to look him in the eyes. "You're more or less a good worker, even if you can't do but a fraction of what the rest of the men can do. And I won't be here forever, y'know."

Calum kept his mouth clamped shut. *Hopefully not.*

"You do a good job with this, you might make foreman someday. Sounds pretty good, don't it?"

Calum raised an eyebrow. *Foreman? Why would I want to be foreman of this miserable place?*

But the more he considered it, the better it sounded. It would sure beat everything else he'd been doing here for the last eight years.

"It's not like you're goin' anywhere else. Might as well get the top job here." Burtis patted his shoulder. "So don't let me down, son."

Calum's blood instantly boiled. "I'm *not* your son."

Burtis glared at him and stood to his full height. "No, you're not. Then again, I didn't get myself killed by the King's soldiers eight years ago, neither."

Calum clenched his fists, wishing he could use the whip on Burtis for his unfair jab. Through gritted teeth, he said, "Those soldiers *murdered* my parents."

"You think I care?" Burtis scoffed. "Don't care what happened then, don't care what happens to you now. Long as I meet my quota at end-of-day, none of it matters. You don't want this job, I can find someone else."

Calum exhaled a sharp breath through his nose. Compared to hauling rocks and cracking stones open, Burtis's offer was practically a vacation. "No. I'll do it."

Burtis folded his arms across his chest. "You don't seem all that interested to me."

"Thought you said you didn't care," Calum muttered.

Burtis raised his hand for another swing, and Calum flinched, but the sting never came.

"Some day, Calum, I'm gonna lose my patience with you," Burtis warned. "Lots of ways a man can die in a quarry, and I've seen just about all of 'em. Keep it up with your disrespect, and you'll find out which one of 'em hurts the most."

Calum yearned to bite back, but he bit his tongue instead.

Burtis turned toward the Saurian, who had just stopped pulling the cart. Muscles rippled in the Saurian's powerful arms and legs as he turned around and lifted the cart up. In his wildest dreams, Calum could never have hoped to be that strong.

Boulders dropped out the back of the cart into a pile, and a group of pickax-wielding workers each quickly grabbed one and began to chip away at them, as if eager to get far away from the Saurian as fast as possible. In return, the Saurian only glared at them.

"Soon as he returns that cart to the lift, you start showin' 'im 'round."

Calum looked down at the coil of whip in his weathered hands. "He got a name?"

"You don't needa know his name," Burtis sneered. "Make one up for 'im, and not a good one, neither. Do *not* be nice to 'im. He's not your friend, and he's not like the rest of the men. He's a slave. *Scum.* Worse 'an that, if there is such a thing."

Calum nodded, though he didn't like any of what he was hearing.

Burtis pointed his finger at Calum's face. "Treat 'im like that for long enough, and he'll eventually *think* like that. And if you can get 'im *thinkin'* like that, he'll be your slave forever. Crystal?"

Just like you do with the rest of us. "Clear."

"Go on, now. I'll send Jidon over with the key to unlock 'im from the cart in a minute."

Calum approached the Saurian, who backed the cart up to the edge of the quarry where a rope-and-pulley system would deliver the next load of boulders within a few minutes.

When the Saurian finished positioning the cart, he noticed Calum. His black pupils—slits instead of round like a human's—darted between Calum's eyes and the leather whip in his hands.

Calum gulped down his rising nerves and stopped ten feet from the Saurian. He could do this. The beast was shackled and chained to the cart. As long as Calum kept his distance, he'd be fine.

"You're gonna come with me now, and I'm gonna show you what's what. Show you what else you're supposed to do around here."

The Saurian's embittered golden gaze persisted, and he exhaled a loud breath through his nostrils. He still wore the leather muzzle around his snout, and his large hands rested at his sides, still shackled and clenched into scale-covered fists. He was still chained to the cart by his neck, too.

Did he understand what Calum was saying? Could he talk? Did they even speak the same language? Calum had seen a keen spark of intelligence in the Saurian's eyes, but that didn't mean they could communicate.

"Jidon will be along soon to unlock you from the cart. Until then—" Calum let the business end of the whip drop from his hand, into the dirt, and he stepped forward.

The Saurian squared his body to face Calum, and a low growl rumbled from his throat.

Now only a few feet away from each other, Calum stared up at the Saurian and tried to hide his wonder—and his primal terror—at being so near to such a monstrous creature. Calum was neither short nor especially tall, but the Saurian towered over him all the same.

Calum squeezed the whip's leather grip tighter. Burtis's direction was clear. He didn't want to whip the Saurian, and he hadn't intended to do so, but he'd already angered Burtis enough for one day.

But would that whip even get the Saurian moving in the first place? Could Calum even swing it hard enough to get the beast moving?

Ultimately, this Saurian wasn't his friend, and Calum needed to establish who was in charge. He had the whip, and he supposed he had to try to make use of it. "Look, you and I—"

"You gonna talk 'im into submission?" A burly brown-haired man stepped forward from behind Calum and snatched the whip from his hand. Jidon. "You'll never get 'im workin' that way."

If Burtis hadn't made foreman, Jidon would have. As it was, Burtis relied on Jidon for extra muscle when he needed it, whether for work or keeping order. After all, who wouldn't want the biggest, strongest worker on his side?

But as big as Jidon was, the Saurian was bigger. Even so, that didn't stop Jidon from lashing the whip at him.

The Saurian recoiled from the blows with his eyes shut but didn't try to shield himself. He withstood eight of Jidon's lashes, each of which carved long red slits into his smooth reptilian skin, some along his chest, some along his arms, and one that stretched from just below his eye down his neck.

When the onslaught stopped, he opened his golden eyes, gave another low growl, and glowered at Jidon.

"*That's* how you do it." Jidon coiled the whip and smacked it against Calum's chest so hard that he had to take a step back to keep his balance. Then Jidon faced the Saurian again. "You stay still when I unlock you from that cart, or you'll get another eight. Crystal?"

The Saurian didn't move, but his gaze narrowed. When Jidon approached, the Saurian's muscles tensed.

Calum's heart seized. "Jidon, he—"

"He's not gonna do anythin'. Not 'less he wants to get lashed again." Jidon reached for the lock that connected the Saurian's shackles to the cart and twisted a key inside. The lock popped open and fell to the ground, and Jidon stepped back. "See? Nothin' to worry about. Now, go on. Take 'im to the pit like Burtis told you."

Calum nodded. He met the Saurian's eyes. "Come on."

ALONG THE NORTHWESTERN edge of the quarry wall, a gaping hole in the ground threatened to swallow anyone who stepped too close. As perilous as the hole appeared from the outside, its true terror resided within. The Gronyx lived inside that hole, though nowhere near the surface.

Of the seventeen or eighteen men who'd entered the Gronyx's pit for gems since Calum first came to the quarry, only three had ever made it out alive. Burtis and Jidon had not only survived several encounters with the Gronyx and lived to tell about it, but they had also recovered the most precious stones Calum had ever seen, and in the highest quantities.

The third survivor was Scrim, the oldest worker at the quarry, but he never said anything about his encounters with the Gronyx. He'd been down there more times than anyone else, but he'd made it abundantly clear that he was never going back again. Now he mostly just kept to himself and stayed quiet.

Hardink once told Calum that whatever had happened during Scrim's last time down there had scarred him permanently. What that was, Scrim didn't say. He *wouldn't* say.

Between Scrim's silence and Jidon and Burtis's stories, Calum hoped he'd never have to go down there.

The Saurian, on the other hand, didn't have a choice. Burtis had decided to send him down, so down he would go.

A few of the men strapped a leather harness to the Saurian's torso then fastened a rope through some iron rings attached to the harness's straps. The rope threaded into an overhead pulley system that hung from a tall wooden A-frame that stretched over the pit.

Prior to that day, Jidon had been the heaviest person strapped to that harness, but the Saurian weighed much more. Nonetheless, Burtis insisted it would hold.

Once they secured the Saurian, he glared at all of the men and let out the same low growl as before.

Burtis grabbed the harness and pulled the Saurian close. "I know you think you're bad news because you're a Saurian. Maybe you are. Here's your chance to prove it. Bring up as much glimmer as you can carry before that thing shows up. You see a green light, that means he's comin' for you. Hurry up and get out, or you're dead, and I'm out a few hundred in gems."

The Saurian's eyes narrowed at him, and a long hiss issued through his muzzle.

"Reminds me. Better take this thing off in case you gotta fight your way out. Same with the shackles." Burtis pulled a key from the ring on his belt. "I'm gonna unlock you, but if you try anythin', I won't just drop you down there. I'll *leave* you down there 'til it gets you. Crystal?"

The Saurian snorted.

"Good enough for me. Jidon, take off his muzzle. I'll get his shackles." Burtis eyed Calum while he worked on the Saurian's bonds. "You stand over there and spot 'im."

Calum glanced at the Saurian. "What do you mean?"

Burtis tossed the shackles aside and hooked the key back to the ring on his belt. "I mean stand there and watch what happens in that hole. You see green light, you holler so we can pull 'im out."

"Got it." Calum took his position about a quarter of the way around the pit from the men who held the rope. Last thing he needed was to get knocked into it by accident.

They began to lower the Saurian into the pit. In one hand he held a pickax, and in the other he held an empty burlap sack, which Burtis expected full of gems before the Saurian came back to the surface. He made eye contact with Calum one more time before he disappeared into the darkness below.

Nothing happened for the first few minutes. All Calum could hear was the intermittent chipping of the Saurian's pickax against the inside of the pit. The rope would occasionally tug twice in succession, which meant he needed more slack. Three tugs meant to pull him up.

By Calum's estimation, they had lowered the Saurian down at least fifty feet into the pit. At sixty feet, the rope tugged three times. Then three more. Then it just kept tugging rapidly, again and again.

"Pull 'im up," Burtis said.

The two men on the other end of the pulley yanked on the rope, but it didn't move.

Burtis blinked, then pointed to three more men nearby the pit. "Go help them."

Calum stepped closer to the hole and peered down, careful not to slip down the steep slopes around it. The pickax sounds had given way to growls and a guttural rumbling.

The rope still wouldn't move.

Burtis snapped his fingers and pointed to a group of six other men working nearby. They hurried over, grabbed the rope, and began to pull. It started to retract from the pit. One foot, two feet, three feet...

A roar ascended from the pit, followed by the sound of two voices in a dissonant shriek. At first, Calum recoiled at the sound, but then he stepped forward and peered into the pit again.

...seven feet, eight feet, nine... then back to eight feet again, then seven.

The men on the other end of the rope lurched forward, and half of them tripped. A chorus of grunts and groans emanated from their direction as the rope continued to pull them toward the pulley, toward the pit.

Burtis's eyes widened. He cursed and darted over to the men holding the rope, all the while yelling for more men. Jidon grabbed ahold of it next and started hauling with all of his might.

When Calum refocused on the pit, a faint green light glowed in the darkness below. Calum's heart stuttered at the sight.

"Burtis!" Calum shouted. "There's green light in the pit!"

"Pull 'im up!" Burtis shouted. The muscles in his big arms rippled with each yank. "More men—we need more men over here, now!"

Another half-dozen nearby men dropped their tools and ran over to the rope.

"Not good enough," Burtis yelled. "We need *more*. We need everyone!"

As more men came running, Calum looked down into the pit again. The green light had brightened, and the shrieking continued.

Something cracked to his right, then above him. Calum looked up.

The frame that held the pulley crashed toward him.

Calum dropped to the ground and rolled away from the pit with his arms shielding his head. When he looked up again, the entire framework capsized and dropped into the pit. The rope followed, and the twenty or so men who held the other end skidded toward the edge of the pit.

"Pull harder!" Burtis yelled. Easy for him to say—he was at the back of the group.

Petyr, the worker at the front of the rope, inched ever closer to the edge.

Let go. Calum's jaw hung down. *Let. Go.*

Petyr didn't let go. His foot slipped over the edge, and he tipped forward, still holding the rope, and his feet dangled over the pit.

Calum's eyes widened. *Don't let go!*

"Don't stop! Pull! Pull! Pull!" Burtis leaned back and pulled with all of his body weight. The other men did the same and synchronized with Burtis's pulls. They managed to pull the rope back far enough so Petyr could find his footing again.

Calum scrambled to his feet and ran over to help, but Burtis stopped him short.

"Get back, Calum!" Burtis hollered. "Back on the edge an' spot for us. *Now!*"

Several agonizing minutes later, the men had made significant headway with the rope, but the Saurian still wasn't out of the pit. All the while, the green light in the pit had intensified, as had the mixture of roars and wails from below. Yet even with the extra light, he still couldn't see anything down there.

The men pulled faster and harder, still keeping time with Burtis.

"That's it!" Sweat glistened on Burtis's bare shoulders. "*Pull.* Don't stop."

All at once, the entire group jerked closer to the pit by two feet. Jidon's eyes widened, and so did those of several others. The pit was pulling back again.

More and more rope slid down into the pit, and the men skidded toward it.

Burtis cursed and swore. "Come on! Pull harder!"

The green light in the pit flared brighter, and the two-toned shriek screeched even louder from below. Men struggled and strained, but they couldn't help but be pulled closer, even though more than thirty of them strained at the rope.

Another wrench from the pit yanked the men forward. Their boots carved into the dirt, but it didn't help. Calum didn't know much about the Gronyx or the pit, but he knew *this* had never happened before.

On the next lurch, Petyr left his feet again, but this time he didn't hold onto the rope. He couldn't have, even if he'd wanted to. It happened too fast.

Instead, in a desperate attempt to survive, he leaped across the pit and grabbed an exposed tree root that protruded from the opposite edge. As he cried for help, the terror in his voice added to the swirl of sounds coming from the pit.

"Calum, help 'im!" Burtis yelled.

Calum rounded the pit and dropped to one knee in front of Petyr. He reached out with his right arm and kept his left behind him as a counterbalance.

Petyr glanced down at the pit, then he refocused on Calum with pure fear in his eyes. "Help me!"

Calum stretched toward him. "Grab my hand!"

Their fingertips touched, but Petyr couldn't get a grip. He latched on to the tree root again and shook his head. "You gotta get lower, or I can't reach!"

Would Calum even be able to pull him up anyway? Sure, he'd worked in the quarry for the last eight years, but Petyr was built of solid, heavy muscle.

It didn't matter. He had to try.

Calum dropped to his stomach and leaned forward as far as he could without falling in. "You gotta reach farther up. You can do it!"

Amid the screams and thundering from below, Petyr jerked upward and grasped Calum's wrist. He smiled. "Now pull me up."

Pull him up? Calum couldn't even get any leverage to get *himself* up.

He tried anyway, but he could barely hold Petyr in place, much less pull him up. "I—I can't—"

"Pull me up, kid!"

"You need to *help me.*" Calum ground his teeth. "You're too heavy!"

Petyr's eyes filled with desperation again.

Calum slid toward the pit, and his bare chest scraped against the rough sand.

"Grab onto something!" he shouted to himself as much as to Petyr, but he didn't have an angle to get a good grip on anything.

Petyr groped for the tree root again, but his fingers scraped past it, and he sunk even lower than before. His body weight pulled Calum closer to the edge. Any more and Calum wouldn't have enough counter-weight to stay out of the pit.

"Help me!" Petyr pleaded. "*Please.*"

Calum shook his head. "I can't! I can't hold you."

Petyr's eyes ignited with fear and—*anger.* He wrenched Calum's arm down and reached with his other hand. He clamped onto Calum's forearm and tried to climb out of the pit using Calum's lean body as a rope.

"No—don't!" Calum's heart jumped as his body slipped forward and pitched over the edge toward a shrieking green hell.

CHAPTER THREE

The drop ended with a sudden impact. Calum's body hit something softer than rock, yet it still cracked upon impact. He rolled off whatever it was onto the pit's gravel floor. His back and arms protested with pain, but he was alive.

Green light blanketed the rocky cave walls around him. The rank odor of decay and stagnant soil hit his nose.

His head swam, and his vision blurred. Dazed, he tried to blink the sensations away, only to see a dark massive form reaching out for him. Something else wailed from behind him. The thing latched onto his wrist and pulled him close.

The next thing Calum knew, his feet left the gravel below, and his body began to ascend. Nausea from the abrupt lift seized his stomach, and he vomited. Some of his meager breakfast hit his boots, but the rest fell past down to the dirt, now a good ten feet below.

Something slithered beneath him, but it shrank away rapidly.

He craned his head and looked up. The blue-white opening of the pit came into focus above him and approached fast. Really fast.

Calum vomited again, this time missing his boots entirely.

The green light and the shrieks gave way to hot sunlight and grunts.

Three pairs of hands hooked under his limbs and set him on the dirt. Fellow quarry workers.

What?

"Get 'em away from the edge." Burtis's bearded face appeared overhead. He reached down and took hold of Calum's left arm along with three other men and lifted him. "And don't let *him* escape."

Calum squinted in the sunlight. He turned his head to where Burtis was looking and blinked several times. The large form, the one that had grabbed him and pulled him to safety, stood to its full seven-foot height.

The Saurian.

Streaked with dirt and something like glowing green ooze, he strained against the men who pulled on his rope and harness while others surrounded him wielding pickaxes and shovels. Now free of his restraints, he had an opportunity to try to escape, albeit not a great one, but he didn't engage the men.

Instead, he let them pin him to the ground, and he exhaled long breaths through his flared nostrils, all the while focused on Calum.

The Saurian had saved him...

But why?

Then Jidon's boot plowed into the Saurian's snout.

"No!" Calum shouted and twisted out of the other workers' grips. His boots hit the ground and he charged at Jidon, lowered his shoulder, and hit him from behind.

It wasn't much, but the impact sent Jidon forward just enough that he tripped over the Saurian's torso. He sprang to his feet in a hurry and stared steel at Calum.

Calum didn't back down. "Don't hurt him. He saved my life."

Jidon snarled and stepped toward Calum with his fist raised, but Burtis caught his wrist mid-swing.

"*Enough.*" Burtis shoved Jidon back with his other hand then turned to Calum. "Don't you *ever* side with that thing over your own kind again, crystal? A man's dead 'cause of him."

The men surrounding them muttered to each other.

Sickness tinged Calum's stomach. "But I'm *alive* because of him. Doesn't that—"

Burtis backhanded Calum hard enough to awaken every latent ache from his fall into the pit. He stumbled backward, stunned but not surprised, as the taste of copper tainted his mouth once again.

"What'd I just say to you?" Burtis snapped. "You don't side with 'im over us, over me. *Period.*"

Calum dabbed at his lip and found blood on his fingers. He scowled at Burtis.

"And if you don't get that sour look off your face, I'll smack it clear off you."

"Do you got any idea what a Gronyx does with its victims?" Jidon stepped toward Calum. "It rips its food apart before it feeds. I've seen it firsthand. That's what happened to Petyr. Shoulda been that Saurian, but instead, Petyr died. You expect us to feel good 'bout that? To let him off easy? No. He's gonna pay. A life for a life."

"Jidon, shut up." Burtis stared at him. "Petyr had bad luck, nothin' more. I paid good money for that Saurian, and he's gonna work here 'til the day he dies. You don't cut 'im off early 'less I say so."

Jidon grunted and folded his arms.

Burtis refocused on Calum. "Either case, I don't want you 'round the Saurian no more. I was wrong to let you try your hand at discipline when you obviously don't got any of your own. From now on, you're back on boulder duty."

Calum glared at Burtis, but he nodded. Burtis stepped away, toward the Saurian, and barked more orders to the surrounding men.

As Calum stood there, Jidon leaned in close. "Watch out, little man. You cross me again, and even Burtis won't be able to stop me from breakin' your neck."

Calum recoiled a step. Then Jidon spat a wad of saliva on the dirt at his feet, snarled, and plodded away.

As Calum watched Jidon go, he saw something small and metal disappear in the Saurian's scaly fist. Calum squinted at it and briefly considered telling Burtis, but after that rebuke, Calum didn't care to ever speak to him again.

Instead, he grabbed a pickax and headed toward the upper level of the quarry. He took one last glance back at the Saurian, just in time to see several workers surrounding him, many of them with whips in their hands. Burtis and Jidon stood among them.

Calum didn't look back again, even when the whips began to crack.

CHAPTER FOUR

Western Kanarah

L illy woke up to find a hooded man crouched over her.
    She gasped and pushed away from him, but her back hit metal
bars. The ground under her bounced, and she stared at the hooded man,
wide-eyed. She groped for something to use to defend herself, but her
fingers found only straw.

"Easy, child." The man raised his hands and pulled the hood of his
tattered cloak from his head. Long silver hair spilled out and draped
over his shoulders. "I'm not going to hurt you. Quite the opposite, in
fact. I was trying to make sure you were alright."

Unlikely. She'd been warned about the kind of indecent men who
wandered Kanarah, men with no allegiance to anything or anyone but
themselves and their own carnal desires. For all she knew, this old man
was one of them.

"Do you know where you are?" the old man asked.

Her mind clouded with dark images and fright, but it finally started
to focus. She remembered the spiky-haired slave trader ordering them
to drug her and another man pressing a foul-smelling rag to her mouth
and nose, but nothing after that.

The old man frowned. "Aliophos Nectar. They use it to drug their fresh captures and, on occasion, to subdue unruly slaves. You've been unconscious for about half a day."

Afternoon sunlight filtered through the trees and down into the cage in patches. She realized she was in a cage atop a wagon, moving along a road of some sort, but not a well-used one. The foliage around them was far too thick and the ride too bumpy for it to be a main road.

"What?" Lilly blinked, and her heart hammered. She'd been abducted by slave traders, but she didn't want to believe it. She couldn't.

"They removed your armor and put you in here with the rest of their haul from the past week." The old man motioned over his shoulder at the wagon's two other occupants: a middle-aged woman with brown hair who kept scratching at her scalp, and a man about the same age— scraggly, dirty, and sound asleep on a mound of hay. "Including me."

The ground rumbled beneath Lilly again, and she jumped.

"Relax." The old man extended his withered hand toward her. "They're taking us somewhere. Don't know where, yet."

Lilly noticed her legs, bare from mid-thigh down to her boots, no longer covered with her light-pink armor. She noted her bare arms and stomach as well, but her white armor-lining undergarments still covered her chest and her hips, tight against her skin.

Still, she might as well have been naked. She hugged herself and retracted her legs until she sat against the bars of her cage, her knees level with her face.

Worse yet, they'd taken her cape. Even if she could get out, without her cape, she couldn't fly away.

Lilly's eyes widened. *What if—?*

"No one has touched you, child." The old man offered a sad smile. "Roderick, for all his cruelty, lives for the next coin more than for momentary thrills. As such, you are wholly intact."

Lilly squinted at him over her kneecaps, but his blue eyes betrayed no aggression, no ill-will. "Who are you?"

"I'm no one of consequence. My name is Colm, but you may call me Grandfather if you wish. I have always wanted grandchildren, but I never settled down long enough to earn them." The old man smiled at her. "And you may regard me as such a person in your life, for I have no desire to harm you or take advantage of you whatsoever."

"I'll stick with Colm, thanks." *Grandfather? Weird.* "I'm Lilly."

"You should eat something, child." Colm reached for a thin leather satchel that hung from the inside of their cage-on-wheels and removed a crust of bread. "It's not much, I know, but the three of us have eaten our share for the morning, and I made sure to save this for you."

Lilly wanted to deny his offer, but her stomach accepted with a loud rumble before she could reply. She reached for the bread. "Thank you."

Colm grabbed her wrist and pulled her close in one quick motion. Warm breath hissed past her ear in a harsh whisper, and his stubble scratched her cheek.

"I meant what I said about not harming you, but don't expect such courtesy from anyone else. You're in a far different world than the one you left, judging by your armor and your beauty. The other slaves, the slave traders themselves, and even—*especially* the slave buyers are not to be trusted. Be on your guard at all moments."

Lilly pushed away from him, more shocked at his words than his actions, but he'd been honest about not harming her. If he'd wanted to hurt her, he could have done any number of things to her while she was sleeping, or just now when he grabbed her, but he hadn't.

When she looked down at her hand, she found the crust of bread in her palm. "How did you—?"

Colm put his index finger against his lips and gave a slight nod. "Remember what I said."

Lilly nodded. She put the bread crust to her mouth.

"If you'll pardon me saying so, it helps if you don't try very hard to chew it. Just let it sit in your mouth until it softens." Colm chuckled. "At least that's what I have to do. My teeth don't work as well as they used to."

Lilly crunched into the crust and leaned back against the bars. While she chewed, the wagon came to a halt. "What's happening?"

Colm shook his head. "Nothing you'll enjoy, I'm afraid."

Three men circled around the back of the wagon, and one unlocked the door with a large gray skeleton key. Two of the others held swords in their hands and began to climb up into the cart.

"Up against the bars, all of you." One of them grunted. Colm complied immediately, as did the woman, and Lilly mimicked their actions.

The man sleeping on the wagon floor didn't move until one of the slave traders kicked his ribs. He jerked awake, yelped, then scrambled toward Lilly. She recoiled as he lunged for her, but he got ahold of her long blonde hair and yanked her over to him.

"Let go!" she yelled and resisted him, but he held her between the approaching slave traders and himself. "Colm?"

Colm didn't so much as look over at her. He just faced the bars, his legs spread, and stayed still.

"Let her go, you sack of slime," one of the slave traders said. "Or we'll gut you right now."

"N-no." The man shook his head so wildly that his long brown hair smacked against Lilly's cheeks. He curled his arm around Lilly's throat, and she caught a foul whiff of body odor. "No, you're n-not gonna t-t-touch me. You let m-me leave, or she d-dies."

"Not gonna happen. Let her go, or you'll get twice the thrashing." The slave trader grinned a crooked yellow smile. "And I'm gonna enjoy it, too."

The man holding Lilly backed against the bars. "I—I'm serious. I'll k-kill her. I know she's w-worth a lot to you. I heard you s-s-say it. You want her alive, d-don't you?"

The slave trader and his buddy glanced to the man's left, to something just outside the cage, then they snickered at each other. "Fine, you win."

"That's right. I w-win. Now—you t-two s-s-step back out of the wagon and let me g-go. She and I are g-going to—"

The wagon shifted. A loud thump, like something hard banging against metal, resounded behind Lilly, and the man's grip around her went slack. He crumpled into a heap behind her, unconscious.

When she turned around, Lilly saw the man in the brown armor with the spiky red hair. He clutched the man's long hair in one hand and held onto one of the bars with his other. A dark splotch stained one of the bars red, and a wound oozed blood on the back of the man's head.

"Get to it, already," the spiky-haired man said. "Take him to the other wagon. No one touches her, crystal?"

"Clear, boss." The slave trader with the yellow teeth sheathed his sword, and together with his buddy, he hauled the man out of the wagon, then out of sight.

The spiky-haired man dropped down from the wagon and grinned up at Lilly with one eyebrow raised. Her stomach churned at the sight. He nodded to the third slave trader, the one who'd opened the cage to begin with. "Go on. Check them. Find it."

The slave trader at the door hopped inside the wagon and drew a dagger from his belt. He bypassed the woman and headed straight for Colm.

"Easy on me, Luggs. I'm just a bag of old bones."

Luggs shoved him against the bars. "You're a thief and a liar, you are."

"Come now, Luggs." Colm shot Lilly a look and a wink—why, she didn't know—and grumbled. "I don't call you names. Seems to me you ought to be nicer to your merchandise. Maybe we'd fetch higher prices if you took better care of us."

"No one would buy your old husk anyway." Luggs patted Colm's arms and legs at regular intervals. "Believe me, we've tried."

"If I'm really a thief and a liar, then surely you'd have found someone in need of those unique skills by now."

Luggs jolted him forward again, and Colm's head smacked against the bars. A line of blood trickled down Colm's pointy nose from a small cut on his forehead.

"Face forward," Luggs ordered.

After three solid minutes of searching Colm, Luggs still hadn't found anything.

The spiky-haired man rapped the bars, and Lilly jumped. "Well? We don't have all day. I want to make the pass sometime before the end of this season."

"He's clean, sorry to say." Luggs huffed and spun Colm around. He pointed a finger at Colm's face. "You sit down and don't move. Crystal?"

Colm nodded and sat, but a smirk curled his lips.

Luggs sheathed his dagger and rubbed his dirty hands together, his gaze fixed on Lilly. He licked his chapped lips. "Alright, missy. Your turn for friskin'."

The spiky-haired man clanged his gauntlet against the bars. "Luggs, don't you lay a grubby *finger* on her."

Luggs's grin melted into a frown. "But what if she's the one who—"

"She's not, Roderick," Colm said. "She just woke up ten minutes ago."

Shing. Luggs's dagger leaped into his hand and lurched toward Colm's neck. It stopped just under Colm's chin, but he didn't so much as flinch.

For a fat guy, Luggs moved well.

"I told you to sit down and *shut up*," Luggs repeated.

Colm cleared his throat and raised his chin. "You told me to sit down and not *move*. You never said anything about talking."

"Well, I'm tellin' you now." Luggs spat a dark glob of something into the hay near Colm's boot. "So *shut up*."

"The old buzzard's right." Roderick eyed Lilly slowly—too slowly—from head to toe. "Just look at her. She's barely wearing anything to begin with. She's not hiding anything. At least nothing I intend to let any of you idiots have a go at."

Lilly shrank away from the bars and huddled close to herself. Now, for the first time in her life, she understood what it meant to be exposed. She might as well be a roasted quail in the center of the Premier's table.

Luggs ogled her too, his gaze somehow even more suggestive and revolting than Roderick's. He pulled his dagger away from Colm's throat. "I'll check the other one, then."

"You do that." Roderick still hadn't removed his gaze from Lilly.

As Luggs approached the woman, she whirled around. Silver flashed in the sunlight—a knife. She stabbed at Luggs's throat, but he blocked her attack with his forearm and bashed the pommel of his dagger into her face. She dropped into the hay, stunned.

"Stupid harpy," Luggs scoffed. "They never learn, do they?"

The woman screeched and slashed at Luggs's leg, but she missed by a solid foot. She lunged for him again, but Luggs stomped on her wrist and she dropped the blade. She wailed and clutched her wrist, and Luggs grabbed her by her hair and wrenched her upright.

"You'll learn one of these days not to fuss." He raised his hand to strike her with the dagger's pommel again.

"Stop!" Lilly didn't realize she'd yelled it until Colm stared at her wide-eyed, his eyebrows up. Now Luggs, Roderick, and the woman all stared at her as well.

"What'd you just say?" Luggs released his grip on the woman, and she shrank into the nearest corner, her eyes aghast.

"I said—"

Luggs stormed toward her. Lilly backed up, but the bars kept her from escaping. He raised his free hand, but this time, she didn't recoil from his blow. She'd watched how he moved when he hit Colm and dealt with the woman. She was ready.

Roderick yelled at Luggs to stop again, but Luggs's arm was already in motion. Lilly ducked under his swat and rolled along the hay. On her way up, she snatched the woman's knife from the floor and darted for the wagon door, which still hung open. Cape or no cape, they'd given her a chance to get out of there, and she intended to take it.

Lilly flung herself through the open door and hit the ground running.

She didn't run often—why should she when she could fly?—but the sensation of her feet thudding along the bumpy road and her legs pumping against gravity's pull invigorated her almost as much as the thought that this nightmare would soon end. She'd escaped the wagon, and soon she would be—

She skidded to a halt in front of three armed men who'd emerged from the trees. She turned to her left, but two more men with bows and arrows emerged from the brush and took aim at her. A quick pivot and she faced the woods on the other side of the road, but two more archers stepped forward, their bows ready.

What she wouldn't give to have her bow in hand right then.

A slow rhythmic clapping sounded behind her. She spun back to find

Roderick approaching. A smile split his square chin. "Well done, Angel. Well done."

She hissed a curse upon him and a prayer to the Overlord in the same breath—wrong on every level except for how honestly they both reflected her feelings. If only she had her cape.

"You didn't really think the wagon was the extent of the precautions we took to contain you, did you?" Roderick shook his head and wagged his forefinger, still coming closer.

He towered over her by almost two feet, and he had to be at least three times as wide. His armor made up some of his girth, sure, but the rest had to be muscle. She hadn't met many humans, but he certainly dwarfed any Windgale she'd ever seen, including General Balena.

"And even if you did escape, where would you go? You're barely clothed, without your cape, and with no weapons in this wilderness." Roderick eyed the knife in her hand. "Oh, *excuse* me. You have a knife. I take it all back. You'd be fine."

Lilly ground her teeth and squeezed her fists tighter.

"Look, Angel, you can either drop that knife and come back with us, and I'll let you off with a warning this time, or you can try to carve our eyes out with that toothpick while we take you back by force, and then you don't eat for two days." Roderick tilted his head and grinned at her. "Which will it be?"

Lilly clenched her eyes shut and exhaled a sharp breath. Carving his eyes out with the knife sounded pretty good, but she had to be realistic about her chances. Without her cape, her armor, and her bow, she didn't stand a chance.

Though she didn't want to do it, Lilly dropped the knife.

CHAPTER FIVE

Eastern Kanarah

A few minutes before sunset, Calum cracked open another rock and then bashed it into small enough pieces for Hardink to sift in his bowl tomorrow. Sixteen more and he'd be done.

He rolled a new rock into place, and this time he imagined it was Jidon's head when he swung the pickax. It was more or less the right size, but the rock was probably more intelligent.

Most of the other men had stopped by the shed to deposit their tools for the evening. Calum garnered more than one surly glare from the group, mostly from the men who'd been closest to Petyr, but he ignored them. It wasn't his fault Petyr had died, and he wasn't about to let anyone guilt him into believing otherwise.

About fifteen minutes later, Calum finished crushing the last of his pile and headed to the shed. He deposited his tools, but as he stepped outside, the plank leading up to the entrance shifted under his foot.

Calum stared at it for a moment, then he bent down to inspect it. Someone would need to repair that tomorrow if it had come loose. He pulled, and it separated from the parallel support rails underneath with little resistance. A glint of something crystalline stopped Calum's heart.

Gemstones shimmered under the moonlight.

Not many of them, but more than enough to bother Burtis. Well, *one* hidden gemstone would be enough to bother Burtis.

But these looked different. Brighter, somehow, and all with a greenish hue. They were stones from the Gronyx's Pit.

Burtis had once explained to him why the gemstones from the Gronyx's Pit were so much more valuable, so much more worth the risk, but Calum couldn't remember why. He'd been just a kid at the time, and he hadn't bothered to ask again.

Regardless, these were Gronyx stones, no doubt. But who had put them here?

Perhaps Calum should take them. Maybe he could use them to get himself out of this place, to start a new life somewhere else.

But if Burtis found out—

"Heys."

Calum dropped the board in place and whirled around.

Hardink stood there with a shovel in his hand, leaning on it to give his bad foot a break. "What're yous doin' there?"

"This board's loose, and I—I found—" *Careful, Calum.* "—I found it like that when I stepped on it. Was gonna try to fix it real quick."

"What're yous gonna fix it withs?"

Calum tapped the board with the corner of his boot. "Maybe there's a hammer and some nails in the shed."

Hardink chuckled. "In all my years, I never seens neither of those things in the shed where just anyones can get at 'ems. Burtis keeps 'ems somewheres else, same as the last foremans, and the foremans before. Yous might as well let someone else find that spots and fix it in the mornin'. Go back to camp and eat somethin's before Burtis gives your rations aways."

Calum squinted at him. "Why are *you* out here?"

Hardink held up his shovel. "Found this on the ways back to camps. Decided I oughta bring it backs. You know how Burtis is in the mornin' when he finds out a tool's missin'. We *all* suffers."

Calum nodded. It made sense... but it didn't completely allay his suspicions.

A smirk cut into Hardink's left cheek. "Yous gonna move so I can put this backs?"

"Yeah." Calum stepped aside. "Sorry. Just watch your step. Don't want you to trip with that bad foot of yours."

"I'll be fines. Yous runs along, now. Don't want yous complainin' that you're hungry in the mornin'."

"Shouldn't I wait for you? If you fall on your way back to camp—"

"Then I'll gets up and keeps goin'." Hardink turned back to him. "My foot's messed up, but I can still walks. I'm not an old lady, yous know."

Calum feigned a laugh, then he regretted it. *Too obvious?*

Hardink shook his head. "Go ons. Gets outta here. I'll be fines."

Sweat trickled down Calum's back. He couldn't stay there. If he did, it would give something away, whether Hardink had stashed those gems or not. He nodded and started walking. He glanced over his shoulder once, but Hardink had already disappeared inside the shed.

Calum sighed and headed back to camp. He'd check the stones again tomorrow night after work. If they were still there, maybe he could make a run for it.

"THIS IS FOR YOU." Axel leaned forward and passed a small pouch no bigger than a man's fist across the table to Calum, then he scoured the tavern with his eyes. A few other quarry workers sat around some of the other tables, but no one seemed to be paying them any mind.

Calum squinted at it, then he met Axel's dark-blue eyes. He loosened the string, poked his fingers inside, and pulled out two small red peppers.

"These two ripened early, before the rest of the crop." Axel smiled. "Well, a few others, too, but these are the ones I managed to hide. Might be able to get you a few more over the next couple days."

"Thanks." Calum matched his smile.

Axel leaned back. "Don't mention it. Ever. Seriously. To anyone."

"Obviously."

"You're like a little brother to me. It's the least I can do. Actually, it's about the most I can do, too."

The men who worked at the quarry got the vast majority of their food from Axel's family farm. Ever since Calum had landed in that quarry camp, he'd gone along with the men every evening to collect their share of food.

When Calum first showed up, Axel was ten and already almost twice his size. Now, at sixteen, Calum had caught up a bit, but Axel, at nearly eighteen, still had three inches of height and a solid fifty pounds on him. Unlike Calum, he had dark-brown hair with a bit of curl to it, a stark contrast against Calum's short blond hair.

Axel had looked out for Calum ever since his first night with the workers, at least as much as he could. He worked on his farm all day while Calum worked the quarry, so they only got to see each other in evenings, and usually not for longer than an hour.

"What else did they ration out for you?" Axel asked.

Calum tucked the peppers back in the pouch and dropped it into his satchel along with the rest of his food. "Looks like a boiled potato, a roasted chicken leg, and a slice of barley bread."

Axel rested his fists on the table. "Heard something happened today. You alright?"

Calum nodded at the sobering reminder of the Gronyx's pit and what had almost become of him. "Yeah. I'm fine. A bit bruised up, but I'm alright."

"Heard a Saurian pulled you out. Big green brute. Might as well be a monster." Axel scratched at a rough patch on the table with his finger-nail. "Lucky for you they're keeping him in line. He had plenty of lash marks all over him."

Calum's stomach soured. The last thing the Saurian deserved was that kind of treatment.

"Hey." Axel reached across the table and slapped Calum's bare shoulder. "After a day like that, you'll sleep real good tonight."

Calum smiled. "Burtis also told me I could be foreman someday."

Axel's grin melted.

Calum exhaled a sigh when he noticed it. What was Axel going to say now?

"He said you might make foreman, huh?"

"Yeah, he did." Calum read the frown on Axel's face. "Look, I know it's not much, but it's as good as it gets in this type of life."

Axel shrugged. "If you say so."

For all of his good brotherly qualities, Axel sure had some bad ones too.

"Not everyone gets to inherit a massive family farm when their parents are gone," Calum said. "Not all of us even have parents anymore."

"Come on, Calum. My parents work for the King, same as you do. Same as I do. This farm may be ours in ink, but we all know it belongs to the King and his soldiers, the same people responsible for what happened to your parents."

Calum shook his head. "Doesn't mean you should look down on me for wanting to accomplish something with my life."

"You think being the quarry's foreman is 'accomplishing something with your life?'" Axel scoffed. "It's the exact opposite of that. It's a waste. I want something better for you than that. I want something better for myself than inheriting a farm that doesn't really belong to me."

Calum rubbed his forehead with his fingers and closed his eyes. "Why? We'll both eat well for the rest of our lives. Does anything else really matter?"

"Absolutely." Axel smacked the table with his palm, and Calum's eyes opened. "I want to get out of here, find some adventure. I want to make some coin, learn to fight, and live life the way *I* want to live it. I want to find a beautiful woman and feel the warmth of her body close to mine. I want children of my own someday. Doesn't any of that matter to you?"

Calum thought back to the stash of gemstones he'd found under the walkway board. If he could get ahold of those and get a bit of a head start, maybe what Axel was proposing was possible.

Or maybe Axel's big dreams had infected them both long enough, and only a dose of reality would cure them.

"It *sounds* good, but I can't have any of it." Calum sighed. "I might as well stay here, do good work, and honor the King—with a full belly every night."

"You want to honor the man responsible for your parents' deaths?" Axel shook his head. "That's no way to live. Not all slaves wear chains. You're no different than that Saurian. You're a *slave.*"

Calum exhaled a furious breath through his nose and clenched his teeth. If he weren't so sure Axel could pound his face in, Calum would have taken a swing at him.

Why did he have to be so weak? Why hadn't he been born stronger? Would he always be this way?

Calum's chest filled with frustration. In the end, all he'd ever be was a quarry worker.

Axel put his hands up. "Hey, don't get mad at me. I'm not the one who sent you to the quarry when your parents died. I just want something better for you. Better for us both."

Calum slung the satchel over his shoulder and stood up. "I need to get going. I gotta get up at sunrise, and I still have to eat. Good night."

"Come on, Calum. Don't be like that."

"No. You're right, Axel," Calum said, allowing his anger to underpin his words. "I'm a slave. I know I am. But I don't know how to be anything else, except maybe foreman someday. It's good enough for me, so maybe you should be happy for me instead of bringing me down."

Axel folded his arms, still sitting. "How can I be happy for you when being foreman is still being the King's slave? Just with more perks?"

Calum shook his head. "Fine. Then don't be happy for me. But don't talk to me about it either."

"Calum, I—"

"Enough. I'm leaving." Calum reached into his satchel and extracted the pouch of peppers. He tossed it on the table in front of Axel. "Here. A *slave* shouldn't get special treatment."

"Calum, those are for you," Axel hissed. "Take them."

"No. I don't want any favors from you."

Axel stood up and rounded the table with the pouch in his hand. He glanced around the room and uttered, "I don't care if you're mad at me. Don't make a scene. You're *going* to take these."

"No, I'm not." Calum ground his teeth.

"*Yes*, you are. Do you have any idea what my parents would do to me if they found out I took these for you?" He eyed the nearby workers, but as before, no one appeared to care. "Or what they'll do if I bring them back and they find them on me or in my room? You're taking them."

"I said I'm—"

"I will beat you *senseless* if you don't take them." Only a hint of humor lined Axel's threat. "I'll beat you senseless, stick them back in your satchel, and dump your unconscious body in your tent if I have to."

Calum glared at him and clenched his fists, powerless to do anything other than refuse.

"You know I will. Take them." Axel extended the pouch again.

Calum loosed an angry sigh. The only way he was getting out of there was with those peppers in his possession. Might as well get it over with.

He snatched the pouch from Axel's hand and dropped it into his satchel. He turned to leave, but Axel caught his wrist.

"Like I said before, you're like my little brother, my best friend." Axel clapped his hand on Calum's bare shoulder, just as Burtis had done earlier that day. It awakened the aches in Calum's body from his fall into the Gronyx's pit. "I only want what's best for you."

"Good night, Axel." Calum twisted out of Axel's grasp and headed out of the tavern.

———

BACK AT THE CAMP, Calum noticed the Saurian chained to a thick wooden post about twenty feet from the nearest tent. Even in the faint light of the dying campfire, Calum could see the red lines that streaked across his green hide. He hunched forward with his head leaned against the post.

Calum glanced at a few of the nearby tents then took a tentative step toward the Saurian. Then a few more. He got within ten feet before the Saurian looked up at him. When he did, the dismay in the Saurian's golden eyes sharpened to fury.

Calum stopped. The Saurian had his muzzle on again. Had Burtis and Jidon bothered to feed him anything after the whipping?

"Hey," he whispered.

The Saurian's gaze sank back down to the dirt, and he leaned his head against the post again.

After another quick scan of the camp, Calum took another step forward.

The Saurian's head swiveled toward him, and he gave the same low growl he'd given earlier that day.

Calum stopped. What was he even doing there in the first place? Maybe this was a bad idea.

But Calum *had* to continue forward. The Saurian had saved his life, after all. He swallowed the lump in his throat and stepped within five feet of the Saurian.

"Hey," he repeated, even quieter this time. "Did anyone feed you anything?"

The Saurian didn't move, didn't blink. He just projected golden-eyed anger at Calum.

Calum reached into his satchel and pulled out the potato. "Do you want this?"

Nothing.

Calum squinted at him. He dropped the potato back in the satchel and pulled out the slice of barley bread. "This?"

Still nothing.

What did Saurians eat anyway? Calum tried the peppers next.

Zero movement.

The only thing left was Calum's roasted chicken leg. It was a big piece too, for once. About half the thigh was still connected, plus the drumstick was a good size. He didn't really want to offer it, but... "How about this?"

The Saurian tilted his head, almost indiscernibly.

Shoot. That's what he wanted. Calum wished he hadn't offered it.

But after how things had gone that afternoon, the Saurian probably needed it more than Calum did. "Well... I guess you can have it."

Now the Saurian glanced around the camp just as Calum had a moment earlier.

"I'm serious. I'm not trying to fool you." Calum stepped closer. "I owe you at least this much."

The chain that connected the Saurian's shackles stretched around the post, but the silver talons on the tips of each of his scaly fingers gave Calum pause. Nonetheless, he took another step forward and extended the chicken leg.

His hand shook. Calum blinked and tried to calm his hammering heart. Hardink and Burtis had both warned him what the Saurian was capable of, and he'd seen it in action up close.

Calum stopped, and the Saurian huffed a sharp breath through his nostrils. Was a piece of chicken worth his *life*?

He was overthinking it. If the Saurian had wanted to harm him, he would've abandoned Calum at the bottom of the pit.

He was a slave. Just like Calum.

And even slaves needed to eat.

Now only three feet away, Calum took another step.

That's when the Saurian lunged forward.

Calum recoiled, but he was too slow. The Saurian grabbed his arm and pulled him forward. The chicken leg dropped to the dirt.

Something sinewy and strong pressed Calum's back and pinned him against the post, and the Saurian's other hand clamped over his mouth before he could cry out.

He'd made a mistake. A terrible mistake. And he was far too weak to pull free.

He should have listened to Burtis. To Hardink.

Too late now.

A long hiss overwhelmed Calum's hearing, and the Saurian's hot breath heated Calum's face. How would the Saurian do it? Would he snap Calum's neck? Would he jam his talons into Calum's gut and let him bleed to death on the ground next to him?

Nothing happened.

Calum just stood there, his heart racing, his breaths short and quick. Wide-eyed, he craned his neck to look up at the Saurian.

The beast nodded at him, then slowly pulled his hand away from Calum's mouth.

What was going on?

The pressure on his back subsided, and the Saurian released Calum's wrist. Calum staggered back and stared at the Saurian, who bent down and reached for the chicken leg, but it lay too far out of reach for him to get it with his hands.

His long green tail, which must've been what he'd used to pin Calum to the post, snaked through the dirt and pulled the chicken close enough that he could grab it. He held it up to his mouth, still covered by that muzzle, and tapped his snout with one of his fingers.

Calum didn't move. He still didn't understand what was happening.

The Saurian rotated his body around the post and tapped his snout with his other hand, the one not holding the chicken. He growled again, but it didn't sound as angry.

Now he wanted help? He'd just attacked Calum—kind of—and now he expected Calum to help him?

The Saurian turned again and tapped the back of his head.

Calum blinked again. "You want me to take off that muzzle?"

The Saurian nodded.

After what just happened, Calum didn't know whether he should trust the Saurian or not. Yes, he'd saved Calum's life, but why had he behaved so erratically when Calum had drawn near? And if Calum got that close again, what would happen?

"You're not gonna hurt me, right?"

The Saurian shook his head.

So it *did* understand Calum.

But if it understood Calum, that meant it could be lying, too.

Calum glanced at the chicken leg clutched in the Saurian's talons. He couldn't just leave the beast there with food in his hands but unable to eat it. It wasn't fair, wasn't humane.

Humane. Did that word even apply to Saurians?

Hardink had called Saurians a type of people, but Burtis's words resurfaced in Calum's head: *Do not be nice to him.*

Whatever, Burtis. He'd already gone this far. And Burtis was an idiot.

Calum swallowed and hesitated, then he closed the distance and started to unfasten the straps on the back of the Saurian's muzzle. A moment later, he pulled it off the Saurian's snout.

The Saurian opened his jaws wide, as if stretching them out, and Calum stumbled back at the sight of his long sharp teeth, his red tongue, and his gaping throat. Definitely a meat-eater.

The chicken leg and half-thigh disappeared in one large chomp, bones and all.

Calum realized how far down his jaw was hanging and shut his mouth. He looked at the muzzle in his hand, then back at the Saurian. "Do you have a name?"

The Saurian squinted at him.

"Do you speak?"

Nothing.

"Do *any* Saurians speak?"

Still nothing.

"Fine. But now I need to put this back on you."

A familiar low growl rumbled from the Saurian's thick throat.

Calum glanced around again. "Look, if they find you without this in the morning, you're gonna get whipped even worse, and then Burtis will start asking *us* questions. That means no more food for you, at least not from me. Is that what you want?"

The Saurian exhaled a long breath through his nose then motioned with his head for Calum to come back over. The Saurian stretched his jaws once, then he allowed Calum to secure the muzzle on his snout.

Calum stepped back and assessed his work. Good enough. "Well, I'm off."

As he turned away, a snort sounded, distinct against the crickets chirping somewhere in the moonlit woods beyond. Calum glanced back, and the Saurian gave him a slight nod.

Calum allowed himself a timid grin and nodded back, then he headed for his tent.

Inside, Calum set his satchel on his bedroll and sat next to it. Good thing he'd gotten a whole potato tonight, or he would've gone more hungry than usual. He unpacked the peppers Axel gave him plus the potato and the barley bread, then he tucked the satchel under his bedroll.

He picked one of the peppers up and studied it—red, with a tinge of yellow and some green close to the stem. He couldn't let them go to waste, no matter how much of a jerk Axel had been to him. Food was too precious a resource.

Still, he couldn't shake the idea that Axel was right. What if Calum just... left? What if he abandoned the quarry and tried to make his own way in the world?

Whenever other quarry workers—other *slaves*—had fled in the past, Burtis, Jidon, and some of the other men chased after them. They looked at it almost as if it were a sport, a welcome interruption to the everyday grind of quarry life.

Thus far, no one had ever escaped. Markham was the last one who'd tried, and it had gotten him sent down to the Gronyx's pit—and he never came back out.

Even if Calum had some of those hidden gemstones, he didn't stand a chance against Burtis and Jidon. So what was the point of even trying?

What he'd said to Axel back in the tavern was true enough: He'd be stuck in the quarry forever. That was the reality of his life, and no amount of dreaming would ever change it.

Calum lay on his side and took a bite out of his boiled potato, and within fifteen minutes of finishing his dinner, he fell asleep.

LIGHT PENETRATED the darkness until it washed out Calum's vision. He tried to shield his eyes with his hands, but nothing he did could block out the brilliance. It shined through him as if his body were made of glass.

From deep within the light, a figure emerged. White armor covered his strong limbs, and a silver-and-gold sword hung from his belt. A golden crown glistened atop the figure's head, and his eyes flickered like two balls of fire above a white half-mask that covered his nose and mouth.

Calum's jaw hung open. *What in the—*

The figure drew his sword and traced a circle made of white fire. In the center appeared an image of three lakes with a path that ran through the middle.

Calum could've been looking at a map, except the image moved as if he was seeing it while flying overhead. The view narrowed onto the path, followed it from one side of the lakes to another, then it centered on the base of some red mountains.

A black hole appeared in the rocks like a yawning mouth.

"Go, Calum. Find the Arcanum. Discover the way to set me free." A voice resonated around Calum. *Within* him. "Go, Calum."

CALUM BLINKED AWAKE, and the figure and the map vanished. What had he just—

"I said *wake up*, Calum." Someone shook him by his shoulders.

Calum blinked again. Rather than the ethereal face from his dreams, Burtis's ugly bearded mug hovered over him, and the sound of men chattering and shuffling around the camp reached his ears.

"What?" He tried to push Burtis's hands away.

"Get outside." Burtis straightened up, his head almost reaching the ceiling of Calum's tent. "The Saurian's escaped."

CHAPTER SIX

Burtis stormed out of the tent, and Calum rubbed his eyes.
What a weird dream.

Calum pulled on his old wool shirt, then his trousers, then he stepped outside.

Sure enough, the camp buzzed with quarry workers, most of whom held torches and pointed in various directions amid a peculiar mix of yawns and frantic conversations. Some of them held ropes, and others held thick tree branches as makeshift clubs.

The weirdness of Calum's dream still lingered in his mind. The blinding light, the white figure who'd appeared, and the map—none of it made any sense.

And what was an "Arcanum?"

Maybe those peppers he'd eaten hadn't agreed with him. Whatever the case, he could sure use a few more hours of sleep.

A yawn stretched Calum's jaw, and he rubbed his eyes again. When Calum's vision refocused, Jidon stood in front of him. Then his fist plowed into Calum's gut.

Calum dropped to his knees and clutched his stomach, overwhelmed by pain and the sudden lack of breath in his lungs. He sucked for air, but his lungs felt like they'd shriveled to a fraction of their original size.

"*Where* is he?" Jidon spat on the ground only inches from Calum's head.

"I don't—" Calum wheezed and looked up at Jidon, wide-eyed. Why had Jidon singled him out? "—know."

Jidon grabbed Calum's wrist and yanked him to his feet. "You sure 'bout that?"

Calum glanced past Jidon at Burtis, who stood by the campfire talking to several other men, including old Scrim and Hardink. Burtis wouldn't be around to intervene this time.

That meant Calum would have to handle this himself... or he'd pay the price by himself.

"*Hey.*" Jidon's stubbled, sour face filled Calum's view. "I asked you a question."

"I said I don't know." Calum tried to pry Jidon's hand free from his wrist, but Jidon wouldn't release him. "Let me go!"

"You spent more time with 'im today than anyone. He didn't say nothin' to you? Didn't drop no hints?" Jidon flicked Calum's cheek with his fingers. "Huh?"

"Cut it out!" Calum dug his fingernails into Jidon's wrist. He doubted it would be enough to make him stop, but to his surprise, it worked.

Jidon retracted his arm and stared at the red marks Calum's fingernails had left. Given their size disparity, Calum only had one option now: he threw a kick square into Jidon's groin, and Jidon doubled over in pain.

"How do *you* like it?" Calum glowered at him.

Jidon roared. He flailed his arm at Calum, who was ready for some sort of wild attack and backed away, and Jidon missed.

But Calum hadn't expected to trip over something behind him. He fell and landed on his back, and the breath almost pushed out of his lungs again.

Meanwhile, Jidon reached for the campfire and wrenched a burning log free by its unburnt end. Embers wafted into the night air, and Jidon started toward Calum.

Every alarm bell in Calum's head rang loud and clear as Jidon stormed closer. Calum scrambled to get back up to his feet, to run, to get away, but the well-worn soles of his boots kept slipping on the dewy grass.

Now looming over Calum, Jidon raised the flaming log high over his head.

Calum shielded himself with his arm.

Then two sets of strong arms wrapped around Jidon's arm and kept him from pulverizing Calum.

Burtis's voice split the night. *"Enough, Jidon."*

The log dropped, and Burtis kicked it back toward the fire.

Jidon twisted out of Burtis's grip and pointed an accusatory finger as Calum hurried to his feet. "He kicked me in my—"

"You got what you *deserved.*" Burtis stood neither as tall as Jidon nor as wide, but he had no trouble yelling louder. "Lay another finger on 'im again, and I'll crack your skull. Crystal?"

Jidon backed away from Burtis, but his steely-eyed focus remained on Calum.

Burtis shoved him and snarled, "I asked you a *question.*"

"Clear." Jidon spat on the ground at Calum's feet again.

"Take a quarter of the men north. I'll take a quarter east. Parkus will take another quarter west, and Scrim will head southeast to get the King's soldiers." Burtis spun around and surveyed the men in the camp. "First group to find 'im gets a double share tomorrow at breakfast. First man who spots 'im gets a whole day off. Now git!"

The men cheered and jogged in four different directions, including Jidon and Burtis. Calum pushed himself up to his feet and started after Parkus's group, but a glint caught the corner of his eye.

There, on the ground next to a set of shackles near the Saurian's post, something glimmered in the light of the campfire. Calum bent down and dug a small piece of metal from the dirt.

A bronze ring, bent straight. One of the rings used to secure the rope to the Saurian's harness before they lowered him into the Gronyx's Pit.

The Saurian had concealed it in his fist after the men hauled him back up to the surface. That's what Calum had seen. Then the Saurian must've somehow used it to pick the locks on his shackles.

A realization hit Calum's mind, stark and bright, just like the dream he'd had only minutes ago.

The plank at the shed. The hidden gemstones underneath. If Hardink hadn't hidden them...

Then perhaps the Saurian had.

The last place Burtis and the men would look would be back at the quarry. Why would the Saurian go back there, of all places? He wouldn't have had a reason to—unless he'd hidden those gemstones on purpose and was using them to escape.

Calum didn't know when the Saurian would've had time to stash them away, but he hadn't been working around the giant lizard at all after the incident at the Gronyx's pit. Maybe he'd hidden the gems then.

Then another realization hit Calum. There would be no better time to flee the quarry than right now. With Burtis, Jidon, and the rest of the men distracted, Calum could just leave. But he would need those gemstones in order to get himself beyond Burtis's reach.

And if the Saurian was already going for them...

Calum made his choice. He ran back to his tent, grabbed his satchel, tied up his bedroll, and secured both to his back. If Calum could get to the gemstones before the Saurian, perhaps he could run and buy his way to freedom once and for all.

WITH ONLY THE moon and stars above, the quarry resembled a blue desert with a massive sinkhole in its center. Calum approached in silence, aware that the Saurian could be hiding somewhere nearby.

The shed looked undisturbed, at least from a distance, but that didn't mean anything. The Saurian could be inside or standing behind it. Or not there at all.

Did Saurians have better hearing than humans? Could they see better in the dark? They were stronger and could regenerate after being injured, but what else might Calum encounter that he didn't already know?

Calum snuck toward the shed, staying low. Nothing moved. What little grass rimmed the quarry's perimeter swayed in a slight breeze from the northwest.

When he made it to the shed, Calum headed straight for the loose plank. He lifted it up without a sound and reached his fingers into the space beneath.

Nothing.

He shifted so his body wouldn't block the moonlight, just to double-check.

Still nothing. The stones had been taken.

Calum's heart sank. Should he still try to run? How far could he get without the gemstones to help him along the way? Where would he even go? How would he find food?

Something rustled behind him.

Calum whirled around, and a thick tree branch slammed into his side. The blow sent him careening against the shed door.

Not a branch—the Saurian's tail.

Calum's ribs ached, and he crumpled to the ground, wheezing. Why did everyone keep knocking his breath away?

In one massive leap, the Saurian closed the distance to Calum and pinned him against the shed door with one massive hand against his chest.

"Wait!" Calum held his hands in front of his head and sank lower against the door, struggling to breathe.

"Do not presume to give me orders, *boy*." The words flowed from the Saurian's mouth like an angry flood.

Calum's eyes widened. "You—you can talk?"

The Saurian glowered at him.

"Just don't hurt me." Even as Calum said it, his gut and ribs flared with pain from the Saurian's tail strike. He added, "Anymore."

"I should *kill* you." The Saurian's deep voice rasped in his throat.

"Please don't!" Calum almost begged, holding his hands up.

"And why should I not?"

"You—" Calum shook his head, his heart thundering. The only response he could muster was the truth. "You saved me today. Why would you kill me now?"

The Saurian's golden eyes narrowed, but he pulled his hand away from Calum, who wheezed and rubbed his aching side. He stared up at the Saurian, who rose to his full height.

"Your life is just as worthless now as it was then," he growled.

In spite of his aching side, Calum pushed himself to his feet. He didn't know which hurt more—his ribs or the Saurian's remark. "Hey, I stood up for you today."

No response. With one arm, the Saurian shoved Calum aside, clearing his path to the shed. Calum tumbled into the prickly grass surrounding it, and the Saurian yanked on the old lock that secured the shed door. It ripped through the door latch and took a chunk of wood with it. The Saurian tossed them both away.

Though the sight amazed him, Calum refused to show it. He quickly stood back up, wincing. "I said I stood up for—"

"I heard you the first time."

"And?" Calum followed the Saurian inside the shed, which was now considerably darker inside at night than during the daytime.

"And what?"

"Doesn't that mean anything to you?"

The Saurian eyed the tools that hung from the walls rather than making eye contact with Calum. "You are alive. According to the laws of Kanarah, we are more than even."

Calum raised an eyebrow. "Why *did* you save me in the Gronyx's pit?"

"Why did you bring me food earlier tonight?"

"Because I didn't like how the others were treating you."

The Saurian reached for a large pickax, one that only the strongest men in the camp could wield. Calum could barely lift the thing, much less swing it, but the Saurian hefted it as if it weighed nothing.

"You didn't answer my question," Calum said.

The Saurian stopped and looked down at him. "What do you want, boy?"

Calum blinked. What *did* he want? "I—"

"If you intend to tell your friends where I am, you had better do it quickly. I will not tarry here much longer." The Saurian strapped the pickax to his back with a leather belt and fastened a coil of rope to another belt that he clasped around his waist.

"That's not what I—"

"Then *what?*" the Saurian snapped.

Calum's mouth hung open. *Maybe we could... but the gems aren't...*

Up until this point, fleeing the quarry had only been a foolish dream for Calum. The hidden gemstones, Axel's prodding, and the Saurian's escape had given Calum hope that maybe he'd actually be able to pull it off.

But now the Saurian had provided a way out, a means of escape—with or without the gemstones. Whether the Saurian had taken the gems or not, he was leaving the quarry. If he could do it, so could Calum.

"*Speak,*" the Saurian grunted.

"I—" Calum's doubts got the better of him. "I don't know."

"Then get out of my way." The Saurian pushed past Calum, heading for the outside once again.

"I want to come with you," Calum blurted, but he wasn't sure he believed it.

The Saurian stopped in the shed's doorway. "You do not even know where I am going."

"I don't care," Calum said, his resolve growing. "I can't stay here. Anywhere is better than here."

"You are in training to become the foreman of this place someday. Is that not what you want?"

Calum frowned.

"Do not act surprised. I am not deaf."

Calum shook his head. Axel had been right all along. There was nothing for him here anymore. There never was.

"I want to go with you. I don't want to stay here. I can't be a—" Calum bit back the emotion rising in his chest. "I can't be a slave anymore. Please let me come with you?"

The Saurian stared at him for a long moment until he finally said, "No."

Calum's heart sank. He'd put himself out there, tried to grab at the freedom just barely within reach, and the Saurian had snatched it away with a single word.

Calum swallowed down his frustration. "Why not?"

"I do not want you around." The Saurian refocused on the wall of tools again.

The pit of Calum's stomach swelled with pain and emotion.

But he wasn't just going to give up.

"Why not?" he pressed, his voice hardening.

"Why do you humans ask so many questions?"

Calum glared at him. "I don't want to stay here anymore. I don't want to live this life."

The Saurian leaned close to Calum and stared into his eyes. "I do not care."

Calum exhaled a long breath through his nose. Was that it? Was the conversation over?

With one last look around the shed, the Saurian headed for the door and stepped outside.

No. Calum refused to accept this outcome. He chased after the Saurian and added some edge to his words. "You don't have to be so—"

"There he is!" a man's voice shouted, followed by a loud whoop.

The sound stalled Calum's words and his steps, and his heart jumped and jiggered in his chest.

The Saurian stopped short as a group of several men, all wielding torches or tree branches, emerged from the path through the trees. Men from the quarry.

Rather than running, the Saurian stood his ground with his fists clenched. Calum stopped just behind him.

When he saw Jidon standing at the front of the group with a smirk on his face, Calum's blood ran cold.

"So it was *you* who helped the beast escape." Jidon sauntered forward, and the other workers followed him. His eyes, lit only by torchlight, fixed on Calum. "You little traitor."

Calum's heart pounded in his chest. He shook his head. "Didn't have anything to do with it. I found him here only a few minutes ago."

"Shut your lyin' mouth, kid. You really expect me to believe that?"

Nothing he said to Jidon would change his mind. That much was clear. But the more Calum tried to justify himself to Jidon, the harder it would be to convince the Saurian to take him out of this place, so he decided to keep quiet.

"I'll deal with you later." Jidon shifted his focus on the Saurian. "First, we got us a slave to capture."

The Saurian stepped into a defensive stance and pulled the large pickax from his back.

"No." Calum darted forward and positioned himself between Jidon and the Saurian. "No one needs to get hurt."

"Get outta the way, Calum." Jidon motioned to the men behind him. They spread out and encircled the Saurian and Calum. "In fact, get in line with the other men, and help us bring 'im in. Maybe I'll forget 'bout how you kicked me back at the camp. Maybe I'll forget 'bout this betrayal, too."

"I didn't betray *anyone*."

The Saurian huffed behind him.

Calum bristled. He needed to fix this, needed to show the Saurian where he stood. To Jidon, he said, "But I'm not helping you."

Jidon shrugged and positioned the makeshift club in his hands and stepped forward. "Fine by me. Burtis isn't here to save you this time, you little rat."

For being such a big guy, Jidon moved quickly. He darted forward and swung the club at Calum so fast that he couldn't have possibly dodged the blow or shielded himself in time.

Were it not for the Saurian, who reached past and caught the end of Jidon's club in his huge hand only an inch from Calum's head, Calum would've met his end right then and there.

Calum blinked and staggered back, breathing frightened breaths.

Jidon wrenched the club from the Saurian's grasp and swung it again, but the Saurian absorbed the blow with his pickax.

"Get 'em!" Jidon yelled.

The Saurian swung his pickax at Jidon's head, but he ducked under it and drove the end of his club into the Saurian's gut.

A worker from the left charged into the fight and swung his torch, but the Saurian sidestepped the swing. Instead, the torch hit Jidon in his bare chest amid the sound of searing flesh.

Jidon hollered and leveled the worker with a wild thrash of his club, then he staggered back with his left hand pressed against the blackened spot on his chest. The Saurian's tail swiped Jidon's legs out from under him, and he landed on his back.

Another worker charged in, this time toward Calum, swinging his club. Surprised, Calum dove to the side, rolled, and quickly sprang back up to his feet.

The worker swung again, and Calum backed away from the swipe, then he ducked under the one that followed.

"Catch!" the Saurian bellowed.

Calum turned in time to see a fiery torch soaring toward him. He shifted his stance and caught it, then he used it to block the worker's next blow. The impact rattled Calum's fingers, and embers spurted from the torch flames and dissipated into the night sky.

What am I doing? He'd never fought anyone before in his life. He was going to get himself killed if he didn't think of something fast.

The worker, a man in his forties with thinning black hair, glared at him and bared his crooked teeth. Calum had known his name once, but that didn't matter now. He wasn't as huge as Jidon, but he still outweighed Calum by at least thirty or forty pounds.

Calum swung his torch at the worker's head, but the worker blocked it with his club and threw a punch at Calum's face. His fist connected, and pain flared through Calum's cheek.

Calum staggered back. He'd been struck and whipped before, but this was a real fight. The stakes were completely different, and Calum couldn't just give in to the abuse like he normally would.

This time, he was fighting for his life. And if he was going to survive, he had to do something drastic. A plan formed in his mind—a crazy plan. It probably wouldn't work.

But if he didn't try it, then it definitely wouldn't work.

So when the worker charged forward and swung his club again, Calum went for it. He dropped to his knees under the attack and jammed the burning end of the torch into the worker's shin, letting the fire do its job.

The worker dropped his club and went down with a yelp, clutching at his seared leg.

It had worked. Calum could scarcely believe it, but now wasn't the time for cheers and celebration. The fight wasn't over.

Calum tossed the torch at him, fiery end first, and snatched up the club instead. Now he had a better weapon, at least.

The worker batted the torch away before it could burn him again, and he grabbed Calum's ankle.

Calum had to make a choice, and he made it quickly. With one heavy swing of the club, he whacked the back of the worker's head.

Crack.

The worker's grip went slack, and his entire body went limp. Blood oozed from a gash on the back of his head, and Calum stepped back, breathing haggard breaths.

Had he killed the man? Or was he simply unconscious?

Either way, Calum couldn't face the truth of it now. He was still in the middle of a fight, and any wrong move could be his last.

With his club at the ready, Calum turned back in time to see the Saurian deliver a stunning blow to the head of another worker with his tail. Yet another went down when the Saurian drove the bottom of the pickax handle into his chin. Several more workers lay unconscious or wounded around him.

The Saurian raised the pickax over his head to finish one of them for good.

Calum's eyes widened. "No!"

The Saurian stopped and glared at him. In that moment, Jidon plowed into the Saurian's chest, and they both went down. The huge pickax hit the ground as the two of them struggled.

Somehow, Jidon managed to straddle the Saurian's waist, and he delivered three solid blows to the Saurian's reptilian jaw. The fourth punch stopped short in the Saurian's big hand, which clamped down around Jidon's fist.

Jidon yelled and gripped his wrist with his free hand, but the Saurian didn't let go, and the gut-twisting sound of crunching bones crackled. The Saurian shoved Jidon off and stood to his feet while Jidon shrank lower, down to his knees, all the while whimpering and screaming.

Calum tightened his grip on the club and started toward the Saurian with cautious steps.

Amid his struggling, Jidon lurched upward and drove his fist into the Saurian's gut. The Saurian released Jidon's hand and staggered back, doubled over. In one fluid motion, Jidon scooped the huge pickax into his good hand and hefted it over his head.

Out of instinct, Calum sprang forward and swung his club as hard as he could. Jidon's wild eyes flickered toward Calum just before a deadened crack split the night air.

Then Jidon dropped to the ground, and the pickax hit the dirt next to him. Blood oozed from a fresh gash on his forehead, and he stared up at the night sky with vacant eyes.

Calum dropped the club, shocked at what he'd just done. When he looked to the Saurian, the beast nodded to him.

Calum shook his head. Jidon was a jerk, and he'd threatened to kill Calum, but… "I can't believe I just—"

"You did." The Saurian stepped toward him. "It is done."

"Is he…?"

The Saurian bent down next to Jidon and pressed his first two fingers against Jidon's neck. "He yet lives."

That gave Calum some comfort, albeit not much.

The three men who'd stayed out of the fight ran off, but they'd seen it all. They'd seen what Calum had done, both to Jidon and the other worker.

"They're gonna kill me anyway." Calum stared at Jidon's motionless body, his hands trembling. "They're gonna tell Burtis, and Burtis is gonna kill me tomorrow. Maybe even tonight."

"Then…" The Saurian exhaled a loud hiss. "…you must come with me."

CHAPTER SEVEN

"I know someone who might help us." Calum led the Saurian through the forest adjacent to Axel's family farm, all while trying to forget what he'd done back at the quarry. "Maybe we can hide until this blows over."

"Hiding is not an option. We must keep moving." The Saurian adjusted his grip on the giant pickax and ducked under a low-hanging tree branch.

Calum exhaled a shaky breath. He was both afraid and relieved to hear the Saurian say that. "If we're actually leaving then we'll need food for traveling. Axel's farm is just a few minutes away from here. He'll help us."

They stopped at the tree line, and Calum squinted into the darkness. An expansive field of corn separated them from a small farmhouse drenched with silver moonlight.

Calum faced the Saurian. "Do you have a name?"

The Saurian nodded. "Magnus."

"Magnus," he repeated. "I'm Calum."

"I know."

"How well do you see in the dark?" Calum asked.

"Better than you, but not greatly so."

"Do you see anyone? Or do you hear anything?"

Magnus shook his head. "If we intend to see your friend, we should make haste."

"Follow me."

They cut across the field, keeping low so the corn stalks would provide them with some cover. When they reached the edge of the field, Calum looked Axel's house up and down. Two floors, a few windows. Nothing special, but a far cry from the tent Calum had slept in for the last eight years of his life.

"Well, we can't just knock on their front door."

Magnus stared at him.

"Can you lift me up to that second floor window?"

"I can, but to what end?"

"I'm pretty sure that's Axel's room. If I can knock on the window and get his attention, maybe his parents won't wake up."

"I see." Magnus nodded. "Very well. I will lift you, but do not fall."

"I won't."

Calum and Magnus cut across the moonlit gap between Axel's house and the cornfield. In the shadow of the house, Magnus hefted Calum up to his shoulders and then hoisted him up to the window.

Calum peered inside, careful not to lose his balance on Magnus's shoulders. There, in bed asleep, lay Axel. Calum looked around the room to see if anyone else was there, then he tapped on the window.

Axel rolled over in bed and faced the other way.

Calum sighed and tapped on the window again, this time louder.

Axel slowly sat up in bed and stared right at him, squinting and blinking. Then he reached next to his bed, pulled a long silver object into view, and flung the sheets off himself.

It was a sword.

When Axel started toward the window with a furious look on his face, Calum glanced down at Magnus.

"Uh... let me down," he said.

"Did you get his attention?"

"Yes—but you need to let me down *now*."

Magnus complied, and Calum's boots hit the dirt just as Axel pushed the window open and stuck his head out.

"Who are you? What do you think you're—" He laid eyes on Magnus. "What in the King's name is going on?"

"It's alright, Axel." Calum put up his hands. "It's me, Calum."

"Calum? What are you doing here?" Axel pointed his sword out the window at Magnus. "And what is that *thing* doing here with you?"

A long low hiss issued from Magnus's nostrils until Calum waved him down.

"It's a long story. The short version is, we're leaving the quarry. There are men after us, and we stopped here to ask if you could spare any food." Calum swallowed the lump in his throat. "I know you don't owe me anything, but I thought I'd ask. As a favor."

Axel shook his head. "Do you have any idea what they'd do to me if they found out I helped you?"

Calum hesitated. He hadn't thought of how he might be compromising Axel and his family just by showing up at his house. "Any chance you could come down here and talk to us?"

"*Us?*" Axel eyed Magnus again. "I'm not coming down there as long as that *thing* is with you."

"Come on," Magnus growled. "We cannot afford to waste any more time."

Calum held up his hands. "Please… let me try something."

Magnus exhaled a harsh breath through his flared nostrils.

"Axel, what if I send him into the cornfield? Then would you come down?" Calum asked. "Or can I come up there?"

Magnus shook his head, but Calum ignored him.

"Fine," Axel said. "Send the beast into the corn, and I'll meet you on the other side of the house at the front door. If I see him anywhere nearby, I'll kill you both."

Magnus huffed. "That is a delusion."

"Stop." Calum stepped in front of Magnus. "Just stop. There's been enough fighting for one night. Let me handle this."

"How long do you expect it will take our pursuers to realize we will seek out food and supplies?" Magnus growled. "This is the next place they will check. Every minute we stand idly by counts against us. We're wasting time."

"Well, we're gonna make time for this."

Magnus snarled at him.

"Are we doing this or not?" Axel asked.

"I'll meet you at the front door." Calum ushered Magnus toward the field and then circled around to the front of the house.

A moment later, the door opened. Axel stood in the doorframe and beckoned Calum forward with his left hand. Once Calum made it inside, Axel shut the door behind him without a sound.

"I'll try to be quiet," Calum whispered. "I'm sure your parents are—"

Axel's sword flashed to Calum's neck. "As bad as the punishment would be for helping you, the reward will be just as good for turning you in."

AXEL NARROWED his gaze at Calum, whose face betrayed his surprise. Calum had really ruined things this time. Now Axel didn't have any choice but to turn him in.

He'd looked after Calum, snuck him extra food, and even patched him up a time or two after a beating, but this was different. Axel couldn't save Calum from something like this.

"Axel?" Calum whispered, his voice strained. "What are you doing?"

Still, a part of Axel wanted to give Calum the benefit of the doubt. "Give me one good reason why I shouldn't hold you here until my father can go for help."

Calum grunted. "I can give you several."

"Then start talking. *Quietly*."

"We're friends." Calum held up one finger, then another. "I haven't done anything wrong. I—"

"Not true." Axel shook his head. "You wouldn't be leaving if you hadn't done something wrong."

"I sided with the Sau—with Magnus. I didn't want—"

"So he's got a *name*, now?" Axel rolled his eyes. Leave it to Calum to befriend a beast instead of an actual person. "You two must be best buddies."

"You already know he saved my life today."

Axel clenched his jaw. He had to admit, that did count for something. "Why'd you have to leave?"

"He escaped after that, and I went to look for him. I found him at the quarry, and a group of the workers caught up to us there. I didn't want him to continue to get abused, so I sided with him, and they attacked us, and—"

"How many did you kill?"

Calum bristled. "I didn't kill anyone, but I—I—"

"Come on. Out with it." Axel leaned forward.

"I hit Jidon and one other man in the head with a club. They both went down," Calum explained. "When we left, they were still down, but Magnus said Jidon was still alive."

"Jidon? Big Jidon?" Axel snickered. "Yeah, right. He weighs more than you and me combined."

"He was gonna kill Magnus. One good swing to his forehead, and he dropped."

Axel huffed. "If you say so. Either way, you helped an escaping slave. That makes you a criminal, a fugitive. As such, if I turn you in, I get a reward."

Calum recoiled from the blade at his neck but couldn't back up thanks to Axel's front door. "What kind of reward do you think you'll get, Axel? At the end of the day, you'll still be stuck on this farm. Just maybe with some extra coin. I'm your *friend*. Doesn't that mean anything to you?"

"You're my friend, but you're also a criminal. The King's men are gonna hang you when they find out what you've done." Axel shook his head again. Calum had *really* messed up. "'Course, that's *if* they get to you in the first place. Burtis seems like he'd just as soon take care of you himself."

Calum's eyes narrowed. "So you would really hand me in for—"

"No. I wouldn't turn you over just for the reward." Axel motioned toward the staircase with his head. "But if I don't, then I'm responsible for not turning you in. That's gonna come back on me *and* my family."

"Then forget I was ever here. Just don't turn me in. Let me leave, and we're gone. Even if they catch us, I won't say a word about being here."

Axel shook his head again. "If I don't turn you in, I get whatever punishment you were supposed to get. You know that's how it goes."

"Come with us," Calum blurted.

"*Quiet.*" Axel pressed the sword against Calum's neck again and glanced over his shoulder. "You trying to wake my parents? You wake them up, and we're done talking. For good."

Calum smirked.

Axel furrowed his brow. "That doesn't mean I'm gonna let you go."

"Come on, Axel. Come with us. We both know you want to. You told me what kind of life you wanted back in the tavern. This is your chance to go live it."

Axel chuckled. "Are you kidding? That's a death sentence for sure."

"Only if they catch us."

"Even if they never did, it's still a death sentence. We don't know the first thing about how to survive in the wild."

"You work on a farm. You know plants and terrain and other stuff like that. Besides, I bet Magnus knows a lot, too."

Axel scoffed and rolled his eyes. "Yeah, 'cause I'm gonna trust that *thing* when we're all alone in the wilderness."

"He's not a *thing*." Calum glowered at Axel. "He's a Saurian. A person. Someone with a name and a history and a life."

"Whatever." Axel shook his head. "I don't trust him. Not in the least."

"You don't know him, either," Calum countered. "My point is, said you wanted to get out of here and do something else with your life. You had big dreams and big plans. This is your chance to do all that. Maybe your best chance." Calum cleared his throat. "Maybe your only chance. Come with us."

Axel shifted his footing and pulled the tip of his sword away from Calum's neck, but he didn't lower it. He'd already made up his mind that he wouldn't—he *couldn't* kill Calum, even if he tried to escape. "I can leave whenever I want to."

"Then do it," Calum urged. "Axel, you were right. I don't want to work at the quarry for the rest of my life, and I don't want to be foreman. I'm done being a slave. I know you don't want to stay on this farm forever. It's like you said to me earlier tonight: I only want what's best for you. So come with us."

Axel bit his tongue. Everything in his heart longed to go along with Calum, but everything his mind resisted the idea. "No way."

"Do you really want to hand us over to Burtis? Or to the King's men? You *hate* them. They murdered my parents, Axel. They treat you and your family like slaves too, just like me. Just like Magnus."

"Don't you *dare* compare me to him."

Calum's voice hardened and his posture straightened. "It's true, and you know it. 'Not all slaves wear chains,' remember? Come on, Axel. We need your help. You need to get outta here. Either let me go or kill me now, because I'm leaving."

Axel scowled at Calum and sighed. Stupid Calum would get himself killed without help. He'd screwed everything up, and now Axel would have to bail him out.

And as a bonus, maybe Axel could finally find that adventure he'd been after.

He grumbled but lowered his sword. "Wait outside. I gotta pack a few things."

"FOLLOW ME IF YOU WANT FOOD." Axel stormed out of his front door dressed for an excursion into the wild. A small satchel and a bedroll clung to his back, and his sword hung from his belt in a sheath.

When Magnus emerged from the cornfield, Axel tossed one empty burlap bag to Magnus, then he cut away from the house into the corn.

"What did you say to him?" Magnus's gaze followed Axel as the cornfield devoured him.

Calum hesitated. Magnus wasn't going to like this. "He's coming with us."

"*What?*"

Calum shrugged. "It was either that or he was going to turn us in, and I barely convinced him to do this."

Magnus growled. "This is *not* part of our agreement."

"We don't have an agreement, Magnus."

"*Hey.*" Axel hissed from several yards into the corn. "You guys coming or not?"

Magnus growled again.

"Come on. We can talk about it later." Calum started after Axel. When he glanced over his shoulder and saw Magnus trailing behind, he smiled.

Within ten minutes, they made it to an old wooden storehouse on the far side of Axel's family property. A thick padlock hung from a latch that secured the double sliding doors on the front. Axel pulled out a key and inserted it into the lock while Calum and Magnus kept watch.

"What is taking so long?" Magnus hissed.

"Mind your own business," Axel shot back. He pulled the key out, blew a puff of air into the lock, and then reinserted it. "This lock was always finicky. Just give me a minute, here."

"We don't have a minute, Axel." Calum scanned the nearby woods. "We need to get going before someone—"

"Look, the more you yammer, the longer this is gonna take." Axel lowered the keys and glared at Calum. "So are you gonna keep talking or—"

Magnus grabbed the lock and yanked it clean off the door along with the latch, just as he had with the one at the quarry shed. As he pulled the sliding doors open, he said, "Let's go."

Axel stood in place, his jaw hanging open. He stepped toward Magnus and jabbed his yellow chest with his index finger. "This is my father's storehouse. You had no right to—"

"You presume to lecture me on breaking the door latch when we are already stealing food and trying to escape a band of angry quarry workers?"

"It wasn't your lock to break. Nor is it your food to steal."

Magnus shook his head and brushed Axel's hand away from his

chest. "Next time you point a finger at me, I may just do to your hand what I did to that latch."

Axel gawked at him, then at Calum, who just shrugged and stepped inside the storehouse after Magnus.

Inside, mounds of food organized by type towered almost to the ten-foot ceiling amid bales of hay and a few farming tools. Calum had never seen so much food in one place before.

He scowled at Axel. "How is it that I barely got enough to eat every night at the quarry, but you have a storehouse full of food?"

"Actually, we have five storehouses. My family eats pretty well, but we gotta be careful with everything. The King's soldiers keep a close watch on what we produce and what we distribute."

Calum and Magnus frowned at Axel, who held up his hands.

"What I mean is that none of this belongs to my family, even though it came from 'our' land and it's on 'our' property in 'our' storehouse. Really, it all belongs to the King, or by extension, to his soldiers. We aren't supposed to touch it."

"Well, we're about to do more than touch it." Calum popped a strawberry in his mouth, which made it the fourth strawberry he'd ever tasted. He'd already decided to pack many more of them into his bag—and his stomach—before they left the storehouse that night. "Let's load up and get outta here."

It only took a few minutes for them to fill their sacks with a variety of grains, dried meats, fruits, and vegetables. By the time they finished, Calum actually had to strain to heft the loaded sack over his shoulder.

Axel elbowed him on the way toward the storehouse doors. "Think you guys got enough there?"

Calum chuckled. This running away thing might not be so bad after all. "Hey, I haven't eaten my fill for as long as I can remem—"

Something yanked him back, and a shovel clanged against the doorframe. Calum hit the wooden boards on the storehouse floor, and half the contents in his sack spilled out next to him. When he looked up, Magnus stood between him and the doorway.

A man, one of the quarry workers, stood in the doorframe and swung his shovel a second time, but Magnus caught the shovel by its shaft and leveled the worker with one vicious punch. He grabbed the worker by his legs and hurled him out of the storehouse, then he pulled the doors shut.

"C'mon out." A gruff voice ordered from the other side. "Surrender now, and I don't gotta kill you."

Calum knew that voice, and fear pulsed through his chest.

It was Burtis.

CHAPTER EIGHT

"Calum, I know you're in there," Burtis called. "Saw you when Khoba almost took your head off with his spade."

Calum glanced at Axel and then looked at Magnus, who shook his head. He stood to his feet and backed away from the door. "We're not coming out, Burtis. You might as well just get out of here and let us pass."

Laughter bellowed from outside the storehouse. "You're funny, kid. Always good for a laugh. That's for sure."

"I'm serious, Burtis."

"You don't know the meanin' of the word, Calum." All the mirth dissipated from Burtis's voice, replaced by primal undertones. "Now get on out here, or I'll kill you my own self."

A part of Calum, the same part that had learned almost a decade ago to fear those in authority, whether the foreman like Burtis or the King's soldiers, wanted to step out and give up.

But another part held him back and loosed his tongue.

The part of Calum that refused to lie down anymore. The part that would no longer be bullied or abused.

The part that longed to be free.

"Burtis," Calum began, "if you kill me, then so be it, but I'm not your slave anymore, or anyone else's."

"You sure 'bout that?" Burtis called back.

Axel nodded and drew his sword. "I've already come this far. I'm not gonna let a bunch of quarry scum—no offense, Calum—keep me from my future."

Magnus growled and drew his pickax. "Nor will I be going back."

Calum smirked at them both, then picked up a wooden rake leaning against the inside of the storehouse. "We're not coming out, Burtis."

"Then we're gonna burn the storehouse down around you. How 'bout that?"

"You won't," Axel yelled. "The King's men will arrest you for treason."

"That the young farm boy I hear? So these fugitives recruited you to their lost cause as well?"

"*Recruited* me?" Axel winked at Calum. "Not a chance. I'm their *leader*."

Magnus huffed.

Burtis cackled. "You bein' in there won't stop us from burnin' it down, and neither will an empty threat 'bout the King's men. Just as easy to say you four burned it down when you were tryin' to escape. Since you'll be dead, you won't be 'round to argue your side."

Axel eyed Calum and Magnus then turned back toward the door. "Why don't you come in here, and we'll find out?"

"Oh-ho! Big words for a farm boy. Why don't you c'mon out here and make me?"

"Go ahead," Axel yelled back. "Burn it down. See if I care."

Magnus grabbed Axel's satchel and pulled him away from the door. "Easy."

"He can't talk to me like that." Axel pointed toward the door. "Without me he'd go hungry. Dumb brute."

Magnus started to say something, but one of the doors swung open. A torch zipped inside the storehouse and landed in a mound of hay. The fire quickly spread to the nearby wall, which caught fire.

Firelight flickered in Axel's wide eyes. "He's... actually burning the storehouse down."

Magnus grabbed Axel and Calum by their shoulders and pulled them close. "Listen to me. We have little time. We must fight our way out of this. Work together. Watch out for each other. Let them attack first. Wait for them to swing, then dodge and hit them with your weapons. They may be older and stronger, but you are younger and faster. Use that. Crystal?"

Calum nodded, but Axel brushed Magnus's hand off. "I know how to do this."

"Then make sure Calum does not get hurt. Keep him safe."

Axel nodded. "No problem."

"Follow me."

When Magnus stepped out of the storehouse, a barrage of clubs, pickaxes, and shovels swung at him. He avoided several and blocked the others with his own pickax.

Calum and Axel followed, ready for battle. One of the workers recovered from Magnus's deflection and hacked at Calum with a spade. He reacted and blocked the blow with his rake, but the impact sent a shock of pain into his hands, and he nearly dropped the rake. Now he understood why Magnus had told him to dodge the attacks instead of trying to block them.

The worker swung again. This time, Calum hopped back away from the swipe and then, while the worker was stuck in his follow-through, Calum whacked him in the side of his head with the blunt end of the rake, and he went down.

Calum stole a glance over his shoulder, and to his surprise, it actually *did* look like Axel knew what he was doing. He waited for the attacks to come, avoided them, and then lunged forward to deliver quick blows to his opponents with his sword, sometimes wounding them.

Magnus did most of the damage. The workers came at him in droves, but he batted them aside as if they weighed nothing.

Within minutes, the only workers still able to fight were Burtis and three of his men. Everyone else was either unconscious, wounded, or possibly dead, depending on the level of mercy Magnus had deigned to show them.

While Burtis and his three remaining men hesitated to come forward, they still blocked Calum and his friends' escape, and the storehouse fire still raged behind them.

"This is your last chance to give up, Calum." Burtis's eyes focused on him, then on Axel. "You too, farm boy."

"Do I look like a *boy* to you?" Axel started forward, but Magnus pulled him back.

"Yes." Burtis chuckled, and Axel scowled. "Either way, I figure you got 'bout ten minutes 'fore ol' Scrim gets back with the King's men. Then you'll really be in trouble."

Calum glanced at Magnus, but he didn't budge. Facing down Burtis and the idiots from the quarry was one thing, but dealing with trained soldiers...

"The King's men don't take kindly to thieves and murderers." Burtis tilted his head. "And neither do I."

Axel huffed. "I didn't steal anything from you."

"No, but them two did." Burtis extended his fingers one by one, listing his claims as he glowered at Calum and Magnus. "There's that pickax in the beast's hand and the belts strapped to 'im. Then there's the matter of the beast himself. I own 'im for no small sum, and now Calum's at fault for his escape."

Calum glowered at him. "He escaped on his own, and you know it."

"Did he?" Burtis asked. "Then why'd you whack poor Jidon in the head when he tried to stop the Saurian from escapin'? Nearly killed the man. As it is, neither he nor most of the men with 'im are gonna be back to work anytime soon. Or the ones with me, for that matter."

"He was gonna kill Magnus." Relief settled in Calum's chest. As awful as Jidon had been, he was glad he hadn't killed the brute. He threw in a smirk for good measure. "And he was a moron."

Burtis blinked and stared at Magnus. "It's got a *name* now?"

Calum's jaw tensed. He didn't have to defend Magnus, but he would nonetheless. "He's *always* had a name. He's a person too, just like you and me. And like I said before, we're not your slaves anymore."

"*My* slaves? You both belong to the King. I'm just one of his many stewards, here to keep you in line."

"You're doing a great job of that," Axel muttered.

"But you sided with the Saurian and ran away." Burtis shook his head. "Did you really think you'd get away with—"

"Enough talk." Magnus hefted his pickax higher. "We are leaving. Let us go, and we will not add you to the number of the dead and wounded. Try to follow us, and you *will* perish this night."

"So he talks after all." Burtis huffed. "Not a word all day, but now you speak?"

Magnus glared at Burtis, then he refocused on Calum. "Let us go."

Burtis didn't move to stop them, but his gaze fixed on something behind Calum, and he smirked. A twig snapped from the side.

"Watch out!" Axel yelled.

Magnus swiveled his hips, pushed Calum to the ground, and swung his pickax. A man soared at him through the air and knocked Magnus to the dirt. When Magnus shoved the man off of him and onto his back, Calum recognized him.

Jidon lay before him with his head bandaged up—and the pick end of Magnus's pickax protruding from his chest. Burtis had lied about him being too wounded to work—but now it didn't matter. He was definitely dead now.

Burtis roared and lashed his sword, but Axel's blade caught the blow just before it could reach Calum. Axel threw two haphazard swings, then Burtis jammed his fist into Axel's gut so hard that it dropped him to the ground, gasping for air.

Already back on his feet, Calum swung his rake at Burtis's head, but Burtis batted it away with his forearm and sent Calum flying back with a wild kick to his chest. Then Burtis turned back to Axel and raised his sword as Calum scrambled to his feet again.

Calum had no hope of stopping Burtis's swing, but he could knock him off-kilter. He charged forward and drove his shoulder into Burtis's huge frame, just like he'd done to Jidon earlier. The impact barely knocked him off-balance, but it jarred Burtis enough that his swing thumped into the soft ground instead, missing Axel entirely.

Burtis retaliated with a ferocious backhand to Calum's cheek that sent him spiraling back down to the ground, his face ablaze with stinging pain.

Magnus leveled the three remaining workers in quick successive blows, then he charged toward Burtis, who rolled out of the way. He slashed at Magnus's gut, and a red line split his yellow belly. A long grunt rumbled from Magnus's throat, and he pressed his hand against the bleeding wound.

His cheek still burning from Burtis's smack, Calum pushed himself to his feet for what felt like the millionth time that day. He started toward the fight, but Magnus caught him by his wrist and pulled him back.

Magnus's fingers left bloody red streaks on Calum's wrist. Magnus winced, pressed his free hand against his gut again, and said, "He is mine."

Calum glanced at the red line across his belly and the blood trickling from it. "But you're—"

"I am fine," Magnus insisted. "Help Axel."

Axel still lay on his side, gasping for air. He somehow hadn't ever released his sword, even after Burtis's punch. Calum darted over to Axel and helped him upright as Magnus started toward Burtis again.

"You may be bigger," Burtis growled at him. "But you ain't never gonna be *meaner*."

Magnus didn't move aside from breathing. His pickax still protruded from Jidon's chest, and Burtis now stood between Magnus and Jidon's body.

Why hadn't Magnus reached down to pick up any of the shovels or other tools that lay all around them? It didn't make sense to Calum.

Burtis waved his sword in front of him. "C'mon, Saurian. You talk like a human. Bleed like a human. Bet you can die like one, too."

When Magnus stepped forward, Burtis stepped back.

Magnus snorted. "Afraid?"

"I ain't afraid of *you*. Not in the least."

"I see torches in the distance." Axel pointed back toward his family's farmhouse, but Magnus didn't look. "Soldiers?"

"Still time for you to give up," Burtis sneered.

Magnus took another step toward him, and Burtis backed up again. This time, Magnus didn't stop, though. He took two more quick steps after the first, and Burtis swung his sword. At the last instant, Magnus hopped back, and the tip of the blade missed his gut by mere inches.

Burtis swung his sword again. Magnus spun away from the blow and whipped his tail at Burtis's head, but Burtis ducked under it. Magnus darted forward again, and Burtis's sword stabbed toward his gut.

From Calum's vantage, it looked as if Burtis had skewered Magnus and his sword now extended out of Magnus's back, but then a loud snap sounded, followed by a wail from Burtis.

Burtis's arm buckled at the elbow—the wrong way—in Magnus's huge hands.

Then the tip of Burtis's own rusty blade rotated toward him, disappeared in the center of his bare chest, and promptly reemerged from his back.

His eyes wide, Burtis dropped to his knees and rolled onto his side.

Magnus spat on the ground next to Burtis and wrenched his pickax out of Jidon's chest. Then, without so much as a word, he grabbed one of the bags of food from the fiery storehouse entrance and headed into the forest.

Calum looked at Axel, who nodded at him.

"Come on." Axel stood to his feet, finally breathing normally again. "I see torches at the edges of the cornfields. The soldiers are getting close. We'd better go."

Calum tossed his rake aside and grabbed the bag of food he'd dropped a few feet from the burning storehouse. After a final look back at Burtis and Jidon's bodies, he headed into the woods and left his old life—and Axel's burning storehouse—behind him forever.

CHAPTER NINE

For Lilly's escape attempt, Roderick ordered that she go one day without food. That night, two of Luggs's goons, Gammel and Adgar, made sure she didn't eat. They were the same two men who'd carried out the male slave after Roderick knocked him unconscious.

Colm had tried to sneak her some food once, but they caught him. They stopped the entire procession, hauled him out of the wagon, and gave him five lashes for trying. Then they took his food as well.

That didn't stop silly old Colm, though. He'd managed to stash some extra bread crusts somewhere within his weathered cloak, and he waited until Gammel and Adgar thought he was asleep to slide one to her.

She thanked him with a sad smile. Part of her considered giving it back. After all, she was young and healthy, and he was just a poor old man.

He flashed her a glimpse at a gold coin he'd taken from Luggs after Lilly had tried to stand up for Sharion, the other slave woman in their wagon. Not just a poor old man—a poor old *thief*.

Under the moonlight, Lilly whispered, "How'd you manage to get that off him?"

"I may be old, but I still have nimble fingers, child."

"I'll say." She frowned. "Too bad it won't do us any good while we're in here."

Colm grinned. "I wouldn't say that. These slave traders love coin more than anything else, and they treasure it even more than loyalty to one another. I know of more than a few men in this bunch who'd trade me an apple, or a bowl of hot soup, or even a chicken leg for this."

Lilly's eyebrows rose.

"I'd share, of course."

A smile cracked her lips, then a chill ratcheted through her body. Without her armor, the night would be long and cold.

Colm scooted closer and spread his cloak over her shoulders. "Here, child. No need for you to shiver in the night."

Part of Lilly wanted to refuse him. It felt awkward and strange to sit so near a man not of her family, someone she'd just met, even in spite of his age—and in nothing but her undergarments, no less—but it was cold. Colm had only helped her thus far, so she inched closer to him, and he curled his arm around her shoulders.

"You might think I'm trying to take advantage of you." He looked down at her. "Well, I am. I confess it."

She gawked at him, ready to pull away.

"Don't look so surprised. I'm old. The heat leaves my body faster than it used to." Colm grinned again. "Never fear. I still harbor no interest in you except that you fare well."

Lilly exhaled relief and leaned into him, and their shared warmth eased her tension. She rubbed the fabric of Colm's cloak between her fingers. "Your cloak wouldn't happen to have any aerosilk in it, would it?"

He shook his head. "Sadly, no. A luxury I could never afford, save for a few times in my life when the Overlord's generous blessings seemed to rain from on high. Why do you ask?"

"If it was aerosilk, I could use it as a replacement cape. Then I could fly out of here."

"Is that how it works?"

"Yes. Windgales need aerosilk in their capes, in significant quantities, in order to fly. The amount can vary from Windgale to Windgale, but in general, about fifty percent or more is necessary." Lilly watched Sharion dig down into the hay. "Sharion?"

Her head popped up and she glared at Lilly.

"Would you care to join us?" Lilly smiled. "There's room to keep warm over here."

"Leave me alone." Sharion dug back into the hay and disappeared beneath a mound of golden-brown straw.

"Well, if you change your mind—"

"I won't."

Lilly smirked, but her amusement faded far too soon. "Roderick mentioned the Pass. Does he mean...?"

"Trader's Pass?" Colm nodded. "That he does."

Lilly's breath caught in her throat. They meant to take her to Eastern Kanarah? So far from her family, from her home. And into what? Slavery? To whom?

"Colm." Her voice broke when she said his name. "What's going to happen to me?"

After a long pause, he squeezed her shoulders. "Easy, child. Best not to ponder a future that may never come. Survive the night, first."

Lilly closed her eyes and stifled her tears.

———

Eastern Kanarah

"Stop." Magnus held out his arms and halted his progress. He'd taken the lead position as they crept through the woods. Calum followed him, and Axel brought up the rear. They all stopped and turned back to Magnus.

"What?" Axel said more than asked.

"*Shhhhh*," Magnus hissed. "We are not alone."

Calum scanned the surrounding trees, but thanks to the darkness he couldn't see much of anything. The moonlight barely broke through the thick tree cover, and where it did, it wasn't much help. "I don't see—"

Magnus grabbed his arm and yanked him down to the dirt behind a rotting log. His voice still a hiss, he said, "*Quiet*. Axel, get down."

Axel took cover behind a small bush, stared into the forest for a moment, and then refocused on Magnus, squinting.

Magnus tapped the side of his reptilian head. "Listen."

Sure enough, a faint rustle sounded several yards away, from the very direction they were heading. Through a hole in the rotted log, Calum saw a dark form materialize in the trees, then another, then another, and many more until a couple dozen men swarmed that portion of the forest.

Calum's heartbeat pounded like war drums in his ears, so hard that the men approaching had to hear it. How could they not?

Their footsteps grew louder, and as the men approached, they sharpened into focus. Black leather armor. Shining weapons in their gauntleted hands.

The King's soldiers.

From what Calum could tell, the first soldier who stepped past Axel's hiding spot didn't seem to notice them. Neither did the second, third, or fourth, but the fifth brushed his sword across the top of the bush in a slow, deliberate motion. The metal of his blade sang with tinkling notes as it scraped against the leaves and exposed branches.

"*Billings.*"

The fifth soldier straightened his posture faster than a whiplash, and he turned to face the speaker.

"Focus."

A big man riding an armored horse came into view—or maybe he just looked big because he was on top of a horse. He held a long spear in his left hand and the horse's reins in his right.

A streak of silver ran across his black leather breastplate, something that none of the other soldiers had. It reminded Calum of Burtis's purple foreman's sash, and he wondered if it meant the man on horseback was their leader.

"Yes, sir." Billings turned back and rejoined the regiment, his sword in the ready position like all the other soldiers.

No one in the group said anything after that. They just continued to advance forward.

Soldiers disappeared from Calum's view as they climbed on top of his log and hopped over. The sound of their feet hitting the dirt shook Calum's chest.

Wood snapped next to Calum's ear, and he froze.

A metal-studded boot broke through the rotten log and crunched down only inches from Calum's face. Musty flakes and dust flecked across his cheeks, and curses rang out above him.

"Billings."

"Sorry, Commander Pordone. I didn't know the log was rotten, and I—"

"*Billings.*" Commander Pordone pointed his spear forward. "Focus."

"Yes, sir."

Calum didn't dare reach to wipe off his face, not with Billings so close. Even so, the beginnings of a sneeze tingled in his nose. He had to do something soon. He didn't know if he could hold it back.

Billings pulled his foot out of the log, and more dust peppered Calum's face. After a few muttered curses, Billings stepped past Calum's position.

Calum reached for his nose without a sound and rubbed it, but that just made it worse. He had to hold back his sneeze. Their *lives* were at stake.

Commander Pordone's horse took the long way around the log and angled back behind the first five men. If Calum could just hold out for one more minute until the soldiers moved out of sight and out of hearing range, they'd be able to escape.

He could do it. He had to. He rubbed his nose again and tried to breathe through his mouth instead of—

Calum sneezed.

He muffled it as best as he could, but it was still too loud.

Commander Pordone twisted his torso and turned his head back.

Calum was certain their eyes met, but the commander didn't move after that.

Calum's eyes watered. No, not aga—

A second sneeze.

"There!" Commander Pordone bellowed. He raised his left arm over his head and then thrust it forward in a vigorous point.

A gleaming spear embedded in the log next to Calum's shoulder.

"*Run!*" Magnus grabbed Calum's waistband and pulled him to his feet, then tossed him the bag of food he'd been carrying.

Calum tried to catch the sack, but it popped open, and half the food spilled out on the ground. He ground his teeth and reached for the nearest potato.

"*Leave it.*" Magnus shoved Calum forward, and three more fruits dropped from the sack. "Go!"

Commander Pordone drew his sword and kicked the sides of his horse, which charged forward.

Calum froze. He had exposed them all, and now they would die. Him first.

Magnus wrenched the spear from the log and hurled it toward the approaching commander. Instead, the spear struck the horse in the center of its head, and it pitched forward.

Commander Pordone toppled off the horse, and his body cracked against a nearby tree. Behind him, soldiers ran back toward Magnus, all of them yelling and shouting threats in the King's name.

"Nice throw!" Axel shouted.

"I was aiming for the rider." Magnus hissed at Calum, "Go!"

Enough. Calum resolved he wouldn't freeze again.

He broke free from the trance and ran alongside Magnus. Ahead of them, Axel beckoned them forward with his sword in his right hand and his sack of food in his other.

They ran through the woods with the soldiers close behind. Axel still led, and Magnus still followed Calum.

"They are gaining on us," Magnus yelled loud enough for both Calum and Axel to hear. "We are carrying too much. We each have to drop something."

"I thought you were supposed to be *strong*," Axel called over his shoulder. "Why don't you carry more?"

"I still tire from running." Magnus grunted from behind Calum. "We must drop the food."

"No," Axel shouted back. "Not the food."

"Either drop the food, drop your bedrolls, or drop the weapons. You are welcome to fight the King's men with tomatoes and melons if you wish, but I do not advise it."

Even amid the chase, Calum had to grin at Magnus's comment.

He dropped the half-bag of food he was carrying. Magnus was right—running was much easier without the extra weight, and they could find more food somewhere else along the way. They would have to.

Axel cursed as he ran, but he also dropped his bag of food. Calum, still following Axel, jumped over it so as not to trip.

Within a few minutes, when Calum looked back, he no longer saw the soldiers behind them. Even so, Magnus urged them on for another five minutes before he let them stop. Axel sheathed his sword, Calum wiped his brow with his wrist, and all three of them sucked in a trough's-worth of air.

Axel spoke first. "What now?"

"We make it through the rest of tonight." Magnus pointed to a ridge to the southwest. "We can take shelter among those trees."

Axel pointed east. "There's a cave right over there. Let's make use of it."

Magnus shook his head. "No."

"Why not?"

"It is not safe."

Axel scoffed. "It's a *cave*. One way in. Easy to defend."

Magnus squared himself with Axel. "You obviously know nothing of strategy or tactics. Given our situation, that cave is a terrible idea."

Axel stepped forward and looked up at Magnus. Calum had stood where Axel was, face-to-face with Magnus, and it was a terrifying place to be. He gained new admiration for Axel's courage.

Or was it stupidity?

"You know nothing about me, *Scales*." Axel practically spat the last word.

Courage or otherwise, Calum didn't want this devolving into an unnecessary conflict. He wedged himself between them with his hands and then his body. "That's enough. Both of you."

"He thinks he knows everything. No *Saurian* is gonna tell me what I can and can't do." Axel folded his arms.

Magnus's eyes narrowed. "If I must, I *will* put you in your place, child."

Axel huffed. "You don't scare me."

"It is your prerogative to say so, that you might appear brave in front of Calum, but your eyes betray the truth." A subtle grin curled up the ends of Magnus's mouth. "You are petrified."

Then Axel proved that it had been stupidity guiding his actions all along.

His jaw hardened, and he reached for the hilt of his sword, but Magnus was faster.

In one quick, jarring motion, Magnus pushed past Calum, knocking him to the side. He big reptilian hands clamped onto Axel, one on his right wrist, and another on his throat.

With a powerful heft, he shoved Axel against a tree, lifted him off his feet by his throat, and held him in place there. He leaned in close and exhaled a long hiss through his nostrils at Axel's face.

Though Axel struggled, he could neither draw his sword nor break free of Magnus's hold on him. He choked and sputtered, and even in the moonlight, Calum could tell his face was turning red from the strain.

"Magnus..." Calum said. "You're hurting him!"

"The next time you dare to pull your blade on me, I will grant you no mercy," Magnus warned. "Weapons are to be brandished only against enemies. If you choose to make one of me, I assure you we will not remain enemies for long. Do you comprehend what I am saying to you, *child?*"

Axel managed a desperate nod and some gurgling noises.

Calum just stood there, helpless to intervene. The more he considered it, though, the more he didn't really fault Magnus for his actions. Axel's brazen attitude had gotten him in this situation.

His response seemed to have satisfied Magnus, because he released his grip on Axel and let him drop to the ground. Axel coughed and rubbed at his throat, sucking in greedy breaths.

"So…" Calum began, "…the trees along the ridge, then?"

"If you think you're so smart," Axel rasped as he finally stood back up, "explain to me why that cave is a bad idea?"

"There are multiple reasons," Magnus said. "It is exposed, out in the open, which makes it visible to the soldiers looking for us. They will expect us to hide in a cave because it is a natural shelter—"

"Which is why we should stay in there," Axel insisted.

Magnus eyed him. "Are you finished?"

Axel motioned for Magnus to continue, then he folded his arms and leaned against the very tree Magnus had just pinned him to.

"It is a natural shelter, but it also presents a danger to us because we do not know what or who might already be in there. Nor do we know if that is the only entrance, and even if it is, if we cannot defend it or get caught off guard, we would have our backs up against a wall on the inside."

"Just like the storehouse…" Calum said as the realization clicked in his mind.

"Correct." Magnus nodded. "Hiding among the trees on that ridge is much safer."

"How do you know all of this?" Calum asked.

"Experience."

The way Magnus said it made Calum want to ask him more questions, because there was clearly a lot more Magnus wasn't letting on, but he held off. Something told Calum he ought to leave it alone… at least for now.

Axel sighed. "So are we going, or what?"

"Follow me." Magnus started toward the ridge.

AFTER TWO FITFUL hours of sleep, Axel hugged his knees tighter, shivered, and half-glared at Calum, but so far he hadn't awakened.

Perhaps I shouldn't have gone along with this scheme after all. Where had it gotten him so far? Cold, lost in the woods, with his best friend and a monstrous Saurian bully. *I could be in my bed right now instead of... this.*

A mix of coniferous and broadleaf deciduous trees encircled their camp—if it could be called that. More like two guys and a Saurian laying on the ground in the woods. Calum stirred, and light from the small fire in the center of the camp flickered in his green eyes.

Either the air had cooled as the night deepened, or Axel's temperature had dropped now that he wasn't running around. Maybe he'd feel warmer if he had something in his stomach.

Too bad they'd abandoned all the food when they were running away from the King's soldiers.

Axel scowled at Calum. "I wish you hadn't sneezed."

Calum broke his gaze at the fire and looked at him. "Me too."

"I could sure go for some of that food I helped you steal." Axel eyed the Saurian. Scales. Magnus. Whatever. "Oh, wait. *Someone* told us to drop it all. Great plan, master strategist."

"You are welcome." Magnus didn't bother to make eye contact. He just lay on the ground and stared up at the stars.

Overhead, the sky had begun to yield to the first hint of daylight, so the stars didn't shine as brightly as they had against the solid black curtain of night.

"What do you mean, I'm 'welcome?'" Axel asked.

"You yet draw breath. I saved your life." Magnus leaned his head forward and squinted at Axel with golden eyes. "Twice."

Axel shook his head. "So starving us to death is your idea of 'saving my life?' And how long do you expect us to last out here without food?"

"You ate dinner before you went to sleep, right?" Calum asked. "You can't be *starving* yet. Don't be so dramatic."

"All this fighting and running builds up an appetite. I'm not like you, Calum," Axel said. "I got to eat my fill every day. It's why I'm so much bigger than you."

"Your *head* is certainly bigger," Magnus mumbled.

Axel's focus whipped toward Magnus. "What'd you say to me?"

"You heard me." Now Magnus looked over at him. "What do you intend to do about it?"

A whole range of ideas cycled through Axel's head, but they all amounted to nothing but his imagination running wild. Though he'd never admit it aloud, he couldn't compete with Magnus on any level.

And that frustrated him most of all. If Axel actually wanted to live the life of adventure he'd always wanted to live, he had to get stronger. He had to learn to fight. He had to learn to survive.

"That is what I thought," Magnus said.

Axel ignored him. Let the lizard have his hollow victory. One day, Axel would grow strong enough to take him on. Then it would be Magnus who'd have to shut up instead.

Calum asked, "What'd you do with those Gronyx stones you stole? We could sell those in a town somewhere and buy food."

Magnus stared at him. "What Gronyx stones?"

"You know what I mean," Calum said. "The gems with the greenish tint from the pit. You stashed a handful of them under one of the boards near the tool shed at the quarry. I found them at the end of my workday yesterday. Do you still have those?"

Magnus shook his head. "I never took any Gronyx stones."

Calum sighed. "Then it was Hardink after all."

Axel tilted his head. "Huh?"

"Nothing." Calum waved his hand. "Too late now."

More nonsense from Calum. Great. Axel said, "Whatever."

"Why don't we hunt?" Calum leaned forward. "Some of the quarry guys used to do it at night until Burtis found out and put a stop to it."

"Uh… look around, Calum. We have nothing to hunt with. No bows and arrows. No spears." Axel rolled his eyes. "Unless you think you can outrun a deer and cut its head off with my sword."

Calum looked at Magnus, but he just continued to stare up at the fading night sky. "The quarry guys didn't have bows and arrows either. Burtis never would've allowed that."

"Then how did they hunt? Throwing rocks?" Axel scoffed and rubbed his arms to try to warm up.

"I think they used snares. I saw one of them carrying a rabbit by a rope attached to its foot once." Calum cringed. "That was the same night Burtis found out. The next morning, he strung the man up by his foot and lowered him into the Gronyx's pit."

"Burtis is no longer a concern of yours," Magnus said.

Calum grinned. "I know. Thanks."

"Snares," Axel said. "Do we have rope?"

Calum looked at Magnus again. "He grabbed some from the quarry, but I don't know if it will work for snares or not. It's pretty thick."

"So much for hunting, then." Axel shook his head.

Magnus sat up, and Axel couldn't help but notice that the lash marks and even the slash across his yellow underbelly had already healed substantially. Apparently, Saurians healed a lot faster than humans.

"Though I am loath to admit it—" Magnus said. "—Axel is right."

Axel raised an eyebrow and waited for the inevitable snide comment.

"We cannot hunt. It will not work. And since we have no food, our options are limited."

No snide comment. Maybe it was still forthcoming. Axel ventured, "So… what do you have in mind?"

Magnus glanced between Calum and Axel. "We need to raid the Rock Outpost."

CHAPTER TEN

Axel would've laughed at Magnus's proposition, but he was too stunned to say anything at first.

Calum tilted his head. "Raid the what?"

"You've gotta be kidding me," Axel managed to say. Sure, he'd left his home on a whim to follow his own silly idea of getting away from the farm, but now things had gone too far. *Way* too far. "The Rock Outpost? You want to raid the *Rock Outpost?*"

"We do not yet possess adequate weapons. Calum does not have one at all." Magnus stared into the woods. "We have no armor. No supplies, no food. You said yourself that we will not last long out here if we are this ill-equipped."

"I'm clearly missing something here. What's the Rock Outpost?" Calum asked.

"When I said we wouldn't last long, I didn't mean that we should *attack* one of the King's fortresses as a solution," Axel said. "Are you crazy?"

"You want to do *what?*" Calum gawked at them both.

Axel held out his hand, palm up. Finally, they agreed on something. "Exactly my thoughts, Calum."

"I do not desire to attack the outpost," Magnus explained. "I want to *raid* it. An important distinction."

"Not enough of a difference to make it a good idea." Axel folded his arms and stared at the shrinking campfire. He might as well be one of the sticks he'd just thrown in. "Not even close."

"It will be easy. Sneak in. Seize what we require. Get out." Magnus nodded. "Simple."

Axel laughed. "You're nuts. You're living in a dream world."

"We will succeed," Magnus said. "I already have it planned out. Originally, I intended to do it myself, but it will be even easier with three of us."

"What do you mean, you already have it planned out?" Calum asked.

"I mean what I said." Magnus looked at him. "When you found me at the quarry, that was my intended destination."

Axel laughed again and stood up next to Calum. "You were gonna raid the Rock Outpost by yourself?"

"Absolutely."

"There have to be at least twenty or thirty soldiers stationed there." Axel hefted a log from the pile of sticks and wood they'd gathered for the fire. "You'd need an army."

Magnus shook his head. "Only if I wanted to *attack* the place. Like I said, I just want to raid it."

"Why even risk it?" Calum asked.

"They are in possession of some property that belongs to me. Some things that I hold very dear." Magnus's voice hardened. "And I want it back."

"*Pfft.* Good luck with that." Axel rolled his eyes and tossed the log into the center of the fire. Embers sprayed into the air toward the trees that hung over the camp and quickly cooled.

"Our only other option is to go back," Magnus said. "And we all know what that means."

Axel folded his arms. "I'm not risking my life just to help you get your stuff back."

Magnus shot a glare at him but returned to his spot around the fire.

"Like I said, it will be simple, and it will equip us for the journey ahead. If we encounter any soldiers, I will deal with them."

"You're gonna take on twenty or thirty trained soldiers on your own?" Axel folded his arms again and leaned back against the log behind him. "You had a hard time keeping a bunch of quarry workers at bay. If it weren't for Calum and me watching your back, you would've—"

"There will not be twenty or thirty soldiers inside by the time we get there. The only hard part is actually getting inside without the rest realizing what we are doing," Magnus said. "Which is where you two will come in handy."

"Why would most of them be gone?" Calum asked.

Magnus grinned and eyed the pile of sticks next to the campfire. It was the first time Axel had ever seen a truly pleasant expression on his reptilian face.

He turned toward the forest. "Follow me. We have work to do before sunrise."

Western Kanarah

A CLANG JOLTED LILLY AWAKE, and someone snickered in the darkness behind her. She quickly shed Colm's cloak from her shoulders and tried to get away from the sudden sound, but she tripped over something in front of her.

"Watch yourself!" Sharion hissed. She swatted at Lilly's ankles and curled closer to Colm's legs—and farther under his cloak. So much for preferring to be alone all night.

Bony fingers clasped around Lilly's wrist. Colm gently pulled her close to him again, and she acquiesced. Back under his cloak, she found renewed warmth.

"Don't mind them," he told her. "They just want to bother you."

Lilly rubbed her eyes. "I'm bothered."

"We'll be on the move for some time, now. Get some more rest if you can."

"I don't think that's going to happen."

"No?"

"I have to... relieve myself." Lilly glanced around her jail-cell-on-wheels. "Am I supposed to do it here?"

Colm shook his head. "No. They don't like changing out the hay. Just rap the bars a few times and ask. They'll take you into the woods."

Lilly nodded and began to stand up, but Colm grabbed her hand again.

"Do not be unaware," he wheezed. "A bunch of men alone with a beautiful girl in the woods may forfeit their inhibitions."

"But Roderick said—"

"That doesn't mean his men won't try. Men's carnal desires often outweigh those of their purses." Colm fixed his gaze on Lilly, stern as ever. "Do not be deceived, and do not let your guard down, even for an instant."

Lilly swallowed the lump in her throat and nodded. She pounded on the bars.

Five minutes later, Luggs, Gammel, Adgar, and another slave trader shoved both Lilly and Sharion toward the woods. In the darkness, she stumbled over an exposed root—normally not an issue since she could just fly over entire forests when she'd had her cape—but she righted herself and continued forward.

"That's far enough," Gammel said. "Go on. Do it already."

Lilly stared at him, her eyes wide. "Here? In front of you?"

Adgar chuckled, and Luggs nudged the other slave trader. She recognized him, not by his face but by the bandage wrapped around his thigh. The one she'd hit with her last arrow.

"Of course, here," Luggs replied. "You don't think we'd just letcha wander off in the dark, do you?"

Next to Lilly, Sharion hiked up her tattered dress and squatted near a bush. Lilly looked back at Gammel, who licked his lips.

"At least let me go on the other side of that tree?" she pleaded.

Gammel, Adgar, and the bandaged slave trader all shook their heads "no," but Luggs nodded. "Let 'er go, boys. She won't get far even if she does run."

Lilly didn't waste time. She rounded the tree, relieved herself, and came back into view of the slave traders within less than a minute.

Except they weren't there anymore.

She looked right and panned left for a moment, then turned back.

Luggs and the slave trader with the bandage stood behind her. Luggs shoved her to the ground and grinned, and his eyebrows arched down.

Colm's warning ratcheted through Lilly's memory. This couldn't be happening.

But it was.

Lilly tried to stagger away, but Adgar and Gammel emerged from the brush behind her with Sharion, whom they thrust to the ground next to her.

"N-no—you can't do this!" Lilly more begged than said.

"Better if you don't resist 'em," Sharion muttered. "Just let 'em do what they do. It'll be over sooner."

Lilly turned to her, horrified. She couldn't be serious.

"Your friend has the right idea," Luggs said. "Except that on a sweet little thing like you, I know I'm gonna take my time. Ain't that right, boys?"

Their snickers chorused around her, and a deep sickness clenched in her gut. They'd ventured dozens of yards away from the wagons by now, and probably out of earshot, but she had to try. She wouldn't just let them take her.

She sucked in a deep breath and let out a piercing shriek—only to have it cut short by Lugg's hand to her mouth and his dagger to her throat.

"Not another peep, or your honor won't be the only thing we take from you." Luggs smelled like a trash heap up close, and brown spots dotted his yellowed teeth. "Besides, you shot poor Lorrence in his leg, here. Seems to me he oughta get somethin' for his troubles, don't you?"

Part of Lilly wanted to cry, and another part wanted to claw Luggs's eyes out. With his dagger to her throat, she didn't dare do either.

"You hold her," Adgar said. "Then I'll hold her for you."

Sharion moaned, but didn't resist.

By the Overlord—this *wasn't* happening. She never should have left home. Never should have disagreed with her parents. She should have just done what they'd asked.

Now it was too late.

Lorrence untied the cord that held his bloodstained trousers to his waist.

"Unless you wanna lose something dear to you, I suggest you cinch your pants back up, Lorrence."

All four slave traders and Lilly turned toward the source of the voice. A towering muscular form stepped out from behind a tree. Even in the waning moonlight, Lilly recognized the silhouette of his spiky hair.

Roderick.

"All of you, step back." When no one moved, Roderick added, "*Now.*"

Lorrence haphazardly retied his pants and limped toward Roderick. With indignation in his voice, he said, "She owes me for my leg, boss. It hurts, and I ain't got nothin' in return for my sufferin'."

Roderick's gaze shifted from Adgar to Gammel to Luggs, all within a matter of seconds. Each of them lowered his head, but Lorrence still approached.

"C'mon, boss," Lorrence's voice oozed. "I oughta at least get a taste for my trouble, don'tcha think?"

Roderick tilted his head, then he grabbed Lorrence by his throat and lifted him off of his feet with one hand. Lorrence gripped Roderick's wrist and sputtered until a loud crack echoed off of the trees.

The sound sent a jolt through Lilly, and she gasped.

Lorrence slumped from Roderick's grasp and tumbled to the ground in a heap. His right arm curled under his body at an awkward angle—but not nearly as awkward as the angle of his neck.

"Anyone else want to protest my decision?" Roderick glared at the other three men. "Anyone else want to try to have a 'taste?'"

No one said a thing. Lilly didn't know if she should breathe a sigh of relief or hold onto the air she'd sucked into her lungs. Roderick's strength exceeded even that of General Balena—by a considerable amount, it seemed. The way he so effortlessly lifted Lorrence from his feet and dispatched him... he might as well be part Saurian.

How could Lilly ever hope to escape from someone like that?

"Good. Next person I catch going after this girl gets worse—much worse." Roderick's eyes narrowed. "Get them back into their wagon."

Luggs pointed his dagger at Sharion. "What about her?"

Roderick stared steel at him. "What about her?"

"Can we at least… you know…"

Roderick's eyes narrowed. "Be quick about it. We have a schedule to keep."

Lilly's mouth hung open. Roderick had saved her but still intended to let them have Sharion?

Not if she could do something about it.

She had no weapons, had no way to fight back against three grown men—*plus* Roderick—but she had to do something.

Was it futile? Yes, probably, but maybe all she had to do was buy Sharion time. Maybe Sharion would be lucky enough—and aware enough—to escape in the process.

Gammel and Adgar still stood near Sharion, the three of them bathed in moonlight. Luggs had maintained his position near her, and Roderick blocked off any hope of running back toward the wagons, but Lilly could run laterally with no problem. It wasn't much of a plan, but maybe it would be enough.

With a roar, she pushed up to her feet and charged Luggs.

Lilly drove her shoulder into his hip so hard that she almost knocked her arm out of its socket and barely managed to keep her footing. Luggs yelled and slashed at her with his dagger, but she'd already started running toward the trees—and toward Gammel and Sharion.

Gammel held onto Sharion's wrist, his eyes large and white like chicken eggs, as she jammed her left fist into his nose with a satisfying crack. Her hand smarted from the blow, but Gammel yelped and released Sharion.

Lilly had no time to help her up. Sharion was on her own now.

Lilly angled into the woods while Roderick barked orders to follow her.

She ran along the moonlit paths, this time more careful to watch her footing, even though it was even harder to see now in the dark. She leaped over fallen logs, ducked under low-hanging branches, and swerved through the trees. Her legs burned from the exertion, but a renewed chance at freedom tugged her heart forward.

A large, dark figure leaped at her from the forest to her right, and she skidded to a halt just in time to avoid his grasp. Adgar. She recognized his twiggish form and the stupid brown hat he always wore, the combination of which made him look like a scarecrow.

Her legs pumped against the hard ground, and she avoided his second grasp, but his jagged fingernails scraped her shoulder as she ran past.

Lilly had no idea how fast Adgar could run, but she had to assume he was faster than her. He stood even taller than Roderick, and his long legs meant long strides. She'd have to do something to lose him or he'd catch up.

Oh, to be able to fly again.

A low branch threatened to smack her as she ran. Perfect. Lilly charged straight for it, and Adgar's heavy footfalls plodded just steps behind hers. With her arms up, she grabbed the branch, pushed it forward and upward, and then ducked under it. A split-second later she heard a loud smack, a grunt, and a slew of curses.

Lilly snuck a look back and saw Adgar clutching his forehead under the moonlight. He'd fallen behind but still pursued her. He wouldn't fall for that again.

She'd slowed him down, but at the cost of some of her own speed. She caught a patch of flat ground and pounded against the dirt until she regained her full momentum.

Another slave trader, this one with a bow, jumped in front of her and took aim. Lilly skidded along the ground and dove to her left as he let the arrow fly.

He missed by several feet, and she tore through the woods away from him. Another arrow thudded into a tree to her right as she ran past. Had she been shooting instead, she wouldn't have missed.

Another man appeared on her right, swinging a gleaming sword at her legs. Lilly somehow managed to hop over his swing and rolled end-over-end until she wound up back on her feet, still running.

She knew what they were trying to do. The slave traders had more or less turned her back toward the direction from which she'd come.

She wouldn't let them divert her path. Lilly took a sharp right and cut deeper into the woods, bounding over rockier terrain. Her lungs strained, her feet hurt, and she was running out of tricks, but when she glanced behind her, no one followed.

Good. Maybe she'd escaped after all—an incredible bonus after only intending to distract the men from harming Sharion.

Brighter moonlight shone down on her, more than there should be in a forest. Lilly realized she'd reached a clearing. The night sky beckoned her forward and not much else—literally nothing else.

Lilly gasped and cut off her stride. She slid to a stop at the edge of a cliff that dropped several thousand feet and stretched in both directions as far as the moonlight allowed her to see. Her every impulse told her to leap into the void and take flight, but she forced her mind to remember that she didn't have her cape.

In the basin below the cliff, she saw the Valley of the Tri-Lakes—a flat, gray expanse, devoid of any vegetation. In the distance one of the Tri-Lakes sparkled under the moonlight.

"Nowhere to run now, Angel."

Lilly knew Roderick's voice without even having to turn around. The way he said "Angel" churned her stomach. She faced him nonetheless with her fists clenched.

"You either come with us, or you take the plunge." Roderick folded his arms at the head of the clearing while Luggs, Adgar, Gammel, and several other slave traders emerged from the dark woods behind him. All of them panted and wheezed, but Roderick showed no indication of strain except for a bit of perspiration that dotted his wide forehead. "What'll it be?"

Lilly stepped back and almost lost her footing on the edge, but she recovered before her instincts—to jump and fly away—kicked in.

She wished she could. She'd trade every moment from now until the end of time in obedience to her parents for her cape, even for five minutes.

But it was hopeless. No amount of wishing would secure aerosilk around her neck, and without it, she couldn't escape these ruffians.

Roderick extended his hand. "Come on, Angel. It's the only way."

Lilly stole a glance down at the chasm behind her—lined with jagged rocks and much, much too far for her to fall and hope to survive. The rebellion in her chest wanted her to jump, but that same rebellion had gotten her in this predicament in the first place.

She bit her lip, raised her hands, and walked toward Roderick.

Eastern Kanarah

AFTER A FEW HOURS of executing Magnus's sprawling preparations for the raid still to come, Calum's exhaustion finally caught up with him. Along with Axel and Magnus, he stole another few hours of sleep.

When they awoke, Axel gave Calum a spare shirt he'd packed. It fit him poorly—more like a tent than a shirt—but Calum was grateful for it all the same.

Then the three of them headed southeast through the forest away from the Snake Mountains, which Magnus had pointed out to them earlier. Calum hadn't ever seen real mountains before, and the few glimpses he'd gotten of them through the forest canopy sent an exciting ripple of chills, wonder, and terror racing across his skin.

Perhaps one day—maybe even one day soon—he'd get to traverse those mountains. What kind of adventure awaited him along their rocky cliffs, among the people dwelling nearby? He couldn't know for sure, but his heart told him to anticipate marvels he'd never known before.

About ten miles south of the quarry, near the edge of the tree line, sat the Rock Outpost, silhouetted against the still-rising sun. From so far away, Calum couldn't distinguish it from one of Axel's family storehouses, except it might've been larger, and it looked spikier, somehow.

Calum wondered if the men who'd murdered his parents had ever been inside. Maybe some of them still occupied the fortress—or maybe not.

"Not what I was expecting," Calum said. "Then again, I didn't know it was there in the first place."

Axel eyed him. "Where did you think all those soldiers came from?"

Calum shrugged. "I figured they had to come from somewhere, but I don't remember much from the first eight years of my life, and for the last eight years, I've only ever been to the quarry, the camp, your farm, and now the forest. Burtis didn't exactly let us travel much."

"Well, you've got your chance now, don't you?"

"Quiet, both of you." Magnus handed each of them a thick stick with fabric wrapped around some twigs secured to one end. "Once these are lit, they will extinguish quickly. We cannot spare more fabric right now, and we have no pitch to keep them burning, so once they are lit, you must make haste. Crystal?"

Calum nodded. "Clear."

"I still don't think this is gonna work." Axel exhaled a long sigh. "But whatever."

"Just do not get yourself caught."

Magnus held out his own stick, the last smoldering survivor from last night's campfire. Calum and Axel held theirs against his, and fire spread between them all.

"Go quickly," Magnus urged. "Remember, light the bundles close to the ground so the flames have more time to climb up to the tree branches."

They dispersed throughout a pre-determined area with Magnus closest to the tree line and the outpost, Calum farther back in the woods, and Axel even farther back. With running between two forest fires and setting one of his own, Calum had the most dangerous job, but he was also the quickest on his feet. He had to light the fires and get out of there fast.

They'd spent most of the rest of last night gathering dry sticks and stacking them against certain trees Magnus thought would burn the easiest. Then they'd stuffed dried leaves inside those sticks as well to help everything catch fire sooner.

Magnus had planned it to create a big enough blaze to get the soldiers' attention—in theory, anyway. Even if the trees didn't catch, someone from the outpost was bound to see smoke rising from multiple spots within the forest and muster some sort of reaction.

Calum ignited the first bundle, then seven more, gradually working his way north. The fire shouldn't spread any faster than he could light it, so if he stayed ahead of it and at least even with Magnus and Axel, if not a bit ahead of them, he'd be fine.

Within ten minutes he'd ignited twenty bundles, and his section of the trees had begun to burn on their own. Thanks to Magnus's good planning, the fire continued to spread.

Calum caught up with Magnus, and Axel showed up not long afterward. They headed for the trees near the outpost's north gate and waited.

Twenty minutes later, ten armored soldiers filed out of the outpost, all with weapons in their hands, accompanied by one officer on horseback who carried a spear in his left hand. For all Calum knew, he could've been the same officer as last night in the woods, just riding a different horse.

"Not as many as I had hoped for." Magnus turned his head toward them. "We may have to do some serious fighting after all, boys."

"Wait." Calum pointed. "Look."

One of the soldiers headed toward the officer. They exchanged some words, the officer nodded, and the soldier headed back toward the outpost. A few minutes later, six more soldiers exited from the outpost and jogged toward the fire.

"Much better." Magnus grinned at Calum and Axel. "Follow me. We are going in."

CHAPTER ELEVEN

Up close, the outpost didn't impress Axel: a roof, twenty-foot stone walls, and a large wooden door on the north side, now shut tight. Then again, in such a remote area, perhaps the King didn't need to get fancy with his soldiers' accommodations.

Magnus led them straight to the main gate.

"Alright," Axel said. "We're here. How do we get in?"

Magnus smirked. "Sheathe your sword."

Axel tilted his head. "What? Why?"

"Trust me."

Axel glanced at Calum, who nodded, and he sheathed his sword.

Magnus grabbed Axel by his waistband and hooked his other hand under Axel's armpit. "Grab the edge of the wall."

"What the—" Before he could resist, Axel found himself soaring through the air. Calum and Magnus shrank underneath him as he flew higher, and his heart sank as he began to drop toward the ground, fast.

On his descent, his frantic fingers latched onto the edge of the outpost wall. His thighs slapped the flat stone and he banged his knees hard, but he held on nonetheless—falling would've been a lot worse. He hauled himself up, stood on the edge, and looked down with fire in his veins.

He shook his finger at Magnus. "If you *ever* do that again, I'll—"

"Just find a way inside and open the door for us," Magnus hissed up at him.

Axel scowled but nodded.

By design, the roof didn't connect to all the walls, and an open space about a third the size of the entire building served as a small courtyard. A pair of horses stood in the small stable in the northwest corner, alone in the otherwise empty courtyard.

Axel headed to one of the corners, jumped onto a wooden post that extended upward about three feet from the edge of the wall, and shimmied down. When his boots hit the ground, he glanced around the courtyard again—still no one but him and the horses.

He scurried over to the door and pulled the bolt back to unlock the mechanism. As soon as it disengaged, the door opened, and Magnus and Calum strode inside the outpost.

"Good work." Magnus patted his shoulder. "Come. We have precious little time."

Axel and Calum followed Magnus's lead, and Calum picked up a sword in a rack leaning against one of the courtyard walls. Axel brandished his own, but Magnus held on to his pickax.

They headed into the interior of the outpost via a large door at the top of a wide staircase made of the same gray stone as the exterior walls. The door fed into a main hallway with wooden floors and stone walls.

As soon as they stepped into the hallway, Magnus held up his hand. They stopped and listened for a moment, and Axel heard at least two distinct voices from one of the rooms that lined the hallway.

His voice barely audible, Magnus said, "I will handle them. When I signal you, keep going. Search for the armory and the pantry."

Axel and Calum nodded.

Magnus crouched down low to the floor and hissed.

"What was that?" one of the voices said.

Magnus hissed again.

"Is... is that a snake in here?" another voice asked. "You know I'm terrified of snakes. This some kind of sick joke you're playing on me?"

"Calm yourself," said a third voice, gruffer than the first two. "Rovert probably just forgot to lock the main gate. You know how things just wander in here if you don't—"

"No, I locked the gate. When Brooks came back for more men, I locked it behind him. I remember it distinctly."

Three of them, not two. Axel bit his lip. Could Magnus handle all three?

Sure, he'd battled multiple quarry workers at once, but these weren't average idiots. They were trained soldiers, well-acquainted with violence and fighting.

"You left the gate open, so you take care of the snake, Rovert."

"No way," Rovert said. "What if it's venomous?"

"You're wearing leather boots. With steel studs," the gruff voice replied. "Haven't seen a snake yet that can bite through those."

"I—I don't do well with snakes, either," Rovert said.

A sharp sigh spilled into the hallway. "You have a sword, don't you? Just cut the thing's head off."

"I—I'm not—"

The gruff one cursed. "*Fine*. Come on, Rovert. I'll show you how it's done. Bring your sword, if it's not too *heavy* for you."

Axel's heart rate tripled. He gripped his sword tighter, ready to jump into the fray and help Magnus if he had to. Then he exhaled a calming breath. Better to not let the excitement of the moment get to him.

When the first soldier stepped into the hallway, Magnus clamped his hand around the soldier's ankle and yanked him off his feet. His sword clattered away. The second soldier got Magnus's pickax in his chest.

"Hold him down," Magnus ordered.

Calum and Axel jumped on the first soldier's chest, and Axel pressed his sword against the soldier's neck.

"Don't move. Don't make a sound," Axel said. "You do, and you'll end up like your friends over there."

To his credit, the soldier complied.

Magnus charged into the room and out of sight. A loud gasp followed, then came a dull thud on the wood floor.

The soldier Magnus had killed lay in the doorway with his lifeless brown eyes fixed on Axel and his chest oozing red blood onto the floor.

Axel stared at him for a moment then looked away. The sight churned his stomach at first, but that soldier had deserved to die.

Anyone who serves in the King's army deserves death.

Even so, Axel didn't have to keep staring at him.

When Magnus returned, flecks of red blood dotted his neck and torso. He knelt down near the first soldier. "Where is your armory?"

The soldier stared at Magnus with wide eyes. "H-how did you—?"

"Escape?" Magnus leaned close. "Easily. You humans are predictable."

Axel shot Magnus a glare.

"This is one of the soldiers who bought me from the slave traders and sold me to the quarry," Magnus said. "Which also means you have my armor somewhere. So where is your armory?"

"Hopefully he didn't sell it like he sold you." Calum picked up one of the swords from the floor and looked it over as if considering whether to switch it out for the one he'd taken from the courtyard.

"If he did, he will die like his friends, here." Magnus glowered at the soldier, and iron filled his voice. "Must I ask you a third time?"

The soldier shook his head. His gruff voice quivered as he replied, "N-no, we didn't sell it. It's still here. It doesn't fit anyone we've ever run into. It's too big."

"That is because it was made for *me*, not for you or any other human." Magnus nodded to Axel, who pulled his sword back, and then Magnus jerked the soldier to his feet. "Show us. Now."

"What about food?" Calum asked.

"Armor first. It will ensure our safe departure from this place."

He led them to the end of the hall to two staircases, one that led up to the second floor and one that descended to a lower level. Axel glanced into each room they passed to make sure no one would sneak up behind them.

"The armory's downstairs with the cellar and the brig," the soldier said.

"What's upstairs?" Axel asked.

"Our sleeping quarters."

"Anyone up there?" Magnus asked.

"Everyone's out at the—" The soldier squinted at them. "*You* started the fire, didn't you?"

"Smart boy," Magnus said. "Where's your pantry?"

"Upstairs at the opposite end of the hall."

Magnus nodded to Calum and Axel. "Take him upstairs. Have him show you the pantry. Collect all the food and supplies you can carry, then find some rope and restrain him. Once I retrieve my armor, I will rejoin you there."

Calum nodded.

"Do *not* speak to him, and do *not* let him out of your sight. Crystal?"

"Clear." Axel poked the soldier with the tip of his sword, and he jumped. "Let's go."

Upstairs they passed several rooms with bunk beds, all neatly made. One room, smaller than the rest, had only one bed inside, with a large chest sitting at the foot of the bed.

"That's the commander's room," the soldier said.

"Keep quiet." Axel shoved him forward with his free hand. Calum scowled at him, but Axel ignored it.

Sure enough, at the far end of the hall on the right side, they found a room with a small iron stove in the corner and a long table lined with about two dozen chairs. Early morning sunlight filtered in through a window on the left side of the room.

The soldier pointed to a door in the corner opposite of the stove.

"Calum, go check it. I'll watch him."

Calum went over and pulled the door open. "Looks like this is it."

Axel gave the soldier another shove. "You. Help Calum load up a few bags."

While Axel watched, they filled three large sacks with a variety of tasty foods. Ultimately most of the food had come from his farm in the first place, so he figured he was just reclaiming what rightfully belonged to him. It wasn't stealing if it was his to begin with, right?

"You know we'll find you," the soldier threatened. "We'll hunt you down and exact the King's justice upon you for killing two of our own, for burning the King's timber, and for stealing from us. You've tied your own nooses."

"Be quiet," Axel said.

The soldier dropped a pair of apples into a sack. "You get marks for courage, though. I don't know of anyone who has ever dared to rob one of the King's outposts before. No one's ever done it and lived to tell about it, anyway."

"I said *be quiet.*" Axel stepped torward him. "Or I'll make you be quiet."

Calum glanced at them but kept stuffing food into his bag.

"And you're doing all of this with a *Saurian?* How can you even stand to be in that thing's company?"

Axel backhanded the soldier's mouth, not out of any sort of love for Magnus, but because he'd warned the soldier twice.

It felt good to hit him. *Really* good.

"*Axel.*" Calum glared at him.

"I warned him." Axel stared at the soldier, who held his jaw and glowered at him. "Say another word, and I'll kill you. Crystal?"

The soldier clamped his mouth shut. He wasn't a big guy—probably weighed somewhere between Calum and Axel. Short brown hair, a long scar across his left cheek. Black armor, but no helmet. Maybe in his forties.

What was taking Magnus so long? They'd been in the pantry for awhile now.

Axel glanced out the window. It didn't look like anyone was headed for the outpost, but the longer they tarried, the more likely they'd get caught inside.

"Hey!" Calum's voice snapped Axel back to attention.

The soldier and Calum grappled in the pantry. The sacks dropped and spilled food across the stone floor as the two fought for control. Somehow the soldier managed to wrench Calum's sword away and now held it instead.

He drew his elbow back, ready to impale Calum with the blade.

106

CHAPTER TWELVE

Axel lurched forward, his sword extended. The blade knifed into the soldier's torso just under his armpit, one of the only openings in his leather armor.

The soldier dropped his sword and cried out, then toppled down to the floor, shuddering but still alive.

Axel adjusted his footing and jammed the sword farther in, and the soldier yelped again.

Calum staggered out of the pantry, almost tripping on one of the sacks as he stared at Axel with wide eyes.

Axel yanked his sword out of the soldier's body and stepped back. The soldier gurgled, and blood oozed down his cheeks.

"That'll shut you up." Axel moved close to the soldier again. Despite all of that, he was still alive.

Axel raised his sword over his head and rammed the tip of his blade through the soldier's leather breastplate and into his chest.

The soldier groaned a final breath and stopped moving. Axel jerked his sword free of the soldier's body and looked back at Calum, who'd clenched his eyes shut. Axel opened his mouth to speak, but a deep voice filled the room.

"What are you doing?"

Axel spun around to face whatever new threat had presented itself.

Instead, Magnus stood in the doorway, his hands full of gear. "What did you do?"

"He attacked Calum, so I killed him." Axel motioned toward the pantry with his head, even though Calum now stood to the side of it.

Magnus set the gear—a variety of weapons, supplies, and even some leather armor—on the table and headed toward them. He looked past Axel at the dead soldier and exhaled a long breath through his nostrils. "Now you know the cruelty of the world in which we live, and you have added to it."

Axel glanced at Calum. Why was Magnus on his case about this? "He was gonna run Calum through."

"You saved your friend's life at the expense of another's." Magnus glanced between him and Calum. "This is what life on the run is like. Kill or be killed. Our foes will show us no mercy. From now on, every one of the King's soldiers is an enemy to be met only with the edge of your swords. We are all fugitives, all wanted men."

Axel nodded. A rush swelled within him. Traveling, living by the sword—it's what he'd wanted his whole life. "I have no problem with that."

Magnus turned to Calum. "And what about you?"

Calum swallowed. "I can do it too, if I have to."

"Only when necessary," Magnus said. "This man died because you two were careless. He saw an opportunity and overpowered you. Fortunately, Axel reacted first and saved you both."

If there was anything for Axel to feel bad about, it was that he'd let his guard down.

"It's partially my fault," Axel admitted. "I looked away for too long, and that's when he got the advantage."

"Your inattention almost cost Calum his life. I told you to watch the soldier at all times." Magnus shook his head.

"Did you find your armor?" Calum rummaged through the pile of supplies on the table, perhaps to distance himself from the bloody scene Axel had caused.

Magnus exhaled a sigh. "No."

"So where is it?" Axel asked.

Magnus stared at him. "Had you left that soldier alive, we could have asked him again."

Axel folded his arms. "Yeah, well, it was either him or Calum, like I said. I didn't exactly have time to think it through."

"Evidently."

Axel rolled his eyes. In the short time Axel had known him, Magnus had already killed like a dozen people. Why did he keep trying to make Axel feel bad about what he'd done?

Sure, some small part of Axel regretted that he'd had to do it, but the soldier had condemned himself by attacking Calum. Even before that, when he'd joined the King's army. Anyone clad in the black armor of the tyrannical King deserved the same fate, and Axel would happily disburse it to any who dared challenge him.

"The commander's room is next door," Calum said. "There's a big chest inside. Did you check there?"

"Not yet. First, I want each of you to select a couple of weapons from that table. Once we get out of here, I will teach you how to fight. Only take what you can carry along with a bag of food and a pack of supplies."

Axel walked over to the table and perused the assortment. "I think I did pretty well just now with my sword."

Magnus snorted. "I have no intention of arguing with you. If you do not wish to learn anything, I will not waste time teaching you."

Calum picked up a spear. "You know how to use all of these?"

Magnus nodded. "Yes, of course."

"What about this?" Grinning, Axel picked up an axe.

"You will be too slow with that. It is too heavy."

"Doesn't seem too bad." Axel hefted it up and down. It did have some good weight to it, but Axel hadn't worked on a farm all his life to be a weakling. "And you said I could pick whatever I wanted."

"You will both learn the sword either way, so pick a second weapon, and I will teach you that. If there is another spear, I would recommend that. Eventually, you can learn to throw it, and then our hunting problem is solved."

"Alright. Fine." Axel tossed the axe back onto the table, and it clattered to a stop. "Ruin all of my fun."

Calum peered out the window. "Whatever we do, we need to do it quickly. Looks like they're coming back."

Magnus growled and stormed toward the door. "Make your choices now. Find some armor that fits, and load up the bags with food."

Axel scooped up a padded shirt, leather armor, a pair of greaves, some steel-studded gauntlet-style gloves, and corresponding armor for his legs. He put it all on as quickly as he could then tucked a length of rope into the bag. Calum did the same, and then they gathered up what spilled food they could.

As they finished packing, Magnus returned to the kitchen, and despite his feelings toward the Saurian, Axel couldn't help but marvel at the sight.

Magnus wore bright blue armor from his legs up to his neck, plus a helmet clearly designed to fit a Saurian's head. Even his tail had armor, and it was tipped with a long blade. In his right hand he held a sword so large that a strong man would have to wield it with two hands. Its silver hilt gleamed, stark against its iridescent blue blade.

The closer Magnus drew to them, the more detail Axel could see in the armor. Up close, the metal, which matched that of Magnus's blade, had an opalescent sheen to it, and it gleamed with hues of pink and green, depending on how the light hit it. The effect was beautiful, but its application in the armor now covering Magnus's body sent chills through Axel.

"Whoa." Axel gawked at him. "Nice armor."

"It is made from Blood Ore, a rare metal found only in the mountains near my home. Much harder and lighter than steel, but supremely difficult to forge."

"Where'd you get it?" Calum asked.

Magnus clacked his talons on his breastplate and looked past Calum and Axel into the ether. "It was a gift."

Axel blinked. "A gift from...?"

"My father." A low growl rumbled from Magnus's throat. "But he is gone now."

Calum glanced between the two of them. "The breastplate is a work of art."

"And supremely necessary," Magnus said. "Saurians are somewhat naturally armored because of our scales. As we advance in age, they grow stronger and more durable, but even so, our underbellies are weak, hence the utilization of this specific piece of armor."

Axel asked, "If it's made from Blood Ore, then why is it blue?"

"We have little time. Walk with me, and I will explain." Magnus slid his broadsword into a long sheath that ran the length of his back and snatched two of the bags from the table.

He led them to the staircase, and they ventured downstairs again, with Magnus leading the way. Calum followed him, and Axel brought up the rear. It made sense to protect the weakest member of their party in such a way.

"Names can be deceiving," Magnus said to them. "The ore itself is a dark blue color, not red like its name suggests, but the rocks from which it is mined are a blood-red color. Once forged, Blood Ore brightens to the brilliant shade of blue you see here."

"Wow," Calum said as they entered the courtyard.

"We can discuss blacksmithing later," Magnus said. "We have already lingered here too long. We need to reach the cover of the forest before it is too late."

THAT NIGHT, Calum exhaled a long breath when they finally finished setting up the camp.

The three of them had made it back into the forest with their loot just in time to avoid the returning soldiers. Another substantial trek through the woods consumed almost the rest of the day, including a hike along the base of one of the Snake Mountains, which Calum could scarcely stop marveling up at.

Carrying all that extra weight had worked Calum's sore legs more than even the toughest day's work at the quarry. As Calum and Axel began unpacking food around the campfire, Magnus stood and started to walk into the woods, but he left his bag of food at the camp.

The sight surprised Calum, and he started to follow Magnus.

"Where are you going?" The thought that Magnus might leave them alone stirred worry in Calum's chest. "You're, uh… you're coming back, right?"

Magnus stopped, turned back, and looked down at him. "I need some time to myself. Time to meditate."

Calum blinked at him. "Meditate?"

"It means I will silence myself and listen. It is a relaxation technique and a means to connect to a deeper power than what any Saurian can achieve on his own."

"Well, you have fun with that." Axel's scoff sounded all the way from back at the campsite, and Calum inwardly cringed.

Ignoring Axel, Magnus gave Calum a slight nod, then he disappeared into the trees.

About fifteen minutes after Magnus left, Axel said, "He's so weird. He's huge and dangerous, but now he's going off to *meditate?*"

"He's not like us, Axel. He's a Saurian. I'm sure their ways are as different from ours as our appearances."

"I don't understand why he's sticking around with us. Why doesn't he just go?"

"Do you *want* him to go?" Calum countered.

"That's not what I mean." Axel leaned back against a tree and gnawed on an apple.

"Then what do you mean?"

"I don't like him, but from what I can tell, he doesn't like us much either. So why is he still here?"

Calum shrugged and reached for a piece of dried pork. He bit into it, and a tantalizing rush of smoky, meaty flavors teased his tongue. "I don't know. If he wanted to leave, we couldn't stop him."

"That's what I'm afraid of. He could do *whatever* he wanted, and we couldn't stop him."

Calum just shook his head at that, but Axel hadn't been there when Magnus saved him from the Gronyx's pit, or when Calum had given

Magnus the chicken leg, or when they'd taken down Jidon and his men together. He wouldn't have the same perspective that Calum did.

Instead of trying to explain all of that to Axel, he asked, "Don't you think he'd have done it by now if he meant us harm?"

"No. He used us to help him get into the Rock Outpost, and now that we've done it, what reason does he have to keep us around? We're some of the only people who know he's on the loose. If he wanted to make sure we didn't talk, he could just kill us."

"But he won't."

Axel sat up. "You don't know that."

"I'm pretty sure, actually," Calum said. "I think we're safe. You have no idea how many times he could have killed me yesterday but didn't. Why would he suddenly want to do it now?"

"Believe whatever you want, but I'm not gonna let my guard down while he's around." Axel folded his arms and leaned back against the tree again. "Not for an instant."

A green foot emerged from behind Axel's tree and stomped the dirt next to him.

Axel jolted forward, groping for his sword, but he couldn't get it out of its sheath. When Magnus stepped into full view, his blue armor glimmering in the light from the campfire, Axel gave up his struggle.

"I have no desire to harm either of you." Magnus eyed Axel. "Whether you are on your guard or not."

Axel glared at him, and Calum stifled a chuckle.

"Did you save me any food?"

Calum nodded and tossed Magnus the rest of the chunk of pork he'd been gnawing on. Magnus popped the entire piece into his gaping jaws, chomped on it a few times, then swallowed it while Axel recovered his position by the tree, still scowling.

"We have endured a long couple of days," Magnus said. "We will eat, then we will sleep. Tomorrow morning, we must continue our journey."

Calum nodded, though Magnus's words came as little consolation. That night, after the biggest dinner Calum had ever eaten, he fell asleep.

BLINDING LIGHT SHONE EVERYWHERE. Just like the night before, Calum's attempts to shield his eyes proved futile, and again, the light seemed to actually penetrate his body.

The same powerful figure emerged from the light. Same golden crown, same white armor, same silver sword, same gigantic white wings. As before, his eyes flickered like two balls of fire above the white armored mask that covered his nose and mouth.

Again, the sight left Calum dumbfounded.

The circular living map appeared again, first from a wide overhead view, and then much closer as it followed a path from one side of the lakes to the other. As before, it centered on the base of a range of red mountains.

A black hole opened among the red rocks.

"Go, Calum. Find the Arcanum. Set me free." The voice resonated around Calum. *Within* him. "Go, Calum."

Calum shook his head. He still held his hand up to shield his eyes from the light. It still didn't do any good. "I don't understand."

"You will," the voice said. "Go. I am with you. Always."

"Who are you?" Calum asked.

"I am Lumen, General of Light."

CALUM BLINKED and the vision disappeared, except for the bright light. He held up his hand again, but this time he actually blocked the light from reaching his eyes. That didn't make any sense.

He tilted his head and a shadow covered his face. It belonged to one of the many surrounding trees in the forest, and the light, he realized, came from the morning sun. A yawn escaped his throat as he sat up.

"Good morning," said a quiet, but deep voice behind him.

Calum spun around and saw Magnus seated on a tree stump, still clad in his armor except for his helmet. In the morning sunlight, his armor glimmered in glorious shades of light-blue with tinges of pink, green, and even some purple undertones.

Magnus held a finger up to his scaly lips. "Axel is still sleeping."

Calum nodded and rubbed his eyes.

"Sleep well?"

"Yes. No."

Magnus eyed him. "Well, which is it?"

Calum stretched a kink in his neck. Should he tell Magnus about his dream? Or would Magnus think he was crazy?

"It is a simple question, Calum."

"I—" Calum paused. He could tell Magnus. They'd saved each other's lives more than a few times each now. Calum owed him an honest answer, if not much more. "I had a strange dream last night."

"Do you dream often?"

Calum shook his head. "Never. Not since last night."

"Two dreams in as many nights?"

"Yes."

"Interesting."

"It gets even stranger," Calum said. "The dream was almost the same both nights."

Magnus leaned forward. "What did you dream?"

Calum glanced at Axel, who still lay flat on his back, his eyes closed. "A figure appeared to me out of the brightest light I've ever seen. He showed me a map and told me to find some place called the Arcanum to set him free. At first he didn't say who he was, but this time he said his name was Lumen, and he called himself the General of Light."

Magnus straightened his back. His mouth opened, revealing his pointed teeth, but no sound came out.

"What?" Now Calum leaned forward. "Does that mean something to you?"

Magnus blinked at him. "Do you know who Lumen is?"

"Um…" Calum stared at his boots, but they didn't give him an answer.

"Lumen, the General of Light. Do you not know your own race's history? The history of Kanarah itself?"

Calum shook his head. "My parents were killed when I was eight, and I spent the rest of my life in that quarry. There's not much outside of rocks, shovels, pickaxes, and hard work that I know."

Magnus exhaled a long breath. "Then there is much you must learn."

"About what?" Axel sat up and stretched his thick arms toward the sky.

"About the King and Lumen, and their battle a thousand years ago."

Axel tilted his head. "Maybe I should go back to sleep."

Calum could hardly comprehend what Magnus was claiming. "The King is... a thousand years old?"

"Some believe he uses a form of sorcery to prolong his life." Magnus sat back on his stump. "According to legend, a thousand years ago, Lumen rebelled against the King to set humans and the other races free from his tyrannical reign."

Calum looked at Axel, who shrugged.

"At the end of a long and arduous battle, Lumen was defeated. Instead of killing him, though, the King banished him to a secret place—the Arcanum—for a thousand years. Legend says he is still there, waiting to be set free.

"When he is released, he will lead an army to save the people once and for all. *All* people, not just humans." Magnus eyed Calum. "And now, almost a thousand years later, Lumen visited you in a dream not once, but twice."

Axel's head swiveled toward Calum. "What?"

Calum repeated the dream to Axel in more detail than he'd given Magnus, including the locations the living maps had shown. "And he showed me a spot at the base of some red mountains across a huge valley with some lakes—"

"Red mountains?" Magnus extended his hand as if to stall the conversation. "You saw red mountains?"

Calum nodded. "A black hole opened, like the mouth of a cave or something, at the base of some mountains, and they were red. Very red, like blood."

Magnus clacked his talons on his breastplate. "You are right to describe them as blood-red. That is their namesake. They are called the Blood Mountains for exactly that reason."

Calum straightened his spine. The places in his dreams actually existed?

"That is where the name for Blood Ore comes from—the mountains are red, even though the ore itself is blue. The path you referenced is also real, as are the lakes." Magnus waited a moment. When Calum didn't say anything, Magnus asked, "Surely you have heard of the Tri-Lakes?"

Calum shook his head.

"I've heard of them," Axel said. "Some of the King's soldiers were talking about them one night at the tavern. Said they're massive, and they're full of dangerous creatures, but the surrounding valley is dead. Nothing lives or grows there."

Magnus nodded. "That much is true."

"How do you know?" Calum asked.

"I have been there," Magnus said.

Silence hovered between them.

"The Valley of the Tri-Lakes connects the eastern half of Kanarah, where we are now, to the western half." Magnus stoked the campfire with a stick. "It is there you will find the Blood Mountains, home to my people. The city of Reptilius sits among the highest peaks in the mountain range. That is where the Saurians live."

Axel glanced at Calum. "So why aren't you there now?"

Magnus's eyes narrowed, then he exhaled a long breath and looked away.

After a long pause, Calum leaned forward. "Magnus?"

"I do not believe your dreams are coincidental or meaningless," Magnus said.

Axel rolled his eyes. "Or they're just dreams."

"Unlikely. The King himself foretold that Lumen would be released at the end of the thousand years." Magnus looked at Calum. "Though no one knows how. No one knows where Lumen is locked away. No one has had any idea—until now."

Calum's eyes widened. "You mean…"

"Yes." Magnus focused his gaze. "Calum, you may hold the key to setting Lumen free and saving all of Kanarah from the King's oppression."

CHAPTER THIRTEEN

Western Kanarah

L illy had succeeded in keeping Sharion from harm, but doing so had cost her.

Roderick had personally assured her that the pair of rusty old shackles now clamped to her ankles would remain on not only while she rode in the wagon but also during trips to the woods to relieve herself. They would stay on her all the time, no exceptions.

What's more, Roderick informed Lilly that he would now personally oversee her trips to the woods—to protect his "investment." She didn't like how he smirked when he told her, but it was worlds better than enduring the threat of his men every time she had to answer nature's call.

As much as she hated to admit it, her life as a slave had settled into a miserable routine. The caravan drew nearer and nearer to Trader's Pass, carrying her farther and farther away from her home.

The night after she'd saved Sharion, she and Colm huddled close together, as always, to stay warm. Sharion had snuck closer to them as well, ever-willing to steal warmth yet never willing to ask for it or accept it when offered.

Then a chorus of loud whoops and hollers sounded from the forest around them, wresting Lilly from the relative safety and tranquility of the moment.

"What is that?" Lilly whispered, shuddering.

"None of your concern, child," Colm replied. "Try to rest. Tomorrow is another long day of travel. We should make Trader's Pass by midday."

The shouts eventually stopped, but about a half hour later, Roderick and several of his men appeared from the moonlit woods. They dragged a net behind them.

Inside, a black form thrashed and snapped at their hands, snarling and growling.

At first they headed toward Lilly's wagon with the thing, but instead of putting the creature into the wagon with Colm, Sharion, and Lilly, they tossed the thrashing pile of net and beast into a separate wagon far behind hers. Lilly caught sight of a pair of angry blue eyes before the beast disappeared out of sight.

She nudged Colm, who remained fixed on the procession. "What is that?"

"A Wolf, I suppose."

"They caught a Wolf?" Lilly gawked. "How? I've heard they can move like shadows through the darkness."

"Apparently you've never met one, then. Surely, there are many who can do as you say, but some are as incapable as the average human or Windgale." Colm coughed into the crook of his elbow. "Catching a Wolf for this bunch isn't that impressive. Not long before they seized you, they managed to capture a Saurian. Now *that's* a feat not easily accomplished."

Colm had seemingly only ever told Lilly the truth, but she had serious doubts about his claim. "These idiots managed to subdue a Saurian?"

"That they did," Colm replied plainly. "Now would you bless me with a few hours of sleep before the night ends? I don't sleep as well once the sun comes up."

"Sure. Sorry."

119

"No trouble. Just shift a bit closer, will you, child? This batch of night air chills me more than usual."

Lilly wrapped her arm around Colm's back and pulled closer. She leaned her head on his shoulder with her eyes closed and drifted off to sleep once more.

COLM HAD BEEN RIGHT. They reached Trader's Pass by midday, but before they headed into the pass, Roderick and Luggs let Lilly and Sharion relieve themselves in the ever-sparse woods.

"Enjoy the scenery while it lasts." Luggs chuckled. "From here on out, it's flat and gray."

Lilly ducked behind a bush so her lower half wouldn't be visible to the men. Sharion did the same right beside her. By now Lilly had adjusted to having to share space, but she still didn't like it.

Sharion remained an enigma. She seemed lucid about half the time, and the other half she scratched her scalp and mumbled nonsense. She'd made no mention of Lilly saving her from enduring Adgar, Gammel, and Luggs's abuse. Perhaps she didn't comprehend what Lilly had done or why she'd done it.

As they walked back toward Roderick and Luggs, Lilly said, "Sharion, I—"

"Don't speak to me. Don't you *dare* speak to me." Sharion hissed her words.

Lilly clamped her mouth shut. *Alright, then.*

While on her way back to the wagon, Lilly saw Gammel and Adgar escorting a lithe black animal toward the woods as well. The Wolf. She wore a muzzle over her snout, and each of the men guided her with ropes looped around her neck attached to the long poles they held. Her blue eyes locked on Lilly as they passed each other, and she issued a low growl.

Not a day for making friends, apparently.

Luggs escorted Lilly and Sharion back to the wagon while Roderick stayed in the woods to keep watch. As Luggs opened the door to the wagon, a howl and a series of snarls sounded from the woods.

"Look out! She's loose!" Gammel shouted.

As Luggs turned toward the commotion, Lilly seized her chance. She grabbed the cage door and yanked it open. Luggs turned back in time for the metal bars to smash into his forehead, and he dropped, stunned and bleeding from a nasty gash above his eyebrows.

Lilly wrenched the keys from the lock and fingered through them until she found one that she thought matched her shackles. Within seconds, she was free. Lucky guess.

"Here." She tossed the key ring to Colm and then bolted up the road, past the other wagons and away from Trader's Pass. By now she'd gotten good at this running thing, and she'd even begun to enjoy it. Arrows thudded into the dirt around her as she ran, but she didn't stop. She couldn't stop.

She'd run forever if she had to.

The men shouted behind her, but she didn't dare turn back. It would only slow her down.

A patch of trees beckoned her forward. Not much, but it beat heading into the barren gray surrounding Trader's Pass where they could easily see her.

She ran deep into the trees. They ended some fifty yards ahead and opened into a clearing of some sort. Based on what she'd seen while running to the trees, it didn't look like it was a drop-off like she'd encountered before. She hoped to find more trees and more woods farther beyond.

Lilly cleared the woods and stumbled into a small field of tall grass. The footsteps of the men behind her still thundered, but she'd put more distance between them. Without the cover of the trees to hide, though, they'd soon find her.

She breathed quick shallow breaths, and her heart drummed. She had to keep running, or she had to hide. The grass was tall, but not tall enough that she could hide. They'd see her if they came within ten feet of her position—maybe as little as five if she were lucky. But if she could make the tree line across the field, perhaps she could lose them.

Her legs burned and her stomach growled for food, but her resolve pushed her forward nonetheless. She bolted into the grass.

"There she is!" a voice shouted, followed by a chorus of rallying cries from even farther behind her.

Lilly kept running.

Halfway into the field, she tripped over something. A boulder. She skidded through the grass and it bit into her knees and her palms.

She chanced a look back. She couldn't see the men following her, but she could hear them. So much for her growing lead.

Lilly leaped up to her feet and kept running. The tree line drew ever nearer. She was going to make it. The wind whipped her face and cooled her perspiring forehead as she practically flew forward—even though running could never compare to the sheer exhilaration of flying.

Thirty yards from the trees, she heard the first metallic thunk, then the second soon after. Heavy, armored footsteps clanked behind her, growing closer, louder with each stride she took. She clenched her teeth and pushed forward even harder, but the sound persisted.

With fifteen yards to go, Roderick's massive form appeared in her peripheral vision as he ran alongside her. He even gave her a wave and a toothy smile. How was he so fast? It should've been impossible.

Lilly cursed and tried to dart to her right, away from him, but he clamped down on her wrist with his gloved hand and slowed them to a halt. She swung her fist at his face. He easily blocked the punch with his forearm and shoved her down onto her back in the grass.

"Why won't you let me go?" she screamed. Tears burned her eyes, and she kicked and punched at him, all to no avail. "I just want to go home!"

"Three escape attempts in what, three days' time?" Roderick whistled. "It all runs together out here in the wilds. I'm tempted just to cut you loose."

Roderick snatched her up, his arms wrapped around hers, restraining her while she thrashed and twisted and tried to break free until she couldn't anymore. Her fight gave way to miserable sobs as he started walking back toward the wagons with her in his restraining embrace.

"Then do it!" Her voice no louder than a pained whisper, she repeated, "I just want to go home."

"You already know that's not how this works, Angel." Roderick shook his spike-haired head. "I'm selling you to an old friend of mine, a longtime client. You're gonna belong to him; but until then, you belong to me. Get used to it."

Lilly bowed her head and whimpered.

COLM HELD LILLY CLOSE, stroking her hair while she sobbed into his shoulder. "There, there, child. Breathe deeply. All will be well."

Lilly jerked upright, filled with rage. She glared at him.

"No, it *won't* all be well, Colm." She wiped the tears from her cheeks. "Roderick means to sell me to some pig friend of his, and every time I try to escape, somehow they catch me. Roderick is faster, stronger, and probably smarter than me, and he knows this area better than I do. I'm doomed to be a slave forever."

She buried her face in his shoulder again and heaved. The wagon jerked forward onto Trader's Pass.

"I'm afraid this new life is one to which you may need to adjust, child."

That was the last thing Lilly wanted to hear. A shudder racked her body, and the sickening twist of hopelessness infected her stomach once again. She released her grasp on Colm, sat up, and wiped the last of the tears from her eyes.

"While I greatly admire your tenacity, there does not seem to be any escape without them noticing or without them catching you again. Were I a younger man, I would fight for your honor and try to buy you time to escape, but these days I'm old, tired, and slow. I'd be a leaf attempting to dam a mighty river."

"If I had my armor and my cape, I could fly out of here. I would fly until they were out of sight, and I'd never look back." Lilly ground her teeth, focusing on calming her breathing next. "If I had my bow, I'd take a few of them down first, before I left. Luggs, Adgar, Gammel. Roderick too, if I had the shot."

"Easy, child. Vengeance is a path from which there is no return."

"It wouldn't be vengeance. It'd be justice. I'm not the only one they've hurt."

"The line between the two is often very thin and easy to cross." He smiled at her. "Forgive me for arguing, but I would hate to see such a beautiful soul blackened by thoughts of revenge."

"If I don't act, my soul will be blackened by something else." Lilly narrowed her eyes at him. "And why don't you want revenge for how they've treated you? You're locked in here, the same as me. You never get angry about anything."

Colm sighed. "Make no mistake, I do not want to be here. Nor do I know the reason why I'm here. But I know the Overlord watches me, and He has sustained me thus far, even in my current circumstance. I believe I am here, now, for a purpose. Perhaps to fulfill some greater good."

Lilly stared at him. *The Overlord wanted Colm here? Unlikely.* "You're locked in a cage. Wouldn't the Overlord rather see you set free to do more good?"

"I don't deny that a part of me wishes that were the case, but when freed I tend to make my way through Kanarah with little reservation about whom I harm in the process. I am a thief, child. Not the most honorable profession, nor the most charitable." He smiled. "But here, I have no choice but to behave and to do good things for my fellow slaves. And if I do steal, it's from people who deserve to be stolen from, and never solely for my benefit."

She frowned. "You have to be locked up to become a good person?"

"Isn't that the idea behind locking people up? To encourage them to become better people?" Colm winked at her.

Back at her home, criminals found within the Sky Realm were tried, convicted, stripped of their capes, and locked in cells under the Aeropolis. To her knowledge, once released, those same criminals almost always returned to their illicit behaviors, with or without their capes. She had no idea how they behaved while imprisoned, though.

"Either way, there's a good chance they still have your armor and your cape stashed somewhere. Probably in one of the smaller wagons without bars, the ones with two wheels and pulled by donkeys instead of horses.

"I've seen them loading and unloading other merchandise to sell, and your armor was quite nice. I imagine Roderick would keep it for its resale value, especially if your cape is aerosilk like you said it was. Plenty of Windgales in Eastern Kanarah would buy an extra cape if they could."

That gave Lilly hope. If she could get out, then perhaps she could get ahold of her cape, at least, if not her armor and her bow as well, and then get out of there. Now that she knew where she needed to look, maybe she could find a way.

She set her face once more and tightened her jaw. She *would* find a way.

"Luggs is pretty sour." Colm chuckled. "Big gash on his forehead. Not a pretty sight. 'Course, he wasn't particularly handsome to begin with."

Lilly smirked.

"Here." Colm glanced around, then under the draping of his cloak, he handed her a roasted drumstick from a chicken's leg.

"Your coin?" Lilly smiled at him.

Colm nodded. "I already ate the thigh. I hope you don't mind. I'm an old man and don't get such delicacies often."

Lilly wrapped her arms around his neck and squeezed him. "Thank you."

CHAPTER FOURTEEN

Eastern Kanarah

Axel rubbed the bridge of his nose and clenched his eyes shut. He was still processing everything that Calum had shared and Magnus had explained, and he wasn't sure he believed or agreed with any of it.

"So your plan for us is to head toward the Valley of the Tri-Lakes, cross it, and find a secret cave at the base of the Blood Mountains so we can release a legendary warrior who's going to defeat the King and free us from his tyrannical reign once and for all?" Axel opened his eyes and folded his arms. "And you're getting all of this from a couple of dreams?"

Magnus glanced at them both and nodded. "Yes. That is precisely what I am saying."

"Right." Axel rolled his eyes. What had he gotten himself into? "I knew I should have turned you two in when I had the chance."

"Do you have something better in mind?" Magnus asked. "Or do you prefer to wander the wilderness aimlessly for the rest of our lives?"

"Well, I wasn't planning on wasting my life searching for something that isn't there." Axel nodded at Magnus. "And besides, what's in this for you? You got your armor and your sword back. Why do you even care?"

"Saurians view the return of Lumen not as a myth but as truth, a prophecy to be fulfilled. We have suffered at the hands of the King's soldiers as well, albeit not for several centuries now. Still, the King has done my people great harm over the years.

"We believe that Lumen's return and subsequent rise to the throne of Kanarah will bring about a time of peace and prosperity our land has never before seen, so we have been waiting, watching, and counting the years until his return. It appears our count was off by a few years, but his return is nonetheless imminent." Magnus clicked his claws against his breastplate. "Besides, my home is in the Blood Mountains. I wish to see it again."

"So what happens when we get there? Are you just gonna leave us in the mountains on our own?" Axel folded his arms again.

"I do not intend to."

"So you'll just walk us up to the gates of Reptile City and introduce us to all your scaly friends?"

"*Reptilius.*" Magnus corrected him with a huff. "You need only concern yourself with finding Lumen."

"*If* he's even there."

"He's there." Calum leaned forward. "These dreams felt so real, Axel."

"I've had dreams that felt real, too, but that doesn't mean I went out and acted on them the next morning." Axel smirked and rubbed his hands together. "Although, if we're thinking about pursuing what happens in our dreams, the other night I dreamed about this gorgeous brunette I met in a town I visited with my father last year…"

"I see no other explanation for his dreams than the one I have provided," Magnus said. "It makes sense. Lumen's return is near, and with it, the salvation of Kanarah."

"Except you said no one was supposed to know how Lumen comes back or where he is."

"I have awaited Lumen's return for decades, and my people have awaited his return since the war itself. Many Saurians believe he will bring true freedom to Kanarah." Magnus pointed southwest. "The answers lie within that cave. Within the Arcanum."

Axel rolled his eyes. "Just two nights ago you said going into caves was a bad idea."

Magnus glared at him. "You know what I mean. All we have to do is visit it, and then we will know."

"Yeah, we'll know that there's nothing there worth finding." Axel scoffed. "And that's *if* we even make it there in the first place. We can't just waltz along the roads and stop at local towns and villages with Scales here out in the open. Won't be long before someone catches up with us, especially the farther south we go, toward more populated cities."

"We will stick to the mountains, to the woods. We can try to descend into the valley from the range if we can find a safe path down, though that may prove impossible." Magnus scanned the forest and scraped his talons across his breastplate. "Once I have trained you to properly use your weapons, the entire journey will get easier."

Calum nodded. "When do we start?"

Magnus refocused on him. "The training? Or the trip?"

"Both."

"Whoa, hold on." Axel held up his hands. This was moving pretty fast for a crazy idea. Then again, most crazy ideas he'd ever heard or come up with tended to move pretty fast as well—it's just that they usually died out fast, too. This one seemed to be gaining momentum. "I never agreed to go along with this. I don't think it's a good use of our time."

"I don't have anywhere else to be. Nothing else to do." Calum looked at him. "Axel, how long have you wanted to get out and see the world? If we free Lumen—if he's real—then you'll get your chance to do exactly that. Plus, we'll be on the move frequently, which means we'll be that much harder to catch."

"I have been absent from my home for too long." Magnus gazed toward the west. "And if we find Lumen, if we can set him free, then we can change Kanarah forever. We will no longer have to flee from the King's men."

Calum and Magnus stared at Axel.

He sighed and folded his arms again. This was a colossally stupid idea, but Calum was right about one thing: Axel didn't have any other plans, nor did he have somewhere else to be. This path would take him on an adventure, at least, and for now, that could be enough.

"Fine," he said. "You two want to go on your little quest? I guess I'll come along to make sure you're safe."

"Speaking of which," Magnus said. "Both of you, grab your swords. It's time for your first lesson. After that, we eat breakfast, then we get on the move."

"Can't we eat breakfast first?" Axel rubbed his stomach.

"Certainly. Calum and I will go through some basics while you prepare breakfast."

Axel frowned. "That's not what I had in mind."

"You are doubtless acclimated to awakening to breakfast on the table, thanks to your mother, but she is not here." Magnus smirked. "I would have packed her, but we were in such a rush..."

"Yeah, yeah. I get it." Axel glared at him. "Just so you know, I hate cooking, so eat at your own risk."

"In addition to combat training, reading, writing, and history, I will teach you both how to cook. The women in your futures—if any are magnanimous enough to tolerate you—will thank me for it." Magnus turned to Calum. "Come over here. Let us begin."

THE LESSON CAME AND WENT, as did breakfast, more lessons, and lunch. That afternoon, just when Calum thought he was getting the hang of swordplay, Magnus announced it was time to head out. With Magnus in the lead, the trio traveled southwest toward the heart of the Snake Mountains.

Days passed, then weeks. Calum's dreams of Lumen persisted. Lumen kept reminding Calum that his time was near and that he'd soon return, but only with Calum's help. Despite the rough terrain, dwindling food supplies, and even less rest than he'd had at the quarry, Calum pressed onward, galvanized by Lumen's call.

The terrain at the edge of the Snake Mountain range proved as unforgiving as Magnus had suggested. Vegetation struggled to grow in the rocky ground, and they hadn't seen many animals, either. It reminded Calum of the desolate interior of the quarry.

Likewise, the Valley of the Tri-Lakes far below resembled a desert of grays with three massive pools of shimmering water spread across the land under the midday sun. Calum could only see two of the three lakes, but Magnus said there was a third much farther south.

After a fourth day of fruitlessly searching for a feasible route down into the valley, they set up camp about forty feet from the edge of the cliff separating them from the valley below.

Magnus shook his head and gulped down his last bite of smoked venison. "It is as I suspected; I do not believe we can find a way down after all."

Calum sighed. The journey thus far had exhausted him. Whenever they weren't hiking, they were training. And whenever they weren't training, they were hiking. And whenever they weren't hiking or training, Magnus made good on his promise to teach them to read and write, courtesy of sticks and symbols—letters—drawn into the dirt to form words.

As a result, Calum had no trouble falling asleep every night, but dreams of Lumen often woke him early. Whenever they did, he found it harder to fall back to sleep afterward.

"So what does that mean?" he asked.

"It means we must head to Kanarah City," Magnus replied. "That is the starting point for Trader's Pass, the only true path through the valley."

The idea of visiting a city, particularly one as big as Kanarah City, excited Calum, but it also worried him. If the King's soldiers were still searching for the three of them, a city might not be the best place to visit. "Where is that?"

"About a month's walk south from here. It would be less on a road, so I am factoring in the terrain."

"We'll never make it there in time. We'll run outta food long before then." Axel folded his arms. "Sure, we could hunt with the spears if there was anything around here worth hunting, but I haven't seen so much as a squirrel in the last four days. We gotta head east and either hunt in the woods or trade in a nearby village."

Calum raised an eyebrow. "Just yesterday, you said you wouldn't want to go into a village with Magnus."

"That's because I *did* say that, and I meant it, too. But you and I can still go in there and see what we can come up with."

"Axel is right," Magnus said. "Someone will need to watch our supplies anyway. I am happy to oblige. Either way, you two are capable enough with your weapons now that I can trust you on your own."

"Got that right." Axel smirked. "So we head east tomorrow?"

"Southeast," Magnus corrected. "Yes."

"Works for me," Calum replied.

They sat in silence for a few minutes and watched their pitiful campfire dwindle even smaller. Calum finally spoke up. "So I think I'm definitely better at throwing the spear than Axel, but I'm not as good at fighting with it as he is."

Axel rolled his eyes. "Whatever. I'm better at both, and you know it."

Magnus just stared into the darkness toward the east, away from the cliff. Calum expected he'd weigh in, but he hadn't said a word. Perhaps he was just lost in thought, or reliving another dark memory from his past, none of which he'd ever discussed with them in any meaningful detail.

Or perhaps it was something else entirely.

Calum leaned toward him. "Magnus?"

"*Quiet,*" he hissed. "Something is out there."

A low growl sounded over the crackling of the dying campfire, and Calum's heart smacked against the inside of his chest. He still couldn't see anything, but the sound had come from the darkness only a few yards away from their position.

Axel slowly pulled his sword from its sheath, and Calum did the same with his own.

Another growl sounded, then another. Then three more.

"Sabertooths." Magnus latched his helmet onto his head and drew his huge broadsword.

"What?" Calum tried to make eye contact with him, but Magnus didn't divert his vision away from the darkness.

"Sabertooth tigers. Wild cats. Big ones. Carnivorous." Magnus exhaled a long breath through his nostrils. "On your feet, boys. Do not back away from them, no matter what. Stand your ground and fight."

Calum nodded. He could do this. He could defend himself. He'd survived a fall into the Gronyx's pit, after all. He'd battled quarry workers, and he'd raided the Rock Outpost. Remembering those things gave him courage, despite the hammering in his heart.

A set of large feline eyes flickered in the darkness. Then another. Then another. Then another. Then another...

Calum counted twelve sets of shining eyes before the first cat emerged.

An orange-and-black blur with large fangs leaped toward Magnus, who reacted with clean alacrity. He both sidestepped the cat and swung his broadsword at the same time, and the vicious blow knocked the cat off its trajectory. It skidded along the rocky dirt away from the campsite until it stopped against a boulder, motionless, with a devastating wound along its flank.

Eleven to go.

The other cats all charged at once. Wide-eyed, Calum sidestepped the first just like Magnus and the cat flew past. It clawed at the dirt as it slipped over the edge of the cliff and disappeared, roaring the whole way down.

But Calum couldn't have avoided the next cat no matter what he did. Its gigantic fangs just missed Calum's head as it tackled him to the ground with its front paws. The fangs had to be at least a foot long, if not more.

Up close, it smelled like rancid meat and the stink of nature gone sour. The cat was gaunt yet powerful, doubtless even more desperate than Calum and the others for a good meal. And if Calum didn't do something soon, he'd *become* the meal.

Calum tried to push the cat off him, but that proved impossible. He wasn't nearly strong enough, and the cat had dug its claws into Calum's leather chest armor, anchoring itself in place.

As the cat leaned its huge head toward his face, Calum plunged his sword into the side of the cat's neck. The cat stiffened and dropped on its side, off of Calum.

He'd done it. He'd actually killed one of them.

No time to celebrate. A third and a fourth cat charged at him, one right after another.

Instead of standing his ground like Magnus said, Calum stepped forward before the front cat could jump, timed his swing, and took it out with a vicious hack to its head. It was a trick he'd used on Axel a few times when they were sparring, and it was one of the only ways he'd managed to win so far.

Axel might've been stronger, but Calum was just a little bit faster.

But there was only ever *one* of Axel to spar with. Calum still had another cat to deal with.

He spun away to avoid the next cat, but by the time he repositioned, the cat reared up on its hind legs and swiped at his head. Calum wasn't fast enough to dodge the blow, but his reflexes brought his left forearm up in time to block the blow.

Sharp pain flared in his forearm as the cat's claws punctured through the thick leather armored gauntlet, and Calum winced. Better there than his unprotected head, but he'd paid the price all the same.

The swipe also knocked him off-balance, but he quickly recovered his footing and held his sword at the ready.

The cat rose up on its hind haunches to swipe at him again, but this time Calum ducked low and jammed his blade up into the cat's chest. The cat toppled to Calum's left and lay still in the dirt.

Magnus's training had served him well. He hadn't hesitated, he hadn't been afraid. He'd just done what he had to do.

No more cats charged him, but two of them now circled Axel from different directions. Not good.

Calum hollered and ran toward the nearest one. It turned and pounced at him faster than he expected, but he managed to raise his sword and intercept its fangs with a loud clang.

Even so, the blow sent him reeling backward. His right foot caught on something and he landed on his back. His sword tumbled away, and as Calum groped for it, the cat mounted him with its fangs angled toward his head.

Calum shifted his torso hard to the left, and the fangs dug into the ground instead of his face. When Calum grabbed onto them with his hands, the cat roared and shook his head, shaking Calum along with it.

It swiped at Calum with both of its front paws and tried to pull him off, but he didn't let go, even when the cat's claws latched onto his right shoulder pad and wrenched him downward.

Calum yelled as the cat thrashed him about. He timed it just right and released his grip on one of the cat's more vigorous jerks, freeing him from the entirety of its weight for just a second.

He rolled toward his sword, scooped it into his right hand, twisted back toward the cat, and jammed it between the fangs, into the cat's gaping mouth. The cat stopped mid-lunge and dropped chin-first, but its upper half pinned Calum's legs to the ground.

Now another cat approached him, snarling. Its spotted face contorted as it spread its jaws wide and roared at him.

Calum yanked the sword from the dead cat's mouth and tried to push it off of him, but he couldn't. Was he really so weak that he couldn't even free himself from the carcass of a dead animal? Was that weakness going to be the death of him?

He managed to wrest one of his legs free, and he pushed with all his might to pull the other one loose, but he was already too late.

As the other cat shifted its weight against its back legs and sprang toward him, all Calum could do was raise his sword in a feeble attempt to fend it off.

CHAPTER FIFTEEN

A green-and-blue blur rammed the cat from the side and sent it spiraling toward the cliff's edge.

Magnus.

Calum exhaled the breath he'd taken in.

The cat's claws stopped its momentum before it reached the drop-off. It righted itself, snarled, and charged Magnus, but he sidestepped again and grabbed one of its fangs with his free hand. He pulled the cat close, swiped its front legs out from under it with his tail, and raised his sword. In one hearty blow he severed the cat's head from its body and held it in his hand.

Axel skewered the last cat through its eye with his sword and a victorious yell. The cat slumped to the ground, and Axel looked around. "That's it? No more?"

"What, not enough for you?" Calum, with one leg still pinned under the dead cat, sucked in some quick breaths. He pushed against it with his other leg until he managed to pull his leg free.

Only when Calum stood to his feet and surveyed the aftermath of the battle did it truly hit him that they'd made it—that *he'd* made it. He'd used what Magnus had taught him, and he'd survived.

Sure, his left forearm was bleeding, and constantly getting knocked down had left his head aching, but he'd made it through.

Axel gave a mischievous grin. "I was having fun."

"Good work, you two." Magnus scanned the darkness around their campsite, then he tossed the sabertoothed cat's head near his spot by the fire.

"Thanks." Calum wiped the blood from his sword on the hide of the nearest dead cat. "So do we just leave these carcasses here, or what?"

"I wanna know if we can eat these things," Axel said. "I mean, it's not my first choice, but I'm pretty hungry."

"I have never tasted the flesh of this beast," Magnus started, "but drag this headless one over to the fire. Perhaps the smell of one of their own burning will serve to repel others, and perhaps we may find them to be edible. I am going to do a quick check of the surrounding area."

As he walked into the main hall of the Rock Outpost, Commander Beynard Anigo could hear the men discussing Commander Pordone's death in hushed tones. It signaled a lack of respect, both for the situation and for the dead, and it represented one of many issues he would doubtless have to correct if he intended to complete his mission efficiently.

The moment Commander Anigo presented himself to the soldiers, all of whom had gathered before the stone fireplace in the common room, they went quiet.

Good, he mused. *They aren't completely lacking in discipline.*

"Greetings, fellow soldiers of the King," he addressed them. "I am Commander Beynard Anigo. In light of Commander Pordone's untimely demise and the business he left unfinished—namely the treason of two quarry workers and one farmhand—I have been sent here as a replacement to see that justice is served."

None of them said anything in response, nor did they dare to move. Perhaps Pordone hadn't been so lax in his standards for them after all.

Ever since their time together in the officers' academy in Solace,

Commander Anigo had never liked Pordone, but he certainly hadn't wished injury upon him, either. However, more than mere injury had found him nonetheless.

The order he'd received a week earlier detailed the escape of two workers from the quarry and one from a family farm nearby. In the ensuing escape, worker casualties mounted, and Commander Pordone had sustained a fatal injury—a fall from his horse in the woods that broke his neck. The horse had died as well, courtesy of Pordone's own spear, as thrown by one of the escaping workers.

"The loss of one such as Commander Pordone is tragic, but it pales in comparison to the escape of the three fugitives responsible for this tragedy," he continued. "It has been made clear to me that our priority is the capture and return of these fugitives directly to Solace for trial and sentencing in the King's courts.

"As your new commander, I am authorized to modify the terms of these orders as they pertain to the situation at hand. Given the violent natures and actions of these fugitives, I hereby declare it also permissible that they be executed in the King's name should they refuse to comply with our orders."

He studied each of their faces. Some of them nodded, others remained still as statues, and still others stared at the floor.

Commander Anigo noted the bloodstained wooden slats both near the hearth and under his own boots—evidence of the escaped workers' incursion into this base—and frowned. The men who'd perished in those spots had died carelessly, and the men who'd tried to clean up the mess had been equally careless.

It disgusted him.

All of it.

The idea of leaving his cushy assignment in Solace, Kanarah's capital city, to serve as commander in this backwater province filled his veins with fury. He hadn't labored his whole career, serving at the pleasure of the King in hunting down the most egregious offenders and bringing them to justice, to be reduced to... *this*.

All that work, all of his successes wiped away by one order, one command relegating him to this rural nightmare. It was disgraceful.

Demeaning. And he'd done *nothing* to warrant such treatment. Nothing whatsoever.

Yet here he was, all the same.

He clenched his fists and tensed his jaw.

But Commander Anigo had always prided himself on thriving based only on his needs, not his wants. He would make do here, in the middle of nowhere, and once he completed his mission, he would doubtless be welcomed back to Solace as a hero, a crusader who had righted the great wrongs inflicted upon this miserable place.

He let his hands and his jaw relax.

"That is all for now," he concluded. "See to it that these floors are cleaned of blood yet again, as they did not receive proper attention the first time. Our search begins tomorrow at dawn, and no later. Anyone who delays us will be whipped for the duration of time he makes me wait."

Commander Anigo strode up the stairs and found Pordone's room—now *his* room. Despite the relative chaos of the last weeks, the bed was made, the floors were clean, and afternoon sunshine streamed through the solitary window. It might've been that Pordone left it in this state before his demise.

The only thing off about the room was the chest at the foot of the bed, whose top stood open rather than being shut. A minor inconvenience, given the circumstances.

He walked forward and tipped the chest's lid forward. Its hinges squeaked as it fell into place and clomped shut, restoring the room to its otherwise acceptable state.

Acceptable, not comfortable.

Needs, not wants.

"Commander Anigo?" a soldier asked from behind him.

He turned around.

The soldier saluted, smiling. "I'm Corporal Bezarion. I dispatched the messenger to Solace as soon as we returned from our search."

"And?" Commander Anigo removed his gauntlets and handed them to the corporal.

"Sir?" Corporal Bezarion tilted his head as he received the gauntlets.

"Am I to commend you for doing your duty, soldier?"

"N-no, sir," Corporal Bezarion replied. "I just figured you'd—"

"Let me make one thing perfectly clear to you, Corporal." Commander Anigo approached Bezarion, who stood two inches shorter than him. When they stood face-to-face, Commander Anigo continued. "You are never to 'figure' anything as far as I am concerned. You will obey orders, and you will do so with haste.

"Assumptions and a lackadaisical attitude toward enforcing the King's law is what landed us in this dismal situation in the first place. Such blatant carelessness is reprehensible and a stain upon the reputation of the King's army. It ends today, with my arrival to this outpost. Crystal?"

Corporal Bezarion nodded. "Clear, sir. Perfectly."

"I will take my supper in my room this evening." The last leg of Commander Anigo's journey from Solace had worn both him and his horse out, though he had no inclination to explain that to Corporal Bezarion or the other soldiers. He added, "Immediately."

Corporal Bezarion glanced at the window and the afternoon sunlight aglow from it. "Apologies, sir, but it is still quite early. Dinner has not yet been—"

"I don't care to repeat myself, Corporal." Commander Anigo stared steel at him. "Ever."

Corporal Bezarion nodded again, this time more frantically. "My apologies again, sir. I'll have it prepared for you right away."

Commander Anigo shook his head and sat on the bed, again lamenting his appointment to this miserable place.

Needs, not wants, he reminded himself. *Needs, not wants.*

———

AT DAWN THE NEXT MORNING, Commander Anigo headed down to the courtyard. His horse, a white stallion he'd named Candlestick, munched on a bag of oats near a water trough with the other horses, already packed with provisions and weapons for their journey into the wild.

If nothing else, at least Commander Anigo had Candlestick with him, here in this backwoods province. Even if he couldn't trust anyone else, he knew Candlestick wouldn't let him down.

To their credit, the soldiers already awaited him with packs in tow and swords sheathed at their sides. Disheveled as they were, given the early hour, they snapped to attention upon his command.

"We will not return until our mission is complete. Mount up, if you have horses." He raised his fist and said, "For the King."

The soldiers shouted the second half of the mantra back at him, "May he forever reign!"

Commander Anigo turned toward the open gates of the Rock Outpost and stared into the wild forest beyond.

The fugitives' time was limited. He would soon find them, and he would bring them to justice.

THE NEXT MORNING, Calum woke up first and stretched his sore limbs. He sat up and checked the gouges in his forearm, which had crusted over in the night. He'd survive.

Axel moaned and pushed himself up to a sitting position. "It smells terrible around here. The cats must be starting to rot."

The remaining cat carcasses still lay around the camp where they'd been slain.

Calum wrinkled his nose at the stench and nodded. "At least we didn't get attacked again."

Axel grunted and muttered something, but Calum couldn't understand even a single word. "What do we have left for breakfast?"

"I think we had a bit of smoked venison left, and maybe a couple of potatoes." Calum scanned the campsite for the bag of food but didn't see it. Maybe it had been moved during the fight. "We definitely need to hunt today, unless you want to eat rotting sabertooth cat meat."

"No thanks." Axel stuck his tongue out. "Give me my spear any day, and I'll get us something. After breakfast, at least. Where's the food?"

Still sitting, Calum looked around again and shrugged. "I don't know. Maybe Magnus moved it."

"Well, get up and help me look for it."

After a few minutes of searching the campsite, they still hadn't found the bag.

"Alright. Enough of this nonsense." Axel walked over to Magnus, who lay in a shallow burrow in the dry dirt, still asleep, and kicked him in his hip. "Wake up, Scales."

"Axel, cut it out." Calum glared at him.

"What? He can regenerate. That cut Burtis gave him last month healed by the next morning." Axel kicked Magnus again. "I said wake up."

Magnus growled and latched onto Axel's ankle, then he yanked.

Axel landed on his rear-end as Magnus stood to his full height.

"What'd you do that for?" Axel glowered up at Magnus, who now towered over him.

"I do not enjoy being kicked."

Axel scrambled to his feet and stood well within Magnus's space. "And I don't enjoy getting knocked on my rear-end."

"Then perhaps you should alter your behavior."

"Enough, both of you." Calum held up his hands, and the two separated. "Magnus, where'd you put the bag of food?"

"I did not put it anywhere. I left it near the campfire where we always keep it."

"It's not there anymore."

Magnus tilted his head. "Then I do not know where it is."

"What do you mean, you don't know?" Axel extended his arms out to his sides. "You had it last. Where is it?"

"I said I do not know."

Axel pointed at him. "You ate the rest of the food after we went to sleep, didn't you?"

Magnus straightened up. "Why do you accuse me?"

"Why don't you answer the question?"

"I did not eat the rest of the food." This time, Magnus stepped into Axel's space. "And I categorically deny all assertions otherwise."

This time Calum physically stepped between the two of them. He had no doubt that Magnus was telling the truth. If anything, Axel's insistence made *him* look guiltier than Magnus.

But even so, Calum didn't believe Axel had eaten the rest of the food, either.

"Maybe we left the bag somewhere and forgot about it," he said, hoping his words would broker a more lasting peace between his friends. "Maybe it got kicked over the edge sometime during the fight with the sabertooths. Maybe something else happened to it."

Magnus's eyes narrowed, and he stepped away from Axel and Calum and examined the ground.

"That's right." Axel sneered. "Back up, Scales."

Magnus's tail whipped toward Axel and whacked his shoulder.

Axel staggered to one side, off-balance from the blow. "Hey!"

"Apologies," Magnus said flatly as he crouched low to the dirt. "I think Calum may be on to something."

Calum raised his eyebrows. "I am?"

"Perhaps. There appear to be some faint footprints here among ours and those of the sabertooths."

"Those cats trampled this whole area, and you think you're seeing footprints?" Axel rolled his eyes. "Sounds like another ploy to distract us from figuring out you ate the rest of the food."

Magnus pointed to a spot in the dirt. "Then how do you account for this?"

Axel and Calum leaned closer.

Axel shrugged. "What? I don't see anything."

"There. A perfect comparison. You can see a large paw print, and next to it, a smaller one." Magnus looked at Calum. "Do you see it?"

"I do, but what does that prove?" Calum asked.

"Proves you're gullible." Axel scoffed. "That's what it proves."

"Someone or something else was here last night," Magnus continued, ignoring Axel.

"So a smaller paw print proves something else was here?" Axel shook his head. "Maybe one of the cats had smaller feet."

"No. The shape of the paw is different. Entirely different." Magnus nodded. "It appears we had a unique visitor last night."

Axel nudged Calum's arm. "How are you falling for this? He's clearly making stuff up."

"I don't think so." Calum had ignored Axel for as long as he could. "Now that he pointed the prints out, I see more of them leading in the same direction, away from the camp. I think he's right."

"You can't be serious."

"The tracks enter the camp from the northeast and then exit due east." Magnus's eyes traced the route. "He was a quiet one, too."

Calum tilted his head. "He?"

Magnus turned to face him. "I'm assuming it is a 'he,' but I don't know for sure."

"It?" Axel squinted at him. "So what is this 'it' that supposedly stole our last bag of food?"

Magnus smirked. "A Wolf."

"Alright, now I *know* you're making this up." Axel scoffed again. "You're trying to tell us that a wild dog ran in here and stole our last bag of food in the night?"

"Exactly, except for the 'wild dog' part. He probably looks like a wild dog, but Wolves are sentient, intelligent beings just like you and me," Magnus said. "They differ greatly from the sabertooths we engaged last night. They are their own species, and they have souls just like we do."

Axel shook his head. "I still think you're making this up."

Magnus swept his hand toward the edge of the cliff. "Unlike me, you have never ventured to the other side of that valley. Humans rule this entire half of Kanarah, but across the valley, three races divide Western Kanarah. A member of one of them, the Wolves, robbed us last night while we slept."

Calum glanced at Axel. In all his sixteen years, he'd never learned about any other race except for humans. He hadn't even known what a Saurian was until the soldiers brought Magnus into the quarry all those weeks ago.

"There are more races than humans and Saurians?" Calum added, "And Wolves?"

Magnus nodded. "Yes. We Saurians live in the north, among the Blood Mountains and in Reptilius. The Windgales have the southern kingdom and the Aeropolis because they can fly. A rocky arid region known as the Desert of the Forgotten divides our two realms. It is controlled by the Wolves, most of whom live there."

"Then how come I've never seen any of these other races?" Axel challenged. "Aside from your ugly mug, of course?"

A hiss issued from Magnus's nostrils at Axel.

"C'mon, Axel," Calum said, again playing peacemaker. "It's not like you got out much before this."

"More than you," Axel countered.

"Yet clearly not enough," Magnus said. "If you had, perhaps you'd be less bigoted and insolent all the time."

Axel frowned and pointed an accusatory finger at Magnus. "I don't know what those words mean, but I don't have to take this kind of verbal abuse from a scaly freak of nature like you."

"The reason you do not see other races is because of the King's soldiers," Magnus explained despite Axel's anger.

"What do you mean?" Calum asked.

"The King claims dominion over all of Kanarah, but his soldiers clearly favor humans over the others to the point of mistreating or even abusing them. We have little reason to spend time on the eastern side of Kanarah in light of such persecution and favoritism." Magnus's gaze hardened and he glared at Axel. "That mentality has pervaded even the outermost fringes of the human race, I see."

Axel rolled his eyes and folded his arms. "Whatever."

"Nevertheless, I am certain our culprit is a Wolf."

"So…" Calum briefly considered what that could mean for them, but he came to very few conclusions. "What do we do now?"

"There is nothing else to do but follow the plan we set yesterday: head east and find some food, then return here and try to find a way down into the valley."

Trader's Pass/The Valley of the Tri-Lakes

THE FIRST TWO weeks of Lilly's journey across Trader's Pass had breezed by without incident.

She had precisely zero opportunities to escape as the slave traders watched her with even more diligence than ever. At least two of them always escorted to her to relieve herself, now only in broad daylight and usually without any hope of privacy whatsoever, as the Valley of the Tri-Lakes entirely lacked for foliage of any kind.

Sometimes she managed to find a large rock or a small hill behind which she could conceal herself when the time came, but rocks and hills didn't keep the men escorting her from indulging themselves in long, lascivious looks. Still, it had become so routine that she didn't even pay them any attention anymore.

Until one of them dropped to his knees in front of her with a spear lodged in his chest.

"Get over here, now!" the other slave trader shouted at her.

But behind him, at least a dozen dark forms leaped over a row of boulders that formed a hedge around the desolate area.

Bandits?

The slave trader whirled around and swung his sword at the first of them. He felled the bandit, but the second, third, and fourth rushed him, knocked him to the ground, and stabbed him repeatedly with twisted and tortured weapons while he screamed.

Lilly bolted back toward the wagons as fast as the shackles on her ankles allowed her to run. Colm had warned her about men like these—bandits who would just as soon kill her as free her. As much as she hated to admit it, she was safer with Roderick and his men.

"Roderick! Bandits!" she screamed as she hobble-ran. *Oh, to be able to fly again!* She rounded a large mound and shouted again. "Roderick!"

He stood near one of the short wagons, gnawing on an apple. Given the vacant terrain around them, he'd given up on personally escorting her anymore. After all, if she ran off, he'd be able to see her for miles in any direction.

As she approached, Lilly noticed the tan fabric that normally covered one of the wagons was pulled back. From inside, she caught a glimpse of shimmering blue fabric and light-pink plating—it had to be her cape and her armor.

She noted the brown color of the donkey pulling the cart compared to the gray donkey that hauled the other, and she committed the information to memory.

Roderick's gaze fixed on her then widened at the sight of the horde that followed her. He tossed his apple aside and drew his broadsword. "Formation!"

His slave traders formed around him with Luggs to his right and Gammel and Adgar to his left, each of them wielding swords. The archers among them took positions and drew their bows back.

Lilly clanked forward, but the huffs and unintelligible shouts of the bandits behind her drew ever closer. She chanced a look back.

The bandits would overtake her in seconds.

CHAPTER SIXTEEN

When Lilly faced forward again, Roderick had already closed to within five feet of her position. He zoomed past her in a blur of brown armor and spiky red hair, and a series of heavy smacks and clangs sounded behind her.

"Archers!" Luggs shouted.

The archers let loose a flurry of arrows in rapid succession, and some of them barely missed Lilly. Gammel and Adgar met her partway and escorted her back to the wagon while the others charged forward and engaged the bandits.

In the center of the fracas, Roderick roared and swung his sword as if he were invincible. As Lilly watched him decimate half the bandits single-handedly, she wondered if maybe he was.

"Child, are you alright?" Colm reached for her with frail and tentative fingers

Behind him, Sharion dug into the hay and covered her head.

Lilly nodded and sucked in several deep breaths, more winded from fear than from running. In the distance, Roderick leveled three bandits in one swing of his huge sword.

Unbelievable.

Within minutes, the fight ended as the last of the bandits, a handful compared to the number they'd started with, fled back the way they'd came. Roderick wiped his sword on the tattered clothes of one of the dead bandits, sheathed it, and started back toward the caravan. Splotches of blood glistened on his armored chest and arms, and more dotted his smiling face.

Is he even human? Or is he something... else?

Eastern Kanarah

To Calum's relief, a few days and a few dead animals later, the trio reached the foothills at the eastern edge of the Snake Mountains and found a small village by the name of Pike's Garrison a few miles south, nestled among a forest full of towering evergreen and broadleaf trees.

As discussed, Magnus hid in an inconspicuous spot on the outskirts of the village while Calum and Axel headed into its heart to see if they could trade for food.

"Is there even a market for sabertooths?" Axel pulled one of the fangs out of the sack he carried. "Er—saber*teeth*?"

Calum shook his head. "I don't know. Guess we'll find out."

Several villagers gave them tentative looks as they walked through the village. Whether it was from their scratched-up soldiers' armor or the foot-long sabertooth fang Axel constantly held in his hand, Calum didn't know.

Most of the homes in the village looked as if they'd been there for a hundred years. The stones that formed the houses' exteriors had long since smoothed from weathering, and the wooden doors and door-frames bore decades-old scars and gashes.

"Ever been in a village like this?" Axel muttered.

Calum shook his head. "Never."

A beautiful red-haired girl about their age walked past them. She wore a flowing orange dress, and a white flower adorned her hair. Her blue eyes lingered on Calum for a long moment, and he couldn't divert his gaze from her even after she walked past and looked away.

A whack to his chest jolted him back to the present.

"Eyes forward, Calum." Axel snickered. "You've probably never seen girls our age, have you?"

"Haven't seen women of any sort for eight years. None worth looking at, anyway." Calum smirked. "Aside from your mother, of course."

Before Axel hit him, Calum braced for the blow. A few traded punches later, their bodies hit the dirt, intertwined in a match of submission wrestling. Calum knew he wouldn't win, but the jibe alone was a victory.

Within seconds, Axel managed to pin Calum down and twist his arm the wrong way. "Submit."

Calum ground his teeth as pain surged through his shoulder. There was no getting out of this. Axel was too strong, and Calum wasn't any good at wrestling.

But his pride wouldn't let him give in—not yet.

Axel wrenched Calum's arm farther, and the pain brightened. "*Submit.*"

"Can I help you gentlemen?"

In spite of the pain, Calum raised his head. A black-haired man, his hair peppered with gray, stood over them. Brown dirt streaked his beige trousers, his green shirt, and his tanned face.

Axel released his grip on Calum, and relief flooded his sore arm. On his feet again, Axel replied, "No, sir. We're fine, thank you. Just some horseplay."

The man gave a slight nod. "You're making some of the townsfolk nervous, carrying on as such. Do you have reason to be here?"

Calum pushed himself up as well and rotated his arm to bring it further relief. "Yes, sir. We're hoping to trade for food and other supplies if anyone's willing."

"You're the King's soldiers, aren't you?"

Calum glanced at Axel. "No."

"You're wearing black leather armor, standard-issue." The man stepped toward them, and his left eye twitched. "Only the King's men wear that kind of armor. If you're not them, then where did you get—"

"We traded some deserters for their armor," Axel said before Calum had a chance to speak. "They fled the Rock Outpost north of here after a forest fire got too close. They were starving and hungry, so we traded them in exchange for half of what we had at the time. A few nights ago we ran out of our own supply, so now we're here to trade, if we can."

The man nodded but eyed them both. His left eye twitched again. "You're welcome to walk around freely with your wares, but we desire no trouble, so kindly do your business and kindly move on."

"Yes, sir," Calum said. "Thank you."

After the man walked away, Axel scooped up the sack of sabertooth fangs he'd dropped. "Old buzzard. He oughta mind his own business."

Calum shrugged. "It's his village."

"I don't even see why we need to trade these things. I doubt they're worth anything. We should just take what we want like we did at the outpost."

Calum stepped in front of Axel to keep him from walking. For him to even make such a suggestion flew in the face of everything Calum had fought against to earn his freedom.

"Absolutely not. These people are just like us," he asserted. "They're under the same oppression. We can't steal from people like this. It wouldn't be right."

Axel rolled his eyes. "If you say so. Come on. Let's visit that apothecary over there and see what we can get for these ivories."

In addition to the modest shops interspersed between the old houses, a few vendors lined the main thoroughfare that divided Pike's Garrison into two parts. Some of them offered food, others flowers, and a few dealt in weapons and traveling supplies, but they all seemed to lack both variety and quantity in their wares.

What few villagers occupied the streets seemed to do so with purpose—everyone darted from place to place. When they noticed Calum and Axel walking past, their paces quickened.

An hour later, having visited every shop and vendor in the marketplace, Calum and Axel still had eighteen of the original twenty fangs they'd brought to the village—plus a small bag of potatoes.

Axel tossed the bag of fangs on the ground behind a house. "This is ridiculous. No one wants these stupid things. We hauled them all this way, and we only got a measly bag of starch to show for it. You won't let us steal anything, so what do you propose we do now?"

Calum sighed. "I don't know."

"Well, one of us had better think of something, and soon, because..."

As Axel prattled on, Calum noticed a silver-haired lady seated in a rocking chair outside of a meager house. She'd sat there knitting ever since they arrived in the village, but now her hands covered her face, and her back heaved up and down, shuddering.

She was weeping.

But why?

Calum's heart went out to her. He'd wept like that before, with great shuddering sobs, when his parents were killed. When the soldiers dropped him off at the quarry. And many long nights for a few years after that, until he'd finally resigned himself to his fate.

He understood the kind of pain that brought a person to this point. He still felt a measure of it, even to this day.

"...back in the forest." Axel smacked Calum's shoulder. "Are you even listening to me?"

Calum looked at him. "Stay here. I'll be right back."

"Where do you think you're going?" Axel's voice trailed off in a flurry of muttering.

The old woman continued to cry even as Calum approached, but she hadn't seen him yet. Perhaps that was for the best.

"Excuse me, ma'am?"

The old woman raised her head. Tears streaked down her cheeks, and her dark-brown eyes were red and puffy. Upon seeing Calum, she pressed her hand against her chest then promptly resumed her knitting. "Oh, I'm sorry, sir. Didn't mean to pause for so long. I'm already back to work, of course."

"No—I mean, I'm not a soldier," Calum explained. "You don't need to worry about that."

She studied him for a moment, hair roots to leather boots. "You're wearing a soldier's armor."

"Well, we traded some deserted soldiers—" Calum bit his lip. Even if he did remember all of Axel's story, he'd probably butcher it as it came out. "Look, I'm not a soldier. It's a long story. I just came over here because I noticed you crying. Is everything alright?"

She hesitated, then she looked down at the yarn in her hands. "You're not from around here, are you?"

Calum shook his head. "No, ma'am."

"Then you don't know the oppression that regular folk suffer from men who wear armor like yours." The old woman resumed her knitting as if that concluded the conversation.

Calum bit his lip. "I have a pretty good idea of how cruel the King's soldiers can be."

"Then how do you justify wearing their attire?"

"The armor keeps me protected in battle and warm at night. It doesn't represent who I am or what I believe in any way."

The old woman chuckled and worked the yarn and needles in her hands. "I believe you, but the image suggests the contrary. Perhaps you ought to consider that when next you decide to—"

"Ma'am, my parents were killed by the King's soldiers when I was eight. I was forced to work in the King's quarry until just a few weeks ago. The only reason I'm standing before you right now is because I fought my way to freedom." Calum immediately regretted his tone, but he couldn't retract his words. He added, "...with some help from a friend."

"By the Overlord..." The old woman stopped knitting. She stood up, her mouth open and brown eyes forlorn, set her project on the chair, and pulled Calum into an embrace. "You poor dear."

Calum didn't know what to do. This woman, who had just chastised him for wearing soldiers' armor, clung to him as if he were her own child.

"I'm sorry." The old woman squeezed him tighter. "I had no idea. Twenty years ago this winter, the King's soldiers killed my only son."

Calum exhaled a sigh. No wonder she'd been crying.

He wrapped his arms around her and returned the hug. In that moment, this woman became the closest thing he'd had to a mother in nearly a decade.

She pulled away from him but kept her hands on his gauntlets. She looked them over and then met his eyes again. "I'm sorry I spoke ill of your armor, though now you understand why it's such an affront to me. We share that horror in common. What's your name, child?"

"Calum." He couldn't hold her words against her. He gave her a half-smile.

"A strong, noble name. I'm Reginia. I can't express how sorry I am for your loss."

Calum nodded. "Your son—is he why you were crying?"

"I'm afraid not. I've cried rivers of tears for him in my time, but not today." Reginia shook her head. She picked up her knitting and sat in her rocking chair again. "Forgive me if I sit down. My ancient legs wear out quickly, and I need to save my strength for making dinner this evening."

"Of course." Calum crouched next to her. He glanced back at Axel, who leaned against a nearby house and yawned. "But there is something going on."

"Our village's problems insidiously complement each other and compound our frustrations." Reginia sat back in her rocking chair and looked up at him. "A couple times a month, a group of bandits raids our village. They take most of our food, any gold or silver we earn from travelers passing through, and whatever else they want."

Apparently, the King's soldiers didn't have a monopoly on cruelty.

"I'm sorry." Calum turned back and motioned for Axel to come over, and Calum introduced him to Reginia. "Have the King's soldiers tried to help you?"

"Not in the least. They don't care about us any more than the bandits. It's gotten so bad that the bandits don't even bother to come at night anymore. They just walk into town and take what they want. They've been here so many times that we don't even bother to fight back now." Reginia sighed. "That's the other reason I'm not fond of your attire."

"But you *have* talked to the King's soldiers about this?" Axel asked.

"It didn't do any good." Reginia gave a sad laugh. "Three weeks ago, they came into town while the King's men were also here. We thought the day of reckoning had finally come, but we were wrong. Their leader nodded to the commander of the soldiers, and he nodded right back and stood by while they robbed us again. They did nothing to help us."

Axel growled and muttered a curse.

While Calum shared every ounce of Axel's rage, he wanted to express it in better terms for Reginia's sake. "What Axel means is that we want to help you if we can."

Reginia smiled. "You do?"

Axel's head turned toward Calum. "We do?"

"Of course. Since the King's men aren't doing what they're supposed to do, we'll do it instead." Calum raised an eyebrow. "For a price."

Reginia's smile faded. "Which is?"

"We get half of whatever we recover. We'll clear out the bandits and make sure they never bother you again."

Axel leaned close to him. "Bold plan, but I don't know if we can—"

"We most certainly can, and we will." He rubbed his hands together and grinned at Reginia. "What do you say, Reginia? Who do we need to talk to in order to make this official?"

The hopefulness in Reginia's eyes had returned at Calum's proposal. "What you suggest seems fair. My husband is the village's elder. If you'll excuse me, I'll go get him."

As she walked away, Axel twisted Calum toward him. "Are you crazy? We don't even know what we're walking into here."

"It's just a group of bandits. We can handle them. It'll be a quick easy payday."

"We've never done anything like this before. How do you know we—"

Calum elbowed him in the gut and turned to face Reginia, who led a white-haired man with a matching beard over to them. A long black chain hung from his neck over his gray-and-white robes. Two black earrings in each ear matched the metal of the chain.

Calum stepped forward and extended his hand. "I'm Calum. This is Axel. We'd like to help you solve your bandit problem."

The bearded man extended a gloved hand, also black, and his green eyes scoured them. "Stavian. Reginia told me of your proposal. I must tell you, she tends to be far more optimistic than me. I have my doubts about your ability to do anything for us, especially if there are only two of you."

"We have another." Calum recalled how Magnus had severed the last sabertooth cat's head a few nights earlier and added, "He's a skilled fighter."

"And you're not?"

Calum's smile evaporated. "No—I mean, yes, we are too, but he's—"

"We're *all* skilled fighters." Axel pushed Calum aside and stepped forward. "Calum meant that our friend is the most experienced of all of us."

Calum glanced at him. *Sure, now he gets on board with the plan?*

"There are at least ten bandits. Possibly twelve or thirteen, but no more than that. They reside in a hideout somewhere west of here in the Snake Mountains. I can show you on a map where we think it is." Stavian cleared his throat. "But even if your friend is as capable as you describe, I doubt you could overcome such a large force."

"We can handle it, alright." Axel held up his hand. "Several weeks ago, we took control of a mighty fortress that housed more than twenty men."

Calum eyed him for the gross exaggeration, but Axel ignored him.

"And you also realize that if you fail, you'll be jeopardizing our village beyond even what we've suffered thus far?" Stavian's icy blue eyes fixed on Calum.

Calum glanced at Reginia. He hadn't considered that, but how could he back out now?

"Yes, of course," he said. "But we're not going to fail. We're going to get your coin back, and—"

The yells of several men and women erupted from the other side of Reginia's house, followed by clashes of swordplay.

Axel and Calum looked at each other, then at Stavian and Reginia. They ran around Reginia's house to the village square, which had crowded with people formed into a loose ring.

There, in the center of it all, Magnus engaged several villagers in battle.

CHAPTER SEVENTEEN

C alum immediately knifed through the throngs of people toward Magnus. At least a dozen men surrounded him, all with pitchforks or hoes or other farming tools, aside from two of them who held actual swords.

Without drawing his own weapon, Calum pushed between two of the offending villagers and stood at Magnus's side. He raised his hands in the air. "Take it easy, people. Calm down."

Axel joined them, but he had his sword out. He waved it at the nearest villager with a weapon. "Back off, or this is going down your throat."

Calum grabbed his wrist. "Put it away. We're not fighting these people."

"Not gonna happen, Calum." Axel jerked free from Calum's grasp. "They're threatening us."

"Axel, trust me. If we want this job, we have to be on their side, not *against* them."

"Then maybe I don't want this job."

Since when had Axel decided to side with Magnus on anything? "You wanna eat, don't you?"

Axel glanced around them. "Not *this* bad."

Calum turned to Magnus. "Will you put your sword away?"

Magnus's eyes narrowed, but he complied. "You had better know what you are doing."

Axel glanced between them and the villagers. "Are you guys crazy? They're gonna kill us because *you* won't fight back."

"*Axel.*" Calum's voice hardened. "Put it away."

Axel shook his head. "You can't be ser—"

"I am. Do it now."

Axel scowled at him for a moment, then he sheathed his sword.

"Put your hands up, like Magnus and me."

Axel complied with a sharp sigh.

"We're on your side," Calum said to the crowd. "This Saurian is with us. He won't hurt you unless you try to hurt him. And if you try to hurt him, I don't envy you in the least."

"Stand down, everyone." Stavian parted the crowd with his gloved hands and headed toward the center with Reginia not far behind. When he reached Calum and Axel, he stared at Magnus for a long moment. "You didn't tell me your friend was a Saurian."

Calum glanced at Magnus and Axel. "You didn't ask."

"Having seen him, I am more confident in your chances for success. I grant you permission to remove the bandits on our behalf." Stavian extended his gloved hand. "May the Overlord bless you with great success. If you will come with me, I can provide you with more details on your task."

Calum shook Stavian's hand. "Thank you."

Magnus leaned his head down next to Calum's. "What kind of foolery did you just commit us to?"

"The best kind." Calum gave him a wink.

INSIDE STAVIAN and Reginia's house, Stavian unrolled a map and smoothed it across a wide oak table. Sunlight filtered in through a skylight in the ceiling above the table.

He pointed to a spot east of the Snake Mountains. "We're here." He pointed to another spot, almost exactly due west of Pike's Garrison. "The bandits' hideout is somewhere near here."

"This will not be a short venture," Magnus said. "We will need at least a day to get there, to get inside, dispatch the bandits, and recover your property, plus another day to return."

Stavian shrugged. "We're not going anywhere."

"We're low on food. Could we trouble you for a good meal before we set out?" Calum asked. "We can offer you some sabertooth cat fangs in exchange for—"

"Keep your cat fangs. We have no use for them here." Stavian waved his hand. "We're low on food as it is, but I'll find something to fill your bellies. And I'll even do one better: you can sleep in actual beds tonight and then set out in the morning. How about that?"

Calum's eyebrows rose. He hadn't slept in an actual bed since before his parents died.

"That would be incredible," Axel said.

Stavian nodded. "So it shall be tonight. In the meantime, while I gather you some food, please make yourselves comfortable. My home is your home. If you require anything, just inquire of Reginia or me."

———

THE NEXT DAY, Calum could scarcely control his excitement. It heightened when, after a day of traversing hills and weaving through thickets of trees, the trio found the hideout more or less where Stavian's map had placed it.

The structure amounted to little more than an old wood-and-stone house, albeit a large one, in the center of a gorge nestled at the intersection of three rocky hills. Natural rock barriers kept it hidden from the outside world and almost totally inaccessible—except for a solitary path that swerved between two of the hills adjacent to the gorge and led up to its front door.

Smoke rose from the stone chimney. The bandits were inside. Of that, Calum had no doubt. And that meant he'd be able to do some good for the people of Pike's Garrison.

"If we approach from that path, they will see us coming," Magnus said. "We need to find another way inside."

"What other choices do we have?" Axel asked. "Those rock walls look pretty steep. I doubt we can get down there without killing ourselves in the process."

"We have rope, right?" Calum pulled off his pack. "We don't have to scale the cliff without a safety system. Magnus could lower me down near the house with the rope. I can get in that way. I'll cause a distraction, and then you two can come up the path, no problem. We'll take them out together, bring back the villagers' loot, and walk away with our reward."

Magnus glanced at Axel. "It sounds good in theory, but—"

"But if we don't get there in time, you could be fighting them alone." Axel challenged, "You sure you're up for that?"

The idea of battling up to thirteen bandits on his own exhilarated Calum—and it also scared the daylights out of him. But it was a moot point, since he'd be careful enough to not attract all the bandits to him at once. Obviously.

Even so, Axel had set him up, and Calum wasn't about to back down.

"I'm a better swordsman than you are, Axel." Calum grinned.

Axel scoffed. "We both know *that's* not true."

Calum shrugged "I don't know. I've been beating you pretty consistently when we spar."

Axel frowned. "I've been going easy on you. If we were fighting for real, you would've been dead a long, long time ago. I'm glad you feel so confident, though, even if it's a false confidence."

That stirred Calum's insides, and he smirked. "I'll prove it to you right now, if you like."

"Bad idea." Axel shook his head. "Getting inside that hideout will be a lot harder if you're dead. We need three people to pull this off."

"If you say so." Calum chuckled. "When you come in, bring me a bag for my share of the loot."

"Sounds like it could work." Axel shrugged. "Just don't get yourself killed."

Calum rolled his eyes. "I'll try to leave some of them alive for you."

———

THEY WAITED until nightfall to move into position. Both Magnus and Axel held the rope to which Calum clung, and they lowered him down into the gorge foot by foot.

For a moment, it reminded Calum of Magnus's descent into the Gronyx's pit and his own subsequent fall. He shuddered and shook the memory away.

When his feet touched the stony ground, he untied himself and tugged the rope three times to signal them. The rope zipped up the cliff and disappeared into the darkness.

Calum was on his own now.

He crouched down and surveyed the house. Maybe he could get in through a window on the first floor, or even on the second floor. Perhaps he'd find a rear entrance somewhere. No matter what he did, he'd do it in silence, and he'd avoid the pair of guards posted at the front door.

Calum darted toward the house and hid behind one of the few tall coniferous trees that stood watch in the gorge. A few more steps and he stood with his back to the house beside a window. He leaned his head over for a look inside.

Burning logs in the fireplace filled the room with yellow light. Gold, silver, and bronze treasures adorned the walls, but Calum didn't see anyone in the room. He tugged on the window, but it didn't budge. No sense breaking it. He'd have to find another way to get inside.

Around the back of the house, he found an unlocked door. He pulled it open, his sword in hand, and peered inside.

An iron stove sat in one corner next to a pile of wood, and a man with curly black hair stood at a counter with his back to Calum. He chopped some dark red meat with a big knife. Without hesitation, Calum stalked toward the man in silence with his sword ready.

The man kept chopping, oblivious to Calum's approach.

Calum closed the distance in less than three seconds. A small part of him wanted to run the man through right there, but he couldn't just stab the poor sap in his back, even if he was a treacherous bandit. Instead, he smacked the back of the man's head with his sword's pommel just like Magnus had shown him a few weeks earlier.

The man's knife clanked on the table, and he wilted to the floor, unconscious.

Perfect. Calum moved on.

He made his way through the halls without making a sound, and he didn't encounter any other bandits. Laughter sounded from upstairs on the second floor, along with the occasional stomp or creak or the scraping of wooden chairs across the floor.

Good. Better up there than down here. Hopefully they'd stay up there until he could get to the guards by the front door.

Now how could he cause some sort of distraction?

The next room he entered was the one he'd seen through the window—the one with the fireplace. Perhaps he could set something on fire again. It had worked in the woods outside the Rock Outpost.

Once inside the room, he dodged the chairs and tables and headed straight for the fireplace. All of the logs were too hot for him to grab, but if he could find something small—perhaps a book or some parchment or something—then he could easily spread the fire.

He found nothing of practical use in the fireplace room aside from the wooden furniture, but he couldn't just break it up; it would make too much noise.

The more he considered his plan, the less appealing it became. If he set the house on fire and it spread wildly enough to burn down, what would happen to the bandits' stash? It might get destroyed in the process.

No, fire wasn't a great idea after all. Instead, he headed to the next door.

When he opened it, he found himself staring up at a pair of confused hazel eyes above a big nose and a thick brown beard.

Instinct and shock thrust Calum's sword arm forward. The tip of the blade pierced the bandit's left shoulder, and he yelped.

His right fist plowed into Calum's left cheek, and Calum staggered back, reminded of Burtis's strikes.

The bandit clenched his injured shoulder with his hand and leaned against the doorframe as blood oozed between his fingertips. He opened his mouth to holler, but Calum threw a haphazard punch at his neck.

To his surprise, his fist connected, and the bandit's scream caught in his throat. Wide-eyed and straining to breathe, the bandit clutched at his throat with his hand, no longer concerned with his wounded shoulder.

Emboldened by his luck, Calum swung his sword in a lethal arc. The bandit backed away and then quickly lurched at him with both hands outstretched, still wheezing and still bleeding. When Calum tried to return with a backswing, the bandit caught his arm in both hands and wrenched it the wrong way.

Instead of yelling, Calum ground his teeth and tried to twist out of the bandit's grip, but the bandit readjusted. He tripped Calum and shoved him to the floor, and his sword clattered away. The struggle didn't last long—the bandit had a size advantage over Calum by at least a hundred pounds.

Now on top of Calum, the bandit drew his hand back for a punch. At the last instant Calum contorted his body and avoided the blow, and the bandit punched the stone floor instead. A pitiful yelp rasped out of his throat, and he clutched his fist.

Calum threw the best punch he could manage from such an awkward position, but he only managed to hit the bandit's stomach bulge. It didn't have any effect.

The bandit leaned forward, clamped his fingers around Calum's throat, and began to squeeze. Calum grabbed the bandit's wrists and tried to pry his hands from his throat, but the bandit was too strong, and he weighed too much.

Out of the corner of his eye, Calum saw the glint of the fire dancing across his sword blade. Could he reach it?

He stretched his right arm out, but the handle lay just beyond his fingertips.

"You're gonna die, kid." The bandit's voice scraped out of his throat, and then he displayed a twisted yellow smile.

Calum's vision darkened. He threw a left hook at the bandit's face and connected with his cheekbone. The bandit took the blow, but his grip didn't loosen. Instead, he laughed.

"Hit me as many times as you want. I'm not lettin' go 'til you're dead."

Calum groped for his sword again. His fingertips touched the end of the pommel, but he couldn't quite get a grip. He tried pulling at the bandit's hands again, but they didn't yield, either.

The bandit snickered. "Keep reachin', kid."

Calum noticed the hilt of something protruding from a sheath on the bandit's belt—a blade of some sort. Maybe a knife or a dagger. Instead of continuing to reach for his own sword, Calum grabbed the hilt and yanked it from its sheath.

He was going out fast. He forced his weakening hand to solidify its grip, angled the blade toward the bandit, and stabbed with everything he had left.

Shick.

The bandit twitched, and the smirk on his face evaporated. His grip loosened, and he rolled off Calum onto the floor with the dagger plunged halfway in his side.

Calum coughed and gasped and strained for air, but he knew the fight wasn't over. He couldn't rest yet. He scrambled over to the bandit on the floor and jammed the dagger deeper until it refused to go any farther. For good measure, he gave the hilt a sharp twist.

With a gasp, the bandit twitched, then he went limp. His wide eyes narrowed and glazed over, and he stared at the ceiling with a vacant expression.

Calum released the dagger and rolled onto his back again. He gulped in haggard breaths, and sweet air filled his lungs. His throat burned, but he was alive.

He lay there, sucking in breath after glorious breath until he finally felt well enough to stand. He headed over to his sword and picked it up, but he left the dagger in the bandit's body.

After all, it had been his in the first place. He deserved to keep it.

Calum realized he'd had no choice that time. It was either the bandit or him. He'd done what he had to do, just as Axel had done back at the

Rock Outpost. Just as Magnus had said Calum would someday have to do.

He wasn't sure how he felt about it just yet, but he knew he didn't love the feeling. Still, he was alive. That counted for a lot.

The floor creaked behind him. Calum whirled around, his sword ready, abandoning any lingering concerns he might've had over his first kill.

Ten angry men, all with weapons in their hands, stood at the bottom of the staircase, glaring at him.

CHAPTER EIGHTEEN

One of the bandits, a lanky man with blond hair and a matching beard, pointed at Calum. "He just killed Norm!"

The group started toward him. He had to do something, and fast.

"Who's in charge here?" Calum's voice rasped against his sore throat. He put his left hand up, and to his surprise, they stopped their advance. Maybe he could stall them long enough for Axel and Magnus to get inside. "I want to talk to whoever's in charge."

The lanky blond bandit tilted his head and glanced at a couple of his comrades. "Norm was in charge."

Calum bit his lip. *Shoot.* "Guess that means I'm in charge now."

"What?" A dark-skinned bandit with long fire-red dreadlocks stepped forward. He carried an axe, and when he spoke, an unusual accent tinged his words. "Not a chance. You kill Norm. Now we gonna kill you."

The group took another collective step toward him.

Where were Axel and Magnus?

"No, that means you're gonna shut up and do what I say." Calum stepped back and put up his hands again, this time including his sword, and the bandits halted again. "I earned it. I killed your leader, so now I'm your new boss. Don't you know anything? That's how it works."

Several of the bandits eyed each other, and then him. A shorter, fatter bandit shook his head with vigor. He held a sword that resembled a large meat cleaver. "No, that *ain't* how it works. You don't belong here. You killed Norm, so now you gosta die."

They started toward him again.

Calum couldn't stretch this much further. Axel and Magnus needed to hurry.

He took several more steps back, but he was running out of room. "If Norm was in charge before, then I wanna talk to the man who's in charge now."

The bandits stopped their advance and exchanged glances.

More uncertainty. *Perfect.*

"You mean you don't know who's in charge now?" Calum smirked. "Then I'm in charge."

The lanky blond one pointed his finger at Calum again. "You're tryin' to confuse us. You killed Norm, so we're killin' you."

"Oh, so you're in charge, then?" Calum pointed back at him.

"He ain't in charge." The short fat one stepped forward and eyed the lanky blonde bandit.

Calum raised an eyebrow. These guys were almost as dumb as he'd hoped. "Then you are?"

The short fat one cracked a smile. "Well, I s'pose—"

"Not a chance. No way are you in charge, Goo." The dark one with the red hair yanked him backward. "Not a chance."

Goo swatted his hand away. "Get yer hands off me, Kumba. I could lead this outfit, no probbum."

"Where?" Kumba chortled. "Into a bakery?"

"*Shaddap.* You know I look like this 'cause I have a condition."

"Yeah." The lanky blond one snickered. "Your condition is that you're *fat.*"

Goo turned toward him while the other bandits chuckled. "What'd you say to me?"

"Must be deaf, too." The lanky blond one leaned forward and repeated the words slowly. "I said you're—"

Goo jammed his sword into the lanky blond bandit's gut before he could finish, and he dropped to the floor face-first. "Yeah? Well, this fat guy just *killed* you."

"*Goo!*" Kumba yanked him away from the lanky blond bandit. "What are you doing?"

Goo spun around and slashed at Kumba next, but Kumba dodged the blow and cut him down with one powerful swing of his axe.

Three down. Calum nodded toward Kumba. "Looks like you're in charge."

Kumba's eyes hardened. "You got dat right, boy. Now *three* of us are dead because of you. And now you gonna pay for it."

Calum opened his mouth to speak, but Kumba didn't stop this time. He swung his axe at Calum's head, and Calum ducked under the blow and rolled away. As soon as he recovered his footing, Calum parried a hack from a black-haired bandit.

A roar sounded behind him. He dropped to the floor in time to dodge Kumba's next attack, which crashed into the black-haired bandit instead. The blow nearly split the bandit's head in two, and it definitely killed him.

Four down, including Norm.

Calum lunged at Kumba and struck his armored greave with his sword.

Kumba grunted and pulled his leg back. Then he swung his axe straight down at Calum, who blocked the blow with his sword. The force of the strike knocked Calum backward, but it didn't stop him from attempting a counterattack. He slashed at Kumba's torso.

The handle of Kumba's axe absorbed the swing, and he responded with a powerful kick to Calum's chest. Calum's back slammed into the wall, and again the axe sliced toward Calum's head, and again he ducked. The axe head stuck in the wall, and Calum found his opening. He drew his elbow back to run Kumba through.

Five dow—

He tried to stab, but something held his arm back. A bandit with vibrant green eyes and matted brown hair anchored his arm in place.

Still only four down.

Kumba cocked his arm, but Calum wrenched his body to the side and moved the green-eyed bandit's head to where his had just been. Kumba's punch thudded into the bandit's face, and he released his grip on Calum amid a colorful cascade of profanity.

Calum tried to swing his sword at the green-eyed bandit, but Kumba's boot hit his shoulder and knocked him off-balance. Before Calum could recover, Kumba delivered a stunning punch to his cheek, and he dropped his sword.

Another bandit kicked him in the gut, and Calum curled forward. The following blow to his back laid him out flat.

The beating escalated with Calum on the floor as the bandits kicked his ribs and punched his arms and face. Every blow hurt; every blow further shriveled Calum's body. It continued until Calum almost couldn't feel it anymore, and then, all at once, it stopped.

His eyes barely opened through the swelling, but Calum still saw what happened next. Kumba yanked his axe from the wall, strode over to him, and raised it above his head.

This was it. Calum had been doing so well, too. Though images of Lumen trickled into his mind here at the end, the prevailing sense in his mind was disappointment, not failure.

Then a spearhead pierced out of Kumba's chest, and he cried out, his face crumpled with pain. His axe clattered to the floor behind him, and he dropped to his knees and face-planted onto the floor next to Calum.

Twenty feet behind Kumba, Axel drew his sword from its sheath and charged the rest of the bandits. Magnus followed him into the room and skewered one of the bandits with his own spear then cut down another with his broadsword.

The bandits spread out and engaged them in battle, leaving Calum behind on the floor. Axel and Magnus each took on two of them at once. Clashing swords and hollers filled the house as bandit bodies fell, one by one.

Axel must've been telling the truth when he'd told Calum he was holding back in their sparring sessions, because he looked like he'd morphed into a seasoned fighter overnight. He ducked under a careless swipe from one of the bandits then ran him through the next instant, and then he proceeded to move on to his next foe without missing a beat.

Just behind Axel, Magnus parried an attack with the blade attached to his tail armor then whirled around with his broadsword extended. The hack leveled the bandit, nearly cleaving him in half.

The remaining two bandits regrouped and stood together, their weapons at the ready but trembling in their hands. Axel feigned an advance, then Magnus barreled forward and felled the one on the right with his sword.

The remaining bandit brought his sword down on Magnus's forearm, but the blade glanced off his Blood Ore armor. Magnus turned toward him as Axel closed in for the kill.

His eyes wide and desperate, the final bandit swung at Axel, who parried the blow, dodged the next one, then drove the tip of his sword deep into the bottom of the bandit's chin. The bandit slumped to the floor, unmoving.

After a quick scan of the room, Magnus and Axel darted over to Calum.

"Are you alright?" Axel dropped to his knees next to Calum and set his sword on the floor.

Magnus joined him. "He needs help. I'll carry him, you gather up those…"

The sound of Magnus's and Axel's voices slowed to garbled nonsense. Darkness encroached on Calum's vision until it was all he could see.

CHAPTER NINETEEN

The scout arrived only two hours after Commander Anigo and his men finished setting up their campsite in the forest. Commander Anigo read the report in the light of the campfire and, at first glance, he frowned. A group of bandits had been killed near a small town called Pike's Garrison.

Nothing in the report definitively indicated the involvement of the fugitives he'd been searching for, but when he reread the words scrawled on the dry parchment, something about them aroused his suspicions.

Pike's Garrison was south of their current location. If the Saurian with them was trying to make his way back to Western Kanarah, then it would follow that he, at least, would be heading south to Trader's Pass, the only known route across the Valley of the Tri-Lakes. If the others had stayed with him, then perhaps the three of them might've been responsible for this event after all.

Strictly speaking, Pike's Garrison was out of Commander Anigo's jurisdiction due to his appointment to Commander Pordone's old post, but Commander Anigo's superiors had tasked him with the unconditional capture of the missing fugitives.

That meant he had the King's authority—at least by extension, via his commanding officers—to do what needed to be done, regardless of where his search led him.

It wasn't much to go on, but it might be just enough.

"Corporal?" he called.

Corporal Bezarion approached. "Yes, Commander?"

"Rouse the men and ready my horse. We're heading south."

Corporal Bezarion's mouth opened, and he glanced back at the campsite. "Commander, we've only been at rest for two hours. I think it would be wise to—"

The stern scowl Commander Anigo leveled at Corporal Bezarion shut him up.

"Right, Commander. You don't care to repeat yourself. Apologies. I will go fulfill your order now, sir."

Within fifteen minutes, everything was repacked. Under the moonlight, Commander Anigo mounted Candlestick and led his men even deeper into the wilderness, heading south.

———

As with every other time he'd appeared to Calum, Lumen crafted the living map with his irradiated sword.

"Calum." Lumen's eyes flickered with white fire. "Release me."

But this time, something about the dream changed. Lumen did something completely new: he extended his sword and touched Calum's chest with its tip.

A warm sensation spread throughout Calum's body, and he sucked in a deep breath. Starting in his chest, strength returned to his exhausted muscles. The sensation extended into his limbs and ended in his fingertips and toes.

By the time it had saturated his entire body, Calum felt totally renewed—almost reborn, in a sense—and infinitely powerful.

"Rise." Lumen's unmistakable voice reverberated throughout the space around him and within him. "You must set me free."

———

CALUM'S EYES OPENED, and he promptly squinted and sat up in bed. Morning sunlight streamed into the room through the solitary window set into one of the walls to his left.

Bed? Windows? Walls? Where am I?

Definitely inside someone's house. A brown wooden chest with six drawers sat in the corner next to the window. Also to his left, beside the bed, a small round table held an unlit oil lamp and a wooden cup of water.

Calum patted the poofy pillows and the heavy quilt that covered him up to his stomach. Where was he? How did he get here? The last thing he remembered was—

"You have awakened."

Calum swiveled his head.

Magnus sat in a wooden chair nestled in the corner of the room to Calum's right. He held a thick leather-bound book in his large hands. He still wore his blue armor, minus his helmet, and his tail tapped the floor at random intervals. His broadsword leaned against the wall next to him, still in its sheath.

He shut the book, sending a plume of dust into the air, and grinned at Calum.

"How's the book?"

"Engaging. A fantastical tale about a ghost haunting a mine on some distant world. Truly fascinating." Without standing, Magnus replaced the book in an open slot between two other books on a floor-to-ceiling bookshelf behind him. "How do you feel?"

Calum stretched his limbs and twisted his back, and a litany of aches and pains awakened throughout his body, followed by a pervading sense of weakness and exhaustion. So much for Lumen's sword restoring his strength. Then again, it was only a dream.

"Sore," he replied. "My ribs hurt, and my face does too. Actually, pretty much everything hurts."

"You took quite a beating from those bandits. Do you feel like you can move around?"

"I'm not sure. My limbs feel stiff, and so does my back. I feel like I could stay in bed for a few days."

Magnus nodded. "You have already been in that bed for nearly three days, in and out of consciousness. We managed to get you to take a little water and some food a few times, but we endured long stretches where we feared you might not wake up."

Calum rubbed his neck. His head throbbed as if someone had dropped a boulder on it. Multiple times. He closed his eyes to try to ward off the pain, but it did little good. "Where are we?"

"We are back in Pike's Garrison, inside Stavian and Reginia's house," Magnus said. "I carried you back while Axel carried as much of the treasure as he could, in addition to his supplies and yours."

"You really carried me all the way down the mountain?"

"Yes."

Calum's mouth hung open. "Why?"

Magnus tilted his head and blinked at him with scaly green eyelids. "Because you are my friend. My only friend."

Satisfaction swelled in Calum's chest, and he smiled. More than once, he'd wondered if Magnus was merely tolerating his presence in the group. After all, their initial partnership had been founded on little more than begging and convenience.

And once Magnus got free of the quarry and got his armor back, he had little reason to stick around Calum and Axel, at least from what Calum could tell. Why he'd bothered to stick around was a mystery to them both, but now more than ever, Calum was grateful that he'd done so.

"Thank you," Calum finally said.

"You would have done the same for me."

Calum chuckled at the thought of him carrying Magnus down an entire mountain. Maybe in Calum's dreams, but not in reality.

"Are you hungry?"

Calum nodded. "Yes. Very."

Magnus stood up, but he had to hunch to fit under the ceiling. "I will return with some food imminently. The good news is that we will not go hungry for awhile. Even with handing over the loot we recovered for the villagers, there is plenty left over for us."

"That much?"

"Yes. Stavian sent a group of villagers to bring their share of the spoils back. Even after they claim their share, there is much, much more to be collected from the bandits' hideout. When you are well, we will venture there together and retrieve more."

"What about Axel? Where is he now?"

"As soon as we arrived here, I sent him back to the hideout to recover more loot with the villagers. He should be back with the others sometime within the next day."

Calum lay back against the pillows again. Aside from nearly being pummeled to death, everything else seemed to have worked out. "Good."

"Rest. I will find you something to eat."

WHEN AXEL REACHED Pike's Garrison with the villagers that afternoon, Magnus met him at the edge of town, grinning.

"Calum is awake."

Axel dropped the huge sack of loot that hung over his shoulder and charged past Magnus toward Stavian and Reginia's house. He didn't stop until he made it inside Calum's room and stood at the foot of the bed, his heart pounding as he stared at Calum's bruised and battered face.

But his eyes were open, and he was sitting up in the bed.

"You're... alright?" He couldn't help but smile.

Calum nodded. "Yeah. I'm alright."

Axel pointed at Calum as he came around the side of the bed. "You had me really worried. After you killed that last bandit, I didn't know what was gonna happen to you."

Calum sat up and scooted back against the bed's headboard. "That makes two of us. Thanks for helping Magnus get me back here. I can't ever repay you for this and everything else you've—"

"Don't start that with me." Axel held up his hand. "We're best friends. Brothers. That's what we do for each other."

"Well, I owe you." Calum smiled.

"I'll be sure to cash in later on." Axel whacked his shoulder, and Calum winced. "Oh, sorry. Still sore?"

Calum nodded and rubbed the spot. "Might be for awhile."

"I know what you mean. After that last fight, everything hurt." Axel sighed. "Of course, since I actually know how to fight, I didn't get the sap kicked out of me like you."

"Keep it up, and I might die of laughter," Calum said, his voice flat. "Anyway, I had another dream about Lumen."

Axel glanced back at the door. "Did you talk to Magnus about it yet?"

"No. It was just before I woke up this morning. I forgot to mention it, and he's been outside helping people with odd jobs around the village."

"And?"

Calum shrugged. "And I think that's a nice thing for him to do. I'd be doing the same if I were able to get out of bed."

"No." Axel rubbed his forehead with his fingers. "The dream, Calum."

"Oh. Whoops." He gave a quick chuckle. "It, uh… it was basically the same as last time, except that this time he touched my chest with the tip of his sword. It felt like fire was spreading through my veins, strengthening me, and then I woke up."

Axel raised an eyebrow at him. "That's…interesting."

"Anyway, he said we—he said *I* am supposed to go release him."

"So you're still on that, huh?" Axel folded his arms. A part of him had secretly hoped one of those bandits had knocked some sense into Calum during that beating. Then maybe he wouldn't have to waste time on what would ultimately be a fruitless quest with a disappointing end.

"Definitely. I feel it inside of me. It's something I *need* to do," Calum insisted. "And if Magnus was right about the thousand-year legend, then we'll be doing Kanarah a favor, too."

Oh, Calum. You and your delusions of grandeur. "If he's even real."

"You're still skeptical?"

Axel shrugged. "In nineteen years I've never even heard of him, and neither had you."

Calum chuckled again. "Yeah, but we didn't exactly get out much."

"Hm." Axel had to concede that one. "True."

"Think about it—it's been a thousand years since Lumen was locked away. Plus, the King doesn't want him released because Lumen's gonna overthrow him and free us from his oppression. So there's the issue of a lot of time passing coupled with the idea that the King is probably stifling any murmurs about Lumen's return."

Axel supposed that made sense, but it still all sounded too farfetched for him to believe. If this ancient warrior was supposed to be so powerful, and if he was going to awaken in a thousand years anyway, what did he need the help of someone like Calum for?

Calum leaned forward. "It all sounds like a good way to hide someone as important as Lumen, if you ask me."

Axel cleared his throat and put his hand on Calum's shoulder, much gentler this time. "Look, Calum. I know you want all of this Lumen stuff to be true, but it's pretty unbelievable. I don't want you to get your hopes up and then find out that you just imagined the whole thing."

"I know you don't," Calum said. "But I'd rather take the chance and see if we can change Kanarah for good rather than keep scraping by every day. I mean, if Lumen is real, and he really will save Kanarah from the King, can you even imagine what'll happen to us if we're the ones who set him *free?*"

The only thing Axel knew for sure was that he was growing weary of this conversation. He shrugged. "I have no idea."

Calum glanced at the window. "We'll be *heroes*. If we set him free, we'll be heroes. We could become generals, or princes, or nobility. We could rule Kanarah with him."

Axel held up his hands. "Alright, even if he is real, we don't *know* that any of that would actually happen."

"So we just shouldn't try?" Calum's blue eyes locked onto Axel. "You have to admit that just making the journey, seeing the Tri-Lakes up close, and visiting the Blood Mountains is gonna be the adventure of a lifetime. That alone is worth the effort."

Axel narrowed his eyes. Though they didn't agree about the whole freeing Lumen escapade, Axel had to admit Calum was right about the adventure part. Traveling and exploring Kanarah was exactly what he'd always wanted to do.

But Calum's irrational desire to go even farther, to venture across the valley to an unfamiliar land in hopes of finding something that may not even exist had less appeal for Axel. What did Western Kanarah even have to offer someone like him?

Wolves, Windgales, and more Saurians. The one he had to travel with was enough of a burden already, thank you very much.

"You don't have to believe it's true to come," Calum said. "I just want you there if we do find him. I want to free Lumen with my best friend at my side."

"Tone down the sappiness, will you?"

"Sorry." Calum chuckled. "It's true, though."

Axel sighed. How could he refuse? At least it was a plan of some sort. He could follow it... for now. At least until something better crested his horizon.

"Then you'd better get healthy soon," Axel said. "I'm not getting any younger, and neither is Scales."

Calum beamed. "Give me a day or two, and we can get out of here."

Axel pointed to him. "You got it. Two days. If you're not up by then, I'm gonna haul you outta that bed and drag you across the valley myself. Crystal?"

Calum nodded. "Clear."

WITHIN A DAY AND A HALF, Calum made it to his feet again, walking and even jogging a bit. The swelling on his face had gone down, and his bruised ribs didn't hurt as much. His limbs still ached, but far less so. By the next morning, he was ready to go on his way with Magnus and Axel.

They said their goodbyes to Stavian and Reginia, their newest and only other friends in Kanarah. Calum shook Stavian's gloved hand, and when he hugged Reginia, he couldn't help but think of her as his mother again.

She'd taken care of him while he recovered, let him sleep in one of her beds, and showed him kindness and compassion unlike anything he'd ever experienced. As they embraced, he realized he would miss her the most.

The journey back to the bandits' hideout took longer since Calum had to walk slower than normal and needed to stop more often. As dusk settled around them after their first day, Magnus began working on the campfire, and Calum unsheathed his sword and challenged Axel to spar.

"Take it easy, Calum." Magnus stacked chunks of wood over a small pit he'd dug out. "It is senseless to risk re-injuring yourself."

"I know, Magnus. I just want to gauge where I'm at in my recovery. You never know when we might run into trouble."

Calum squared his body with Axel's, and the sparring began. He circled Axel and threw a few quick jabs—though not as quick as before he'd taken his beating. His body just refused to cooperate exactly as it had before.

He wondered if he'd sustained any permanent damage. Hardink's bad foot came to mind, but that was an injury. Calum was just sore and needed to loosen up and reeducate his body in the ways of fighting.

To his credit, Axel took it easier than normal too—mostly.

A few strokes into the match, Calum overreached with his sword. Axel sidestepped the swing and drove his shoulder into Calum's, sending a bone-rattling shock throughout Calum's whole body.

Off-balance, Calum tottered to one side, but by the time he recovered, Axel had already moved behind him. The next thing Calum knew, he'd fallen to his rear-end, and fresh pain ignited throughout his body.

"That is more than sufficient for now," Magnus said. "We still have at least a half-day of travel until we reach the bandits' hideout. Save your strength."

Axel extended his hand down toward Calum, who grasped it and allowed Axel to help pull him up to his feet.

"At the end, there, what did you do?" Calum asked.

Axel smirked. "I grabbed the back collar of your armor and pulled you down. Once I had you, I could've done anything. Stabbed you. Cut off your head. Drove my knee into your spine. If you let your enemy get behind you, you're in for a world of hurt."

Calum glanced at Magnus, who nodded. *I'll remember that.*

DESPITE HIS LINGERING ACHES, around noon the next day, Calum was the first to crest the edge of the gorge that concealed the bandits' hideout. When they closed to within three hundred yards, Magnus yanked them both behind a row of pine trees and told them to be quiet.

"What's wrong?" Calum stretched his back after the harsh jerk on his armor.

"The King's soldiers." Magnus snarled. "Have a look, quietly."

Calum and Axel parted some of the conifer branches with their arms and peered down at the house. Even from far away they could see men with black armor patrolling the grounds, including one man on a white horse.

Magnus huffed. "They found the hideout."

CHAPTER TWENTY

A xel cursed, and Calum couldn't blame him for doing it. He thought they'd struck a vein of good fortune—at least up until now. The King's soldiers had complicated everything, as usual.

"What're we gonna do now?" Calum asked.

"We cannot go down there," Magnus said. "So put any such thoughts out of your mind."

"That's exactly what I'm thinking." Axel rubbed his hands together and smirked. "Let's take them out."

"Are you serious?" Calum shook his head. Sometimes Axel came up with the worst possible ideas. "There are at least two dozen men down there, and maybe more inside. We can't handle them, even with Magnus."

"We just brought down eleven bandits without any problems."

Calum eyed Axel.

"Alright, *you* got beat up, but you're fine now."

Calum kept eyeing him.

"Mostly fine." Emphatic, Axel said, "*Come on*. We can take them."

"Keep your voices down, both of you." Magnus glanced over his shoulder. "Royal soldiers typically deploy a minimum of one scout for every five to ten men in a given area, so there is likely one nearby. If he finds us, we will quickly encounter a surplus of trouble. If you wish to discuss our options, we must find somewhere safer to talk."

Axel frowned, but nodded, and Calum nodded too.

After a ten-minute walk to the southeast, all three of them hunched behind a boulder about half the size of Stavian and Reginia's house.

Axel pointed toward the bandits' hideout. "That's our coin in there. *Ours*. We earned it. We can't just let them take it."

As much as Calum wished otherwise, he couldn't deny the truth. "I don't think we have a choice anymore."

"We can take them by surprise, just like we did the bandits."

Calum's voice flattened. "Yeah, we know how *that* turned out."

Axel shrugged. "Hey, *you* wanted to go in alone."

"I went in alone to make it easier for you guys to get inside."

"Yeah." Axel looked him up and down. "And we know how *that* turned out."

Calum scowled at him. "Maybe if you'd gotten inside *faster*, I wouldn't be in this sorry state."

"Not my fault you can't fight worth a—"

"Leave him alone, Axel," Magnus said. "He defeated four of them on his own before they overpowered him. I doubt you would have done as well."

"I would've done *better*." Axel folded his arms.

In fairness, based on how well he'd fought the other bandits once they finally *did* get inside, Axel probably would've done better, but Calum wasn't about to admit that.

"The point is, we cannot engage twenty-five of the King's soldiers at once. With only three blades, it is folly to think otherwise," Magnus said.

"Come on. You're as strong as ten of them, plus you can regenerate if you get injured, plus you have that incredible armor. What are you worried about?" Axel scoffed. "This should be *easy*. If there are twenty-five men inside, then twenty-five swings is all you'd need to end this, *plus* you'll have Calum and me to watch your back."

"I'm in no condition to fight." That, Calum could admit. Even the thought of doing battle again sent fresh aches throughout his body.

"Our sparring today proved that. I can walk or even run, but I'd rather wait a bit longer to heal up before I jump back into fighting."

Axel raised his hands and smacked them on his thighs. "Then we wait a couple of days and then go in."

"I warned you to keep your voice down." Magnus hissed. He clicked his talons on his breastplate. "If we wait that long, the soldiers may be gone, but so will our spoils."

"Then you and I can go." Axel nudged Magnus with his elbow. "We'll stash Calum somewhere safe and go in ourselves and—"

"Evidently, you have no understanding of what is transpiring down there." Magnus squared his body and stared down at Axel. "Those soldiers are not there by accident. They have almost certainly been pursuing us since we hit the Rock Outpost. Before that, even—since we left your family farm. They are *hunting* us, Axel, which means they are on to our trail."

A shock of terror filled Calum's chest. "They're tracking us?"

What did that mean? Were the soldiers going to catch up? If they got caught, would they send Calum back to the quarry, or would they just kill him outright?

Magnus nodded. "I have been tracked by the King's soldiers before. They will probably stop at Pike's Garrison next, and then they will head back into the forest to look for us again. As such, we need to disappear *now*. That means no more spoils."

Axel's jaw hardened. "That's unacceptable."

"It is *reality*," Magnus countered. "If they find us, I expect they will surround and kill us. The best I could hope for in such a dire situation would be escaping with my own life, not protecting yours as well."

Calum shuddered at the thought of fighting to the death, only to be the one dying at the end of the fight.

Magnus exhaled a long sigh. "It is not as easy as twenty-five swings of my sword. If it were, everyone would be a warrior. After all of our training, I thought you would have learned that."

Axel glared at him. "I learned enough to take out *half* of the remaining bandits in that house on my own, without your help. I could've taken all of them had *you* not been there."

"Your delusions know no limits," Magnus muttered.

"Alright. That's enough." Calum held up his hands. Why did Calum always have to get between these two? "I'm sick of this pointless arguing. It's not getting us any closer to a solution."

"He needs to realize he is not as capable a fighter as he believes," Magnus said, "or he may soon find himself wandering the afterlife with his ego in tow."

"I said *enough*, Magnus."

To Calum's surprise, Magnus didn't say anything else after that.

Calum refocused on Axel. "We're not going down there, Axel, so forget it. We'd just get ourselves killed. There's no scenario in which we'd win against those odds without serious help."

Axel shook his head. "You don't know that."

"I'm telling you," Calum firmed up his voice, "we're *not* going down there. Crystal?"

Axel stepped in front of him, his brow furrowed. "No, it's not *crystal*, Calum. You want me to go with you to find some fairytale warrior that probably doesn't even exist, but you won't back me when it's our lives and our livelihood on the line?"

Calum stood his ground, something he probably wouldn't have done had they been back at the quarry or on Axel's farm. "I'm not asking you to walk into an instant death-trap. That's what you're asking here. It's just a bad idea."

"And your little quest *isn't?*" Axel spat.

"Why are you attacking me?" Calum held his hands out to his sides.

"Because you think you're in charge, but you're not."

"No one is in charge," Magnus said.

"Easy for you to say." Axel scoffed. "You two always side with each other."

Calum sighed. Why was this so hard? "We're not trying to team up against you, Axel."

"Well, it sure seems like it."

Magnus snorted.

Axel held up his hand and started to walk away. "Whatever. You said we're not going down there, so there's no point in wasting time here.

Gotta find Calum's mystery warrior and save the world before the thousand years is up, right?"

As Axel disappeared behind some trees, Calum sighed again and looked up at Magnus. "What am I supposed to do?"

Magnus patted him on his back. "He will come around. Come on. The last thing we need is to lose him in the forest when he is upset."

AXEL EXHALED a long sigh and tossed a piece of gristle from dinner into the campfire. The only reason he hadn't left these two jokers behind was because he had literally no idea where he was. Without Magnus to guide him, he'd get lost in the woods.

Frankly, he was already lost in the woods, just with other people who weren't. It frustrated him all the more to realize he was essentially trapped with Scales and Calum. He resolved to learn how to navigate using the stars so he'd never find himself in such a miserable position ever again.

"Do you intend to be sour all night?" Magnus asked.

Axel rolled his eyes. Didn't the Saurian realize that asking questions like *that* just made him angrier? "Yes."

Magnus shook his head and sat down next to Calum on the opposite side of the camp. "I suggest we set watches tonight."

Back in Pike's Garrison, before they'd tried to collect the rest of their plunder from the bandits' hideout, they'd traded their meager amount of loot for the King's royal currency—gold coins with his insignia stamped on them. Much easier to carry around a skull-sized leather pouch stuffed with gold pieces than a sack bulging with various trinkets and valuables.

"We cannot afford to get robbed again," Magnus continued. "If we each sleep four hours at a time and leave one man up, we can all get a good night's rest. I will gladly take the middle shift so you can both sleep without interruption."

Calum nodded. "Sounds good. You want the first shift or the last shift, Axel?"

"Whatever." If it mattered, Axel would've given a better response.

Magnus turned and stared into the dark forest. "Tomorrow we can head west toward the edge of the range again. We can continue our search for a way down."

"According to Stavian's map, we should be almost to Trader's Pass by now." Calum leaned toward the fire, extended his hands, and rubbed them together. "Why not just head straight to Kanarah City and use the pass?"

"Given our recent escapades, it is likely the soldiers there will be looking for us. If not, they will at least be aware of who we are. If they recognize us, it will complicate our journey, to say the least." Magnus smacked a beetle that had landed on his leg, then he licked it off his hand with his long, red tongue.

Axel wrinkled his nose and frowned.

"Excuse me." Magnus added, "Granted, I'm not certain they will come after us, but I'd rather not risk it unless we have no other choice."

"I understand." Calum looked at Axel. "What do you think?"

Axel rolled his eyes. "We all know that neither of you actually care what I think, so you don't have to keep asking my opinion."

"Axel—"

"Just drop it," Axel snapped. "From now on, I'm just gonna cooperate and do whatever you guys want me to do, alright? Like a dutiful soldier. An obedient slave."

And we'll see how everything turns out then.

Calum sighed. "Fine, then. You take the first watch. I'll take the last watch. I'm beat."

Axel nodded. "Sure thing, boss."

Now Calum rolled his eyes.

———

SOMETHING SHOOK CALUM AWAKE. When he opened his eyes, he saw a big green hand on his chest, connected to a matching arm. An imposing reptilian face startled him at first, until he recognized Magnus.

"Your turn for the watch, Calum." Magnus extended his hand and pulled Calum up.

"Thanks." Calum yawned and stretched his sore arms, grateful that they felt better now than when he'd gone to sleep.

"It will be sunrise soon, but I intend to sleep my allotted four hours. If Axel wakes up early, please ask him to keep quiet."

Calum nodded and yawned again, then he sat down on a boulder near the campfire. Despite the chilly night air, the fire warmed him up. The boulder, which had absorbed some of the fire's heat also warmed his bottom.

"The bag of gold is right here next to you. Guard this especially. It is paramount. Wake me if you need help. I seriously doubt anyone or anything will come after it with the fire burning and with you awake, but those sabertooths came for us under these same conditions, so be on your guard anyway."

"Yeah, yeah. I got it, Magnus." Calum waved him away and rubbed his eyes. "Go to sleep. I'll be fine."

Magnus nodded. "Good night, then."

An hour passed. Calum stoked the fire, added a few more logs from the pile they'd gathered, and considered all that had transpired since he left the quarry.

He'd traveled the Snake Mountains. He'd fought and killed saber-tooth cats. He'd run away from soldiers and raided one of their outposts, and he'd gotten clobbered by a group of bandits almost to the point of death.

And he'd killed people—at least two for sure. Granted, everyone he'd fought had meant him harm or wanted to kill him instead.

Magnus had warned Calum it would happen, that he'd have to make those kinds of choices, and he'd made them. Now those men would never draw breath again because of his blade. Still, he took comfort in knowing that he'd spared lives when he could.

On top of all of that, he'd had multiple dreams of Lumen. Perhaps when Calum finally found and freed him, all of this strife and violence would end. Maybe peace—true peace, not the kind manufactured by the King's tyranny—would reign in Kanarah, and everyone would just—

A shadow moved beyond the campfire.

Was it a shadow? Or was he imagining things?

Calum stared at the spot, and his eyes traced around the camp in the direction he thought he saw it move.

Nothing.

Yeah, right.

Something was out there. Or at least that's the stance he intended to take. He wouldn't convey it, though. Better to give the thief confidence and let him try something.

Still, if this was a Wolf like Magnus had thought, how would Calum fare if he had to face off against it? Were Wolves vicious? Intelligent versions of the sabertooth cats they'd faced? Or did they prefer to remain in the darkness and avoid confrontation? Calum would soon find out.

If he'd actually seen a shadow move.

Calum patted the bag of gold with his fingers then leaned back and stared up at the stars for a moment. They shimmered against the night sky like glistening drops of water stuck in place, unable to fall.

Something rustled behind him.

Calum swiveled his head and peered beyond the darkness, but it was only Axel, shifting in his sleep. Calum turned back and stared at the flickering campfire for a moment. Again, he wondered if he'd actually seen a shadow move in the first place or if his mind and the flickering campfire were playing tricks on him.

It didn't matter. He needed to behave as if he hadn't seen it. Then he could get the drop on whoever was—

A twig snapped to his left. The thief—or whatever it was—wasn't very quiet, and now Calum knew for sure that he wasn't alone.

Calum turned his head and stared in that direction for a moment, then he thought better of it. Perhaps he was feeding into the thief's plan. Well, as long as he kept his hand on the—

His fingers grasped only air where the pouch should have been.

When he looked down, it was gone.

CHAPTER TWENTY-ONE

"Magnus! Axel!" Calum's voice split the quiet night.

Magnus sprung to his feet and his sword sang into his hand. "What is it? Are we being attacked?"

"Someone took the bag."

Axel stirred from his sleep as well, but much slower.

"*What?*" Magnus stepped toward him. "Did you fall asleep? Were you not guarding it?"

Calum shook his head. "I was awake the whole time. It was sitting here next to me. I heard a sound over there, so I looked. I didn't see anything, and when I turned back, the bag was gone."

"Wait, what?" Axel stood. "What happened?"

Magnus glared at Calum, then he turned to Axel. "The bag is gone. Someone took it."

Axel's eyes widened. He stomped toward Calum. "You let someone take our coin? *All* of it?"

"He stole it when I wasn't looking," Calum explained. "I didn't hear any footsteps. I didn't hear the coins clinking when the pouch got stolen. I didn't hear or see anything. I couldn't have known—"

Axel grabbed Calum by the sides of his leather breastplate and shook him. "I'm gonna *kill* you."

Magnus pulled them apart and eyed Axel. "Channel your anger into finding the thief. He is already on the run, so he has a head start on us. Do you remember what the Wolf paw prints look like?"

Calum nodded, but Axel just kept glaring at him.

"Axel." Magnus jerked him. "Do you remember what the—"

"*Yes.*" Axel's jaw tensed. "What does that have to do with anything?"

"I think, perhaps, that we may have fallen victim to another Wolf. Let us see what we can find. Grab a stick from the fire and use it to light your way. Look around."

Within a minute, they found the footprints and started to follow them.

"Shouldn't someone stay with the rest of the supplies at the camp?" Calum asked. "That bag isn't the only thing of value we had."

"No, but it was *most* of the value," Axel grumbled.

"Stop it. Calum is only as accountable as either you or me, Axel. We could have divided the coins or taken further precautions to prevent something like this, but we did not." Magnus turned to Calum. "You are right that you should stay at the camp. Axel and I will search for the thief."

Axel shook his head. "He just let our gold get stolen, and now you want him guarding everything else?"

"He is still recovering from his injuries, so he is not as mobile as you are. Quit arguing, bring your torch and your sword, and follow me," Magnus said. "Calum, stay at the camp until we get back."

To CALUM'S DISMAY, Magnus and Axel returned an hour after sunrise with nothing to show for their search.

Axel slammed his sword down on the ground and glared at Calum. "I hope you at least had the good sense to start breakfast."

"Come get some stew." Calum tossed him a pewter bowl. It would take much more than a bowl of stew to appease Axel, but it was a start. "You didn't find him, I take it?"

"He must have realized we were following him. The trail circled back over itself and branched into four different directions. I could not tell where it began and where it ended." Magnus reached for a bowl of his own and sat down next to Calum. "I knew we had to get back, so I called it off."

Even now, after traveling with him for so long, Calum still marveled at Magnus's size.

"I'm really sorry," he said.

Magnus shook his head and filled his bowl from the small pot Calum had perched over the fire. "Wolves are skilled thieves. They are quick, and they can all but disappear in darkness. I doubt I would have done any better than you."

Calum knew Magnus was just trying to make him feel better. "If you say so. Recently I've felt like the weak link in this group."

Axel walked over and ladled some stew into his bowl. "That's because you *are* the weak link."

Magnus sprung to his feet and knocked the bowl from Axel's hand in one quick motion, splattering stew on the ground.

Axel, wide-eyed, dropped the ladle.

Then Magnus grabbed Axel by the throat and lifted him clear off his feet, all while still holding his own bowl of stew in his other hand, even as Axel thrashed and struggled to get free.

Calum gawked at the sight. "Magnus, what are you—"

"Do not *ever* say anything like that again. Calum is the *soul* of this group. Without him, I would have gone my own way a long time ago and left you to fend for yourself."

Axel squirmed against Magnus's grip and clenched his arm with both hands.

"Calum is our leader, without question. I may have said otherwise, but I was wrong. Either you will begin to treat him with the respect he deserves, or you will leave the group. Crystal?"

Axel sputtered and managed to reply, "Clear."

Calum stifled a smile. He didn't like being at odds with Axel, but Magnus standing up for him felt good. Great, even.

Magnus dropped him, and Axel's boots hit the dirt. Once he sat back down, Magnus resumed eating his breakfast.

Axel rubbed his throat, coughed, picked up his bowl, then slumped against a tree several feet from the others with his arms folded.

"You didn't have to do that, Magnus," Calum said.

Magnus swallowed a large gulp of stew and turned his focus to Calum. "Did you hear what I just said to Axel?"

Calum glanced at Axel, who didn't make eye contact with him. "Yes."

"Everything I said was true. You *are* this group's leader and its soul, regardless of what I have said in the past. Without you, both Axel and I would be dead by now. You alone have seen visions of Lumen, and you alone have been called to free him. We are following *you*. We need you here, mistakes or otherwise."

Calum stared at the fire, digesting Magnus's words. Even if it was all true, the thief had left them in a tight spot. "But what are we going to do about the coin?"

"We can find another village. There are plenty of bandits in these mountains. Maybe they have wronged others whom we can help." Magnus gazed into the woods. "Or we could try to pick up the thief's trail and follow him until we catch up, but that may never happen."

"We could probably chase him forever, but we need to keep heading toward the valley," Calum said. "These dreams of Lumen aren't going away. Each time I dream of him, I sense more and more urgency for us to free him."

"Perhaps if we stop at one of the villages south of Pike's Garrison before Kanarah City we could hire out for some manual labor. We could—"

"No." Axel looked up. "I'm not going back to that life."

"I do not recall asking your opinion." Magnus turned his reptilian gaze toward him.

"Easy, Magnus," Calum said.

Magnus hissed a sigh. "It would only be for a few days at the mo—"

"I said *no*." Axel's voice hardened.

"I'm with Axel on this one," Calum said. "I don't want to go back to manual labor unless I have no other choice. Eight years in a quarry was long enough."

Magnus hissed again but nodded. "Then what do you suggest we do?"

Calum glanced between them and stood to his feet. "After you guys finish eating, we'll pack up and head west toward the edge of the range. We'll keep trying to find a way down, farther south along the range. If we can't find anything, we go to Kanarah City and cross over Trader's Pass."

Magnus glanced at Axel, then downed the rest of his stew. "I will start packing, then."

———

BRILLIANT LIGHT FILLED Calum's vision, and Lumen appeared once again.

Another night, another dream.

"Go to the Arcanum," Lumen said in his all-pervading voice. "Time is short. Set me free, and I will bring justice to those who have done you and your friends harm."

Lumen had been watching them? Was he referring to what had happened to Calum's parents, or something else entirely?

"How do you know all of this?" Calum asked.

"I see many things," Lumen replied. "My power is burgeoning. Free me, and I will defeat the King, claim my rightful throne, and grant you the desires of your heart."

The living map snapped into view, and a grand city came into view. Towering gray walls surrounded it, and within its walls people bustled throughout its streets and buildings.

"What is this place?" Calum asked. "Is it Solace?"

"No," Lumen replied. "Solace is a far greater city. This is Kanarah City. Here you will find the entrance to Trader's Pass."

Calum nodded.

"Time is short, Calum." Lumen repeated. "You must reach Trader's Pass soon. I have chosen you to free me, and when you do, I will glorify you above all others." The living map swirled and evaporated into the light that outlined Lumen's powerful form. "Go forth. Find the Arcanum, and learn the secret to releasing me."

Lumen and his light spiraled into the blackness of Calum's dreams once again.

———

"I DON'T THINK we have a choice." Calum rubbed his sore neck and straightened his back. "It's been a week. Lumen told me we were supposed to go down to Kanarah City. We've already searched almost the entire edge of the range, and we still haven't found a way down. Kanarah City is the easiest way get to Trader's Pass, and then we can cross over to find the Arcanum."

Magnus shook his head. "We are certain to encounter trouble. I know it."

Axel rolled his eyes. "Look, if you ever wanna get across the valley, that's the way we need to go."

"Since when are you so willing to make the trip?" Magnus asked. "Or provide a useful opinion about… well, anything?"

"Didn't say I was, but I'm sick of wandering the woods without a reason to be here. I'm sick of rationing our food. I'd rather get to Kanarah City and try our luck there."

Calum smirked. Since Magnus's confrontation with Axel, they seemed to have reconciled their differences and meshed into more of a team, and Axel had grown much more cooperative. Hopefully, he'd stay that way.

"Besides, if Calum's having dreams about Kanarah City, then maybe we *are* supposed to go there," Axel said.

Calum's smirk widened into a smile. "Axel is right, Magnus. We need to get out of here and make better progress in reaching the Arcanum. There just isn't a safe way down to the valley from here or anywhere along the range."

Magnus huffed. "Then lead the way."

"Regret that you made me the leader yet?" Calum elbowed Magnus's armored ribs. He didn't even flinch.

"Moderately, yes."

Calum led them east through the woods for the next few hours until they reached a small clearing. Sunlight emblazoned the tall green-and-gold grass from above, and the entire color range of autumn leaves swirled in the wind.

About ten steps into the clearing, Magnus grabbed Calum's shoulder. "Stop."

Calum knew what that meant, and his blood tingled in anticipation. "What do you hear?"

"We are not alone. Axel, get over here."

Axel plodded over and scanned the tree line. "I don't see anything."

"They are not in the trees." Then, cryptically, Magnus added, "We have walked into a trap."

Dark forms rose from the tall grass all around them. First five, then ten. By the time all of them stood up, Calum counted twenty men surrounding them, all brandishing gleaming weapons.

Calum, Axel, and Magnus drew their swords.

This was bad.

Calum was still learning about strategy and tactics from Magnus, but he didn't have to be an expert to know that three fighters, surrounded by twenty in an open field with no cover and no chance of escape, had little chance of surviving, much less winning.

Yep. Definitely bad.

One of the men, clad in dark-red armor, sauntered toward them. He stroked his curly black beard with his left hand, and in his right, he gripped a shining sword with a slight curve at the end of its red blade. A long burgundy cape with a black lining hung from his shoulders.

Definitely not one of the King's soldiers.

He pointed a finger at Calum. "You killed my cousin."

Calum held his sword at the ready but glanced at Magnus and Axel. "Who are you?"

"My name is Tyburon, leader of the Southern Snake Brotherhood. You killed my cousin."

"Bandits and assassins," Magnus hissed.

Calum swallowed the lump in his throat. "Who was your cousin?"

"His name was Norm. He led the Northern Snake Brotherhood." Tyburon's gaze hardened, and Calum immediately recognized a resemblance to Norm.

Tyburon could have passed for a taller, thinner version of his cousin, but the way he carried himself suggested he was far more dangerous.

"You broke into his hideout and killed him along with most of his men."

Most of his men? Calum's eyes widened.

Tyburon tilted his head. "Thought you killed everyone, didn't you?"

Magnus and Calum glanced at each other.

"Nicolai, come here." Without shifting his gaze from Calum, Tyburon motioned with his left hand.

One of the men walked over. He wore dark-green armor and held what appeared to be an oversized meat cleaver in his left hand. The man removed his helmet, revealing curly black hair and dark eyes.

Calum had knocked him out in the kitchen at the bandits' hideout.

"You see," Tyburon patted Nicolai's armored shoulder, "Nicolai escaped through the back door before you three could finish him off, although it came at the cost of a nasty bump on his head. He came straight to me and told me what had happened, and we've been tracking the three of you ever since."

"What do you intend to do?" Magnus stood between Tyburon and Calum.

Tyburon smiled. "I'm here with twenty armed men, and you're asking what I intend to do?"

Calum pushed past Magnus. "Your cousin and his bandits preyed on innocent villagers, people who barely had enough to get by without suffering extra loss from your cousin's men."

"Hence the term 'bandits,' mmm?" Tyburon shrugged. "It's a living. Not a noble one, but a living nonetheless. In this age, everyone has to look out for themselves and their families. Now I'm looking out for mine."

"Killing us won't bring your cousin back," Calum said, now well within striking range of Tyburon.

"No, it won't," Tyburon said as Nicolai put his helmet back on. "But it will make me happy, and it will serve as a warning that anyone who dares to oppose the Brotherhood will meet the same fate."

Tyburon lashed his red-bladed sword at Calum, but Magnus jerked Calum back just in time. Magnus counterattacked with his own blade. Tyburon blocked the blow, but it forced him back a step.

They stood at odds, opposing each other but not approaching.

All Calum could think of was how fast Tyburon's blow had come at him. If Magnus hadn't yanked him out of the way...

Calum concluded that unlike Norm, Tyburon was a skilled and ruthless fighter. He probably had to be in order to maintain his authority over a bunch of murderous, thieving bandits. And he was fast —deadly so.

When Nicolai started forward, Tyburon put his hand against Nicolai's chest to keep him from advancing. "Not yet, Nicolai. You'll get your chance soon enough. Fall back in line with the others... and close the noose."

As the bandits backed away, Magnus said, "Let me handle Tyburon."

Calum nodded. "What are we gonna do?"

Magnus pulled Axel closer to them. "Put your backs against mine. Stay nearby. We are going to fight."

Axel nodded. "You'd better believe we're gonna fight."

"Let them come to you. Let them do the work," Magnus muttered so only they could hear him. "When they get close enough to strike, then strike, but not before then. Do not let them get any of us from behind. And most importantly, when I yell 'switch,' rotate one quarter turn to your left and take down whoever ends up in front of you."

"Will that even work?" Disbelief lined Axel's voice.

"It is worth a try. It will catch them off guard, but it will only work once."

"Alright," Axel said. "Let's do this."

As the bandits closed in around them, Tyburon yelled, "Save the little one for me. He killed Norm. He's mine."

Great. So much for avoiding Tyburon.

Six of the bandits, not including Tyburon or Nicolai, drew in closer, almost within the range that Magnus had referenced. Some of them wore mismatched armor, mostly on their chests and arms, and some of them wore robes or animal skins instead. Each of them wore a confident snarl.

Calum wanted to peek over his shoulder at Axel and Magnus, but he didn't. He kept his eyes focused on the two bandits in front of him.

One of them stepped within range.

Calum lunged forward and swung his sword in a broad swipe at the bandit's exposed left ankle, but the bandit jumped back just in time to avoid getting hit.

"You telegraphed your swing, Calum," Magnus hissed at him from behind. "I cannot even see you, and I knew what you intended to do. Conceal your intentions before you move. Let him do the work for you."

The first bandit stepped within range again. This time Calum waited.

The second bandit sprang forward and jabbed at him with a spear. Calum parried, then he ducked under the first bandit's sword. The clanging of weapons sounded behind him as Magnus and Axel engaged their foes, too.

Another spear jab just missed Calum's arm. He batted the spear toward the first bandit, and it stalled his next attack. Calum rolled under his next swipe and cut him down at his knees. The first bandit dropped, screaming.

The second bandit thrust his spear at Calum's face. Reflex jerked Calum's sword upward, deflecting the attack, but he'd wandered away from his friends.

He stumbled back closer to Magnus and Axel and waited for the next attack to come. He traded several swings and swipes with the spear bandit, but he couldn't get close enough to do any damage. The spear had the length advantage, and no matter what Calum did, he couldn't get past it.

"Switch!" Magnus roared.

Calum took three quick steps to his left and intercepted a haphazard axe meant for Axel. The bandit's axe skidded off Calum's incoming sword, but Calum's return swing caught the bandit just under his ribs.

If the bandit had been wearing armor, it would've saved him, but instead he wore only animal skins and fabric. He sputtered then dropped to the ground.

Calum stole a glance back in time to see Magnus wrench the spear away from the spear bandit he'd been fighting. Weaponless, the bandit turned and tried to flee, but Magnus hurled the spear at him. It skewered through the bandit's back, and he went down.

"Fall back," Tyburon hollered. "Fall back *now*."

Only two of the original six bandits had survived. They retreated back into their circle, now four men thinner than before.

"No more child's play. This time we *all* go in at the same time." Tyburon pointed his sword at Calum. "But the boy is still mine."

"Then come and get me." It sounded fierce and confident when Calum said it. Whether he actually felt either of those things was a different matter.

The noose tightened so that all sixteen of the remaining bandits plus Tyburon stood almost shoulder-to-shoulder around Calum, Magnus, and Axel.

Definitely, definitely bad.

"What do we do now?" Calum muttered.

"We kill them all," Axel said.

Magnus exhaled a long sigh. "No matter what happens, it has been an honor to know you both."

Calum tightened his grip on the handle of his sword.

A horse whinnied in the distance. Calum glanced in that direction, but he didn't see anything. He refocused on Tyburon and his advancing men, except now Tyburon had locked his eyes on something far away.

"By the Overlord." Tyburon's eyebrows arched lower.

"What is it?" Calum asked.

"Soldiers." Axel shielded the sun from his eyes with his left hand but didn't lower his sword. "A lot of 'em."

Calum grumbled, "As if things couldn't have been worse."

"They're coming this direction," Axel said. "What do we do?"

"Stay put, and stay on your guard," Magnus said. "Things are about to get very interesting, very quickly."

CHAPTER TWENTY-TWO

"**B**rothers, regroup to me," Tyburon said.

To Calum's surprise, the bandits abandoned their circle and formed two orderly lines with Tyburon in the center. He hadn't expected them to demonstrate that level of discipline.

"We should make a break for it," Axel said. "We're not surrounded anymore."

Magnus eyed him. "First you want to fight, now you wish to flee?"

"There are at least two-dozen soldiers approaching, plus seventeen bandits. Forty-one is too many to risk fighting on our own."

Calum chuckled. "So forty-one is your cut-off for too many enemies to fight at once?"

Axel scowled at him and quipped, "No, it's actually more like thirty-seven. Maybe thirty-eight if I'm feeling especially spunky."

Calum rolled his eyes. "Axel raises a good point. Why don't we just run for it?"

"If we flee, both sides will pursue us, and we will be killed," Magnus said. "If we stand our ground, perhaps it will end differently. Besides, the soldiers are too close now. It is too late to flee."

Calum wanted to say something else, but a yell stayed his words.

"By order of the King and with his full authority, I, Commander

Beynard Anigo, command all of you to lay down your arms and surrender for crimes against the Crown."

Calum turned back. A commander on a white horse extended his spear as he and two-dozen soldiers approached.

"Do it," Magnus said.

"*What?*" Axel's tone could have shattered a boulder.

"Just *do it*, but keep them within reach. Trust me."

Calum and Magnus dropped their swords to the ground, but Axel hesitated.

"*Axel.*" Calum nudged him.

Axel grunted but dropped his sword at his feet, then he unslung his spear from his back and tossed that to the ground as well.

"Raise your hands, too." Magnus raised his hands into the air, and Calum and Axel mimicked him.

Commander Anigo reined in his horse about ten feet from their position, and the soldiers stopped just behind him. He looked them over and smirked, and Calum took in his handsome face and dark eyes. He exuded confidence, much as Tyburon or Magnus did, only in a more polished, official sense.

Commander Anigo eyed the bandits behind them next. "You men, drop your weapons as well. I order you in the name of the King."

As if on cue, Calum, Axel, and Magnus rotated so they could see both the soldiers and the bandits.

Tyburon stepped forward. "We will not relinquish our weapons. Our quarrel is not with you, but with these three villains."

Commander Anigo's voice hardened. "I said to drop your weapons."

"We will do no such thing."

"A violation of an order given by the King's representatives is equivalent to disobeying the King himself," Commander Anigo said. "You are hereby under arrest. Drop your weapons and surrender."

Calum glanced at Magnus who gave both Axel and him a wink. Whatever Commander Anigo wanted to achieve, he wasn't going to succeed at it.

Tyburon smiled and shook his head. "Commander, do you have any idea who I am?"

"Your identity doesn't factor into this matter." Commander Anigo narrowed his gaze. "Only the King's does."

Unfazed, Tyburon continued, "I am Tyburon, leader of the Southern Snake Brotherhood."

Now it was Commander Anigo's turn to look unimpressed. "So?"

Tyburon chuckled. "You really have no idea who I am, do you?"

"Like I said—" Commander Anigo pointed his spear at Tyburon. "—it doesn't matter who you are. You're still under arrest."

"Alright." Still holding his sword, Tyburon raised his hands in the air as if to dismiss Commander Anigo's words. "You obviously don't know what you're saying, so I'll grant you a pass for your ignorance… just this once. If you run along, you and your men don't have to die today."

Commander Anigo went stone-still, and his face warped into a mask of rage mixed with disbelief. "Did you just *threaten* me?"

"Threaten you?" Tyburon scoffed. "No, Commander. I'm trying to show you mercy."

The ranks of soldiers stirred behind Commander Anigo. He held up his right hand, the one that didn't hold the spear, and they fell silent. "No, sir. You threatened me. To threaten one of the King's representatives is to—"

"To threaten you is to threaten the King himself," Tyburon interrupted. "Yes, I get it. If you want to take it as a threat, fine. But I assure you that not a single one of your men will escape this field alive should you try to disarm and arrest us."

"Soldiers, prepare for battle." Commander Anigo raised his spear, and every soldier behind him drew their weapons and stepped into a balanced fighting posture.

"Last chance, commander. These three belong to me. They killed my cousin and his friends, and I'm here to do right by my kin." Tyburon extended his hands out to his sides. "I have no desire to spill your blood on this field as well."

"These three are wanted for the deaths of multiple quarry workers, the ransacking of one of the King's outposts, and for the murder of at least three of the King's soldiers. We have been pursuing them for weeks." Commander Anigo's jaw hardened. "Their penalty is death."

Calum's stomach twisted. He'd considered that the consequences of his escape and his actions since might end his life, but hearing Commander Anigo proclaim it aloud somehow made it more real, more ominous.

But the fear quickly yielded to obstinance. Why should he pay for the sins of others? He hadn't enslaved himself at the quarry. He hadn't subjugated people and forced them to work in order to better his own life. He hadn't ordered the death of anyone's parents.

The sheer gall of the King to rule his subjects in such a way kindled a righteous anger within Calum that he hadn't known was there before. Those four words passing sentence on him and his friends made him realize, for the first time, exactly why Lumen needed to save Kanarah.

Calum would do everything he possibly could to ensure that it happened.

"But it shall not be at your hands," Commander Anigo concluded.

Tyburon readied his red-bladed sword. "Then we have a serious problem."

"Soldiers, take the three outlaws into custody immediately."

About half the soldiers marched forward, still battle-ready, toward Calum, Axel, and Magnus.

Tyburon waved his left arm in a big arc. "Brothers, forward."

"Great. Now they're closing in on both sides," Axel muttered. "We're in worse shape than before."

"That is precisely why I instructed you to keep your weapons close." Magnus's golden-eyed gaze darted between the two forces. "When I say the word, grab your weapons and back away from the main fight. Let them thin each other out, and we will clean up the rest. Only fight those who come directly for you. I will handle Tyburon."

"Good. That leaves the big-talking commander for me," Axel said.

Calum nodded. It sounded like a good plan, at least. "I hope this works..."

"If not, we will perish anyway," Magnus said. "At least I bought us a few more minutes to watch a good show on our way out."

Axel huffed.

Tyburon and his men charged forward. In response, Commander

Anigo and his men also charged forward, including the twelve soldiers who'd already started marching in.

"Now!"

At Magnus's shout, Calum and Axel snatched their swords from the ground, and Axel grabbed his spear as well. All three of them retreated straight back.

About a quarter of the closest soldiers followed them, as did a quarter of the bandits, but the rest plowed straight into each other, their weapons flashing in the midday sun.

Axel fended off two of the bandits while Magnus handled two of the soldiers, and Calum had one of each. They stood in an awkward triangle, each of them glancing between the other two, but none of them moved.

The bandit swung his axe at Calum's head, but Calum dodged the attack. The soldier jabbed at the bandit with his spear, but the bandit parried the attack and returned with one of his own, and they continued to fight each other. Perfect.

Calum ducked away from the fight and snuck up behind Axel's opponents. Two swings of his sword from behind them dropped them to their knees, and Axel finished them off from the front. He and Calum exchanged nods and repositioned themselves to look for new enemies.

Magnus felled one of the soldiers with his sword, grabbed the other by his throat, and hurled the soldier toward three approaching bandits.

They all hit the dirt hard upon impact, and when the bandits made it back to their feet, they ganged up on the soldier. He didn't last long, but another soldier joined the fray and quickly cut down two of the bandits. He faced off with the one that remained.

Axel and Calum partnered against the next batch of soldiers and bandits. They had a good system: they waited until one of the soldiers attacked one of the bandits, or vice-versa, and then they threw a quick barrage at the attacker. Each time it happened, the initial attacker got himself wounded or killed.

In the distance, Calum saw Tyburon at work. He took down opponents with broad, sweeping swings, and otherwise walked through the battle as if strolling through a vacant field admiring the flowers and butterflies.

But when their eyes met, Tyburon's entire countenance changed to one of limitless fury. He started toward Calum, now walking much faster than his previous casual pace.

"I'm gonna take on the commander, alright?" Axel said.

Before Calum could respond, Axel stormed into the battle toward Commander Anigo, who deftly battled the bandits from atop his white horse.

Meanwhile, Tyburon drew even nearer.

"Magnus!" Calum cried.

Magnus carved through his opponents like a gigantic green-and-blue blur, but he'd ventured too far away from Calum. Instead, he engaged what appeared to be a mixed force of seven or eight men from both sides combined. He showed no indication of having heard Calum's call, so Calum started toward him.

A soldier whirled and swung his sword at Calum. He dodged the stab, clamped his left hand on the soldier's opposite wrist, and ran him through.

A second soldier came at him with an axe. Calum yanked his sword free and raised it to block the blow, but a red blade with a curve at its end intercepted it. One swift motion later, the soldier dropped to the ground, dead from a savage hack.

Tyburon stood in the soldier's place and glared at Calum with blood-lust in his hazel eyes.

CHAPTER TWENTY-THREE

"I would kill every man on this battlefield to get to you," Tyburon said.

Calum glanced past Tyburon. Both Magnus and Axel still fought others, too occupied to even notice him, much less help.

He was on his own.

"Your friends can't save you now, *boy*."

Tyburon's first attack came so fast that Calum barely had time to avoid it, but somehow he managed to back away just in time. The second was predictable—a hard chop down at his head. Calum blocked it easily, but he couldn't do anything when Tyburon's boot slammed into his chest.

Calum skidded through the tall grass on his back. He pushed himself upright in time to bat away a series of quick strikes from Tyburon's sword.

A brick hit his face and pain flared in his right cheek. No, not a brick —Tyburon's fist.

Calum staggered back and shook his cognition back into place. Tyburon would maintain his advantage unless Calum could do something to interrupt it.

He knew one thing for sure—if Tyburon expected to kill him easily, Calum intended to disappoint him. Magnus hadn't trained him over the last few months for nothing, and Lumen hadn't called him for no reason, either.

Calum had been chosen, and he'd resolved not to fail, no matter what.

Tyburon laughed. "How does that feel, boy?"

"Not as good as killing your cousin." Calum cracked his neck and leveled his sword.

A solemn wave washed Tyburon's glee away. "First, you kill my cousin. Then you make me track you through the woods, away from my home and my bed. Now you're joking about it? By the time I'm done, no one will even be able to *recognize* you."

"You talk too much."

Tyburon slashed at Calum's head, but Calum rolled under the blow and swung at his legs. Tyburon blocked the attack and kicked Calum again. Calum's breastplate absorbed most of the kick, but the impact knocked him off balance. He fell to the ground, totally vulnerable.

Tyburon's red blade chopped at Calum's left leg, but Calum jerked it away. When Tyburon followed up with a chop at Calum's right leg, Calum shifted, dodged the blow, and planted the sole of his left boot on Tyburon's knee. He pushed off, and Tyburon's knee buckled as Calum rolled backward onto his feet.

Grimacing, Tyburon came at him right away with another swing, and sharp pain knifed across Calum's chest. Had Calum's sword not been there, and had his leather armor not absorbed some of the hack, the slash would've killed him.

As it was, Tyburon's red blade remained where it was, partway digging into the flesh of Calum's chest. Only Calum's sword and his strength kept it from delving any deeper.

With gritted teeth, Calum shoved his sword against Tyburon's, and the blade barely dislodged from Calum's leather breastplate. He staggered back a few desperate steps and dabbed at his chest. Blood tainted his fingertips.

"I hope it hurts," Tyburon said. "It's only the beginning."

Calum glanced at Magnus and Axel again. Magnus had whittled the number of his opponents down to three—all of them the King's soldiers.

Axel no longer held his spear, but he had somehow managed to get Commander Anigo off of his horse, which then bolted for the tree line. They now fought face-to-face in a flurry of clashing metal that made Calum glad he wasn't fighting Commander Anigo.

Then again, he still had Tyburon to deal with.

Tyburon smirked. "Truth be told, I'm impressed you even made it this far."

"That makes two of us." Calum swallowed the lump in his throat and sucked in several quick breaths.

"Not so confident anymore, are you?" Tyburon angled his sword so the tip pointed at Calum's face.

"It's just a cut."

"It's a harbinger of your demise," Tyburon said. "A promise of things to come."

To Calum's surprise, he defended Tyburon's next several attacks without incident, and he even managed to throw in a few of his own. He actually struck Tiburon's left thigh once, but the blow didn't pierce his armor.

Tyburon staggered back and shook his leg, all while calling down every curse and hurling every profane name under the sky at Calum. "You're gonna pay for that."

"Add it to your list of grievances." Calum sucked in quick breaths, trying to ignore the pain in his chest.

"Funny thing is…" Tyburon huffed and waved his sword through the tall grass, for now keeping his distance. "I didn't even like Norm."

Calum's jaw tensed, and anger briefly overpowered the pain in his chest. "Then why are you taking this so personally?"

Tyburon shrugged and began to circle Calum, still teasing the grass with his red blade. "He was my family, and part of the Brotherhood."

Calum wanted to sling a curse or two at him, but Tyburon didn't grant him the time. A hailstorm of attacks rained down on Calum. He parried some and dodged the others, straining to meet each blow.

"Just give up, already," Tyburon said between thrusts. "I'll make it quick and painless for you. Mostly."

"Why don't *you* give up?" If Calum could survive just a bit longer, then perhaps Magnus could come and assist him. "You're old. I'm only sixteen. I have a long life ahead of me. You're basically worthless now."

Tyburon glared at him and scoffed. "Kid, I'm only thirty-eight. That's not old."

As they'd fought, one thing in particular stood out to Calum—Tyburon was aware of everything happening around him in the battle. At one point, he even backed away from the fight to grab a soldier from behind and run him through, thus saving Nicolai, then he reengaged Calum the instant he released his grip on the soldier.

Perhaps Calum could use that to his advantage... but how?

Tyburon lashed at Calum's head, and he leaned back and out of the way. The red metal of the blade missed his nose by inches, and Tyburon continued to spin around for another hack.

As Magnus had taught him, Calum stepped into Tyburon's swing and met his sword with his own instead of falling back. The blades met, and Calum earned a slight advantage by catching Tyburon off guard.

The advantage didn't last long. Though Calum's blade blocked Tyburon's sword from harming him, Tyburon's other elbow freely slammed into Calum's right cheek. The blow stunned Calum, and Tyburon freed his sword with another hard shove to Calum's chest.

In that moment, he realized he'd never beat Tyburon outright. Despite Calum's words to the contrary, the effects of the fight fatigued his body. Even though Tyburon wasn't much stronger than Calum, he was just as fast, if not faster, and he had another twenty-plus years of experience reinforcing his every decision.

No matter how hard he fought, no matter how fast he tried to be, Calum couldn't win—at least not that way. But if he could use the surrounding battle to his advantage, perhaps he'd have a chance.

"Magnus!" he called. "Magnus, help me!"

He knew Magnus wouldn't hear him. The distance between them and Magnus had actually increased since he first called for help.

Sure enough, Tyburon turned his head toward where Calum was looking, although only very slightly. His gaze flitted away for just a moment then refocused back on Calum's.

"The Saurian can't help you now." Tyburon showed him a twisted smile. "You're going to die just as you are now: all alone."

"That's what you think." Calum diverted his gaze from Tyburon's for just a moment, looking over his shoulder, then looked at him again. When he did it a second time, Calum cracked a faint smile.

It worked.

Tyburon's head swiveled that direction for an instant, and his eyes followed, but that was all Calum needed. He sprang forward.

Calum anticipated the kind of reaction he'd receive. Tyburon's head and eyes jerked forward again, and he swung his sword at Calum on a downward angle from his right shoulder down to his left hip.

While still in motion, Calum ducked low and twisted his body away from the slash but toward Tyburon's right side. As Tyburon's blade streaked just over Calum's head and back and started his follow-up swing, Calum drove his shoulder into Tyburon's midsection.

As simple as it was, the move had worked before to knock both Burtis and Jidon off balance. It worked this time against Tyburon, too.

Tyburon pitched off-balance, and as the bandit tried to right himself, Calum found his opening. Just like Axel had done to him, he quickly rotated around Tyburon, grabbed him by the back collar of his armor, and yanked. Tyburon lost his footing and landed on his rear-end, just as Calum had in the woods.

As Tyburon struggled to regain his footing, Calum jammed his sword through Tyburon's burgundy cape and into his back. The blade punctured deep into Tyburon's body, out his chest, and through his breastplate.

Tyburon's struggle stopped, and he sat there, stunned as he stared down at the steel protruding from his chest. When Calum wrenched his sword from Tyburon's body, Tyburon rolled onto his back.

His blood-tinged mouth hung open, and his eyes widened as he wheezed, "I don't believe it."

Calum looked down at him. "If it's any consolation, neither do I."

With one mighty swing, Calum severed Tyburon's head from his body.

ASIDE FROM MAGNUS, Axel had never fought anyone so skilled before. Commander Anigo had proven to be more than a worthy opponent—he was dangerous and even downright scary at times. The guy was just intense… and really vicious and determined to win.

That didn't mean he was going to, though. Not if Axel had anything to say about it.

Axel threw a haphazard slice at him, but Commander Anigo ducked under the attack and jabbed his spear at Axel's chest. Axel parried it away with his sword, but as he did, he stepped back, and something rolled under his heel.

He staggered to stay upright and find his footing again, all while defending two subsequent jabs from Commander Anigo. Then he backed up to get a glance at what he'd stepped on.

His spear. He'd dropped it earlier and lost track of it, but now it lay at his feet.

Axel refocused on Commander Anigo, but positioned his feet on either side of the weapon. He'd practiced the move before and managed to fool Calum a few times, but he'd never tried it in a real battle.

Only one way to find out if it'll work.

Axel tossed his sword, blade-first, at Commander Anigo, not as an attack, but as a distraction. Sure enough, Commander Anigo's eyes followed the sword, not Axel's movements. While Commander Anigo dodged the weapon, Axel kicked his spear up into his hands.

By the time Commander Anigo refocused, Axel's spear was already headed for his chest. The spearhead pierced the commander's breastplate and dug even deeper still, and his eyes widened. He dropped his spear, clamped his hands around the spear shaft, and slumped to the ground.

Axel retrieved his sword, then once Commander Anigo stopped moving and went limp, he bent down and pulled the commander's sword from its sheath on his belt. He couldn't have counted the number of dents and chips in the edges of his old blade, but Commander Anigo's sword looked as if it had been sharpened that morning, so Axel swapped them.

He also took Commander Anigo's spear and left his behind, still lodged in the commander's chest.

Axel grinned and exhaled a long, relieved breath. "Thanks for the steel. Feel free to keep mine right where I left it."

Magnus had just finished off the last of the men battling him, so Axel scanned the field for Calum. It didn't take him long to find him since everyone else was dead.

Apparently, that included Tyburon.

Unbelievable. I really didn't think he had it in him.

Axel waved to Magnus and they both jogged over to Calum. When they arrived, Axel gawked at the sight of Tyburon's bearded head lying next to his body. "You beat him all on your own?"

Calum nodded. Between haggard breaths, he said, "Yeah. I still can't believe it. I used that move Axel showed me the other day. The one where he got behind me and pulled the back of my armor? It worked."

Axel glanced and Magnus and smirked. "Our baby is growing up."

Magnus frowned at him. "Even if Saurians and humans could procreate, you are the last person I would ever care to raise a child with."

"Ew. Not at all what I meant." Axel shook his head. "It was supposed to be a joke."

"Interesting. Are human jokes not designed to include humor?" Magnus asked.

"No, they are, but—" Axel caught Magnus smirking this time. "You're a big jerk. You know that?"

"I think I'll take his sword as a memento of today." Calum picked up Tyburon's sword and examined it. Its red blade glistened stark against its black handle, hilt, and the garnet set into the pommel. Definitely the most impressive sword Axel had ever seen.

Axel and Magnus glanced at each other. Still in disbelief, Axel asked, "You sure you didn't have help?"

Calum's brow furrowed. "You don't believe me? I swear it's true."

"That's... incredible," Axel said.

"Come on. Give me some credit here. I know what I'm doing." Calum bent down and unfastened Tyburon's belt, removed the sword's sheath, and slung it to his waist. He nodded to Magnus. "After all, I had a great teacher."

Axel cleared his throat.

"Oh, yeah. And an amateur sparring dummy to beat up on."

"One good kill, and his ego's as big as a house," Axel said.

"Reminds me of someone else I know," Magnus said.

Axel glared at him, then he shifted his glare to Calum. "We both know I could kick your brains out if I wanted to."

"Just be happy we survived this in the first place." Magnus's gaze fixed on something in the distance, and he threaded his broadsword between the two of them. "Gentlemen, it appears we have a straggler."

Axel and Calum followed Magnus's line of sight.

About fifty yards away, a man in dark-green armor with curly black hair hobbled toward the tree line.

Nicolai.

"Should I go after him?" Axel asked.

"We all will," Magnus said. "Come on."

RUNNING across a field wasn't exactly how Calum would've chosen to celebrate his victory over Tyburon, but Nicolai had left him with little choice. He followed Axel through the tall grass, and they caught up to him in just a few minutes, right before he made it into the woods.

Axel kicked the back of Nicolai's knee, and Nicolai fell to the ground. Calum reached them not long after. By then, Axel had his knee on Nicolai's gut, one hand pinning his chest down, and the other holding his sword to Nicolai's throat.

"Oh, please—" Nicolai shielded his face with his hands. He didn't have a weapon on him as far as Calum could see. "Please don't kill me!"

Axel glanced at Calum, who crouched down next to Nicolai with Tyburon's—now *his* red sword in his hand. He couldn't have been much older than Axel—maybe three or four years, tops. Calum couldn't help but wonder what had led someone so young to join up with a bunch of thieving bandits.

"*Please.*" Nicolai clasped his hands together, and tears streamed down his face. "Please—please don't—"

"Quiet." Calum glared at him. "From this point on, you don't say another word unless I give you permission. Crystal?"

Nicolai nodded at least six more times than necessary.

Axel stood up now that Calum had the situation under control.

"You brought this on yourself." Calum tapped Nicolai's chest with the tip of his new sword, and a bit of blood dotted Nicolai's dark-green breastplate. "I let you live, and you ran off to tell your friends about us?"

Magnus approached them from behind, and he, too watched the scene unfold.

"I'm sorry. I'm so, so sor—"

Calum pressed his sword against Nicolai's lips. "I don't recall giving you permission to talk."

Again, Nicolai nodded a bunch of times. When Calum pulled his sword away, someone else's blood tainted Nicolai's lips red. It made him look even more foolish than he already did, but he made no effort to wipe the blood away.

"Now," Calum continued. "I'm gonna let you go."

"What?" Axel stepped forward. "You can't let him go. He's just gonna run back to some other group of bandits, and they'll come after us next. We need to kill him."

Calum understood Axel's reservations, but he wasn't going to kill an unarmed man in cold blood. Even the thought of it sickened his stomach.

"If he convinces more bandits to come after us, we'll just handle them like we did these guys. He knows that." Calum stared daggers at him to emphasize his point. "Don't you?"

Nicolai nodded again.

"So instead, Nicolai is gonna find the nearest village, get help for his injured leg, and find a profession that keeps him out of trouble from now on. Right?"

Nicolai didn't move.

Calum rolled his eyes. "You can talk, Nicolai."

"Yes," Nicolai blurted. "I'll never do anything bad again. I swear. Plus

I'll make up for all the wrong I've done by giving to the poor, by helping people, by—"

"We get it." Calum held up his hand. "Now listen, because I'm only gonna say this once. If I ever see you again, or if I hear you've joined another group of bandits, or if I find out you're oppressing common people or *anyone* less fortunate than you, I will drop whatever I'm doing, I'll find you, and I'll end your miserable life."

Nicolai swallowed, and his bulging Adam's apple jumped up to his chin.

Calum's voice hardened. "Crystal?"

Nicolai nodded for the hundredth time. "Clear."

"Then get out of my sight."

Nicolai struggled to his feet. "Thank you. Oh, thank you, thank you, thank—"

Calum pointed to the trees. "*Now.*"

Nicolai gave a slight bow, then he stumbled into the woods, heading southwest.

Axel shook his head. "You should've killed him. You didn't last time, and look what that got us into."

"I disagree," Magnus said. "The mark of a true warrior, as my father always told me, is not evidenced through his displays of strength and prowess, but through his acts of kindness, charity, and mercy."

Axel folded his arms. "Yeah, maybe if 'kindness,' 'charity,' and 'mercy' are the names of my sword, spear, and axe."

"I might actually name this sword 'Kindness,'" Calum said. "Because then I can kill people with Kindness."

Axel smirked and pointed at him. "That's actually pretty good."

Magnus just shook his head. "Come. Let us return to the battlefield to collect what we can. Perhaps these brigands have some coin on them or something we can trade when we reach Kanarah City."

Axel grinned and rubbed his hands together. "Maybe both, if we're lucky."

ABOUT FIVE MINUTES after he heard the last of the survivors' voices fade into the distance, Commander Anigo wrenched the spear from his breastplate and let it fall to the ground next to him. He pressed his left hand against his wounded chest, and blood oozed between his fingers.

He chanced a look down. The spear had pierced through his armor and into his flesh, slowed only by the chain maille he wore underneath. The spear may have plunged deeper still, but he couldn't be sure. However bad it was, he needed to get help, and fast.

With his right hand, he pushed himself to a sitting position. His chest ignited with fresh, sharp pain as if he'd been stabbed all over again. He inhaled several quick breaths, then he raised his right hand to his lips and whistled.

The clop-clop-clop of approaching hooves sounded behind him, and soon a horse—Candlestick—sidled up next to him.

Even if he couldn't count on anyone else, he could count on Candlestick.

Commander Anigo grabbed one of Candlestick's stirrups and pulled himself up, then he gripped the saddle and sprang atop Candlestick's back. Everything hurt, but he'd mounted his horse.

As he prepared to ride off, he caught sight of Corporal Bezarion laying face-up in the field, staring at the blue sky with one vacant eye. An axe head protruded from the left side of his face, literally dividing it from the other side.

It appeared Commander Anigo wasn't the only one who'd underestimated the ferocity of the bandits and the fighting and strategic acumen of the fugitives. Even so, Commander Anigo had no sympathy for him. He couldn't afford to.

He urged Candlestick south toward the main road by which they'd initially found this field. From there, he could head to Kanarah City and get proper medical aid. Every bump and jolt of Candlestick's gallops sent fresh pain into Commander Anigo's chest, but he refused to let this wound kill him.

More importantly, he would remember every jolt of pain when he finally caught up to the three fugitives.

CHAPTER TWENTY-FOUR

Trader's Pass/The Valley of the Tri-Lakes

A week and a half had passed since the bandits' attack. As they drew nearer to the end of eastern Trader's Pass and Kanarah City, Roderick's men camped for the night.

Then, early in the morning while it was still dark, they blindfolded Lilly, Sharion, and Colm and shackled them, hand-and-foot. But instead of riding in the wagon, this time they walked.

"Do not be alarmed," Colm whispered while the slave traders locked the wagon door. "When we last traveled this way, they did this. It is to conceal the path we will take from now on."

"Why conceal it?" Lilly asked, now unable to see him.

"It isn't supposed to exist." Colm huffed. "Slave-trading isn't exactly a noble vocation, and it is generally frowned upon by the public."

"What about the wagons?" Lilly leaned close to him. "My cape and armor are still in one of them. They're my only hope for getting out of here."

"Your optimism never ceases to amaze me, child."

Lilly didn't know whether it was truly optimism or not, but she knew with certainty the alternative wasn't something she wanted to endure.

"I wish I held as much faith in myself as you do in yourself," Colm continued. "The wagons will advance as they always do: a small group of men will lead them through the western gate of Kanarah City while the rest accompany us through the tunnels below the city. Once we exit the tunnels, we will rendezvous with the rest of the group."

So she *would* still have the chance to be reunited with her cape and armor. Good.

Colm nudged her hip. "Above all else, child, hold the end of my cloak. Try to step where I step. These tunnels make for perilous passage, but we have no choice but to comply."

Roderick and his men marched them through the darkness of the tunnels for several hours, stopping only to rest when one of them couldn't walk any farther. Usually it was Colm who'd worn himself out, but after so much time sitting in a cart and being transported everywhere, Lilly found that even she grew fatigued faster than usual.

Or perhaps she just wasn't used to walking so much in general. Why walk when she could fly?

Their shackles clanked and the sound echoed around them as they walked. Fatigue aside, the repeated *step-clank, step-clank* of their footsteps and shackles nearly drove Lilly to scream. Just when she thought she couldn't take the repetition anymore, Roderick ordered them to stop, and Luggs distributed a few crusts of bread.

As she ate, she noticed a nauseating odor permeating the tunnel.

"What's that smell?" Lilly asked.

"Nothing good," Sharion replied from Lilly's left. "Nothing good at all."

Lilly turned toward her, but she still couldn't see anything thanks to her blindfold.

Colm piped in, "I imagine she's right, but I can't say for sure."

"It smells like something died."

"Perhaps something did," Colm said.

"It would have to be a very big *something*." Lilly wrinkled her nose.

"Or lots of things. I suppose with so little airflow in here, a dead thing might smell bad forever."

"We're not far from Kanarah City's sewers," Colm said. "That's a stink you won't soon forget."

"Quiet, all of you," Luggs hissed. His voice had an edge to it when he spoke. "Not another word, hear? Next one who talks gets a thrashin'."

"Come on," Roderick said from ahead of them. "We're halfway there."

Within a few more hours, Colm's prediction came true. Lilly's boots squelched in the muck under her feet, and the stench around them changed from death to that of bile, feces, and urine. They'd reached the sewers. Lilly wished she could reach her nose to pinch out the smell, but while walking upright, her chains and shackles didn't allow it.

The clanking of their shackles gave way to the ever-present dripping of something in the distance, splashes and squelches through puddles, and the skittering of something—probably rats—all around them. Lilly shuddered at the thought, but she pressed on. She had no other choice.

A couple hours later, something heavy and metal groaned, and Luggs guided them up a short staircase and over a hump of some sort. A breeze of fresh air relieved Lilly's nostrils, and she sucked in the clean air in big gulps.

"Where are we supposed to meet 'em?" Luggs asked.

Roderick replied, "Follow me."

Another fifteen minutes of walking, and they ordered the slaves to halt. Someone yanked Lilly's blindfold from her head so hard that it tweaked her neck.

Luggs. She glared at him, but he didn't even bother to look her in her eyes. He just moved on to Sharion and tore off her blindfold next.

At least he wasn't leering at her anymore. Perhaps Roderick's numerous warnings that she wasn't to be touched had finally gotten through his thick skull.

They stood inside a large room big enough to house a fleet of wagons but empty except for a few bales of hay, a small platform topped with some wooden posts, and several torches, only two of which burned. Brown planks of wood formed the large room's walls, and the ceiling reached at least thirty feet at its highest point. A warehouse of some sort.

"Child, are you alright?" Colm whispered from her right.

Lilly nodded.

Half the warehouse away, Roderick spoke to a white-haired man in a red robe. Silver rings adorned his fingers, and a large silver medallion with what appeared to be a large ruby in the center hung around his neck. He laughed a raspy laugh and shook Roderick's hand, then Roderick placed a bulging pouch into his hand.

"Who's that man Roderick is talking to?" Lilly asked.

"If memory serves me correctly, his name is Wandell Thirry. I've not dealt with him personally, but his reputation is known in what you'd call Kanarah's underworld. He's sort of a go-between. He helps slavers get from Trader's Pass to auction houses. Arranges other things too, like auctions for stolen goods."

And slaves, Lilly realized. "So that's where we are? An auction house?"

"Yes. A secret place for the purpose of selling questionable merchandise."

"Us," Sharion grumbled. "They're gonna sell us."

Lilly's heart drummed in her chest. "Now?"

"Not until later. It's too early in the evening, yet. These types of deals are arranged in the latest of hours just before dawn." Colm sighed as he looked around. "I have only bad memories of this place."

"Don't get too excited, Angel." Roderick's velvety voice slithered down Lilly's spine as he approached. "No one's getting their hands on you until tomorrow night. We have to notify our usual clients that there's an auction happening first. Colm forgets these little details in his old age."

As much as Lilly wished she could punch Roderick in his throat, she just exhaled a quiet breath through her nostrils and reminded herself that she still had an entire day to find a way to escape. The slave traders may have managed to corral her while on the road, but this was a new environment, and that meant new opportunities for escape.

On his way out the door, Wandell Thirry gave Lilly a lingering look, and he raised his eyebrows. Though Lilly actually found him quite handsome for an older man, his occupation and the lascivious kiss he blew her soured her stomach.

"Come on," Roderick said to Luggs and the other men. "Let's get these darlings to their cells, and then we've got interviews to conduct."

Lilly turned to Colm and eyed him.

"New recruits," he said. "Replacing the ones they lost on our way here."

"Enough chatter." Luggs pushed between Colm and Lilly. He nodded to three other men, two of whom were Adgar and Gammel, and they took hold of Lilly, Colm, and Sharion. He gave Lilly a crooked yellow smile that made her cringe. "Time for bed."

The slave traders shoved the three of them into an adjoining hallway, down some stairs, and into a dark corridor lined with barred cells. The place reeked almost as bad as the sewers, and several moans sounded from the cells as they passed.

Forlorn faces of either Windgales or humans—Lilly couldn't be sure since none of them wore capes—Wolves, and even a Saurian pressed up against the bars as the slave traders escorted the three of them past. A few dying torches mounted to the stone walls between the cells provided mediocre light for the space.

Luggs unlocked a cell in the middle and shoved Lilly, Colm, and Sharion inside. He removed their shackles while Adgar and Gammel watched.

"Do we get anything for dinner?" Colm asked.

"What makes you think we'd give you dinner?" Luggs spat on the floor. "Feel free to lick that up if you're hungry."

"The last time I was here, we had a feast. Roasted duck, boiled potatoes with butter and bits of ham, fresh vegetables and fruit, and the dessert was—"

"Last time you was here, things was different, wasn't they, Colm?" Luggs huffed. "But you're where you belong now, you thieving derelict."

"That I am, Luggs. That I am." Colm's smile wilted into a frown and he bowed his head.

Luggs left the cell and locked it behind him, sealing them inside.

"Come on, boys." Gammel nudged Luggs's belly. "We've got ale to drink."

Luggs shoved him. "I'll come when I'm good and ready."

Adgar grinned and clapped his hand on Lugg's shoulder. "And wenches to woo."

"Good luck with that one." Luggs chuckled. "You couldn't pay a woman enough coin to spend the night with your ugly face."

Luggs had a point, Lilly decided. Just having to listen to them prattle on was miserable enough.

Adgar's jaw tightened. "Look who's talkin'. Your face looks like a bear mauled you."

"That's *her* fault." Luggs pointed at Lilly. "And you all know it."

Adgar grinned and raised his eyebrows. "I wasn't talkin' 'bout the gash on your forehead. I was talkin' 'bout your face in general."

Luggs swung for Adgar's head, but Adgar sidestepped the blow and darted up the corridor. Luggs gave chase amid a slew of profanity, and Gammel followed.

"At least it's not cold in here." Lilly squinted at the cell's contents: a few tattered rags that could double as blankets, plenty of hay, and not much else between the stone walls and the bars.

Sharion snatched one of the rags and dug under a mound of hay like she always did. With another furious scratch of her head, she curled up and started to snooze.

"For now, anyway," Colm said. "At least we're not here in the winter."

Lilly eyed him. He'd made an awful lot of comments about having been here in the past. But if that were the case… "Colm, when you were here last time, were you a slave?"

Colm's lips curled into a sad half-smile. "No, Lilly. I regret to say that I was one of the slave traders."

Lilly's hands balled into fists, and rage erupted in her chest. She had come to trust Colm, even to admire him, only to find out now that he'd been a slave trader himself.

The revelation shouldn't have come as such a shock to her, given how he'd managed to convince some of the slave traders to share extra food with him in exchange for whatever trinkets or coin he managed to pilfer from the guards. And he'd known a surprising amount about what to expect at various points along the way.

Still, Lilly became an inferno at the thought that she'd ever been close to him. She physically took a step back to separate herself from him.

"This whole time," she began, her voice low but furious, "you've been helping me, but you used to be one of *them*? You used to capture people and *sell* them? And the women—"

"I never touched any of the women, child." Colm held up his hand. "That flame inside of me extinguished a long time ago."

"But everything else... you did those things too?" Lilly glared at him.

Part of her refused to believe it was true, but he'd admitted to it openly. Her stomach churned with bitterness and anger. She'd been betrayed by the only person she'd come to even remotely care about since her capture.

Colm exhaled a shaky sigh. "Yes, child. And I regret my decisions every day."

"You told me you were better off being in here, that the Overlord *wanted* you here so you could do good." Tears burned the corners of her eyes. "Was that all a lie?"

"No. Not a single word. If I'm in here, I'm unable to hurt people out there. People like you and Sharion and others caught in this life." Colm stared into her eyes, pleading with his own.

She gave him no quarter in her heart. Lilly would listen to his miserable tale, but it wouldn't make her forgive him. As far as she was concerned, he was just as guilty as Roderick and the others, and he always would be.

"I know what I did was wrong," he continued. "I tried to expose Roderick's entire band to Captain Fulton, one of the local officers in the King's army, but when I did, he betrayed me and handed me back to Roderick, who locked me up.

"That was almost a year ago. Roderick has tried to sell me as a slave twice since then, but no one wants an old man like me, much less one only trained as a thief." He gave a mirthless chuckle. "Apparently, the slave market in Eastern Kanarah is already saturated with enough old thieves."

Lilly narrowed her gaze at him. Her anger had begun to give way to a deep profound sadness instead. "I trusted you, Colm, but I shouldn't have. You're a thief and a liar. For all I know, you're lying to me now."

Colm shook his head. "I wish I could convince you otherwise, but you're exactly right. I'm a thief and a liar, and that's all you can be certain of."

She'd sat next him, shared her warmth with him while he shared his cloak with her. They'd shared food, shared long conversations on boring wagon rides, shared dreams of freedom in the evenings. He'd even asked her to call him "grandfather."

No way that would happen now.

Colm reached for her. "Lilly, I—"

"No." She pulled away. "I have nothing more to say to you."

"I understand." Colm's hand sank to his side and he nodded. "I'll leave you alone, then."

Lilly hugged her knees and leaned against the far wall, as far away from Colm as she could get.

From now on, all they would share was a cell.

LATER THAT NIGHT, a commotion sounded down at the end of the corridor. Lilly opened her eyes, having only flirted with the idea of sleep, but she didn't move. She recognized three familiar voices: Luggs, Gammel, and Adgar, all of them drawing nearer to her cell.

Why would they have come back? And so late? Lilly bristled at the possibilities, but only one of them mattered. She knew what these three were capable of.

Luggs led Gammel and Adgar into the corridor, each of them swaying to the rhythm of inebriation. They guffawed and laughed, oblivious that some of the slaves might be trying to sleep. Luggs stopped in front of Lilly's cell and stared inside, his eyes scanning for her, and he grinned when he noticed her.

"There she is, boys. Roderick's sack-o'-gold." Even from several feet away Lilly could smell the stink of alcohol on Lugg's breath.

Gammel and Adgar chuckled. Lilly tried to recede deeper into the hay, but she didn't dare take her eyes off them.

"Drunk again, Luggs?" Colm stirred from his spot across the cell and sat upright. "The drink has never once served you well since I've known you."

Luggs slurred, "No one's talkin' to you, old man. So shut up."

"I will as soon as you let me get back to sleep."

"Then you'd better learn to sleep through noise." Luggs pulled his key ring from his belt, wobbling on unsteady legs.

Gammel clamped his hand on Luggs's arm. "Roderick will kill you if you touch 'er. The auction's *tomorrow*."

Luggs yanked free from Gammel in overdramatic fashion. "Don't touch me. I know the auction's tomorrow. Why else you think we're here tonight?"

"I—I don't want to face any more wrath from Roderick." Gammel rubbed his bald head. "He's still mad 'bout that she-Wolf breakin' free before we reached the pass."

"He's not mad at you." Adgar leaned against the bars and folded his long arms across his chest. "He's just not all that personable to begin with."

"You ladies really ought to take your conversation elsewhere," Colm said. "I'm sure it's fascinating to you dimwits, but we're not all that interested."

Luggs pointed a stubby finger at him through the bars. "What'd I say? You need to *shut up*."

"Doing my best, Luggs." Colm leaned back against the cell wall. "But you make it so easy to sling stones that it's hard to resist."

"You'll do better, or I'll smack you. No one's gonna buy you anyway, so it don't matter if you're beat-up and bruised."

"I still don't think we should go in there." Gammel shook his head. "Plenty of wenches back at that tavern lookin' to share a night with you or anyone else."

"That's exactly why we're *here*." Luggs smiled his wretched yellow smile through the bars at Lilly as his stupored fingers continued working the key into the lock. "Because she ain't like those wenches. She's cleaner. Prettier, too."

Lilly's heart thudded faster. Trying to escape tomorrow wouldn't matter if they came at her tonight.

They were drunk, though, so perhaps she could outmaneuver them and run away once the cell opened? Or maybe she could get ahold of the dagger hanging from Lugg's belt and use that to fend them off?

Across the cell, Sharion peeked out from under her mound of hay, then she promptly disappeared back under it.

"And that's exactly why we're here," Luggs repeated as he finally inserted the key into the lock and twisted it. The lock clunked, and the door inched open. Luggs turned to Gammel. "You don't like it, then get outta here. Crystal?"

Lilly stood up, her fists balled. Her muscles tensed. She would bite, kick, scream, scratch, shout, and thrash to get away from them. And if they gave her the chance, she would run.

Luggs stepped inside the cell with a twisted grin on his face and his hands on his belt. "Hey, cutie."

Colm stepped between him and Lilly. "Luggs, don't—"

Luggs lurched forward and grabbed Colm by his shoulder.

Shick.

Red spattered on the stone floor between them. Colm staggered backward, his mouth hanging open, his hands clamped over his stomach.

Luggs stood in place, his dagger in hand instead of in its sheath at his belt.

Its tip dripped with blood.

CHAPTER TWENTY-FIVE

Colm slumped to the floor, his eyes wide, his stomach wet with blood.

Emotion overwhelmed Lilly, and she shrieked and rushed to him and clutched him in her arms. "Colm? *Colm!*"

Luggs huffed and wiped the blood from his dagger with the corner of Colm's cloak. "I warned you not to touch me." He spat on the floor near Colm's face but didn't put his dagger away.

"You *stabbed* him!" Lilly shouted. She cradled Colm and helped him to lean up against her, and he moaned. His blood stained her undergarments, her skin, her hands. She tried to put pressure on the wound, but it continued to bleed. "Get some help—please!"

Gammel took three steps.

"*Stay* where you are," Luggs snapped, and Gammel stopped. "We're not done here."

"Yes, we are." Gammel scowled at him. "I'm gettin' Roderick. You just *killed* some of the merchandise."

"I didn't kill nobody. Just pricked 'im a bit," Luggs slurred. He wobbled even more, but he caught himself on the cell's bars and stabilized his footing.

"That's no prick, Luggs. Look at all that blood, you idiot." Gammel shook his head. "He won't survive that, old as he is."

Lilly's heart plummeted into her churning stomach. *Colm—not going to survive?*

Luggs grabbed Gammel by his shirt and threatened him with the dagger. "You tell Roderick, I'll run you through like I done to him."

"You really think Roderick won't notice anyway?" Gammel shot back. "You kill me, it's *two* deaths on your head. He'll skin you alive."

"*Fine*. Go tell Roderick. See if I care." Luggs shoved Gammel against one of the cell walls.

"Tell Roderick what?" A deep voice filled the cellblock.

Luggs whirled around, his reddened eyes wide.

Roderick stood outside the cell, his gray eyes fixed on Luggs. His gaze shifted down to Lilly and Colm, and he frowned. His deep voice flattened. "Come out of the cell. All three of you."

Luggs sheathed his dagger and followed Gammel and Adgar out, staggering. "It ain't what it looks—"

Roderick backhanded Luggs. "Did I say you could speak?"

Luggs rubbed his reddened cheek. His head slumped forward. "No."

"Gammel, what happened?"

"Well, uh…" Gammel hesitated. "We came in here after a few ales at the tavern and—"

"Give me the short version."

"Short version?" Gammel glanced at Luggs. "Well… Luggs stabbed Colm."

"He attacked me," Luggs said. "I had to—"

Roderick raised his hand again, and Luggs shrank away.

"He didn't attack Luggs," Lilly blurted. "Not at all. He was trying to protect me."

Roderick turned his attention to Lilly. For a long moment, he seemed to study her, then he squared his body with Luggs. "Why were you after her?"

Luggs swallowed and gave a nervous chuckle. "Come on, Roderick. You know why."

"I specifically said she was off-limits. Why do you insist on provoking me?"

Luggs backed up a step so Lilly could no longer see him from her vantage inside the cell. In her arms, Colm wheezed. She didn't know what else to do for him.

Luggs stammered, "It—it's just such a waste to not—"

"Come here."

"But—"

"*Now.*"

Luggs stepped back into view. Roderick raised his hand, and Luggs flinched.

Finally, justice for Colm, justice for everything Luggs had done to Sharion and Lilly since they'd captured her. With his power, Roderick could kill Luggs in one solid strike. Lilly had seen him do far more impressive things than that, and now Luggs's reckoning had come.

Instead, Roderick only swatted the back of Luggs's head.

"Don't do anything like that again. Stay away from her and the rest of the merchandise until after the auction," Roderick scolded. "And next time, lay off the drink the night before an auction. Crystal?"

Luggs nodded and rubbed his head. "Yeah, boss. Clear."

"Now, get out of here. All of you." Roderick pointed toward the exit.

As the men shuffled out, Lilly gawked at Roderick. Colm had just been stabbed, and all Roderick did was smack Luggs on the back of his head and chew him out?

"As for you—" Roderick pointed his finger at her. "—I don't want to hear another peep from you, ever. You've been more of a problem than any slave I've ever transported. If you weren't so valuable, I'd have let those dogs gnaw the meat from your bones weeks ago."

Lilly tensed her jaw and glared at him.

"I still might. Try something else, and find out."

Colm moaned in Lilly's arms.

Frantic, she asked, "What are you going to do about Colm?"

Roderick stared at him then shrugged. "I'll send someone to collect the body later."

Lilly's eyes widened. "That's it? You're just going to let him *die?*"

"Nothing to be done for him now, Angel." Roderick smirked. "But knowing him, I'm sure he's already weaseled his way into a far better afterlife than any other criminal ever could hope for."

Part of Lilly wanted to lash out and claw his face to shreds with her fingernails, but the other part knew she'd never be able to. She might cut Colm's life even shorter by trying it. Instead, she scowled at him and swore she'd exact justice for Colm.

Roderick winked at her and shut the cell door, then he locked it with his own set of keys. "Sleep well, Angel."

The door to the cellblock latched shut, and Lilly looked down at Colm. Even in the miserable light of the cellblock, she could tell he'd gone noticeably more pale.

Regret filled her chest. Before Luggs had stabbed him, Colm had yet again tried to protect her, and that was after she'd chastised him for his past. Now he was dying, and it was her fault.

"Lilly…" Colm motioned for her to lean closer. She bent over him. "Inside the inner lining of my cloak."

She hurriedly reached into it, expecting to find something she could use to help him. Instead, she pulled out a small knife and a familiar ring of skeleton keys. She couldn't help but gawk at them. "Where did you get these?"

"Took them off… Luggs when he stabbed me. Almost got his coin purse too, but given the circumstances…" Colm managed a weak smile. "Keep them… Use them to escape."

Lilly's heart shattered. Even after he'd been stabbed, Colm's only thoughts were of protecting her and ensuring her safety. He'd risked his life to protect her, and he'd paid the ransom for her escape with his life.

"Oh, Colm." Lilly's voice cracked when she said it. Sorrow flooded her core, and she didn't restrain her tears. "You can't die. I'll be all alone here."

"Nothing to be done… about it now." Colm grunted, then coughed. Blood tinged the corners of his mouth. "Besides… you'll still have Sharion."

Lilly glanced at Sharion, who still crouched in the corner of the cell farthest from them and clenched handfuls of hair while she rocked back and forth. "Not helpful, Colm."

"It's better than... nothing." Colm wheezed again, and his body shuddered in Lilly's arms. Somehow he seemed even older and frailer than before. "My time... is near, child."

"*No*." Lilly sobbed. "You can't go. I—I—"

"I can... and I must, child." Colm closed his eyes. "When you escape... avoid Roderick at all costs. He... will sell you separately from... the auction. Do not flee... now. Too many... night guards posted. You must... use the distraction... of the auction... to escape."

"Enough about that. I—I owe you an apology." Lilly bit her lip.

Colm shook his head. "Don't want the last words... I hear in this life... to be an apology—from either my lips... or yours."

Lilly sniffed. She knew what he wanted. At first, the idea had struck her as strange, but now it seemed wrong not to say it. Given everything he had done for her, some simple words to carry him into the afterlife was a small price to pay, and she would pay it gladly.

"I love you, Grandfather."

Colm's blue eyes cracked open and welled with tears. He smiled at her, closed his eyes again, and one long exhale later, he was gone.

Lilly pressed her forehead into Colm's neck and sobbed.

"Quick," Sharion hissed from behind her. "Hide that stuff before someone comes back."

As much as Lilly wanted to continue to mourn Colm, Sharion was right. She reached for the keys and the knife and tucked them inside her boots.

"What are you doing? We need to get outta here!" Sharion scratched her head.

"You just told me to hide them."

"Forget what I said." Sharion glowered at her. "Aren't you going to break us out? It's the middle of the night. Everyone's asleep. Let's go."

"Now's not the time. Colm said to wait for—"

"I don't care what Colm said. You've got keys and a knife. We're getting outta here now."

"Keep your voice down." Lilly held her hands out. "If you keep talking so loud, they'll find out. Then we'll never escape."

"Gimme the keys." Sharion held her dirty hand.

Lilly shook her head. "No. Colm said—"

Sharion flung herself at Lilly, and they tumbled into the hay near Colm's body.

"Get off of me!" Lilly tried to push Sharion off, but she couldn't. Sharion thrashed and snarled at her, clawing at Lilly's face. "Sharion, stop!"

"Give 'em to me!"

Enough defending. Lilly couldn't afford this kind of problem on top of everything else. She balled her fingers into a fist and drove it into Sharion's chin.

Sharion's teeth clacked, and she rolled off of Lilly with her hands on her face. She whimpered, and Lilly pushed herself up to her feet.

"I'm sorry, Sharion, but you gave me no choice." Lilly backed away from her and leaned against the wall of bars opposite of where Sharion had curled into a ball. "When the time is right, I'll help you escape, but not before then."

Sharion muttered what Lilly assumed were curses, but she couldn't make out anything discernible. Lilly just shook her head.

She stared down at Colm. Once she worked up the courage, she stepped over to him, bent down, and covered his face and body with his cloak so only the soles of his boots showed.

Given his status as a slave and previously as a thief, he likely wouldn't get a proper burial according to human customs. Had they been back at Aeropolis, they would've burned his body, as was the Windgale way.

He'd been a scoundrel and a liar, but he'd done right by her and deserved better than what Roderick and his men would afford him, even if Lilly couldn't give it to him.

Lilly stole a glance at Sharion. She now sat huddled against the wall, her gaze vacant but not focused on Lilly. Regardless of what Sharion said or did from then on, Lilly would not sleep for the rest of the night.

She tried not to pay attention to Colm's sticky blood all over her hands, arms, legs, and torso. Even if she didn't sleep, she could still rest, so she leaned against the back wall of the cell and exhaled a ragged sigh.

"Wʜᴀᴛ'ᴅ you say your name was?" Roderick's voice stirred Lilly from her rest.

So much for not sleeping.

She jerked back to cognition and stared at Sharion, wide-eyed, but the woman hadn't moved from her spot against the wall.

A second voice started to answer Roderick. "It's—"

"Never mind. I don't care," Roderick interrupted. "You wanna work for me, you gotta prove yourself before I give two fruits what your name is."

They were definitely in the cellblock.

Lilly patted her boots. The rough metal of the keys pressed against her left ankle, and she felt the smooth knife blade against her right.

"There. That one." Roderick's hulking form moved into view beyond the bars. "The cute one, not the ugly one. She's the one I was telling you about."

A young man about Lilly's age with curly black hair stepped into view. Next to Roderick and his brown armor, the young man's dark-green armor made the two of them look like the beginnings of a metal forest.

"Yeah, I see her."

"I'm assigning you to watch her from now until the auction. You'll deliver her to the buyer personally, and watch out, because she's a tricky one. She's tried to escape several times since we caught her."

Lilly sat up and glared at them both.

"Alright."

"Don't 'alright' me. This is serious. The most serious thing you've ever done."

"Yes, sir," the other man replied, his voice shaky.

Roderick positioned himself right in front of the new guy and towered over him. "Your references are good—if they're true—but since

I can't verify anything you've told me, you're gonna have to prove your-self. You make sure she gets to the buyer and that he's satisfied, and then I'll learn your name. Crystal?"

The new guy swallowed, and his Adam's apple bobbed. "Clear. Who's that under the blanket?"

Roderick craned his head. "Oh, him. He's dead. I'll have someone pull him outta there before he starts to stink."

"I can do it, if you want."

Roderick grinned at him and folded his arms. "It's about time someone started to show some initiative around here. I'll send one of the others to help you. You ever lugged a dead body around before? They're heavier than they look."

"I did some butchering back at my last—"

"It was a rhetorical question."

"Oh," the new guy said. "Sorry."

"Anyway, the buyer will be here an hour before the auction starts," Roderick said. "Meet him where we discussed. Don't cut corners, and don't touch her except to get her to him. She needs to be as pristine as possible, or he'll want a refund, and that's *not* gonna happen."

Roderick turned and winked at Lilly, then he whacked the new guy's chest. "In the meantime, she's not going anywhere. Come with me, and I'll introduce you to the rest of the idiots. You can come back for the body later."

Roderick walked out with heavy steps. The new guy gave Lilly a sullen half-smile, then he followed Roderick out of the cell.

Sharion groaned, then she glared at Lilly.

"What's wrong with you?

"You know what's wrong with me. You *know*." Sharion rubbed her chin.

Lilly met her eyes, unfazed. "Maybe you shouldn't have attacked me."

Sharion grunted.

A half-hour later, the new guy in the green armor returned with Gammel, and they entered the cell. Sharion shrank into the corner away from them, but Lilly stood her ground. Gammel wouldn't try anything after his hesitance last night, and the new guy seemed to want to please Roderick. Together, they wrapped Colm in his cloak and picked him up.

"Are you going to bury him?" she asked.

The new guy stared at her with dark eyes and his mouth hung open a bit. "Uh…"

"I don't know what Roderick's gonna do with him." Gammel glanced at the floor where Colm's blood, now dried and darkening to brown, had pooled. "But *I'm* not digging a grave for an old thief."

The new guy glanced between them and shrugged.

"Please bury him. It's the right thing to do." Lilly fixed her gaze on the new guy. "Every man deserves at least that, no matter what he did in life."

"I—I'll see what I can do." The new guy looked away.

"Come on. Let's get 'im outta here," Gammel said.

CHAPTER TWENTY-SIX

Eastern Kanarah

To Calum's surprise, Kanarah City's population did not resemble that of the northern region in either numbers or diversity. Then again, with Kanarah City being the only viable access point for crossing the Valley of the Tri-Lakes into Western Kanarah, Calum should've expected that more races populated the city.

Saurians roamed freely among the humans. While the humans had the clear majority, the two races frequently walked past each other in the street without so much as a foul look or an extra glance. Quite the contrast to Pike's Garrison, where Magnus had still gleaned some glares even after they restored the villagers' wealth.

In addition, Calum saw his first Windgale. He'd swooped down from above, cape and all, and landed in front of their trio in the street. He offered Calum a head of lettuce and a tomato. For sale, of course. *Good price. Low price. Cheap price.*

All Calum could say was, "You can fly?"

"Tourists," the Windgale muttered and zoomed away.

Magnus had been right—they really did look just like humans. Humans who could somehow fly, thanks to their capes.

Tall towers and spike-topped walls formed the city's imposing perimeter, and rows of buildings lined its numerous streets. Soldiers stood guard at regular intervals just inside the city walls, while merchants and shops beckoned travelers with offers of pleasure, luxury, or necessity.

But contrary to Magnus's fears, no one so much as blinked at them, much less tried to attack or arrest them. Apparently, the sight of two armed men walking through the city with a seven-foot Saurian in gleaming blue armor wasn't all that unusual.

Calum and Axel had also upgraded their armor by piecing together some of what the Southern Snake Brotherhood had worn, so they no longer looked like they had robbed one of the King's outposts. Instead, they looked like they couldn't match armor or colors to save their lives, but Calum liked to think it aided in keeping them anonymous.

"We need to unload as much of our spoils as possible." Magnus shifted a large sack from one shoulder to the other. "The trip across Trader's Pass is very long, and there are no animals to hunt or vegetation in the valley, so it is imperative that we plan accordingly."

"Shouldn't be too hard. There are dozens of vendors and merchants lining the streets who want to trade." Axel pointed to a small wooden shop with a weathered sign overhead that read *Garon's Fine Goods, Armory, and Exotic Antiquities* in what appeared to be a lousy attempt at a cursive script. "We could try in there."

Calum nodded. "Looks as good as any of the others."

"When we get inside, let me do the talking," Magnus said. "I have done this before. He will proffer a low price, and we will have to negotiate it up from there. You two hold onto your bags since they contain the soldiers' weapons and armor. I would rather not risk trying to sell those until we know for sure he is amenable to dealing in that kind of merchandise."

Inside, they found an older man with black-and-gray hair hunched over a counter. He wore fine white linens and a purple robe. Gold necklaces, gold rings, and a large gold hoop hanging from his left earlobe topped off his attire. At the sound of the bell jingling over the shop door, he looked up.

"Welcome, welcome. Name's Garon. What can I do for you gentlemen?" His raspy voice filled the small shop as he gestured to the walls lined with shelves of trinkets, weapons, and a variety of other things. "If you need something, I probably have three of it."

Magnus set his bag on the floor. "Do you purchase goods?"

Garon smiled at him. "I purchase, I trade, I sell, I deal, I beg, I barter. I even give, on occasion, but you fellows don't meet the criteria for that one."

Calum glanced at Magnus. "What criteria?"

"I give to the poor and needy, and, on occasion, to very, *very* beautiful women." Garon laughed, but it sounded more like he was wheezing. He waved his hand at them. "I'm just joking around. I don't give to the poor and needy. They're a bunch of gutter leeches. Alright. Let's see what you've got. Put it on my counter here."

Magnus dumped the contents of the sack onto the counter.

Garon sorted through it with his fingers, then shrugged. "Ehhh. Nothing special."

Axel gripped the edge of the counter with his hands. "What do you mean, 'nothing special?' That's high-quality steel and—"

Magnus held up his hand, and Axel went quiet. "What is it worth to you?"

Garon stared at the ceiling and counted his fingertips. "Seventeen gold coins for the whole lot."

"You've gotta be kidding me." Axel folded his arms and exhaled a sharp sigh.

"Axel," Magnus said. "Let me handle this."

Calum didn't show it, but he agreed with Axel. Seventeen gold coins was a pittance for all they'd brought in with them.

"That set of armor alone is worth twenty coins," Magnus said.

"Maybe if it was *new*." Garon shook his head. "Look, you seem like nice young men..." He looked up at Magnus. "...and a nice large lizard-person. I'll make it eighteen."

"No." Magnus folded his burly arms. "I want fifty."

Garon grabbed his chest. "By the Overlord—my heart stopped for a moment there. At my age, my hearing's not so good. Could you repeat that number?"

"Fifty."

Garon grabbed his chest again, feigning agony. "Yep. That's what I thought you said. In what world is this junk worth *fifty* gold coins?"

"In this one."

"Yeah, this one," Axel echoed.

Magnus shot him a glare, then he refocused on Garon. He pointed to each item. "Twenty for the set of armor, including the helmet, a coin for the two lengths of rope, five apiece for the two swords, nine for the axe, and ten for all that leather, including the four pairs of boots and the belts."

Garon counted his fingers again.

"It adds up to fifty," Magnus asserted.

Garon stopped and narrowed his gaze. "Yes, thanks. I can add. If I couldn't, I wouldn't have lasted forty years as a merchant and another eight as a shopkeeper."

"So do we have a deal?"

"The only reasonable price you just quoted me was for the two lengths of rope—" Garon grabbed the ropes, dropped them behind his counter, then pulled a gold coin from his pocket. He slid it across the counter. "—for one coin. You're too high on everything else."

Magnus took the gold coin and handed it to Axel, who dropped it into a small coin pouch. "Then we will pack up our things and go."

"Where do you expect to get forty-nine coins for the rest of that?"

"We will visit one of the bigger shops. I expect they have more capital to trade with." Magnus reached for the suit of armor while Calum held open the sack.

Faster than Calum would've expected, Garon rounded the counter and held up his hand to stop them. "They'll rip you off. They're bigger, so they spend more on bigger items, but they always rip off the little guys. Always. Bunch of scoundrels and predators. You can't trust them. Not at all."

"Better than arguing with you," Axel muttered.

"Do you have another offer?" Magnus asked.

"Twenty even. Best deal you'll get for this stuff."

Magnus motioned to Calum. "Pack it all up."

Garon's hand clamped down on Magnus's wrist as he reached for the helmet, but he let go just as fast. "Wait. You don't have to leave yet. Let's try a new number. How about twenty-five?"

Magnus leaned toward him. "How about forty-nine?"

"King's *mercy*." Garon clenched his eyes shut and clutched his chest a third time. "Your expectations are unrealistic. No one with half a brain is going to give you forty-nine gold pieces for... *this*."

"How about forty-eight?"

Garon glared at Magnus and pointed at the door. "Get out."

Magnus nodded. He reached for the helmet again, and again, Garon grabbed his wrist then quickly let go.

"I'll give you five coins for both swords."

"Five each?"

"Five total."

"I said five each."

"And I said five *total*." Garon held one of them up, and sunlight from one of the windows glinted off the blade. "They've been used. I'll have to sharpen them, shine them, and oil them up before I can resell them."

Magnus folded his arms. "Fine. Eight."

"Six."

"Seven, plus a bigger coin pouch than the one we've got, and you have a deal."

"And you have a deal if I get to keep the smaller coin pouch." Garon smirked.

Magnus smirked as well. "Deal."

They exchanged the goods and the coins, and Axel double-checked to make sure he'd removed all of their own coins from the small pouch before he traded it for the new one.

"Now about that axe," Garon said. "It's not worth nine coins. Not a chance. I mean, if the handle were bejeweled with priceless diamonds, then maybe. So I'll give you three."

"*Three?*" Magnus shook his head. "I can get more than that by selling it to a blacksmith for the metal. Eight."

"Look, we can haggle all day over this, but I'm an old man and would rather sit outside my store and watch beautiful young ladies walk on by." Garon laughed his wheezy laugh again and smacked the counter with his palms. "I'll give you six, which is more than it's worth, just to shut you up."

"Deal."

"The leather's not worth ten, either. How about six for that as well?"

Magnus huffed. "Would you do seven?"

Garon shook his head. "No."

"Then I accept your six."

"Now about that armor—"

"You will not get it for ten coins. You could sell it for double or even triple that, new or otherwise. It is in good shape."

"I'll give you twelve."

Magnus clacked his talons on his breastplate. "Eighteen."

Garon sighed. "Look, son. I'm going to put a price tag of thirty coins on it. I'll tell customers it's on sale for twenty-five, and I'll probably settle for a sale price in the low twenties. So you asking eighteen for it is excessive, offensive, and just plain ridiculous. I'll give you thirteen."

"How about you give me sixteen, you price it at thirty-five and sell it for twenty-six or twenty-seven?" Magnus asked.

Garon waved his hand. "If I price it at thirty-five, it'll sit there until I'm dead and gone and for the next three generations that follow me. Unless there's a war that engulfs all of Kanarah, no one would pay that much for a used set of armor. At least not that one. Thirteen's as high as I can go."

"Fifteen, then, but I keep the helmet." Magnus picked it up and held it in his hand.

"Fifteen?" Garon groaned. "*Fifteen?* Preposterous. And what are you going to do with a random helmet, anyway? Toss rocks into it when you're bored? Look, to shut you up, I'll do fifteen if I get the helmet *with* the armor, and then you can get out of my store. My heart can't handle any more of your badgering."

"Deal."

After their final exchange of goods for coins, Magnus nodded to Calum, who brought over one of the other sacks.

"We have some… other goods," Magnus said. "But I do not know if you are willing to deal in them."

Garon squinted at him. "Just now pulling out the good stuff, eh? After I've spent all my money on your boring junk?"

Magnus raised an eyebrow. "Like I said, I do not know if you are willing to risk dealing in what we have to sell. Is there anything you refuse to buy?"

Garon smiled and raised an eyebrow. "I can't think of anything in particular."

Magnus reached into the bag and removed a soldier's helmet. "How about this?"

The smile on Garon's face flipped upside-down, and his other eyebrow rose. All the mirth left his voice. "Get out of my store. Now. And don't you ever come back here again. Never. Ever. Never ever."

Calum glanced at Axel. Garon's reaction was exactly what they'd feared, and Calum couldn't help but wonder if they'd made a critical mistake.

Magnus dropped the helmet back into the bag and handed it to Calum. "One last question. Do you know of anyone who might deal in this type of merchandise?"

Garon rounded the counter again, this time with his hands up. He shooed them toward the door. "I don't know anything about anyone. I don't know who you are, and I don't know what you've got in that sack. I've never seen you before, and we've never done business. Crystal? Now get out of my shop, and don't ever come back."

"Thank you for your time." Magnus nodded to him and stepped out the door behind Calum and Axel. Once they made it outside, Magnus grabbed them both by their shoulders. "We need to get out of here. Now."

"What?" Axel held his hands out, palms up. "Why?"

"Because Garon is about to find the nearest soldier and tell him what he has just seen."

CHAPTER TWENTY-SEVEN

"Are we bringing the soldiers' gear with us?" Calum hefted the bag over his shoulder. He hoped they wouldn't have to keep lugging it around.

"No. It will slow us down, and if they catch us with it, it will only incriminate us. Better to leave it behind and gain some ambiguity in the process. Nor do we need it anymore anyway. We have enough coin to purchase supplies for the journey across Trader's Pass and then some."

"This is totally unnecessary," Axel said. "We can just go back in there and make sure he doesn't say anything."

Magnus eyed him. "We have no time to argue about this. We do not know this city like the King's soldiers do, and I have only been here once before. As far as I know, we are about as close to the center as we could possibly get, which means that no matter what direction we go, it will be hard to get out of here."

"Like I said, we won't have to worry about this hassle if I go back into the shop and—"

"And what?" Magnus stepped in front of him. "Kill him?"

Axel didn't back up. "If it came to that, sure."

"You cannot just kill your way out of every problem, Axel."

"Beats running from them, don't you think?" Axel smirked. "But that's what works for you, isn't it, Scales? You still never told us why you left your homeland. Are you *running* from something?"

Calum gawked at Axel's audacity. He'd been curious about Magnus, too, but he hadn't dared ask him about it. And he certainly wouldn't have challenged him about it like this, either.

Magnus glared at him. "That is not a conversation we have time for, nor is it any of your concern."

"Oh, so you *are* running from something." Axel tapped his chin with his fingers. "Let's see… you have special armor, a special sword… From what I've seen here in the city, no other Saurians have anything like it, do they? You must've been someone important, or rich, or both. I wonder what—"

"*Enough*, Axel," Magnus hissed. "I have nothing to say to you. Nothing. We must go. Now. Every minute you waste talking is another minute we could use to make our escape."

"Both of you, stop," Calum said.

Axel nudged Calum. "Got you kind of curious now, doesn't he?"

"Calum, please." Magnus turned to him. "This is not helpful. We must flee."

"And now he's being defensive. Must've been something pretty juicy if he's getting all worked up about it, huh?" Axel laughed.

Magnus grabbed Axel by his breastplate and lifted him off of his feet. "You know nothing about me. *Nothing*. So do not pretend you do."

"Put him down, Magnus." Leader or not, Calum was getting tired of mediating Axel and Magnus's tiffs. More importantly, if they had to run, carrying Axel wasn't ideal.

Magnus let him drop but turned away from Axel, who managed to land on his feet. "We need to go. Now. There is no time."

Calum nodded. "We're going. Axel, you're not killing anyone. We'll dump the bags in a trash heap behind one of these buildings, and then we'll head north back to the Snake Mountains for a few days until everything calms down here. Let's go."

"Whatever you say, oh great leader," Axel gave a mock bow that grated on Calum's sense of calm, but he forced himself to ignore it and started to move.

Everything went as Calum had intended, including dropping the sacks of gear on one of the trash piles, until they reached the city's north gate, the same one through which they had entered. A dozen soldiers who weren't there before now stood at the gate, huddled around their commander.

"Back. Back. Now." Calum swiveled on his heels and headed the opposite way.

"Oh, come on. We can get through them, Calum." Axel stopped him mid-stride. "We just handled more than double that number a week ago."

"There are other soldiers nearby. This is home to the third largest contingent of the King's soldiers in Kanarah, after Solace itself and the Border Fortress farther east," Magnus warned. "We cannot instigate any more trouble than we already have."

Axel exhaled a long sigh. "Whatever. I'm not gonna argue. I know it won't make a difference. Never does."

Calum sighed. *Not this whiny "woe-is-me" garbage again.*

"Whatever we decide to do, let's not discuss it in the street, in plain sight," Calum said. He glanced at the group of soldiers again.

One of them was watching the trio. He leaned to his side and said something to the soldier next to him. The soldier's head rotated, and he looked at Calum as well.

Definitely time to go.

They scampered behind a nearby building. Calum looked up at Magnus as they walked down an alley. "Is there an east gate?"

"There is, but I have never been there." Magnus glanced over Calum's shoulder. "They are pursuing us. Do not turn around."

Axel swore. "How many?"

Magnus growled. "All of them."

Calum eyed him. "What do you mean, *all* of them?"

"Too many to fight. More than were standing around at the gate. It is time to run."

"You ready?" Calum nodded at Axel.

"If you're not willing to fight, then I guess I don't have another choice."

"East gate it is. If we get separated, meet up there." Calum nodded to Magnus. "We're ready. Say when, Magnus."

Magnus paused for a moment, still watching over Calum's shoulder. "Now."

All three of them bolted from their spot behind the building and into the street.

From behind them, the cries and yells of several soldiers filled Calum's ears. He stole a glance back. Magnus hadn't exaggerated—the entire dozen soldiers who'd been standing at the gate now chased after them, plus many, many more. Too many to count with only a quick look.

Definitely too many to fight.

Calum faced forward in time to see a pretty young lady carrying a basket full of flowers step in front of him. She squeaked, and he barely skidded to a stop in time. Then he sidestepped her and kept running.

"Pardon me!" he called back to her.

With Axel in the lead, Calum chased Magnus's green tail through the streets.

A soldier emerged from an alleyway to his right. Calum reacted by slamming his gauntleted fist into the soldier's nose. The impact stung his hand, but the soldier got it way worse.

And it meant one fewer soldier chasing them.

Magnus took a hard left down an alley, and Calum followed. On his way in, Calum drew his sword and severed the leg of a cart full of apples, oranges, and walnuts. It tipped over, and its contents spilled in front of the alley. Calum hoped it would slow the soldiers down, though he didn't love hearing the angry shouts of the cart's owner behind him.

The alley drained into another street, one far more crowded than the one they just left. Calum had wanted to sheathe his sword, but he opted to keep it out in case he ran into any more soldiers while on the run.

Due to the thick traffic on the street, Magnus got in front of Axel and roared, and a path cleared through the crowd as people scattered away from the admittedly frightening sound. The trio continued to run.

Ahead of them, three soldiers emerged from the base of a watch-tower in front of Magnus, but he couldn't stop in time. Instead, he whipped his tail around and sent all three of them crashing through the wall of a nearby shop. The surrounding civilians screamed and recoiled from Magnus, and Calum couldn't blame them for it.

They passed about ten more streets and came up to the east gate, but Magnus stopped short. Then he cut south, right past Calum and Axel.

"More soldiers. South gate," was all he said as he barreled past them.

Sure enough, a contingent of soldiers about the same size as the one at the north gate now ran toward them.

Calum's burning legs propelled him after Axel and Magnus. If they couldn't get out through the south gate, what would they do then?

Just run, Calum, he told himself. *Worry about the rest later.*

The three of them rounded a corner and stopped short. A platoon of soldiers four rows deep blocked the street. Had the soldiers in pursuit cut them off, or were these totally different soldiers?

Magnus faced Calum and Axel. "Rooftops. Now."

Before Calum could ask what that meant, Magnus grabbed him by his collar and his belt and hurled him into the air. Blue sky filled his vision, then his body smacked against something hard, and everything snapped to white, then black. His eyes reset in time to see Axel flying through the air down at him.

As if Calum's body didn't already hurt enough from running through the city and landing on the rooftop, all two-hundred-plus pounds of Axel landed right on top of him. The impact pushed the air out of Calum's lungs and sent fresh pain through his torso.

They both let out a loud "oof," and then Axel jumped up.

"Thanks for breaking my fall. Always knew you were a big windbag." He grabbed Calum by his wrist and yanked him up to his feet. "Come on. We gotta keep moving."

Wheezing, Calum headed for the edge of the roof. "Is Magnus coming after us?"

A gigantic green head popped up over the side of the building, followed by two big green hands. Magnus's talons dug into the wooden edge, and he shouted, "Go! Do not tarry on my account!"

Calum nodded, sheathed his sword, and spun around. He chased Axel, who deftly bounded from rooftop to rooftop. They ducked under clotheslines, sidestepped small chimneys, and even jumped over a pipe-smoking roof-dweller reclining in a low chair.

"Southwest, Axel!" Magnus yelled from behind them. "Calum, tell him!"

Calum repeated the words.

"I heard him the first time!" Axel corrected his course and cleared a wide gap between two roofs.

Calum jumped as well, but he didn't make it quite as far. He managed to grab onto the edge of the building, but his chest, knees, and thighs smacked the side. It would have hurt a lot worse had he not been wearing armor, but it still left him stunned and weakened.

Overhead, Magnus cleared the jump with no problem. Just when Calum thought his grip would falter, Magnus reached down, grabbed his wrist, and hauled him up onto the roof.

"Thanks," Calum said.

Magnus's eyes focused on something behind him, down at street-level.

Calum turned back. Down below, the masses of soldiers nocked arrows and drew them back in their bows.

"Get down!" Magnus yelled.

Both he and Calum dropped, and a flurry of arrows zipped through the sky.

Axel.

Calum hollered his name. "Take cover! Arrows!"

Axel spun around for a look, then he rolled behind a brick chimney just in time to avoid at least a dozen arrows that dug into the rooftop where he'd just been standing.

"Draw!" The cry came from below, in the street.

Magnus pulled Calum to his feet and shoved him forward. He shouted, "Axel, move!"

Axel burst from his cover and bolted for the next roof, and Calum and Magnus made the jump as another barrage of arrows plunged into the rooftop behind them.

A pair of soldiers kicked open a rooftop door in front of Axel and swung their weapons at him. He ducked under both attacks and kept going. The soldiers turned to follow him, but by then, Calum and Magnus came up behind them.

Calum bashed one in the back of his helmeted head with his elbow, dropping him immediately. Magnus leveled the other one with a punch that could've felled a horse.

The soldier's head jerked to the side with a sharp crack, and he slumped to the rooftop, but instead of continuing to run, Magnus stopped and scooped the soldier into his arms.

Calum eyed him and started to ask what he was doing, but Magnus yelled, "Keep going!"

Calum caught up to Axel at the edge of one of the rooftops. Below them, the south gate, set into the tall city walls between two watchtowers just like the north and east gates, was shut. A small army of soldiers stood guard down below.

Calum turned back to Magnus, who had just made it onto their roof with the motionless soldier still in his arms. "They're waiting for us at the south gate, too."

"Have they realized we are on the roof?"

"No," Axel replied. "They're focused on the street."

"Good. Then we need to—"

An arrow plunged into the base of Magnus's neck, just above his armor, and he went down.

CHAPTER TWENTY-EIGHT

"No!" Calum yelled. A few more arrows smacked the rooftop around him, all from the two watchtowers on either side of the gate, but Calum didn't care. He ran to Magnus and dropped to his knees, ignoring the arrows thudding into the roof around him. "Magnus?"

"I'm fine," he growled. "Just pull it out."

"Are you su—"

"*Pull it out.*"

Calum wrapped his fingers around the arrow and yanked it from Magnus's neck.

Magnus roared, then hissed, and blood burbled out of the wound and trickled down toward Magnus's breastplate.

Calum recoiled and stared at the bloody arrowhead for a moment, thankful it wasn't barbed, then he tossed it aside. "Can you move?"

Magnus grunted but stood to his feet. "Hurry—to the edge."

Calum headed back to the roof's edge, all the while shielding his head from the sporadic arrows that the soldiers in the watchtower now launched at them. Magnus came up behind him and stood there with the soldier in his arms again.

"You alright?" Axel asked.

"It was not deep. My skin is getting thicker, I think. It will heal quickly," Magnus said.

Calum wanted to ask about how Magnus could heal so much faster, but now wasn't the time. Instead, he asked, "What do we do now?"

"We jump."

"Where? Down to the street?"

Magnus shook his head, and more burgundy blood bubbled out of his arrow wound. "No. Over the gate."

From their position on the roof, the jump was manageable, at least from a distance standpoint. They had already cleared wider jumps between rooftops—the problem was the long metal spikes that lined the top of the walls and the gate. Calum had noticed them atop the walls when he first entered the city.

"I will go first," Magnus said.

Axel grabbed his shoulder. "Wait—you'll skewer yourself if you hit those spikes."

Magnus smirked. "That is what our friend here is for."

It made sense to Calum right before Magnus jumped.

Magnus flew through the air with the soldier in his arms, and as he approached the wall, he positioned the soldier's body under his own. As they landed, the spikes knifed into the soldier's body, and thanks to the weight of the soldier's body combined with Magnus's momentum, the spikes bent away from Calum and Axel.

Magnus rolled off and dropped out of sight behind the wall, seemingly unscathed.

Calum smacked Axel's breastplate with the back of his hand and backed up to get a running start. He charged full speed, planted his right boot on the edge, and leaped toward the wall. When his feet hit the soldier's armor, he tucked into a roll and dropped down outside the city walls.

The fall ended with no pain and no jarring impact. When Calum opened his eyes, he lay in Magnus's arms.

Calum blinked.

"It was a long drop. I figured you would not mind some assistance."

"Not at all. Thanks." Calum grinned. It had worked. Now they were just waiting for—

A raucous yell sounded above.

"Excuse me." Magnus set Calum on his feet and shifted his footing, then Axel tumbled from the wall down into Magnus's arms.

Axel rubbed his eyes. "What in the—"

"You are welcome." Magnus set Axel on his feet.

"I'm never doing that again," Axel said.

"No time to dally now," Magnus said. "Before long, they will deduce what happened, especially with you screaming like a little girl when you jumped."

Axel glared at him. "No time to fool around, but you're making jokes?"

"I could not help myself. In all seriousness, as soon as they get that gate open, we will yet again find ourselves in peril." Magnus pointed west. "We will head to the southern end of the Snake Mountains and take cover until this trouble subsides."

"What about Lumen and the Arcanum?" Calum asked.

"This is a temporary precaution. We need to allow this tension to cool down, and then we will head for Trader's Pass again."

"How long?" Calum asked. "My dreams are getting more and more urgent."

"A few days, at most. These things have an ebb and flow to them. They will lose interest soon enough."

"Alright. Three days, tops." Calum started west, and the others ran alongside him.

"Any chance they can cut us off from the west gate?" Axel asked.

Magnus shook his head. "No. The only way in or out of the west gate is via Trader's Pass. Everything around it is mountainous and lined with the same steep cliffs we found along the western edge of the range to the north. They can only chase us if they open the south gate or come at us over the Snake Mountains from the north, which they will not do."

"Good," Calum said.

Within minutes, they disappeared into the woods southwest of Kanarah City.

COMMANDER ANIGO RUBBED his sore chest, now bandaged and on the mend, but by no means restored to full health. A new leather breastplate covered his torso, and a local blacksmith had mended the chain maille shirt underneath as well.

When a soldier by the name of Corporal Jopheth reported a sighting of three fugitives—two young men and a Saurian in bright blue armor—Commander Anigo had to restrain every impulse to go after them, even in his weakened state. Now the corporal had returned with yet another update.

"Captain, we've lost sight of them." Corporal Jopheth pointed to the south gate. "We think they went over the wall. Should we open the gate to pursue them?"

"No." Captain Leonid Fulton, the commanding officer of the entirety of the King's forces in Kanarah City, yawned and waved his hand. "They're rabble-rousers. Nothing more."

Commander Anigo resisted the urge to correct him and remind him of the very specific orders he'd received prior to leaving Solace. Instead, he turned to the corporal. "Aren't the walls lined with spikes?"

Corporal Jopheth nodded. "Yes, they are."

"How did they manage to get over without getting impaled?"

"What does it matter?" Captain Fulton adjusted his breastplate, made of polished silver instead of black leather, for the umpteenth time.

Ever since the other day when Commander Anigo met him after leaving the infirmary, Captain Fulton continued to shift the breastplate every so often. It just didn't fit him the way it should.

Probably because he was a fat lush who refused to do his job properly.

But Commander Anigo couldn't say that to him, either.

"They're gone," Captain Fulton said. "They're of little consequence."

Commander Anigo narrowed his eyes. "Captain, they have killed or been party to the killings of dozens of men, including at least ten of the King's soldiers. They assaulted and robbed one of our outposts in the north, and they—"

"Yes, yes. I'm aware of their crimes." Captain Fulton yawned again.

Commander Anigo clenched his teeth. "My point is that they've ascended far beyond the level of a mere nuisance. I recommend we pursue them."

"Montrose?"

Corporal Jopheth stepped aside, and a slender lieutenant gave Captain Fulton a slight bow.

"Yes, Captain?" When Montrose looked up, his emotionless gaze met Commander Anigo's for a moment, then they fixed on Captain Fulton again.

"Are our dinner preparations ready for this evening?"

"Nearly, sir," Montrose replied.

Preparations? Commander Anigo fumed. He was trying to catch a trio of wanted fugitives known for their violence and cunning, and Captain Fulton was more concerned about his dinner plans for that night.

"Captain, I—"

"That will be all, Commander." Captain Fulton didn't even look at him. Instead, he was trying to adjust his breastplate again. "Head back to the barracks and rest your injured chest. Your vagrants are gone, and if they are foolish enough to return, we will swiftly bring them to justice then."

"With respect, Captain, I'd like to request a contingent of men to accompany me while I search for them outside the city walls."

"Your request is denied, Commander. Unlike you, I did not manage to get the men assigned to me killed."

Commander Anigo bristled at that remark. He could hardly be held responsible for the deaths of those men, especially in light of their rampant incompetence. If they'd fought harder and smarter, perhaps they would've survived. And perhaps he wouldn't have to be here now, either.

No, their failure and deaths reinforced what he'd believed about them upon his arrival to the Rock Outpost: Commander Pordone had been a pitiful excuse for a commanding officer. If anyone could be blamed for the demise of those men, it was Commander Pordone and his lax attitude toward enforcing the King's law.

"Besides, I require my men to remain here in Kanarah City to continue to ensure the safety of our citizens. These brigands you're pursuing have left the city, and therefore they are no longer our problem."

Commander Anigo gritted his teeth. "I respectfully disagree. If they were to—"

"You may disagree all you want, as long as you do so in silence," Captain Fulton said, his voice hard. He struggled to rise to his feet from his chair until Montrose took hold of his arm and pulled him up. "Now I take my leave. Rest and recover, Commander, and when you are well enough to travel, you may return to the north for more men. You surely shall not take any of mine."

With that, Captain Fulton waddled away. Both Lieutenant Montrose and Corporal Jopheth followed, leaving Commander Anigo standing there, snarling. Captain Fulton's lack of regard for his own office sickened Commander Anigo. Worse still, the pain in his gut persisted.

EVENING CAME SOONER than Lilly expected.

When the new guy showed up with a small sack tied with twine and slipped it through the bars, Lilly eyed him, but she didn't move.

"Roderick's orders," he said. "Your garments are old and soiled. These are new ones."

It was true. Lilly's skintight top and bottoms, once pristine and white, bore a myriad of dirt, sludge stains from the sewers, and now, Colm's blood.

Hardly appealing to a prospective buyer. She shook her head at her own distorted humor.

Lilly's stomach churned, but she snatched the sack from the new guy's hand and recoiled into the cell. She untied the twine and spread the sack open on the floor. Sure enough, a clean set of undergarments very much like the ones she wore lay before her.

"There's more." The new guy stepped aside and returned with a bucket and a cream-colored bar of soap. "He wants both of you to wash up before the auction tonight, and he said *you're* supposed to wash first." He pointed at Lilly.

The new guy unlocked the cell and slid the bucket and the soap inside, then he locked it again.

Lilly eyed the bucket and the soap then glared at him. "Do you really expect us to just strip down and wash in front of you?"

The new guy's eyes widened. "Uh—no?"

"Then could you please give us some privacy?"

He nodded. "Yeah. Sure. Sorry."

As the new guy headed toward the cellblock door, Lilly stared at her reflection in the bucket. Yes, she wanted more than anything to scrape the grime off of her skin, but the idea that doing so would fetch a higher price sickened her.

Still, she needed to do it. Once the new guy shut the cellblock door behind him, she peeled her soiled undergarments off and started to wash. She couldn't do anything about the other prisoners in the cells, but at least she'd managed to keep Roderick's new puppy from staring at her while she did it.

An hour after Lilly finished scrubbing the blood and grime from her body and re-clothed herself in the new undergarments, the new guy returned and peered at her and Sharion through the bars. "You ready yet?"

What did he expect her to say? Lilly wanted to bash his head in. Instead, she just sighed.

The new guy swallowed. "I mean—are you dressed?"

"You've got eyes, don't you?"

"Well, yes, but—"

"I'm ready."

"Alright." The new guy stepped into full view and inserted his key into the lock.

Lilly eyed Sharion, but she didn't give any indication that she intended to reveal Colm's parting gifts. Perhaps she'd realized that Lilly was her only hope of escaping this place.

The new guy produced a burgundy gown and held it out for Lilly to take. "Here. This is for you. Roderick's orders."

She took it and rubbed the burgundy fabric between her fingers, then cursed to herself. Not aerosilk. Roderick knew better than to give a Windgale something made of aerosilk, or even an aerosilk blend.

And to top it off, burgundy really wasn't her color.

"Why?" she asked.

"He said he wants you to look your best for tonight."

"I couldn't care less what Roderick wants."

The new guy gawked at her. "What? But—"

"Where's *my* fancy dress?" Sharion folded her arms and glared at the new guy.

"I—I don't—"

Sharion spat on the floor in front of him.

His brow furrowed and he pointed at Lilly. "Just put it on, alright? We've got a schedule to keep."

As the new guy left the cellblock, Lilly traced her finger along the dress's black lace neckline. She'd never wear anything like it if she had the choice, but it beat staying in just her undergarments. She pulled it over her head and adjusted it on her body.

It fit well, but she hated it just the same, mostly because of what it represented.

Something tugged at her back. She turned and—

"Hold still," Sharion grunted.

Lilly went rigid. "What are you doing?"

"The back of this dress won't tie itself." Sharion pushed Lilly's cheek and faced her forward. "I said to hold still."

Lilly smirked, and she relaxed as Sharion did her work.

By that night, Magnus's accelerated healing had already sealed and begun to repair the arrow wound in his neck. Calum marveled at the sight and wished he had that same ability. In the kind of life he and Axel were now living, quick healing like that would change everything for them.

In the end, it only amounted to wishful thinking. That healing remained exclusive to Saurians, so Calum would just have to be cautious.

And speaking of cautious, when they made camp deep in the wilderness that night, they tied the moneybag shut and kept it near whoever was designated to stand watch. They'd cleared a decent amount of coin from Garon's shop, but they still only had limited supplies and no food to speak of. With little else to do, they went to sleep early.

Calum took the last shift again, and again, about two hours before sunrise he heard noises and thought he saw movement in the shadows.

This time, he was ready, though.

He gripped his sword in his right hand and listened, always with his left hand on the bag.

Something snapped to his left, just like the last time he'd let the bag get stolen. But he wouldn't get fooled twice. Instead of looking toward the sound, he stared right at the bag of gold coins. It couldn't get stolen if he kept his eyes on it, right?

A low growl sounded from the opposite side of the campfire. Calum glanced in that direction, but he didn't remove his hand from the pouch.

Perhaps he should rouse Magnus or Axel? Or both of them?

No. He needed to stick to the plan.

The growl stopped. Calum tightened his grip on his sword and stared over the campfire. If the Wolf attacked, he'd kill it, no question, and then that would solve the thief problem for good.

The pouch zipped out of his grasp and into the darkness.

"Now!" Calum yelled.

Magnus jumped to his feet and yanked a cord he held in his hands. Axel had attached it to the string that tied the bag shut through a small hole he'd cut into the bottom of the pouch. It functioned like a fishing line without a proper hook—they were counting on the Wolf refusing to let go of the bag once he got his jaws on it.

It worked.

The cord tightened, and a mass of brown-gray fur soared toward them from the darkness. It landed hard and skidded along the grass until it stopped about three feet away from Magnus. Gold coins flickered in the night sky and pinged along on the rocky ground, but they were of secondary concern compared to the thief now among them.

The Wolf released the bag, hopped up to its feet, and tried to dart away, but Magnus already had it by its tail. It pulled against his grip at first, then whipped its head around and chomped on Magnus's fingers.

Magnus hissed and winced, but he didn't let go. He pulled the Wolf closer and drew his sword. As Magnus raised the blade, fright flickered in the Wolf's eyes.

CHAPTER TWENTY-NINE

"No!" Calum stepped between Magnus and the Wolf, and Magnus stayed his hand.

The Wolf twisted free and darted into the woods.

"What are you doing?" Axel yelled. "We had him!"

"I—I don't know. I just couldn't let Magnus do it. He's a thief. He didn't try to kill us. It just didn't seem right to kill him for it." Calum shook his head. "I don't know."

"Well, now he's gonna come back, and he's gonna find a way to steal from us again." Axel glared at him. "Sometimes I just want to punch you, Calum. Hard."

"I'm sorry. I don't know what came over me." He glanced at Magnus. "Maybe I should've let you do it. I'm sorry."

"You should be." Axel threw his sword on the ground and dropped back into his spot. "I'm going back to sleep. You can pick up the coins without me."

Calum sighed. He deserved that. He'd botched the whole plan, and it had been working. He looked at Magnus again. "I'm sorry."

Magnus nodded. "Everything happens for a reason, Calum. Your compassion is something you should not lose if you can help it. It is the reason we are friends."

"If you say so."

"Indeed I do." Magnus patted him on his shoulder. "Come. Grab a stick from the fire. I will help you gather the coins."

———

A FEW MORE HOURS PASSED. Lilly assumed that night had fallen, but she didn't know for sure because the cellblock had no windows.

The new guy stepped into the cellblock and unlocked Lilly's cell. "It's time."

Lilly sat on the floor, wearing the burgundy dress. She stared at the patch of Colm's dried blood on the stone in front of her and shifted her foot in her boot. The knife blade pressed against her ankle as it had the last dozen times she'd checked for it. Good.

"Well, come here." The new guy extended his hand.

She could shift her leg under the hem of the dress and remove the knife, conceal it along the back of her wrist, and then jam it into his throat when he didn't expect it. From there, she could unlock the other cells and free the other slaves, and together maybe they could find a way to escape.

"*Come here.*" The new guy's dark eyebrows arched down. It was the first time he'd been stern with her so far.

Lilly lingered on the floor and moved her hand closer to her boot.

"What's the holdup?" Roderick's voice sent tremors into Lilly's stomach. He stepped into view behind the new guy and grinned at Lilly. "The show's about to begin."

Lilly froze, but she managed to scowl at him. The meager dinner of soup and stale bread they'd given her churned in her stomach at the sound of Roderick's voice.

She ignored the knife and instead pushed up to her feet. No chance of escaping now, not with Roderick around. She'd have to find another moment.

"Come on." Roderick motioned with his head. "We don't want to keep your buyer waiting."

Roderick shackled her wrists—but not her ankles this time. Then he shut the cell door behind her, and escorted her and the new guy to the auction house.

A row of thick black curtains prevented her from seeing the bustle on the other side. Through the occasional crack in the curtains she caught glimpses of a smattering of people in fine clothes. They held drinks and mingled like old friends at a wedding.

Didn't they realize what was about to happen? That people's lives were about to be changed forever? They had made the slaves' suffering into a social event, something to be celebrated. It sickened her.

Through the next opening in the curtains, she saw a fat, bearded man pat a thick pouch that hung from his belt, and the ugly woman talking with him laughed so hard that she almost spilled her drink.

Pigs. No—worse than that. Vermin. No better than the rats that had nipped at her ankles and squeaked around her as she traversed the city's sewers.

"That's not for you, Angel. Your buyer's better than any of them." Roderick stepped between her and the curtains. "At least he will be, until he resells you after tonight. If I were you, I'd try to make him really happy. Then he might just keep you around instead of tossing you to someone else when he's done with you."

Lilly's stomach lurched, and she vomited bile on Roderick's hip and down the side of his right leg. She hated the feeling, but at least she'd doused him in the process.

Roderick hopped back at first, then grabbed her by the back of her neck. His gray eyes burned and he raised his hand to strike her.

"Careful, Roderick." She glowered at him, then smirked. "You wouldn't want to forgo a higher price over a little vomit on your armor, would you?"

His jaw tightened and his eyes narrowed, but he let her go. He eyed the new guy. "You two keep going. He's waiting outside in a wagon. You'll know it when you see it. I have to get cleaned up before the auction."

The new guy nodded and yanked Lilly forward. "Come on."

"And wash her mouth out before you get to him. Can't have her smelling like—whatever it is she ate tonight."

"What do I do about the coin?"

"Don't worry about that. We already agreed on a price. He'll hand you a sack of gold once he sees her. Bring it straight to me once you get it." Roderick started toward them again and pointed his finger at the new guy. "And it's a lot of money. If you run off with it, I'll make you sorry you were ever born. And you know I can find you, too."

"Got it." The new guy nodded. He tugged on Lilly's arm. "Let's go."

They rounded a corner and stopped at a table behind the curtains. The new guy poured her a goblet full of cool water from a bronze pitcher. Lilly swished it around her mouth then spat it all back into the pitcher instead of on the floor.

The new guy pulled her away from it. "You wench! Don't you know there are people out there who were going to drink that?"

Lilly stared into his dark eyes and grinned. "Yes."

The new guy glared at her and shook his head. "Enough. We're going."

He led her back the way they had come and then out of the building. Sure enough, a large wagon adorned with purple awnings and gold trim awaited them under the moonlight.

Lilly's heart hammered in her chest. *When do I go for my knife? Do I feign being sick again and hunch over for it? What do I do?*

A thin man dismounted from the front of the carriage and started toward them. He wore black armor—the same armor the King's men wore—but no helmet, and he held a bulging leather pouch in his hands. A sword, sheathed, hung from his belt. He stared at her with vacant brown eyes, as if he was more dead than alive.

"This is her?" he asked, his voice monotone.

"Yep." The new guy urged Lilly forward.

She couldn't reach for her knife now. Not while there were two of them.

The soldier tossed the new guy the pouch. "That's all of it. The captain will be pleased. *Very* pleased."

"Oh," the new guy said. "So you're not—"

"Run along, boy." The soldier grabbed the chain between Lilly's shackles and pulled her away from the new guy. "The transaction's done."

The new guy eyed them both, nodded, then turned back toward the auction house.

The urge to call him back swelled in Lilly's stomach, but he couldn't help her now even if he wanted to. And he wouldn't help her anyway.

What was she about to get herself into?

"Come on, wench." The soldier shoved her toward the back of the wagon, pulled back a fold of purple fabric, and opened the wooden door. He ushered her inside.

The wagon compared in size to one of Roderick's caged wagons, but the similarities ended there. Soft light glowed from the candelabras mounted on the interior walls of the carriage, illuminating the space. Plush purple fabric lined the walls and ceiling, and a layer of blankets and furs covered the floor.

In the center reclined a rotund, balding man clad in a fine white robe. What little hair adorned his head took on a reddish hue in the candlelight, but Lilly noted several gray hairs mixed in as well. A small gray mustache hung under his arched nose, and he clutched a golden goblet in his left hand.

He grinned at her with lust in his dark eyes.

She'd decided the people attending the auction were rats instead of pigs, but this man was truly the latter. Even the sight of him churned her stomach.

The soldier removed Lilly's shackles and shoved her toward the hairless ogre lying on the furs.

"That will be all, Montrose. You know the routine. Take a walk. Be back in an hour." The captain took a gulp of wine from the goblet, then licked his plump lips. "On second thought, make it a half-hour."

"Yes, Captain Fulton."

Fulton? Lilly remembered that name. *The officer who betrayed Colm to Roderick?*

Montrose shut and latched the carriage door, and his footsteps faded into the distance.

Captain Fulton pushed himself up to his feet and started toward

Lilly. She tried to retreat, but the back of the carriage stopped her. There was no escape.

"My, my." Captain Fulton reached for her. Lilly recoiled, her eyes shut, but she still felt his thick fingers stroking her cheek. "Roderick wasn't lying. You're the most beautiful creature I've ever seen."

Lilly almost reached for the knife then, but she stopped herself. *Not yet.*

Then again, she didn't know how much time she had left.

"Did Roderick tell you about me?" He took another greedy slurp from his goblet, and Lilly noticed two thick golden rings, one on his little finger and one on his ring finger of that hand. "Hm? He must've said *something*. Roderick is a loquacious sort if I ever met one."

Lilly had no desire to respond to anything he said. He reeked of wine and a pungent floral fragrance that overwhelmed Lilly's nostrils.

"I'm sure you're frightened, child, but I mean you no harm." He tangled his fingers in her blonde hair. "By the moon, you are *radiant*."

Disgust swirled in Lilly's stomach. She thought she might vomit again, but she managed to hold her composure.

"I can assure you, I'm very experienced. You could enjoy this if you wanted to." He tossed his empty wine goblet behind him and it clunked against the wall, empty, then cupped her shoulders in his hands. "I know I will."

That's it. Enough. Lilly drove her knee into Captain Fulton's groin and shoved him back.

Red-faced, he dropped onto his hands and knees on the blankets with his teeth bared.

Lilly spun around and grabbed for the carriage door, but it didn't have a handle, only a keyhole. How would she—

Something jerked her head back. Captain Fulton had her hair.

He yanked her away from the door and thrust her onto the carriage floor. The lust in his eyes had given way to rage.

"You had your chance, pretty one." He towered over her, his fists clenched. Perspiration dotted his forehead and rolled down his cheeks. "I don't mind a little fight in my girls, but that was too far."

Captain Fulton untied the front of his white robe and exposed his hairless chest—and a silver skeleton key that hung from a thin chain around his neck. The carriage door key?

Now or never. Lilly skinned the knife from her boot and scooted away from him until her back rested against the carriage wall opposite of the door.

"My, what a twist. You think one small knife will keep you safe from me?" Captain Fulton scoffed. "You obviously don't know who you're dealing with."

"Stay away." Lilly held up the knife, which kept Captain Fulton well beyond arm's length away.

"Ah, so she does speak." Captain Fulton stalked closer, one cautious step at a time. "A lovely voice to match her lovely exterior. I wonder how she'll sound when she *screams?*"

"I said to stay back!" Lilly drew the knife back slightly, but her elbow hit the wall. She turned her head—a mistake. General Balena would have chastised her for it.

Captain Fulton sprang forward faster than she expected, given his girth, and clamped his hand around her wrist. She couldn't move her hand with the knife because of his grip, so she drove her fist into his round belly. It rippled, and he grunted, but he didn't stop his advance.

He grabbed her other wrist, wrenched her around, and pulled her close to him.

The stench of sweaty flowers almost suffocated her, and he squeezed her tight. She screamed, but he didn't release his grip.

"Roderick was right about you being wily, too." He chuckled. "I may have gained a few pounds since my prime, but I'm still a trained soldier. I know how to disarm a child with a knife."

He jerked her right hand downward at an awkward angle, and she dropped the knife with a yelp. He kicked it away and it plunked against the carriage wall, well out of reach.

A snort sounded over her shoulder, then another behind her neck. Was he—*smelling* her?

Lilly cringed and twisted in his grasp, but she stood no hope of breaking free. She shrieked.

"The less you fight, the easier this will be for both of us." He spun her around and pushed her down onto her back.

Every curse and insult she'd ever learned teased her tongue, but they all dissipated in dread when he crouched down over her. He clasped his thick hand around her throat and leaned in so close that his gut pressed against her abdomen, pinning her down.

His dark eyes narrowed and his nostrils flared. "I could just snap your neck, you know."

Lilly craned her neck in spite of his grasp until she got a view of the knife, and she stretched her arm toward it, but it lay a solid foot out of her reach.

"Still resisting? Very well. I don't like to do this, but I suppose I'll have to this time." Captain Fulton pinned her under his full weight and pulled a small vial of violet liquid from his waistband. "Aliophos Nectar won't kill you. It won't put you to sleep either, unless I give you half the vial, but a drop should make you more cooperative."

Aliophos Nectar—the same stuff Roderick had used to knock her out when he'd first caught her. Not again. Lilly strained for the knife, but no matter how she writhed against him, she couldn't reach. "I don't care what you do. I won't cooperate with *this*."

Captain Fulton grinned. "We'll see about that."

He released his grip on her throat to uncork the vial and she lashed her arm toward the knife, but his gut kept her pinned in place. She screamed and clawed at the floor for it, all to no avail. She couldn't reach the knife.

"Easy, little one. Soon you'll see things my way." Captain Fulton grinned.

Lilly summoned all the rage in her body into her mouth, and she spat in Captain Fulton's left eye. He recoiled with a snarl, and it freed Lilly to move.

She snatched the knife handle with her right hand.

Captain Fulton wiped the saliva from his face and groped for her throat. As he leaned down, Lilly plunged the knife into the left side of his thick neck.

He screamed, and as he clutched at the wound, blood oozed from between his fingers.

Lilly shoved against his chest with all her might and he rolled off of her onto his back. She jumped to her feet, yanked the key from the chain around his neck, and dashed to the carriage door. She jammed the key into the lock and began to—

Captain Fulton's hand clamped around her ankle, and he jerked her back. Her footing dropped out from under her, and she hit the floor chest-first. Lilly's breath pushed out of her lungs, and she gasped as Captain Fulton reeled her back toward him.

She twisted so she lay on her back. Even though the knife was still lodged in his neck, he still tried to press the fingers of his other hand against his wound. With her free leg Lilly kicked at his arm and his stomach and his chest, but he didn't relent. He kept pulling her, his wide eyes rabid with rage as red gurgles sputtered through his clenched teeth.

The sight gave Lilly a new target: his teeth.

She adjusted her footing and slammed the heel of her boot into Captain Fulton's mouth, then again into his nose. He lost his grip for a moment, and she recoiled, but he lunged forward and grabbed her other ankle instead.

Would he *never* give up? Why wouldn't he just die already?

Now that he had her other ankle, it meant her right leg was free. The knife still protruded from his neck, just where she'd left it.

It was her way out of this horror.

In one savage motion, Lilly shifted her body hard to the right and drove the heel of her boot into the end of the knife handle. Captain Fulton gasped, released her, and clutched his throat with both hands, his bloody mouth wide open.

Lilly drew her leg back again for another kick and let it fly, but Captain Fulton blocked her leg with his forearm and latched onto it. She wrenched her body to the side and hurled another kick with her left leg at his face, and it connected. He let her go again.

One more shift, one more brutal kick to that knife would finish it.

She glared at him as he slumped to the floor again, a look of pained desperation in his eyes. "This is for Colm."

She delivered a blow so hard to the knife hilt that her foot hurt afterward.

The knife hilt all but disappeared into Captain Fulton's thick neck, and his mouth widened even farther. He coughed and hacked up specks of blood onto her torso and face, then he slumped onto his side. His eyes rolled back, and he stopped moving entirely.

Either he was dead or he wasn't—Lilly had no desire to find out—but either way, he wouldn't be chasing her anymore. She whirled around and twisted the key in the lock, and the carriage door swung open. A gust of cool night air washed away the combined scent of sweat, flowers, and blood, and it renewed Lilly's spirit.

Freedom.

Part of her wanted to retrieve the knife from Captain Fulton's neck, but another part of her, a part she knew was totally irrational, worried he might come back from the dead if she pulled the knife out. She left the knife, but snatched up the vial of Aliophos Nectar that lay next to his motionless body.

She never would've expected it, but she found herself thanking the Overlord for the color of her burgundy dress. It disguised the spattered blood that coated her upper half, and she used the fabric near the hem to wipe off her face, neck, and hands.

Enough. It doesn't have to be perfect.

Lilly let the hem drop back down and peered out of the carriage into the night. From what she could tell, Montrose hadn't finished his walk and wasn't yet nearby. Maybe she could make a clean escape.

No. Not yet. She still had to find and recover her armor and her cape, or she'd have no chance of getting home safely.

She crept back toward the auction house, but instead of going inside, she rounded the side of the building. If her armor was still in Roderick's wagon, the one pulled by the brown donkey, then perhaps she wouldn't have to go back inside at all.

Sure enough, she found a row of familiar wagons, some of them big barred boxes like the one the slave traders had confined her to during her trip across Trader's Pass, and some of them small and loaded with crates and barrels and other supplies.

The only problem was that all the donkeys and horses pulling the carts had been unhitched and now lingered in a small stable adjacent to where the wagons were parked.

Lilly cursed under her breath. A man emerged from the stables with a shovel in-hand. Lilly ducked behind the nearest wagon and crouched by the wheel.

The man shut the door and set the shovel next to it, then he walked in her direction. He stopped at the wagon just ahead of hers and leaned against the bars.

How would she get to the wagons with a guard posted there? The Aliophos Nectar wouldn't work unless he breathed its fumes or drank it, and the only thing around that could've served as a weapon was the shovel, but she couldn't get to that without him seeing her either.

Lilly cursed silently again.

"Hey," the man hissed. He craned his head and bent down, his eyes fixed on her location. "Who's there?"

She ducked behind the wagon wheel again and bit her lip. Apparently, she hadn't cursed silently enough.

Hurried footsteps approached her position.

CHAPTER THIRTY

L illy had no time—she just reacted.
"Who are y—"

Lilly uncorked the vial, sprang at him, and tossed the full payload of the Aliophos Nectar at his head. The violet liquid splashed on his face, and he recoiled a step, sputtering.

"What is... what did you...?"

It was the new guy, the one who had escorted her to Montrose and Captain Fulton. The one with the dark eyes, green armor, and curly black hair.

He blinked at her and pointed an accusing finger. "You're... not supposed to..."

His legs wobbled, gave out, and he slumped to the ground, unconscious and snoring.

No time to enjoy the sight. Montrose would find Captain Fulton any minute now, and who knew how long the Aliophos Nectar would keep the new guy unconscious? She shuffled over to the wagons and began to rummage through their contents.

Three wagons in, she found her armor, her bow and arrows, and her cape. Joy and relief and excitement cascaded through her veins at the sight.

She sliced her dress down the center of the bodice with one of her arrowheads and shed it from her body, then strapped her armor on, piece by piece. She hooked her cape onto her back, and slung her bow across her chest.

Time to fly.

For the first time in nearly two months, her feet left the ground, and she ascended into the night air as effortlessly as taking a breath. She hovered ten feet off the ground, then twenty, then she matched the height of the building. Exhilaration swelled in her chest the higher she climbed. Now she could zoom away and leave all of this behind as nothing more than a bad memory.

But what about Sharion? What about the other slaves?

No. She didn't have time. Montrose had to be close to the carriage by now. More importantly, she had responsibilities to her family and her parents back home. She couldn't linger here.

But was she truly willing to condemn all of the other people in those cages to fates like the one she'd just escaped?

It wasn't condemnation, she rationalized. She'd escaped. They could do the same if they wanted.

Could they? She pulled the keys from her boot and jingled them in her gauntleted hand.

"When the time is right, I'll help you escape, but not before then."

Lilly had said that to Sharion after Colm died, after she'd clocked Sharion in the chin for trying to use the keys and the knife to escape then and there.

Was it a lie?

Or was it a promise?

Lilly's jaw hardened, and she exhaled a sigh through her nose.

Then she drew an arrow from her quiver, nocked it in her bow, and headed back toward the auction house door.

LILLY PUSHED the cellblock door open. Thanks to the black curtains and the commotion on the other side, Lilly had made it through the auction house all but undetected, and the one guy she did encounter went down with an arrow to his throat, unable to call for help. At least she hadn't lost her accuracy.

She trotted down the cellblock, her head swiveling.

The cells were empty. Every single one.

She was too late.

She stopped at her cell and peered inside. Maybe Sharion had huddled in the corner and they had missed her?

No such luck. She was gone.

Well, she'd tried. Nothing left to do now but escape herself, once and for all. She turned toward the cellblock door and—

"Hey!" a voice, hushed, hissed from behind her.

She whirled around and drew her arrow back, ready to skewer whoever had found her, but found no one. The corridor was empty.

"Down here." The voice sounded from the end of the cellblock, in the last cell. Almost no light entered that cell from the torches in the cellblock. No wonder Lilly hadn't seen anyone in there.

Still, Lilly didn't move. She squinted and kept her arrow trained on the source of the sound—at least as best as she could tell. "Who's there?"

"Come closer."

"Why?"

"Your friend isn't here. They already took her." The voice took on a feminine tone, but it didn't sound like that of a human or another Windgale. "But if you free me, I can help you find her."

"Who are you?"

"My name is Windsor. Hurry—there's little time."

Lilly glanced over her shoulder, then she started toward the end of the cellblock. She relaxed the tension in her bowstring and pulled the keys from her belt. "*What* are you?"

"Unlock the cell, and I can show you."

Lilly pushed the key into the cell's lock but didn't turn it. "How do I know you won't try to hurt me?"

"You don't. But if you want to see your friend again, you'll let me out."

Did she want to see Sharion again? They weren't exactly *friends*, after all…

"Open. The. Cell," the voice growled.

Lilly's eyes narrowed. She'd do it, but she'd be ready if the prisoner came at her. She turned the key, nocked her arrow, and—

The cell door burst open, and a black blur knocked her onto her back. Teeth flashed under a set of vivid blue eyes and a furry snout.

The Wolf. The one that had almost escaped Roderick's men and given Lilly one of her failed opportunities to escape.

She snarled at Lilly, and her forepaws gripped the top of Lilly's armor. "You shouldn't have tried to shoot me."

Lilly glared up at her and tried to shift, but Windsor was heavier than she looked. Bigger than Lilly had expected, too. "You shouldn't have been so brusque. Now tell me where my friend is."

Windsor growled. "You're in no position to make demands."

"I let you out. I held up my end. Now tell me where she is." Lilly raised an eyebrow. "Or does the word of a Wolf mean nothing?"

"I should kill you for saying that." Windsor leaned in close, and Lilly smelled rancid meat on her breath. "I could tear out your throat right now and I'd be none the worse for it. You'd be the first fresh meat I've had in a month."

"I don't have time for this." Lilly's voice sharpened. "If you're going to kill me, then either do it, or let me up so I can get out of here. If your word means nothing to you and you're not going to help me, then I'll find her myself."

"You're brave—for a Windgale." Windsor growled again, then she stepped off of Lilly's chest. "I'll help you find her, but then I'm out of here."

Lilly pushed herself up to her feet and recovered her bow and arrow. "Lead the way."

Windsor headed to Lilly's old cell first to pick up Sharion's scent from a scrap of the rags she'd worn, then she led Lilly out the cellblock and back into the auction house. Lilly noted a patch of white fur on the tip of her tail, the only part of her coat that wasn't black. It didn't seem to affect her ability to hide in darkness in the least.

273

Windsor hid in the shadows seamlessly while Lilly slunk along the wall in the main room of the auction house. The commotion on the other side had subsided, now replaced with Roderick's voice.

"...you can see this isn't our finest crop ever, but at least the opening prices are competitive." The crowd laughed, and Roderick continued, "As usual, we start at the low end and save the good stuff for later. We've got a gorgeous black she-Wolf locked up, but she's a handful, so she'll be the last prize for you to bid on. For now, let's start with this guy, here. He's got bad teeth, but he's cooperative. Who'll make me an offer?"

"One gold coin," a man from the audience called.

"Jethro bids one gold coin, but he always was cheap." The crowd laughed again. Roderick said, "Any other takers?"

The auction had begun, and patrons perpetuated it with shouts of various amounts of money.

"Your friend—" Windsor motioned toward the curtains with her head. "—she's already out there."

Lilly's jaw tightened. "How do I get her away from them?"

Windsor shook her head. "Not my problem. I'm out of here."

"But you—"

"I said I'd help you *find* her, and I did," Windsor snapped. "I'm not sticking around any longer than I have to. Neither should you. It's too late for her. You should get out while you still have the chance, before they find you again."

Windsor trotted toward the auction house's door, but Lilly took to the air and beat her there—how good it felt to fly again, even for a short amount of time. "Don't you want to take revenge on these guys for what they did to you? They locked you up. Abused you."

"And now I'm free, and I'm out of here." Windsor growled at Lilly. "Move aside, or I'll move you aside."

"I need your help, Windsor. I have to free them. Not just Sharion, but all of them. This is wrong, and you know it."

"What I know is that it's none of my business," Winsdor snarled, "so get out of my way."

Lilly scowled at her but stepped aside.

"Have a nice life." Windsor nudged the door open with her nose and disappeared into the night.

"You should get out while you still have the chance," Windsor had said. Perhaps she was right.

No. Lilly had made a promise to Sharion. She had to find a way to free her.

She rounded the corner of the curtains and spotted the table where the new guy had gotten her water after she'd retched all over Roderick. A big man stood there, his arms folded, but he wasn't looking her direction. A half-dozen slaves, all of them human, stood near him, shackled and chained to each other.

Sharion wasn't one of them.

Lilly drew her bow back and launched an arrow at him. It embedded in the side of his head and he slumped to the floor, dead. She swooped over and landed next to him, careful not to ascend above the curtains. The slaves gawked and gasped at her, but she shushed them.

"Easy, easy." She held her hands up to quiet them. True to Roderick's words, they looked healthier and more capable than some of the other slaves she'd seen. He really was saving the "good stuff" for later on. "I'm here to help you, but I need your help as well."

They ogled her with wide eyes and mouths agape.

"I'm going to unchain you. When I do, I need you to rush through the curtains to create a distraction so I can free the other slaves."

"Why in the Overlord's name would we do that?" one man hissed. "You're setting us free. We're leaving."

The others murmured in agreement.

Lilly shook her head. "How far do you think you'll get without money or food? The crowd will have bags full of money in their possession. These slave traders took your freedom from you so they could sell you to those pigs out there. You might as well get something in return, right?"

"B-but the s-slave traders have w-weapons," another slave stammered.

Lilly removed the dead slave trader's sword from his belt and tossed it to the slave. "Now you do, too."

"That's great, but what about the rest of us?" The first slave jammed his fists into his hips.

"You'll have to make do."

The slaves looked at each other, then at her. The first slave shook his head. "Sorry, miss, but we'd rather just be on our way."

First Windsor, now these people, too? "I need your help. What about the other slaves?"

"Beggin' your pardon, but if you had a chance at freedom, wouldn't you take it?"

"This *is* my chance at freedom. I was caged up with the rest of you not an hour ago, but I'm still here, trying to help all of you and those who are out on that platform right now."

A brief pause lingered between her and the slaves.

"Look, you're a good shot with that bow and all, but six of us against almost double the number of slave traders and dozens of other people? It's lunacy. Just unlock us and we'll leave."

"You're not goin' anywhere," a voice behind them said.

Lilly whirled around. She knew that voice.

Montrose stood there, sword in-hand, with Luggs, Gammel, and Adgar at his side, each wielding weapons of their own. Two other slave traders also stood with them, bows nocked and ready.

They were trapped.

CHAPTER THIRTY-ONE

The slaves huddled together behind Lilly, and the one to whom she'd handed the sword dropped it.

"Drop the bow, pretty one." Montrose pointed his sword at Lilly.

"And if I don't?"

"*Sold*," Roderick crooned on the other side of the curtains. "This one with the bad teeth goes to Jethro for five gold coins. As usual, you can claim your prize after the auction has concluded."

Montrose glanced at Luggs, who raised his arm. The archers drew back their arrows.

"If you come quietly," Montrose said, "I assure you that all of them will live, and so will you, though you must answer for Captain Fulton."

Lilly hesitated. She could bolt into the air and evade their arrows if she had to, but she couldn't let the other slaves die because of her.

Windsor had been right. She should've left when she had the chance.

She dropped her bow at her side.

Montrose nodded toward her. "Take her."

The archers relaxed their bowstrings, and Gammel and Adgar started forward.

A black blur launched out of the shadows and collided with

Montrose. His sword clattered toward Lilly. The two forms tumbled to the floor, but the shadow mounted him and lunged for his throat as he screamed. Its tail waved with delight as Montrose thrashed, and Lilly noticed a patch of white fur on its tip.

Windsor. She'd come back.

Pandemonium seized the room. Lilly tossed the key ring to the first slave, and he began to unlock his shackles, then she snatched up her bow and skinned an arrow from her quiver.

In the chaos of the moment, the archers alternated surprised glances between Windsor tearing at Montrose's throat and face and at the slaves. One of them took aim at Lilly again, but her arrow hit him in his face before he could get a shot off. Thanks to Lilly's second arrow, the other went down right after noticing the first archer's fate.

Meanwhile, Luggs swung his dagger down at Windsor, but she darted away from Montrose, and Luggs's dagger lodged in Montrose's chest instead. Luggs staggered back, horrified, until Lilly's arrow hit his shoulder. He yelped and went down, and Lilly regretted not hitting him as squarely as she'd hit the archers.

The curtains spread wide, and Roderick's towering form filled the open space. "What in the Overlord's name is—"

Lilly aimed her next arrow at him right as he noticed her. He glared at her, and she let the arrow fly.

Roderick sidestepped the arrow and charged at her, but she burst into the air, well out of his reach. By now the freed slaves had scattered, and Roderick yelled for more slave traders.

The set of keys Colm had given her lay on the floor near a pile of shackles. Lilly angled down and scooped them into her hands, bolted toward the ceiling again, and then she dropped down onto the platform in front of the slaves.

She landed in front of Sharion.

Sharion's eyes widened, and she recoiled a step.

Lilly smiled at her. "Told you I'd get you out."

Movement rushed behind Sharion.

"Get down!" Lilly yanked Sharion to the floor and a sword lashed where her head had just been. Adgar.

He swung at them again, but Lilly and Sharion rolled opposite directions, and his blade clanged against the platform instead.

Lilly sprang off her feet and drove her shoulder into his side, and Adgar lost his footing and fell. Still on her side, Sharion bashed him in the face with her elbow then got to her feet.

Adgar lay there, clutching at what appeared to be a broken nose. The stupid hat he always wore had tumbled off his head and lay next to him on the platform.

Lilly crushed it under her boot as she handed Sharion the keys. "Can you take it from here?"

Sharion nodded and smiled. "Thank you."

Lilly gave Adgar a kick to his ribs for good measure, then she turned toward the crowd—or rather, what remained of it. Windsor and some of the other slaves, including the Saurian she'd seen locked up in the cells below, had overrun them and caused a ruckus.

Lilly grinned. It was exactly what those pigs deserved.

A primal roar erupted behind her.

She spun around in time to see Roderick barreling toward her.

Lilly zipped away, but Roderick pursued her nonetheless. She wove through the crowd and arched toward the row of curtains, then angled up and over them.

Roderick's sword severed the rod that suspended the curtains in place, and he tore after her. He moved faster than she remembered.

She flew down the corridor toward the auction house door. Another archer stepped into view at the opposite end of the hall and took aim at her, but she dropped her flight path low and the arrow knifed past her. Roderick grunted behind her, but when she looked back, the arrow hadn't hit him.

Lilly just had to get outside, and then she could get away. The archer nocked another arrow and let it fly as she zoomed toward the door, but on instinct, she stopped short.

The arrow thudded into the doorframe just inches from her face.

She pushed through the door and pulled her bow from her shoulders as she took to the night sky.

The city dropped out from beneath her, but an arrow whizzed past her, then another. She looped and twisted and whirled, but they kept coming. She drew an arrow of her own, turned back and took aim.

Pain stabbed her left shoulder and her arrow loosed, but it hit nowhere near her intended target. Instead, someone else's arrow protruded from her shoulder, right between her breastplate and her shoulder plate. She looked down.

Far below, Roderick fired more arrows at her in quick succession. Despite the pain, Lilly spun away from the next barrage and ascended above the cloud line.

She'd made it. She'd escaped, and she'd freed the other slaves, too, but not without cost. Blood trickled down her armor.

Lilly wanted nothing more than to rip it from her flesh, but she recalled General Balena's instructions about arrow wounds: she had to leave it in until she could get proper care, or she'd risk bleeding out.

It burned like no pain she'd ever felt before, but she could still fly, and she'd flown well clear of the auction house and Roderick and his men by now. All she had to do was find her way home.

Easier said than done. She'd never been to this half of Kanarah before, and she had no idea where she was. And it was nighttime, and she'd never really learned how to navigate using the stars.

Her head swam with disillusionment. Something wasn't right. Her vision wavered, and her body quivered as she flew. Not normal.

She looked at her bleeding shoulder and at the arrow sticking out of it. She hadn't lost enough blood to grow faint, so why would she—

Aliophos Nectar. It had to be. Roderick must've coated the arrow-heads with it. Whether he had or not, she couldn't risk flying while only half-awake.

She descended below the cloud line and saw a small forest below her, and beyond that a sprawling field of gold drenched in silver moon-light. Wheat, maybe?

Her head throbbed, and her vision blackened. She couldn't see.

She blinked hard as she continued to drop lower and lower, and her vision returned in intermittent glimpses of what lay before her. She wanted to slow down—she needed to. Most of all, she needed to land face-up so the arrow wouldn't lodge any deeper in her shoulder.

The land rose up to meet her as her feet touched the ground, but her legs melted underneath her. Lilly managed to twist as she fell, and she landed on her back among the wheat.

Then everything faded to darkness.

CHAPTER THIRTY-TWO

The sun hadn't yet risen when Corporal Jopheth burst into Commander Anigo's room.

He jerked upright in his bed, and a jolt of pain stabbed his chest—a reminder that while he was still alive, he was also still mortal. "What is the meaning of this, Cor—"

"I'm sorry for the interruption, Commander," Corporal Jopheth blurted. "Captain Fulton and Montrose have been killed."

Commander Anigo's rage iced over. "What happened?"

"It reeks of scandal, sir. It appears Montrose brought Captain Fulton to a slave auction and helped him procure a Windgale girl to… to…"

"I'm familiar with the concept of prostitution, Corporal."

"Anyway, it appears she brandished a knife and killed him, then she loosed the other slaves and escaped with most of them. The warehouse where it all happened has been vacated, but a man named Wandell Thirry alerted us to several dead bodies inside. Fresh bodies."

Commander Anigo's eyes narrowed. "At an auction? Were they purchasers?"

"Some, yes. Also some slaves and some slave traders, we presume."

"What about the other slave traders?"

"After the pandemonium of the auction, they cleared out. I have men watching the west gate to Trader's Pass right now in search of anything suspicious."

"Well done." Commander Anigo didn't care for Corporal Jopheth, but at least he'd proven somewhat competent.

"I'm afraid Captain Fulton's death means you're now the ranking officer in Kanarah City, Commander. I have dispatched a messenger to Solace requesting instructions on how we are to proceed," Corporal Jopheth said. "In the meantime, what are your orders?"

The ranking officer in Kanarah City? He'd lamented having to deal with Captain Fulton's insolence and disregard for the effective rule of law just yesterday.

Perhaps this was providence—the means and manpower to catch the three fugitives he'd been chasing for the last few months. He grinned.

"Sir?" Corporal Jopheth leaned forward.

Commander Anigo threw the sheets off his legs and stood. "Bring me breakfast. We have much work to do."

AXEL'S STOMACH grumbled for what had to be the third or fourth time that morning. They'd gone yet another day of camping in the woods with no food, so when Magnus suggested they head southeast toward the Golden Plains rather than staying in the mountains, the idea immediately appealed to Axel—at least at first.

"We can harvest some grain from the King's fields," Magnus said. "And if we travel far enough east, we can collect some fruit from his orchards. Along with our weapons and armor, we should be able to make the trip across the valley if we pack enough food. From there, we can begin our search for the Arcanum."

"I said I didn't want to go back to manual labor." Axel folded his arms and frowned. He'd done everything he could to get away from that life, and now Magnus was suggesting he go right back to it. Even if it was only temporary, the idea still grated on him. "I'm done with that life."

"We are enacting this plan precisely because of your farming background. You get to lead this expedition. You know the soil, the plants, the trees. You know the fruits and vegetables better than either Calum or me," Magnus said. "You know what will keep and what will spoil."

Axel's eyebrow rose. Everything Magnus had said was true, but the only thing that had any appeal to it was his suggestion that Axel lead this part of the journey.

"And besides, at this point, we cannot afford to spend any extra time in Kanarah City. I want to get us to Trader's Pass as fast as possible, so having food already packed is essential to our progress. This way, we do not need to linger in a populated area any longer than necessary."

Axel huffed, but he couldn't really argue with Magnus's logic. "I still don't like it, but I'll do it."

Magnus smiled. "We leave at your command."

EVEN AS A FARMER, Axel had never seen anything like it.

Expansive fields of gold shimmered under the afternoon sun. Wind rippled the grain like waves in a lake, a lake that never ended, for all he knew.

In a way, the fields made him long for home, but in another way, they reminded him that he could never go back to the life of a farmer.

"Do you think we're far enough away from Kanarah City?" Calum asked.

Magnus nodded. "Even though we can see it in the distance, we're too far for them to muster any actual response, even if they could see us. We just need to watch out for patrolling soldiers or workers who might be in the area."

Early that morning, they'd taken a circuitous southern road mostly devoid of travelers to the King's Orchards. There, they filled two sacks with various fruits, based on Axel's instructions on what would stay fresh the longest.

Then they'd headed northwest along the edge of the fields, back toward Kanarah City. Once they harvested a couple bags full of grain, they'd be ready to head for Trader's Pass.

"Stay near the edge, at least at first," Axel said. "If we venture too far into the heart of the crops, it'll be that much harder to find our way out if someone finds us."

"I don't know how the King's men could safeguard such vast fields, anyway." Calum scanned the fields. "But we can stick to the edges. The grain should be just as good, right?"

Axel nodded. He plucked a head of grain and held it up for them to see. "This is the part we need. Anything else is just plant fiber, and while we can eat it, it has no nutritional value, so try not to drop them in the bag."

Magnus nodded, and Calum said, "Got it."

They harvested for about a half hour and almost filled the first bag halfway.

"Hey," Calum said. "I'll be right back. Gotta pee."

"Don't stray too far," Axel said. "It's easy to hide or get lost in fields like these. All you have to do is crouch or lay down, and the grain does the rest. Watch yourself."

Calum nodded and stepped a few feet deeper into the sea of gold.

Axel elbowed Magnus in his ribs. "Remind me not to harvest over there, right, Scales?"

Magnus smirked. "No question."

"Uh… guys?" Calum said.

"What's wrong? Can't get it out on your own?" Axel chuckled and dropped another head of grain into his bag.

"No. I found something."

Axel glanced at Magnus, then they both walked over to where Calum stood.

There, among the golden grain, lay a beautiful young woman with blonde hair and an arrow sticking out of her upper chest between her left shoulder and her collarbone.

She wasn't moving.

THE GIRL WAS BEAUTIFUL—*REALLY* beautiful.

285

Definitely the most beautiful girl Calum had ever seen.

While he hadn't known many women throughout his life, he'd certainly seen a fair number in the last month or so of traveling with Magnus and Axel through the few villages they'd visited. But none of the others even came close to this girl.

Calum bent down next to her. Detailed white engravings of eagles and hawks adorned the pale pink armor that covered her legs, arms, and torso. Blood oozed from around the arrow in her shoulder, but her chest moved up and down slightly.

"She's breathing," Calum said.

"How did she get here? It looks like someone dragged her through the grain and left her here." Axel picked up the ornate bow and a pristine quiver of arrows that lay next to her and looked them over. "And who is she?"

"That does not matter right now." Magnus brushed her long blonde hair away from the wound. "Find me something I can use for a bandage."

"From where?" Calum asked.

"Anywhere. Just find me something." Magnus clasped his fingers around the arrow.

Axel knelt down, set the bow and quiver down, and pointed to the shimmering blue fabric spread out under her body. "What about this?"

Magnus grabbed his wrist. "Do *not* touch her cape."

"Cape?" Axel's eyes widened with the same realization Calum was having. "You mean she's—"

"She's a Windgale." Calum looked at Axel. "She needs it to fly."

"Bandage. Now," Magnus grunted. "Keep looking."

When Magnus pulled the arrow out of the girl's shoulder, she jerked awake and screamed. Her blue eyes darted between Calum and Axel, focused on Magnus, and then she screamed again. She clawed at the dirt and grain around her and tried to get away from them.

Magnus clamped his hand around her ankle and pulled her back, but when Calum and Axel reached down to try to help, he warned them to stay back. Though she kicked and hollered, he held her in place by her shoulders. He leaned in close and stared right at her.

"Be silent."

Her mouth clamped shut, but her blue eyes opened wider.

"I will not hurt you," he said, slowly and pointedly. "Do you understand?"

She glanced at Axel and Calum.

"Neither will they hurt you," he continued. "You have taken an arrow to your shoulder. I removed it, but you are still bleeding. I need to stop it. But first, I need to clean the wound so you do not get an infection. In order to do that, I need you to stay as still and as calm as you can."

She nodded.

"Press your hand against your wound to help stop the bleeding." When the girl complied, Magnus dug his fingers under the armor along his wrist and pulled out a small vial of orange liquid.

Calum eyed the vial. "What is that?"

"It's veromine."

"Vero-what?" Axel asked.

Magnus eyed him. "Veromine. It fights against infection and speeds up the body's natural healing process. We Saurians have it in our blood. It is the reason we can regenerate from wounds so quickly. Did you find me something to use as a bandage?"

"Uhhh…" Calum and Axel eyed each other.

"Both of you remove your gauntlets and shoulder armor. Rip off your shirtsleeves and give them to me." While they complied, Magnus looked down at the girl. "What is your name?"

She glanced at Calum again, and her voice barely registered above a whisper. "Lilly."

"Calum." Magnus's voice broke Calum's stare.

"Huh?" Calum blinked.

"Sleeves."

"Oh. Sorry." He hadn't realized he'd stopped moving. He tore off his sleeves and handed them to Magnus, who was already at work on Lilly's wound with Axel's sleeves.

Lilly winced when Magnus dabbed at the wound. Once he cleared most of her blood, Magnus opened the vial and poured in a few drops.

"Calum, Axel?" Magnus eyed them both. "Turn away, please."

They exchanged glances with each other then looked at Magnus again.

"I must tear away some of her undershirt to secure the bandage, so for her sake, please divert your eyes."

Calum nodded, and he and Axel turned around. As he slid his armor back onto his arms, Calum leaned over to Axel and whispered, "She's beautiful."

"Yeah, but she's beyond you," he whispered back.

Calum tilted his head. "What do you mean?"

Axel shook his head and secured his gauntlet to his left forearm. "A girl like that? You don't have a chance, brother."

On one level, Calum had never had a relationship with a girl before, and Axel knew more about life in general. He was older and wasn't confined to just his farm like Calum was to the quarry, so Calum felt inclined to believe what Axel said.

Yet a part of him wanted to believe that Axel was lying, or just plain wrong.

"Why not?"

"Someone that beautiful? Are you kidding me?" Axel scoffed. "By the look of her armor, her bow, and her quiver, she's probably rich, too. You're more likely to get struck by a bolt of lightning than to end up with her."

Calum's jaw hardened. He didn't want to believe it, but Axel was probably right. Even though he'd earned his freedom, he was still just a poor nobody.

But if he managed to free Lumen, then...

Axel put a gloved hand on Calum's shoulder. "I'm not trying to be harsh. I'm just trying to keep you from getting your hopes up."

"What's wrong with hoping?"

"I don't want you to get hurt. It's not a good feeling." Axel frowned. "Just trying to look out for you."

"There. Finished," Magnus said.

Axel rotated his head. "Can we turn around?"

"Just a second—there. Now you may turn around."

Lilly still lay there, now with one of Calum's and one of Axel's sleeves tied around her shoulder to cover the wound. Her undershirt was tied together over her shoulder where Magnus had ripped it, its white fabric now stained red.

"Are you alright?" Axel asked before Calum had a chance to open his mouth.

Lilly nodded. Her blue eyes still exuded distrust.

"What happened to you?"

Lilly stared at them but didn't say anything. The thought that she might be a mute crossed Calum's mind, but she'd told them her name. And as far as he knew, Windgales spoke the same language as everyone else in Kanarah.

Calum looked at Magnus then refocused on her. "Look, we're not going to hurt you. We'll even let you go, if you want. But if you need help, maybe we can help you."

After another pause, Lilly stood to her feet with Magnus's help. "I was captured outside my home by slave traders."

Magnus growled, and Lilly recoiled from him. He held his hand up to her. "Forgive my reaction. It is out of disdain for them and for your plight. Please continue."

She nodded. "They brought me across the valley and tried to sell me, but I escaped. I remember getting hit by an arrow as I was flying away, but I kept flying. Then my vision began to darken. As I coasted toward the ground to take a rest, I blacked out."

"You're from across the valley?" Calum asked.

"Yes," she replied. "My home is Aeropolis, in the Sky Realm."

"Calum." Magnus stared to the west. "Someone is coming."

All of their heads swiveled at once.

From the northwest, ten men approached them from deeper within the Golden Plains.

"Soldiers?" Calum reached for his sword, and so did Axel.

"No." Lilly shook her head. "They're the slave traders who abducted me."

"Do we run?" Calum asked.

"No, but back out of the field and into the clearing. If we run, they will continue following us. They want Lilly." Magnus turned to her as the four of them backed out of the grain. "Do not worry. I will not allow them to take you again."

"Me neither," Axel added with an overconfident smile.

Calum wanted to chime in as well, but it felt awkward to try to follow up Magnus's sincere promise and Axel's goofy addition. Instead, he gripped the handle of his sword tighter, but he didn't remove it from its sheath.

As the slave traders approached, Magnus squinted. "I do not believe it."

"What?" Axel looked at him.

"They are the same slave traders who captured me."

CHAPTER THIRTY-THREE

Calum studied the group of slave traders. He noticed four archers among them, which would make the forthcoming conflict more difficult if it came to blows.

"I recognize their leader," Magnus said. "His name is Roderick."

Axel shifted his stance. "You're so strong, though. How'd they even manage to capture you in the first place?"

"I was foolish. They had been pursuing me for days, and I had grown weary. I thought to steal a few hours of rest one night, so I headed into a cave where I expected I'd be safe. I was wrong."

"So *that's* why you don't like caves." Axel folded his arms.

Magnus glared at him. "In part, yes. While I was asleep, a dozen of them pinned me down with a large net, and Roderick held his sword to my neck. We Saurians can heal from a lot of wounds, but we cannot reliably recover from mortal wounds without true medical aid."

"That's how they caught me, too," Lilly said. "They tried to get me with a net. I almost escaped, but Roderick grabbed me."

"They are brutal, treacherous people." Magnus drew his sword and turned to Lilly. "Today marks their final day of oppressing you or anyone else. That, I promise."

The slave traders stopped at the edge of the grain, about twenty feet from where Calum and his friends stood in the clearing. One of them, a man almost as tall and as broad as Magnus, stepped forward. He had spiky red hair and brown armor.

"Well, well. I don't believe my eyes." He displayed a big white smile. "Never thought I'd see you again, Magnus."

Calum glanced at Magnus, who didn't move. The man must be Roderick.

"It *is* you, isn't it?" Roderick said. "I mean, all you Saurians look the same to me, but no one has blue armor quite like yours."

Magnus exhaled a long breath through his nostrils.

"Ah, and there's our prize. How's your shoulder, Angel?" Roderick winked at Lilly, and she withdrew behind Axel and Calum. "Oh, don't be afraid. We aren't gonna hurt you—anymore."

"Yeah, you just wanna sell her to the highest bidder," Axel said.

"You're absolutely correct." Roderick leveled his gaze at Axel. "She's my property, and I'll do with her what I please."

Calum glared at him. "She's *not* your property."

"I beg to differ." Roderick tilted his head. "When I found her, she was all alone. Cold and hungry. I rescued her, fed her, gave her shelter. I even—"

"You held her against her will." Calum's grip on his sword tightened again.

Roderick raised an eyebrow, then he shrugged. "What's the difference?"

Axel drew his sword and started toward him, but Magnus caught him by his collar.

"O-ho! Did I say something you didn't like?" Roderick held his hands out to his sides. "Hey, I'm not such a bad guy. I could've done anything I wanted to that girl after we found her. *Anything.*"

Axel strained against Magnus's grip, but he couldn't get free. Calum didn't blame him. He wanted to rip Roderick apart, too.

Roderick put his left palm out toward them. "Easy, easy. Like I said, I *could have* done anything I wanted to her, but I didn't. You know why?"

Calum's stomach churned. He didn't want to guess at the answer.

"Because I can get more gold for her if she's unspoiled."

Now Calum brandished his sword and took a step forward.

"*Calum.*"

Calum stopped, but he didn't take his eyes off Roderick.

"He is *mine*," Magnus rumbled.

Roderick squinted at him. "Is that right, Magnus? Because last I checked, *you* belonged to *me*, and I sold you to a group of the King's soldiers several leagues north of here."

Magnus just stared at him.

"But I'm willing to let you and your friends go if you hand over the girl."

"No," Calum and Axel said in unison.

Roderick frowned, then smirked. "The alternative, of course, is that I take her back after killing you and your two human friends."

"Try it," Axel said.

Magnus didn't move except to narrow his eyes and exhale a hiss through his flared nostrils.

"You know, I may not kill you three after all. Magnus still has plenty of value, and you boys have some flavor in an otherwise bland world. It's usually more of the King's purview to enslave humans, but in your cases, I think I'll stake my own claim."

Roderick drew his sword and motioned to his men. The four archers raised their bows and nocked arrows.

"Last chance," he said.

One of the archers yelped and dropped to the ground. An arrow protruded from his neck.

Everyone looked at Lilly, who stepped forward with a bow in her left hand and rubbing her injured shoulder with her right. "I'm *not* going back."

Roderick pointed his sword at her. "Go get her. Leave the lizard to me."

The three remaining archers launched their arrows, but Calum and Axel managed to dodge them.

Calum turned back to Lilly. "Stay back and cover us. We'll protect you."

She nodded and pulled another arrow from her quiver, wincing but undeterred.

The slave traders with swords charged past Magnus toward Axel and Calum. Axel parried the first blow that came at him then ducked under the second.

A slave trader swung his ax at Calum's head. He sidestepped the blow and cut the slave trader down with one vicious slice.

Another slave trader jabbed at him with a spear, and Calum parried the blow. The slave trader's second lunge seemed like an over-lunge at first, but at the last second, the slave trader drew a dagger from his belt with his left hand and jammed it at Calum's throat.

Calum blocked the stab with his sword and gripped the shaft of the slave trader's spear with his left. They locked in a grapple, but neither could overpower the other.

Something moved to Calum's right—one of the archers taking aim at him.

Calum shifted his weight and forced the slave trader to the right as the archer let loose another arrow. Instead of hitting Calum, it zipped through the air and plunged into the slave trader's lower back. He dropped his dagger and released his grip, and Calum ran him through.

As the archer drew another arrow from his quiver, Calum switched his sword to his left hand and snatched the spear from the dead slave trader's hands with his right. The archer let the arrow loose, and it whistled by Calum's ear.

The archer jerked another arrow from his quiver and nocked it in his bow as Calum cocked his right arm back. He'd been practicing his throwing technique ever since the fight with Tyburon, and he'd gotten pretty good at it. Now he'd find out if he could do it in the heat of battle.

The archer fired at Calum, who dove to the right. The arrow skipped off of Calum's left shoulder-plate as he hurled the spear. Calum hit the ground on his side, but the spear plunged into the archer's right thigh, and he also fell.

Calum jumped to his feet, charged over to the archer, and finished him off with his sword.

"Calum, behind you!" Axel's voice split the air.

Calum whirled around, but the incoming slave trader dropped face-first to the ground before Calum could react. An arrow protruded from the center of his back.

Twenty feet beyond the downed slave trader, Lilly lowered her bow and rubbed her injured shoulder again.

Pretty handy to have an archer on their side—especially one so pretty.

Calum smiled at her, perhaps a bit longer than he should have while in battle, then he engaged the next slave trader.

LILLY WATCHED A NOW-HATLESS Adgar and Gammel fall under Calum's and Axel's swords, respectively, along with the three remaining archers who'd attacked them as well, but Luggs had managed to get past them. Now he approached Lilly with his dagger in-hand—the same dagger he'd used to kill Colm.

A bandage around his shoulder bore a dark red stain from where her arrow had hit him last night. Luggs bared his revolting yellow smile at her as he stalked closer. "You're comin' back with me, and this time, you're mine. Now that Roderick's got his money, he's got no reason to stop me."

Lilly nocked an arrow and aimed for the center of his chest. This time, she would hit him with a killshot. "Not a chance."

She let it loose, but Luggs shifted his considerable weight out of the way, and the arrow disappeared into the sea of grain behind him. Lilly nocked another arrow, but Luggs had closed too much distance. She leaped into the air, pulled back her bowstring—

Luggs caught ahold of her ankle and jerked her downward.

Terror seized her chest, but she didn't let go of her arrow this time. She wouldn't go back. She couldn't. Luggs wouldn't get his filthy hands on her ever again.

As Luggs pulled her toward the ground, she adjusted her aim and stared him right in his wretched eyes.

"This is for Colm." Lilly let her arrow fly, little more than two feet from his face.

Luggs's eyes widened, and her arrow plunged into his left eye. His mouth hung open, he released his grip, and he toppled onto his back, dead.

Lilly shot three more arrows into his chest just to make sure.

EVER SINCE HE'D been captured, Magnus had yet to face a truly worthy opponent. Now, as he stalked toward Roderick, Magnus realized he might, in fact, be outmatched due to Roderick's hidden advantage—unless Roderick had rid himself of it.

"Do you really want to do this?" Roderick sashayed toward Magnus with his broadsword scraping the dirt behind him. "You know I'm at least as strong as you are. Maybe stronger."

"Are you?" Magnus challenged.

"I still have it. I haven't sold it like I told you I would." Roderick grinned and raised his sword, ready. "So you know I can kill you."

Magnus squinted at him. Regardless of Roderick's strength, Magnus couldn't let him continue to operate as a slave trader any longer. And more importantly, for the sake of all Saurians, he had to recover what was rightfully his. "If you have it, I will take it back from you."

"You're welcome to try." Roderick swung his sword.

Magnus blocked the attack, but the force of the blow shook his arms all the way up to his shoulders. *Unbelievable.*

Roderick swung again, and Magnus parried. They exchanged blows until Magnus ducked under a slash and whipped his tail at Roderick. It smacked against Roderick's shoulder and knocked him to the ground, but he recovered before Magnus could take the advantage.

"You always were a tricky one with that tail." Roderick clanked the pommel of his broadsword against his chest and smirked. "Strength or otherwise, I guess you still have that advantage, small as it may be."

He jabbed at Magnus, then moved in close. Magnus deflected Roderick's left fist with his elbow and halted Roderick's next slash by catching his wrist in his left hand. Roderick locked his left hand around Magnus's right wrist, and they grappled for control.

At first, Magnus controlled the struggle, but Roderick pushed back until Magnus's knees buckled. He growled and tried to wrench Roderick's arms to the left, but he couldn't.

Roderick smirked at him and delivered a kick to Magnus's chest that sent him skidding twenty feet back into the wheat field. Magnus jumped to his feet quickly, but found he didn't need to.

Roderick sauntered toward him, his broadsword down again, smiling.

Magnus glowered at him. Roderick had always been arrogant, but that would end today. Strength wasn't the only way to win a battle, especially against a stronger opponent. He would find a way to defeat Roderick.

Magnus leaped forward and swung his sword, but Roderick blocked the blow with his sword and delivered a stunning left hook that almost dislocated Magnus's jaw.

Roderick's sword knifed toward Magnus's gut. Had Magnus not shifted his body in time, it would have skewered him. Instead, the blade glanced off his abdominal armor.

Roderick pitched forward, and Magnus grabbed him by the throat. One jerk of his wrist, and—

A gauntleted fist smacked Magnus in the side of his head, and he lost his grip on Roderick. Then a kick under Magnus's chin blacked out his vision.

He swung his sword in a wild arc to put some distance between Roderick and himself, but his sword clanged against something hard.

When his vision reset, Magnus saw Roderick's broadsword flashing toward him. He ducked, but the blade smacked into his helmet.

The force of the blow alone would've killed Magnus if he hadn't been wearing his helmet, let alone the blade cleaving through his skull. As it was, he dropped his sword and toppled onto his side in the grain, stunned.

By the time Magnus regained his cognition, Roderick stood over him.

"Told you I was stronger." Roderick raised his sword over his head for a final slash.

CHAPTER THIRTY-FOUR

Magnus lurched upward and caught Roderick by his forearms, stalling his mighty overhead swing, but no matter how hard he pushed, Roderick's blade still sank toward his neck.

Magnus's tail swept Roderick's legs out from under him, but he landed on top of Magnus and mounted him, pinning him to the ground. All the while, the edge of Roderick's sword inched ever closer.

"I meant what I said, Magnus. I don't like to waste money." Beads of perspiration dotted Roderick's forehead. "Surrender. I'll let you live, and I'll sell you to someone nicer this time. You don't have to die."

"*Never.*" Magnus strained, but no matter how hard he pushed, no matter how considerable his Saurian strength was, he couldn't stop Roderick's pressure. The quivering sword continued to descend toward his throat.

No. He would *not* die here, not at the hands of a slave trader. Not before he reckoned with his past and with those who had harmed him. His vengeance would not stall today; Roderick would fall first, soon to be followed by the rest of Magnus's enemies.

"Strength cannot be the only asset you rely on in a fight." Magnus clenched his teeth and pushed back.

"Funny thing for you to say now, with my sword at your neck." Roderick laughed. "Looks like I'll always own you, one way or another."

"Remember..." Magnus strained to get the words out in time. "...how you said my tail was my only advantage?"

Roderick's gray eyes darted to Magnus's tail, which he'd already pinned down under his left knee. "Yeah?"

Magnus smirked. "You were wrong."

Roderick scowled. He jerked his sword down even harder, but at the same time, Magnus yanked Roderick's arms down toward his chest. Instead of it cleaving into his neck, the edge of the sword skidded off of Magnus's breastplate, and Roderick's torso pitched forward, toward Magnus's open jaws.

His teeth fastened on Roderick's exposed neck, and he bit down hard. Metallic blood splashed across Magnus's tongue, but he didn't release his vice grip on Roderick's throat.

Roderick gurgled, convulsed, and let go of his sword to try to tear Magnus's teeth from his neck, but it was already too late. Within seconds, he stopped moving altogether.

Magnus pushed him off and stood up. He spat out the blood in his mouth and stared down at his vanquished foe. "So much for you owning me."

He spat a glob of Roderick's blood in the dirt next to his head, then he reached down toward a pouch that hung from Roderick's belt.

———

CALUM BREATHED quick breaths as he and Axel finished off the rest of the slave traders. They made made eye contact, then turned back to Lilly. She nodded and slung her bow over her shoulder.

All in all, they'd made a pretty great team. Calum hoped she'd consider sticking around now that her pursuers were all dead. They could use her in spats like this.

Though, if he were honest, he would've wanted her around anyway.

"Come on." Calum had definitely grown accustomed to fighting—

he'd overcome the slave traders without much difficulty, especially compared to his fight with Tyburon. "Let's regroup with Magnus."

When they made it over to Magnus, he held an emerald the size of a grapefruit in his hands.

Even though Calum had spent the majority of his life harvesting precious stones from rocks, he couldn't help but gawk at it. The emerald was the biggest gemstone he'd ever seen. It was a rich dark-green color, so deep that the sunlight couldn't even reach its center.

"Where did you find *that?*" Axel's eyes widened.

"Roderick had it," Magnus replied.

"That'll fetch a small fortune. I could retire. We all could." Axel rubbed his hands together.

Magnus shook his head. "No chance."

Axel's brow furrowed. "Hey, the agreement is that we split whatever we find."

"Except this was mine to begin with," Magnus said.

Axel scoffed. "Yeah, right. How do I know you're not just saying that?"

Magnus glared at him.

"Fair enough." Axel nodded.

"What is it?" Lilly asked.

All three of them looked at her, and Magnus held it up. "This is one of the last Dragon Emeralds known to Kanarah."

"A Dragon Emerald?" Calum raised an eyebrow.

"Yes." Magnus stared at it. *Into* it.

Lilly leaned forward. "What does that mean?"

Magnus smiled. "Dragon Emeralds have three phases. This one is in its first phase. When in a human's possession, it amplifies their strength to that of a Saurian's, or even greater. That is why Roderick put up so much trouble when I was fighting him."

"Yeah, I saw that." Axel chuckled. "Looked like he was beating you senseless, Scales."

Magnus ignored him. "Once a Saurian reaches a certain point in development, he or she can use a Dragon Emerald to transform into a Sobek."

Calum and Axel stared at him, but Lilly nodded.

"That's the second phase of Saurian development," she said. "I've seen a few in Aeropolis before. Kahn sent them as emissaries to Avian, the Premier of the Windgales."

"Who's Kahn?" Calum asked.

Magnus's eyebrows arched down, and he exhaled a long hiss through his nostrils. "He rules Reptilius."

"And he's the only dragon in Kanarah, at least since Praetorius died about a year ago," Lilly said.

Silence hovered among them as they stared at the Dragon Emerald. As before, Calum knew there had to be more to the story, but he didn't want to ask. Magnus didn't seem to want to talk about it.

Calum glanced at Magnus. "So… can you use it?"

Magnus lifted his golden eyes to Calum's. "Perhaps."

"Perhaps?" Axel tilted his head. "You don't know?"

"My skin has hardened some, which means I am showing the necessary signs of growth—" Magnus shook his head. "—but I cannot be sure."

"So why don't you just try it?" Axel asked.

"I am not sure I'm ready."

"What happens if you try it and you're not ready?" Axel pressed.

Magnus shook his head. "I do not know. For all I've learned in my two hundred and three years, I never learned how to tell when I would be ready to use this. It is a carefully guarded secret."

"Wait. Stop." Axel shook his head. "You're two *hundred* years old?"

The news had come as a surprise to Calum, too, so much that he couldn't speak.

Magnus blinked at Axel. "Two hundred and three."

"*What?*" Axel almost screeched the word.

"Saurians live a long time," Lilly said. "Ten times longer than humans or Windgales. Before he died, Praetorius was over five hundred years old."

"Older," Magnus muttered.

Lilly glanced at him. "Really? I learned about him in—well, growing up. I was taught he was just over five-hundred. How old was he?"

"I never had occasion to ask him."

Silence reigned anew as Calum and Axel processed the news about Magnus's age.

"I thought you were forty," Axel finally said. "Maybe forty-five. But two *hundred?*"

"And three," Magnus added. "If it helps, just pretend I am forty. It makes no difference to me."

Axel raised his hands. "I don't know what to think anymore."

Calum had to agree with him, but even more so, he found new admiration for Magnus. It was pretty incredible that he'd lived so long, and Calum could only imagine the things he'd seen in his lifetime—things that Calum would only ever know as a part of history.

"What do you have to do to try it?" Lilly asked. "The emerald, I mean."

Magnus's tone lightened up, as if he were glad for the change of subject. "I hold it in my hands and press it against my bare chest."

Axel nudged him. "Do it. See what happens."

"No." Instead, Magnus dropped the Dragon Emerald in a leather pouch and tied it to his belt. "It does not feel right."

Axel rolled his eyes. "Whatever. I still think we should sell it."

Magnus turned to Lilly. "How does your shoulder feel?"

She gave him a half-smile, rotated her left shoulder, and winced, though not as dramatically as before. "Better. Thank you for your help. And thank you all for stopping Roderick and his men."

"Our pleasure." Calum couldn't help but smile at her.

Axel stepped in front of him. "*Anything* for you."

Calum's jaw tensed, but Lilly's smile quelled the frustration rising in his chest.

"You're welcome to come with us, if you like. We're heading across the Valley within the next week or so," Axel said. "We can make sure you get there safely."

Lilly nodded. "I'd like that."

"Great." Axel smiled.

Calum thought he looked like an idiot, but he was also glad Axel had asked her to join them. He wasn't sure he would've found the courage if it had fallen to him.

"Let us collect our bags of food, loot the slave traders for weapons and supplies, and get out of here." Magnus's head swiveled. "I do not care to linger here any longer than we must. If any soldiers show up, count on a multitude of trouble."

They spread out and began to gather what supplies they could. With a sack in his hand, Calum approached one of the downed slave traders but stopped short when he moaned.

Calum brandished his sword, but the slave trader just lay on the ground with his hand on his forehead. Calum set down his pack and walked over to him. Better to put him out of his misery than to let him suffer.

Calum stopped short when he noticed a sword that resembled a large meat cleaver on the ground next to the slave trader. Now that he'd stepped closer, Calum recognized the slave trader's dark-green armor, his curly black hair, and his dark eyes.

Sure enough, there, staring up at him, was none other than Nicolai, the bandit he'd allowed to go free after defeating Tyburon.

"Axel?" Calum called. "Come over here. You're not gonna believe this."

When Axel saw Nicolai's face, his eyes widened. "You've gotta be kidding me."

Upon seeing them, Nicolai exhaled a breath and closed his eyes. "Oh, no."

"So much for promising to stay out of trouble," Axel said. "He stops being a bandit and ends up a slave trader. He couldn't have done much worse with his second chance."

Nicolai opened his eyes and rubbed his forehead with another moan.

"Well, I guess this time we have to finish him off." Axel unsheathed his sword, and Nicolai let out a yelp.

"Wait." Calum's hand kept Axel from swinging. "He's unarmed, and he's mostly harmless. We can't just kill him."

"His weapon's right there." Axel huffed and didn't lower his sword.

"Calum, you need to move. This lurch had his chance. *Two* of them. He wasted them both. His time has come."

"You're not killing him, Axel." Calum's firm voice sounded more convincing to him each time he employed it, and he'd employed it a lot recently.

"Who's gonna stop me?" Axel scoffed. "You?"

Calum had no desire to measure sword lengths with Axel. Instead, he said, "Maybe the reason he keeps falling in with a bad crowd is because he doesn't know any good people."

Axel eyed him. "What are you suggesting?"

"I'm not saying we're the purest souls around, but we're certainly not slave traders or bandits." Calum tilted his head and stared down at Nicolai, who moaned again. "Maybe if we bring him with us, we'll rub off on him. Maybe there's hope for Nicolai yet."

Axel had started shaking his head even before Calum finished talking. "No way. He's not coming with us."

Calum waved Lilly over, then he refocused on Axel. "You need to start looking for the good in people, Axel. When we started out, you didn't want to travel with Magnus just because he was a Saurian."

"Yeah, and now we get along *so well*."

Lilly walked over and stood near them, her eyes locked on Nicolai. She seemed ready to bolt into the sky if he so much as looked at her wrong.

"My point is that Magnus, even though *you* may not like him, is valuable to the group. He's saved both of our lives on countless occasions." Calum stared down at Nicolai. "Who knows what Nicolai might become if we spare him?"

"If we finish him off, I know for a fact he won't be a bandit or a slave trader anymore."

Calum sighed. Magnus started toward them from a couple dozen yards away, where he'd been sifting through a slave trader's pack.

"Am I allowed to say something?" Nicolai raised his hand from his forehead a few inches, revealing a nasty red bump.

"*No.*" Axel pointed his blade at Nicolai.

"Yes," Calum countered.

Nicolai gave him a slight nod. "Please don't kill me. I know I made a mistake by joining this bunch of—"

"Got that right," Axel muttered. He folded his arms but still held onto his sword.

"—of slave traders, but this is the only type of life I know." Nicolai swallowed and sat up, his dark eyes fixed on Calum. "I'd be honored to join your group, if that's what you're offering."

Axel rolled his eyes. "You've gotta be kidding me."

Calum glanced at Lilly, then he focused on Magnus, who stopped short when he noticed Nicolai on the ground.

"Is that who I think it is?" Magnus squinted at him.

"Yeah. We were just discussing how we should kill him," Axel said.

"Actually, we were discussing how he might join our group." Calum cleared his throat and looked at Lilly. "If that's alright with you, Lilly."

She glanced between Magnus, Calum, and Nicolai. "He was new to Roderick's outfit. He didn't mistreat me, but I'm not inclined to trust him. I put him out with Aliophos Nectar when I was escaping. I could've killed him then, but I didn't." She exhaled a sharp sigh. "I hate to say it, but maybe there's a reason for that."

"Right, but he's still one of them, and he was a bandit before that." Axel raised an eyebrow at her. "Surely you don't want him traveling with us after all of that."

Lilly stared at Nicolai. "Like I said, I don't trust him—"

"Me neither." Axel raised his sword again, and Nicolai recoiled.

Lilly stepped between them. "—but we can't just execute him. We all make mistakes. If he wants to change, he will. Everyone deserves a second chance. "

"Last time *was* his second chance," Axel muttered.

"I want to change." Nicolai nodded. "Believe me, I *want* to change."

"Really?" Axel huffed and lowered his sword. "Come on, guys. You don't actually believe him, do you?"

"Here's how I see it," Calum said. "Either he changes, or he's on his own again. It's only a matter of time before he meets a foul end with the way he's been living."

"Yeah, like right now," Axel grumbled.

"Please give me a chance. I'll show you I can be different." Nicolai tentatively stood to his feet and stepped toward Calum, then he turned to Lilly. "I was just following orders. I'm so sorry. I won't do wrong by you anymore."

Lilly rubbed her wounded shoulder. "We'll see."

"You mess up, we toss you out on your own." Calum glanced at Magnus, who nodded, then he looked back at Nicolai. "Crystal?"

"Clear," Nicolai replied.

Calum extended his hand. "Welcome to the group, Nicolai."

THAT NIGHT, Commander Anigo tugged on the reins, and Candlestick slowed to a halt. Sure enough, as the message had read, he found the moonlit bodies of nine slain men near the western edge of the Golden Plains.

He'd only taken five soldiers to investigate the claims of the farm-hand who'd deserted his post to deliver the news. He left the rest under Corporal Jopheth with orders to watch all of Kanarah City's gates at all times should they return. They were to be killed on sight if necessary, or captured if possible.

Under almost any other circumstances, he would've had the farm-hand thrashed, but instead, Commander Anigo wrote him a decree that granted him the remainder of the day off. The catch, of course, was that he had to show Commander Anigo the location of the bodies.

"You said you saw the fight?" Commander Anigo asked.

The farmhand—Commander Anigo hadn't bothered to learn his name—stood at the edge of the fields and rubbed his arms. The night wind carried a harsher chill with it than previous nights, and the farm-hand had neglected to don a shirt before running to Kanarah City.

"Yes, sir." He shivered. "Heard metal clashing. Knew somethin' was up. Ran over to see what was happenin' and caught the end of it."

Commander Anigo's eyes narrowed. "What did you see?"

The farmhand rubbed his shoulders. "Looked like a bunch of men swingin' weapons around. I didn't care to get too close. Hid in the grain. Safer there."

"The winners—did you see them?"

"Yeah. There was a girl with them. I think she was a Windgale. Saw her flyin' around at one point. Either that or she can jump higher than anyone I ever seen."

Captain Fulton's killer? The slave girl?

If so, then these slain men might've been the slave traders responsible for the debacle at the auction. Had they chased her and run into some other force? Surely she hadn't slain nine strong men on her own. "What else?"

"I saw two armored men and a Saurian."

Commander Anigo's eyes widened. "Which way did they go?"

The farmhand's teeth clicked. "They headed west, toward the road."

Commander Anigo urged Candlestick to face west. Had his three outlaws come to the aid of the Windgale girl? If they had left together, he'd be hunting four fugitives instead—convenient, given Captain Fulton's untimely death.

If Commander Anigo could bring all four of them to justice in one fell swoop, he was assured a glorious return to Solace, indeed. Perhaps even a promotion; after all, he'd been eligible for promotion to captain for nearly a year now.

"That's all I saw, sir. Do you—can I go home now?"

"You are released." Commander Anigo glanced back and saw the farmhand disappear into the grain. He turned to two of the soldiers accompanying him. "You two, go with him. Make sure he returns to his assigned post. I don't intend to chase another escaped worker."

The soldiers nodded and rode their horses after the farmhand.

Commander Anigo looked at the two other soldiers accompanying him. He pointed at one of them. "You, ride back to Kanarah City and have Corporal Jopheth ready a platoon of soldiers for a long-term search." He pointed to the other one. "You, come with me."

As the other soldier rode north, the remaining soldier asked, "Where are we going, sir?"

Commander Anigo faced the mountains to the west. "We're going after them."

―――――――

AT THEIR CAMPSITE for the night, Calum sat on Lilly's left, constantly battling his emotions and feelings. Part of him was thrilled to be sitting next to her, another part was terrified of saying something stupid to her, and another part was enraged that Axel was sitting closer to her than he was—much too close to her for Calum's comfort.

Across from Calum sat Magnus, and Nicolai sat next to him, dabbing at the bump on his head with ginger fingers.

"So, unfortunately, we cannot just walk into Kanarah City and head straight to Trader's Pass," Magnus concluded the story of their journey from the quarry all the way through their rooftop escape from Kanarah City. He clacked his talons against his breastplate. "We cannot risk the soldiers recognizing us."

"But now that you're here—and Nicolai, too, I guess—we can get across." Axel winked at Lilly.

Calum noticed it and wanted to knock the smug expression off his face.

"I would not go that far, Axel," Magnus said. "Even if we divided up and entered the Pass using Lilly and Nicolai as extra people to throw off the soldiers, and even if I removed my armor, it is still a considerable risk. I would rather not put Lilly in any more danger, especially considering what she has just endured."

Lilly smiled at him. "Thank you, but I'm capable of handling myself."

"Forgive me. I did not mean to suggest otherwise." Magnus turned to Nicolai and sighed. "And Nicolai... well, I fear we cannot fully trust you yet."

Nicolai shrugged. "I'm not offended. I know I'm good at ruining things."

"So what are we gonna do?" Calum asked. "Try to go individually?"

Axel leaned forward. "We could try to—"

"Shh," Magnus hissed, his golden eyes wide. "I hear something."

Calum and Axel froze.

A low growl emanated from the darkness on the north side of the camp.

All five of them jumped to their feet and drew their weapons.

Out of the darkness emerged a mass of gray-and-brown fur with four legs, two light-blue eyes, a black canine nose, and sharp white teeth.

The Wolf had returned.

CHAPTER THIRTY-FIVE

When the Wolf emerged from the shadows, Calum had expected Lilly to cling to his arm or take cover behind him—or worst case, she'd cling to or hide behind Axel instead of him.

But instead of doing either of those things, she snatched her bow into her hand, nocked an arrow, and took aim at the Wolf.

At first, Calum didn't know how to react. He glanced at her, looked at the Wolf, then repeated the motion until Axel took Lilly by her arm and pulled her away. She glanced at him, confused, then relaxed the tension in her draw.

"Get behind me, Lilly." Axel ushered her back, then stepped between her and the Wolf with his sword in hand.

Calum shot a glare at Axel, but he didn't seem to notice.

"There's no need to be alarmed."

Calum blinked. Had the Wolf actually just *spoken?*

Magnus stepped forward. "You are not welcome here, *thief.*"

The Wolf growled at him, low but more annoyed than threatening. "Believe me. If I could be anywhere else, I'd be there. But you know the Law as well as I do."

Axel shifted his stance. "Law?"

A sharp sigh exhaled from the Wolf's mouth. "You humans created the Law—or at least your King did—and you don't even know it?"

Axel eyed Calum, but he could only shrug. He was still trying to figure out how the Wolf could talk. Magnus had called them intelligent beings, but he hadn't mentioned they could *talk* too.

"He means the Law of Debt." Magnus lowered his sword but didn't sheathe it. "If anyone saves the life of another, the one rescued is indebted to the rescuer for the remainder of his life. Not as a servant, but as a comrade."

Calum smirked. He'd saved the lives of both Axel and Magnus multiple times, and they'd saved him as well. Apparently that meant they were indebted to each other forever.

Magnus focused on Calum and smiled. "And as a friend. The bond is only broken upon mutual release, death, or betrayal—and betrayal is only acceptable if one party becomes an agent of evil. As children, Saurians are taught this Law above all others. I suspect it is the same for the Wolf tribes.

"Even so, not everyone subscribes to or follows the Law strictly, which is perhaps why you have never heard of it," Magnus continued. "And your upbringing in such a remote area of Kanarah was doubtless a hindrance as well. In any case, the Law is upheld by those who choose to do so, and it is incumbent on the one who was saved to accept the terms or not."

The Wolf nodded. His voice flattened, and he stared at Calum. "So... I'm here to fulfill my duty."

Calum raised an eyebrow, but he also lowered his sword. "And since I saved you from Magnus's sword, your duty is to me?"

The Wolf nodded again, somehow managing to frown—another thing Calum didn't know Wolves could do. "Yeah."

"Do you still have any of the property you took from us?" Calum asked.

"Um... no?" The Wolf squinted at him. "Why would I?"

"So you spent *all* the coin and ate *all* the food?" Axel glared at him.

The Wolf tilted his head. "A dog's gotta eat."

Calum sighed, sheathed his sword, and stared into the Wolf's sky-blue eyes. He motioned toward the rest of the group. "We've all saved each other more than once, but no formal obligation binds us. So I release you from your debt, if you so desire."

"I... uh..." The Wolf glanced between them. His eyes lingered the longest on Axel, who still held his sword in his hands as if he meant to cleave the Wolf in two. "I guess I'll be going, then."

Magnus followed suit with Calum and also sheathed his sword, and so did Axel. Lilly replaced her arrow in her quiver, and Nicolai sat back down near the fire. His new sword, one he'd taken from a dead slave trader to replace his old meat cleaver, hadn't even made it out of its sheath.

After a few steps, the Wolf turned back. "You know, I could be of use to you guys. I'm fast. I can hide in the dark. I'm good at stealing stuff."

"Yeah, we figured all of that out already," Axel said, his voice edged with sarcasm.

"You said you would rather be anywhere else but here, yet now you do not wish to leave?" Magnus asked. "Which is it?"

The Wolf's mouth hung open. "Well, I mean... I don't have much else going on."

"So you figure you'll just stay here with us?" Axel folded his arms.

The Wolf growled at him then sat his rear down like any normal dog would. He was definitely larger than any normal dog Calum had ever seen, but he didn't strike Calum as being especially large for a Wolf. In fact, he seemed somewhat on the small side from what Calum would've expected.

"Seems you could use someone like me in your group, especially if you actually wanna get to Trader's Pass."

Calum glanced at Magnus. "What makes you think we need to get to Trader's Pass?"

With another sigh, the Wolf rolled his eyes. "I just overheard you talking about it. Plus, I heard you talking about it the night the Saurian almost killed me. And the night you let me steal your first bag of money. And the night you killed the sabertooth cats. It's pretty much all you guys talk about."

Calum held up his hand. "Alright, we get it. You've been following us for awhile now."

"And robbed you twice, successfully."

Axel huffed. "And you failed once, spectacularly."

The Wolf growled at him.

"Let's get back on topic," Calum said. "You're right that we have to get to Trader's Pass. If you've been listening to us, then you know what we're up against. So how can you help us get past the King's soldiers and to the pass?"

"Simple," the Wolf said. "There's a secret path to get there."

Axel tilted his head. "There is?"

"No," Magnus said. "If there were another way to access the pass, I would have known about it."

The Wolf scoffed. "I don't think I'd be calling it a 'secret' path if a lot of normal people knew about it."

Magnus folded his arms. "What makes you presume I am normal?"

"Alright," the Wolf said, "what makes you different from any other Saurian?"

Magnus didn't say anything.

The Wolf raised one of his front paws, just like a dog begging for a treat. "It's like I said: the path is secret."

"Then how do *you* know about it?" Axel asked.

"It's how I got here from across the valley without drawing a lot of attention to myself. Also, some of my tribe helped dig the tunnels long, long ago."

"Tunnels?" Calum looked at Magnus. "There are tunnels?"

The Wolf growled. "Shouldn't have told you that. Look, even if you find them, there's only one path that actually connects from Kanarah City to Trader's Pass. The rest? Well, you'd probably rather not find out where they lead."

"Wait, wait." Axel held up his hand. "You said the secret path leads to Trader's Pass. Now you're saying it's in Kanarah City? I thought we were gonna bypass Kanarah City."

"Then you thought wrong." The Wolf shook his head. "I never said I could help you avoid Kanarah City. I said I could help you get to Trader's Pass via a secret path that very few people know about. You access it through the city's sewers."

"He's right," Lilly said.

Everyone turned toward her.

"Roderick and his men brought me over the valley on Trader's Pass along with some other slaves. At one point, they blindfolded us and took us on a secret path. I knew we'd gone underground by the horrible smell and the lack of wind, and we eventually wound up in the city's sewers before they brought us out. He's telling the truth."

"Nicolai?" Calum asked. "Have you ever been in those tunnels?"

Nicolai shook his head. "No, but Roderick and some of the other slave traders mentioned them a few times. I joined after they'd already made it over to this side of Kanarah, literally only a few days ago. My opinion? I think he's telling the truth."

"Well, no one asked *you*," Axel sneered.

"Cut it out, Axel." Calum shot a glare at him. "Nicolai made mistakes, but you need to start treating him like a member of the group nonetheless."

Axel scowled back at him. "Whatever."

Nicolai gave Calum a grateful nod.

"I'm... not touching that one." The Wolf gave Lilly a nod. "She's right that some slave traders have been known to use the secret path."

"Helps them avoid the King's soldiers, right?" Calum said.

"It would be awful hard to bring slaves through Kanarah City's west gate." The Wolf scratched behind his left ear with his left hind paw. "It's not unheard of, though. Certain guards will accept bribes, for example."

The five of them stared at the Wolf.

"But... that's not really pertinent right now, I guess."

"How far does the tunnel go?" Magnus asked. "Where in the sewers does it start, and where does it end?"

"Depends on which direction you're going."

Magnus glared at him. "You know what I am asking."

The Wolf exhaled another sharp sigh. "You access it through the sewers on the western side of Kanarah City, and it ends about five miles along the pass."

Magnus turned to Lilly. "Does that sound about right?"

"I can't say for sure on the distance, but the stench down there started out like death and gradually changed to more of a sewer-type stink before they brought us above ground," she replied. "And it took several hours from the time we entered the tunnels to the time we got out."

"Like I said, though, you need a guide to make sure you don't go the wrong way." The Wolf stood on all fours and walked past the campfire toward one of the bags of food. He pawed at the opening with his front right paw until an apple fell out onto the ground.

Axel snatched it away before the Wolf could get a bite and then he cinched the bag shut. "That's not for you."

The Wolf growled at him. "Don't you think that all the information I just gave you is worth one little apple?"

"Sure, puppy." Axel held the apple out in his hand, but yanked it away when the Wolf tried to take it with his teeth. "Ah, ah. Do you know how to play fetch?"

The Wolf half-barked, half-snarled at Axel, who startled, dropped the apple, and jumped back. The Wolf bit into it, reclined back on his haunches to lie on his stomach, and dropped it between his front forelegs.

While Axel swore and cursed, the others chuckled. Axel's glare landed on each of them before it stalled on Nicolai.

"No, I don't play fetch." The Wolf licked his chops. "Just be glad I'm not insisting on *meat* instead."

"Don't *ever* do that again. You hear me?" Axel pointed his finger at him, but the Wolf just rolled his eyes and started gnawing on his apple.

"What else is in those tunnels?" Magnus asked. "The ones that don't lead to the exits?"

The Wolf raised his head between bites. "Whatever it is, it's not something nice. Better if we don't run into it. I've heard of men going in and never coming back out, and the ones who survived to tell about it weren't in great shape, either."

After a long pause, Calum looked at Magnus. "Well, what do you think? Can we trust him?"

Magnus released a long sigh through his nose. "I do not like him, and I do not trust him. I think he is a treacherous cheat and a thieving fleabag who—"

"You do realize I'm sitting here in front of you, right?" The Wolf eyed Magnus. "Even if I didn't have exceptional hearing, which I do, I could still hear everything you're saying about me because you're standing like five feet away from me."

"—but I think he may be the only chance we have for getting to the pass without causing a ruckus that could get us killed," Magnus continued, unfazed. "Right now, I cannot conceive of a better option. I say we do it."

Calum nodded. He faced Axel.

"Don't look at me." Axel held up his hands. "My response is going to be the same as usual: whatever."

"What about you, Lilly?" Calum asked.

She shrugged. "I don't want to mess up your plans or anything, but I want to get home. If you're telling me that going through the west gate won't work—well, I'm not thrilled about going back into those tunnels, but I'd rather do it with all of you.

"Besides that, the trip across the valley is too long and too dangerous for me to make alone, and since you're already planning to head across, it makes sense for us to stay together. After my escape, the King's soldiers might be looking for me, too, so a few more blades on my side wouldn't hurt, either." Lilly concluded, "So I'm in."

"Any thoughts, Nicolai?" Calum asked.

"Uh…" Nicolai stared at him, and Axel scoffed. Nicolai glanced at him for a moment then refocused on Calum. "I'm just along for the ride. No one wants to hear what I think anyway."

"That's not true," Calum said, specifically to spite Axel. "It's like I just told Axel—you're a part of this group now. It means you have a say."

"I agree. Tell us your opinion." Magnus's reptilian gaze fixed on Nicolai.

Nicolai swallowed and ran his fingers through his curly black hair. "Based on what you already told me about your run-ins with the soldiers in Kanarah City and before that, I don't think you—*we* oughta risk running into them again."

"So you'd rather take your chances with whatever's killing people in those tunnels?" Axel folded his arms then nodded at the Wolf. "And with this Wolf, who robbed us twice?"

Nicolai shrugged. "He didn't rob *me*."

"No, I guess he didn't." Axel scowled at him. "It'd be too ironic for a thief to rob a bandit."

"I think it's clear what we've decided." Time to change the subject before Axel got any more riled up. Calum looked at the Wolf. "What's your name?"

"Riley."

Calum moved next to him and extended his right hand. "Welcome to the group, Riley."

Riley stared at Calum for a moment, then he sat up, reached out his right front paw, and placed it in Calum's open palm. "Glad to be here."

"How soon can we leave?" Calum asked.

"How soon will you be ready to go?" Riley lay back down and chomped into his apple again.

THE NEXT MORNING, Commander Anigo and the soldier with him crouched on the edge of a rock face. Far below them, six figures moved through the sunlit trees. He couldn't quite make them out, though he thought he glimpsed a Wolf traveling with the group, three men, and a distinctly feminine shape with blonde hair and pink armor.

When he noticed a set of vivid blue armor covering a green torso and tail, he knew he'd found them. They were heading north, toward Kanarah City.

But Commander Anigo and the soldiers in Kanarah City would be ready for them.

He got up and led the soldier to their horses. They mounted them and galloped down the mountain with abandon.

Soon he'd bring them all to justice. Soon he'd be restored to his former glory in Solace.

THE TREK from the mountains back to Kanarah City took a couple of days, and the group waited until nightfall again before they tried to re-enter the city. Riley knew a secret way into the city through an old drainage tunnel, so they avoided both the gates and the soldiers who stood guard there altogether.

They half-walked, half-jogged through the city under the moonlight. A few people moved about in the streets, but far fewer than in the daytime. Those who did were mostly drunks, vagrants, and beggars. Thanks to Riley's knowledge of the city's standard patrol routes and times, they managed to avoid running into any soldiers as well.

Riley led them on a complex but covert path to the city's west side through secluded back alleys and in the shadows of buildings. He finally stopped at a rusty iron grate at the bottom of a hill with a large pit just beyond. The opening behind the grate was barely wide enough for two large men to walk through if they stood side-by-side.

Calum's nose threatened rebellion at the stench. "This is the way into the sewers, I take it?"

Lilly's nose wrinkled. "I recognize the smell."

Riley let out a short, sharp sigh, something Calum had grown accustomed to but still didn't appreciate. "Yes, Calum."

"This is an overflow outlet," Magnus said. "Reptilius has a similar setup. If the area ever floods and the sewage rises, it flows out here and wherever else it gets too high, and it fills that pit. The stench is perpetually foul, but it keeps the sewage from ever rising to street level."

Axel tugged on the grate, and it barely moved. "You'd need at least two strong men to get this thing open. How did you get in and out?"

"I only came out of there once, and I haven't gone back in since. When I did come out, I waited for someone else to come along, and I just snuck out behind them before it could close. I think they were slave traders."

"It does not behoove us to waste any time. I would rather the soldiers—or anyone else—not realize what we are doing." Magnus reached for the grate. "I will open it, and you five can go inside. Then I will ensure it shuts behind us."

What would've been a challenge for Calum and Axel looked easy when Magnus did it. While Nicolai gawked at him, Magnus pulled the heavy grate open, hefting it over his head with ease and holding until all of them made it inside, and then he shut it in perfect silence.

Calum extended his hand toward Riley. "Lead the way."

COMMANDER ANIGO DROPPED a small pouch into Wandell Thirry's hand. "Your cooperation is much appreciated, Mr. Thirry."

"It's my pleasure, Commander." Thirry stirred the silver coins inside the pouch with his index finger adorned with a silver ring that shone under the moonlight. "And we agree that you'll make an introduction to your replacement when he arrives from Solace?"

"Gladly." Commander Anigo forced a smile.

Dealing with underworld scum wasn't something he was accustomed to anymore, and he'd forgotten how greasy it made him feel. In Solace, he'd already forced the disbanding of every major criminal enterprise, but here in Kanarah City, dealing with undesirable people seemed necessary to accomplish anything of significance.

In any case, Corporal Jopheth had recommended Thirry—which certainly said something about Corporal Jopheth—and Thirry had shown him the entrance to the tunnels under the city, originating almost five miles beyond the city's west gate along Trader's Pass.

It was a hunch, and nothing more, but if the fugitives he'd been chasing meant to use the tunnels to bypass his soldiers, they'd certainly be in for a surprise.

But in his exceptional career, his hunches had more often than not proven to be the deciding factor between success and failure. He wasn't about to abandon his instincts now, after they'd served him so well so many times in the past.

319

"Two of my men will escort you back into the city along the pass." Commander Anigo would've just as soon had his men kill Thirry and leave him along the pass as a message to other underworld slime seeking to avoid dealing with the King's men, but for now, he elected to let Thirry go.

Until his mission was complete, Commander Anigo couldn't be sure he was done dealing with Thirry. The thought of having to engage the man in the future brewed like soured stew in Commander Anigo's stomach, but he would no sooner discard a useful tool because it was covered in grime.

Needs, not wants.

"Many thanks, Commander. I hope your excursion is as profitable for you as it has been for me." Thirry smiled, and his white teeth almost glowed in the moonlight. His white hair certainly did.

Two of the soldiers mounted horses, Thirry mounted another, and they rode off toward the city.

Given the narrow opening and the steep decline into the tunnels, Commander Anigo had left Candlestick back in the army barracks stable for safekeeping. It meant that on this mission, he could only rely on himself. The pain in his chest from his last encounter with these fugitives no longer ached as it did, but it still ached enough to reinforce his caution this time around.

Commander Anigo looked at the twenty remaining men he'd brought with him, half of whom held burning torches, and said, "One lit torch for every four men, plus one near me. We'll find a place to hide, then we'll ambush them."

The soldiers nodded, and half of them snuffed their torches.

"Let's go." Commander Anigo led them down the dark stone stairs into the tunnels.

CHAPTER THIRTY-SIX

Calum and the others followed Riley through the labyrinth of the Kanarah City sewers, all while wielding makeshift torches. Even though they walked along a rocky slab next to the slow-flowing river of waste in the center, muck and waste still clung to their boots. At times the stench grew so pungent that Calum almost vomited.

At one point, Axel stumbled and planted his hand against a brick wall to brace himself, but the ancient brick wall crumbled under the pressure, and his hand went through it instead. A few dozen rats poured out over his shoulders and skittered away in the sludge.

Axel yelped and whooped and danced away from them, and he lost his torch in the river of sewage in the process.

"There you go, screaming like a girl again." Magnus glanced at Lilly. "No offense, Lilly."

She laughed and shook her head. "None taken."

Axel called down a curse on the rats, then he glared at Magnus. "Yeah? Let's see how you react when a thousand rats jump out at *you* in a dark sewer."

"I will do one better." Magnus walked over to the hole Axel had just inadvertently made in the wall, stuck his hand inside, and pulled out a thick rat almost the length of Calum's forearm. "Lilly, you may wish to turn away for this part."

She pursed her lips and then complied.

As soon as Lilly's back was turned, Magnus dropped the rat into his mouth and crunched down on it with his pointed teeth. He swallowed it in two gulps.

Nicolai covered his mouth with his hand. "Did I really just see that?"

Axel closed his eyes and moaned. "I think I'm gonna throw up."

"Me too," Calum said.

"I dunno what the problem is," Riley said. "It's just meat. Not good meat, but meat nonetheless."

"Can I turn around now?" Lilly asked.

"Yes, it's over." Magnus licked his lips with his long red tongue.

She wrinkled her nose at him.

Magnus smirked. "Saurians are inherently carnivorous, but we can function on an omnivorous diet if we need to. Rodents make for a pretty standard meal on the streets in Reptilius."

"That's disgusting." Axel shook his head and covered his mouth with his hand. "I gotta keep moving. Come on."

Magnus just grinned.

A half-dozen turns later, Riley stopped in front of a large opening.

Calum and Magnus came up beside him and held their torches ahead to get a better look while Axel stood behind them with Lilly and Nicolai. Calum would've preferred to stand by Lilly, but with only two torches left, he had to stay near the front so they could see where they were going.

Even so, he preferred to have Axel with Lilly when around Nicolai, just in case. Nicolai had proven trustworthy so far, but it had only been a few days.

The torches revealed an opening about twenty feet high and twice as wide that narrowed to a tunnel about fifteen feet high and thirty feet wide farther inside.

"This is it." Riley sat down and scratched behind his left ear with his corresponding hind foot.

"This is a huge opening. How do more people not know about this?" Axel asked.

Riley exhaled another one of those short sharp sighs. "It's really not that complicated. We're in the sewer. Not many people come down here for evening promenades. It's also in a specific place inside the sewer.

"Sure, you might stumble upon it after a long search, but again, who just walks around a sewer for fun? Plus, it's dark down here. You could walk right past it and never know it. And on top of all that—"

"Alright, alright." Axel held up his hand. "I gotta be honest. You lost me at 'promenades.'"

"It means 'taking a walk,'" Riley explained, aggravated.

"The path is massive," Nicolai said.

"Scared?" Axel asked.

Nicolai turned to him, wearing the beginning of a scowl. "A little bit, yeah."

Axel rolled his eyes.

Riley nodded toward the opening. "Once we get inside, we go for about ten miles in pitch-black tunnels. Then we climb some makeshift stairs carved into the rocks before we finally pop out a little less than five miles west of Kanarah City along Trader's Pass."

Calum nodded. "Let's go."

"Remember," Riley said. "Stay close, and follow me. If you go the wrong way or step somewhere you shouldn't, you might as well be dead, so pay attention, and walk where I'm walking. Crystal?"

Everyone else nodded and followed Riley inside the enormous tunnel.

Nicolai hung back next to Calum while they walked. "Calum, I just wanted to tell you again how grateful I am that you spared my life. I really—I don't want to live my life that way anymore, so this second-second chance means a lot to me."

Calum smiled. He found it interesting how someone only a few years older than him had already found so much trouble this early in his life. "I'm happy you feel that way, Nicolai."

"Look, as far as I'm concerned, I'm indebted to you forever, just like what that Wolf was saying back at the camp." Nicolai unsheathed his sword.

The action set Calum on his guard at first, but Nicolai didn't threaten him with the weapon, though he did wave it around a bit.

"And I'm glad Magnus made me leave that old meat cleaver behind," he said. "This sword hardly weighs anything by comparison."

"I held that cleaver of yours after Magnus made you drop it, just to see how heavy it was," Calum said. "Honestly, I can't imagine how you or anyone not as strong as a Saurian could wield something like that. The blade was dull too."

Nicolai chuckled. "No wonder I was never any good in a fight."

"Have you had any training of any sort?"

"Not really." Nicolai shook his head. "I'm pretty observant though. Picked up a few moves from Tyburon and Norm, but they mostly kept me on menial tasks. I'm not what you'd call athletic by any means."

"Don't worry. With our luck, you'll get some experience in no time."

"Yeah, or I'll be dead in no time."

"Don't think like that." Calum patted Nicolai's shoulder, still a bit wary of his unsheathed sword. If Nicolai tired anything, at least Calum had his torch in hand. He could probably fend Nicolai off until the others came to help if it came to it. "We're a team. We watch out for each other. Sometimes we even bleed for each other. Just remember, we're here to help you."

Nicolai pursed his lips and sheathed his sword. His voice lowered, he said, "I don't think Axel feels the same way you do. Frankly, if a venomous spider was crawling on my nose, I don't think he'd walk three steps to punch me in the face."

Calum grinned. "He might surprise you with that one. He really hates spiders."

"You know what I mean. He doesn't like me."

"Yeah, I know." He stared at Axel's back as he walked next to Lilly. Together, they followed Magnus and Riley, while Calum and Nicolai brought up the rear.

When Axel's hand brushed against Lilly's arm, Calum wanted to charge forward and step between them, but he resisted the urge. He still didn't exactly know how he should behave around Lilly, but he knew enough to realize that kind of reaction wouldn't do him any good.

"So…" Nicolai started. "Any suggestions on how I can get on his good side?"

Calum refocused on Nicolai. He'd been happy to bring Nicolai along, but he hadn't expected so much conversation.

"Just give him time," Calum said. "He was grumpy when we started out on this journey, and he's still grumpy now. It's kind of just how he is. He didn't like Magnus, he doesn't like Riley, and most of the time I'm not sure he even likes me, even though I'm supposed to be his best friend. So far Lilly's the only one he's really taken an interest in."

Nicolai smirked and nudged Calum's armored ribs. "Can't blame him there."

Had Nicolai injected sleaze into his comment, Calum would've decked him with the burning end of the torch, but he'd said it so it didn't convey anything threatening or ominous at all. He'd said it very matter-of-fact, as if he had agreed to Calum's assessment of the weather or something equally mundane.

Nicolai stammered, "N-not that I'm thinking of—"

"I know what you meant, Nicolai." Calum exhaled a quiet breath and glared at Axel from behind again. "She is beautiful. That's for sure."

As they walked, every so often they had to adjust their path to avoid the occasional hole in the floor. Where they'd come from or how they got there, Calum had no idea, but he didn't want to get too close to any of them to investigate, either. With a burning torch in his hand, he had more than enough light to avoid them, and that was good enough for now.

"Do you think you could teach me some fighting basics some time?"

Calum blinked at him. "You want *me* to teach you?"

Nicolai shrugged. "I trust you more than anyone else in the group. I think you'd be less likely to 'accidentally' kill me while we were sparring."

Calum chuckled. "I know what you mean."

"…well?" Nicolai pressed.

Calum sighed. He'd come a long way since Magnus had started

training him, but was he really ready to pass along that knowledge to someone else? What if he taught Nicolai something wrong, and it got him hurt... or killed?

Then again, what if he refused, and not teaching him got him killed instead?

"I'm flattered, Nicolai. I really am," Calum said. "But Magnus is the expert. He taught Axel and me. It's really him you should be asking."

Nicolai shook his head. "I don't want to learn from him. I'd be too embarrassed at how bad I am to work with Magnus."

"*Ha.*" Calum could certainly relate to that. "You should've seen me when I first started. I got lucky my first few fights, or I'd be dead too."

"Look, I want to learn from you." Nicolai stepped in front of him so Calum couldn't walk any farther. "Just get me through the basics that Magnus taught you, and then I'll learn the rest from him. That way I won't be squeamish or awkward when he's teaching me."

Calum stared at his dark eyes. "Alright. As soon as we stop for a break, I'll show you a few things. Probably a good idea anyway in case we run into whatever's lurking down here."

Nicolai beamed, then stepped aside. "Thanks, Calum. I won't let you down."

Let's hope not. Calum showed him a half-smile and kept walking.

TWO LEFTS and one right turn later they stopped for a meal break, probably about six miles into the tunnels. Just like Lilly had said, the tunnel smelled just as foul as the sewers, but in a different way, as if something had died in there awhile back and had just been left there to rot.

Stench or no stench, they still had to eat. Calum handed Lilly his torch so he could unpack some food, and after their meal, Calum showed Nicolai some basic attacks as promised. To Calum's surprise, Nicolai caught on quickly; then again, he had mentioned he was observant.

About fifteen minutes into their training, Magnus pulled Nicolai away so the two of them and Riley could scout another area a bit. Riley hadn't been completely sure which path was the right one, so he wanted to investigate with someone to back him up.

For whatever reason, Axel had decided to go with them, possibly to keep an extra eye on Nicolai, or possibly because if something did attack them, he couldn't trust Nicolai to have Magnus's back in a fight.

Whatever any case, it meant Calum finally had some time to talk to Lilly without anyone else listening, without anyone else around. The idea of it sent shudders through his chest, but he couldn't deny his glee at having the opportunity.

"How's your shoulder?" he asked.

She still carried the torch he'd given her in her right arm, and she smiled and rotated her left shoulder. "A lot better. I think it's almost totally healed. Whatever Magnus gave me—that veromine, or whatever he called it—it worked fast."

"That's good. Great. I'm glad to hear it." He mentally kicked himself. Why was he jabbering so much?

"Yeah." Lilly nodded and her smile widened. "I guess you are."

"You able to fly again, yet?"

"I never lost that ability. I just haven't because I haven't needed to, and until we got into the tunnels the ceiling's been too low to make flying of any real use." She tugged on her shimmering blue cape. "As long as I have this, I can fly."

"Oh. Good to know."

Lilly leaned over, across Calum's chest, and peered into the food pouch. "Can I have one of those oranges?"

Her proximity to him sent chills rippling down his back and arms. His breathing quickened, and he struggled to find words.

He blinked and self-chastised his way out of the sensation. She was asking for an orange, not requesting his hand in marriage.

Still, he found his mouth refused to form words right away. Instead, Calum reached into the pouch and traded her an orange for his torch.

As she started to peel it, he found his voice again. "So you're from the Sky Realm?"

Lilly nodded. "Yep."

"How long have you lived there?"

"All my life." She pulled a big chunk of orange skin off and dropped it on the ground. "Seventeen years, at least until the slave traders got me. It's been almost two months since they first captured me."

"Your parents must be terribly worried by now."

Lilly sighed and leaned against the tunnel wall as she pulled the first segment of orange from the cluster. "I know. If he could, my father would conscript the entire Sky Realm's population to look for me."

"Maybe they're already looking for you."

"I have no doubt that they are. There was a chance they'd find me right after I left, but when Roderick and his slave traders took me across Trader's Pass, that chance all but disappeared."

"Why'd you leave in the first place?"

Lilly stared at him with her mouth open, then she shut it and looked away.

Idiot. Calum had thought he'd been doing well. The conversation was flowing, natural, easy. Then, with one question, he'd ruined it all.

"I'm sorry," he said. "It's none of my business."

She shook her head, but she still didn't look at him. "It's not your fault. It's a fair question."

"Yeah, but I didn't have to ask it. And you don't have to answer, either."

She looked at him with no lack of self-confidence in her eyes. "I know."

"I'm really, really sorry."

"Don't be." She gave him a small but kind smile. "I have my reasons. I made the choice to leave, and now I just want to get back. That's all I can say."

Calum nodded and leaned his shoulder against the tunnel wall, facing her. "Don't worry. We'll get you home soon."

"Thanks." She smiled and handed him half of the now-peeled orange. "Want some?"

"Sure, thanks." He leaned the torch against the tunnel wall, popped a segment into his mouth, and savored the burst of sweet citrus flavor. It almost negated the wretched smell of the place.

"So what about you?" Firelight from the torch flickered in her keen blue eyes.

He swallowed the orange pulp and licked his lips clean. "What about me?"

She chuckled. "How'd you end up working in that quarry?"

Memories of his parents flooded Calum's mind. "Actually, I—"

"We should keep moving," Riley's voice split the darkness. He trotted back toward Calum and Lilly with Axel close behind. "Something's not right. I think we should go."

"Did you find the right path?" Calum asked.

"I'm pretty sure," Riley replied, "but either way, we shouldn't linger here."

"Yeah," Axel said. "Puppy's got a bad feeling about this part, so we're moving along."

Riley growled at him. "Call me 'Puppy' one more time, and I'll rip your throat out in your sleep. Crystal?"

Axel rolled his eyes, unconcerned. "Whatever. Nicolai and Magnus are waiting for us up ahead. Are we going or not?"

Calum cinched up his food pack and tossed it to Axel. "Hey, do you mind carrying this for a bit? My shoulder's getting sore."

"Like I said: whatever."

"Thanks." He turned to Lilly, but before he could say anything, Axel called to her.

"Lilly, got a question for you," he said. "Care to walk with me for a minute?"

"Sure." She walked next to Axel as if Calum had never existed in the first place.

Calum sighed and started walking at the rear of the group. He let them get some distance between them so Axel wouldn't hear the things Calum muttered about him.

Three steps later, the ground under his feet gave way.

Calum's left hand caught the edge on the way down, but his torch kept falling. It dropped farther and farther down until it finally struck a large gray boulder and bounced off onto the dirt floor below. It had to be at least a fifty- or sixty-foot drop.

If he let go, it was over.

"Help!" he yelled. "Come back! Help me!"

Though higher quality, his upgraded metal armor weighed more than the old leather armor he'd worn before the fight with the Southern Snake Brotherhood. He strained to reach up to grab hold of the edge with his other hand, but his fingers had already begun to slip.

"Help!" he called again.

No one came.

The rock under his left hand shifted as if it were giving way, but he managed to hold on.

Calum glanced down at the torch again. If he fell, he'd follow its trajectory. His body would smash against that big gray boulder, then he'd bounce off and probably land facedown.

If the impact didn't kill him, broken ribs, punctured lungs, and internal bleeding eventually would. And even if he didn't sustain any major injuries, he'd never find his way back up.

He would land ten feet away from the boulder where the torch still burned, now surrounded by dozens of small sparkles. They reminded him of the gems he'd mined at the quarry not so long ago.

Great. He'd die among rocks, boulders, and gemstones, just as if he'd never stopped working at the quarry.

Calum's fingers slipped a bit more.

"Help!" he called again, his voice weaker. "Axel, Magnus—help me!"

The edge crumbled under his fingertips, and he fell.

CHAPTER THIRTY-SEVEN

A dark hand clamped onto Calum's wrist.

He looked up and saw Nicolai's face, illuminated by the torch in his left hand.

"I've got you," Nicolai said. He clarified, "I—I think I've got you."

Good thing Calum had decided to spare Nicolai's life after all, despite Axel's objections.

Magnus appeared behind Nicolai. He reached down, clamped onto Calum's bicep, and pulled him out of the sinkhole in one fluid motion. He set Calum down against the tunnel wall. "What happened?"

Lilly landed next to him and touched his shoulder. "Are you alright?"

Calum nodded and sucked in several deep, quick breaths to calm his racing heart. "I'm fine. I was just walking, and the ground gave way. I grabbed onto the edge on my way down, but I dropped my torch. Thank the Overlord that Nicolai was there or I'd be dead."

"It's like you said—we're a team. We look out for each other." Nicolai smiled.

Axel huffed, but he nodded at Nicolai. "I guess you are good for something after all."

Nicolai's smile shrank to a smirk. "Thanks, Axel."

"Guess that explains the holes we saw in the ground," Calum

quipped. "Now I know where they lead, and trust me—we don't want to end up down there."

Riley growled. "Well, we're down to one torch now. I can see in the dark just fine, but you all can't. You'd better not lose the other one."

Axel stepped near the sinkhole and peered into it. "I can still see it down there. You weren't kidding, Calum. That's a *long* way down."

Calum patted Lilly's hand, which was still on his shoulder, and nodded to her, then he stood up and walked over next to Axel. "No kidding. Plus that huge boulder down there would've broken my fall."

"Where?" Axel tilted his head. "I don't see any boulder."

Calum leaned over the hole for a look.

"Do not fall back in, Calum," Magnus said. "Nicolai may not be able to grab you in time if it happens again."

"Yeah, I'm only good for saving one life per day." Nicolai laughed. "I've reached my quota."

"I'll be alright," Calum assured them. He wouldn't have fallen in there in the first place had it not caught him by surprise.

Far below, the torch still flickered along with some of the shining flecks, but he couldn't see the gray boulder anymore. *Weird.*

"Well, when I fell in, the torch smacked a boulder on the way down. Maybe the torch has faded too much to see it now."

"Come on. Enough dawdling." Riley nodded into the darkness of the tunnel. "We need to move."

"He's right," Calum said. "Let's go."

As Calum and the others followed Riley, the ground shuddered beneath Calum's feet. He jumped to the side for fear that he'd drop down again, but he didn't fall, nor did another hole open underneath him.

"Did you guys feel that?" Calum asked.

Nicolai glanced back at him and nodded, as did Axel and Lilly.

"Tremors are normal in here," Riley said from the lead, his voice flat but firm. "Just keep moving."

As Riley said the word "moving," the ground shook again, this time with more force.

Nicolai glanced at Calum. "I sure felt that one."

"Just keep moving," Riley repeated. "We'll be fine."

After another mile or so of tremor-free progress through the tunnel, Riley stopped and sniffed the air. Within seconds, he began to growl.

"What is it?" Magnus stopped too, and the rest of the group stopped behind him.

Riley stepped back and snarled. "We're not alone."

"Now!" Commander Anigo yelled.

His twenty men poured out of shallow crevices in the tunnel walls not more than fifty feet from the Wolf's position with their weapons drawn.

Commander Anigo came out last, holding a torch. One of his men approached and sparked it to life with a flint and a knife, then the soldier took the torch and passed the fire to a few of his comrades.

The added light allowed Commander Anigo to see his catch with significant clarity. He couldn't help but grin. His plan had worked perfectly.

"We meet again," he said.

One of the men with the group, the one whom he'd fought and lost to, stepped forward. "You—I *stabbed* you with my spear. You should be dead."

Commander Anigo shook his head and took a few steps forward, into the torchlight. The high ceiling of the tunnel seemed to yawn open around them, trying to drain the additional torchlight away as if to preserve the inherent darkness of the space.

"I'm sorry to disappoint you," Commander Anigo said. "I've been pursuing you three for some time, as I said when we first met. But now I'm after the girl, too. She's wanted for the murder of my superior officer, Captain Fulton."

"Fulton was a backstabbing liar and a rapist pig," the girl spat. She'd drawn her bow and nocked an arrow. From what he'd read of the carnage that had ensued during her escape from Thirry's warehouse, she was quite an impressive shot with it.

"I am well aware of Captain Fulton's dealings, but you stand accused nonetheless. Lay down your arms, all of you."

None of them moved.

Commander Anigo pointed to the Saurian, two of the men, and the Windgale girl. "You four are under arrest for crimes against the King." He pointed to the other man in the green armor. "If you do not interfere, we will allow you to pass."

The Wolf growled.

"And you, Wolf—" Commander Anigo pulled his spear from where he'd secured it to his back. "—if you so much as twitch in my direction, I'll skewer you like the stray dog you are."

"We won't comply," the blond young man said.

Commander Anigo's eyes narrowed. "We have you outnumbered, and we *will* kill you if necessary. This is your last chance. Lay down your weapons and surrender, or face the King's justice—right here, right now."

CALUM GLANCED AT MAGNUS. Of course they would try to fight their way through the soldiers, but they were in for a difficult battle. This time there weren't any bandits to help them thin out the soldiers' ranks, and they only had scattered torchlight to help them see their enemies.

"We can take 'em," Axel whispered.

"I'm not so sure about that," Nicolai whispered back.

"No one asked you," Axel hissed.

As Riley backed toward them, Magnus addressed the soldiers. "We have not come this far to give in now. You may try to take us if you wish, but you will do so at your own peril. I will *never* surrender."

Magnus drew his sword, followed by Calum, Axel, and Nicolai. Lilly already had her bow out with an arrow nocked, and Riley crouched low as if ready to pounce.

Commander Anigo huffed. He pointed his spear at them. "Bring me their heads."

All twenty of the soldiers stepped toward them slowly with their weapons raised for battle.

As the soldiers approached, the ground shook with even more vigor than it had before, only this time it didn't stop.

Lilly toppled over into Calum, who caught her but struggled to keep his own footing. Together with Axel, they staggered over to one of the tunnel walls and braced themselves as the tunnel continued to shake.

Dust trickled down from the ceiling overhead, and a few small rocks clacked onto the ground. More rocks trickled down the cavern walls, knocked loose by the quaking.

Some of the soldiers fell over, and others moved nearer to the tunnel walls as well. Calum caught sight of Commander Anigo clinging to a rock protrusion, but it broke loose and crumbled at his feet, and he fell along with it.

Sinkholes opened up in the ground in the center of the tunnel. Calum saw at least three soldiers fall in, and he watched another get crushed under a cow-sized boulder that dropped onto him from the ceiling.

But he heard far more screams than that.

Riley, Nicolai, and Magnus made it to the opposite wall and leaned against it for support.

Amid the ruckus, Riley shouted, "This isn't normal. It didn't happen like this the last time I was here."

The shaking continued for another minute, then it stopped altogether.

Magnus stepped away from the wall first with his sword and his torch raised. He walked into the center of the tunnel, faced the direction they had come from, and held his torch out in front of him. The others filed in behind him, and Riley and Lilly kept watch on the soldiers who'd started to recover from the quake.

About thirty paces away, a large gray boulder, one that looked very similar to the one Calum had seen in the sinkhole, blocked most of the tunnel.

"How did that get here?" Nicolai asked.

"Heck of an earthquake, huh?" Axel shook his head, then turned back to face the soldiers, as did Calum. "We can't go back that way."

Calum nodded and raised his sword. "Now we have to fight."

"*Shh,*" Magnus hissed, still facing the boulder. "Listen."

A faint sound permeated the tunnel, almost like the rats' squeals when they'd poured out of the wall and all over Axel. It intensified in volume and focused into two distinct voices, both of them wailing like old women in pain.

Axel, Lilly, and Riley turned back first, and at the sight of the horrified looks on the soldiers' faces, Commander Anigo included, Calum did as well.

When he did, he understood why no one was moving.

As the wails escalated to shrieks, the boulder began to change. It split down the center and slowly folded over until it touched the ground. Then the two halves split, and four rocky points touched the ground. From the center of the segmented boulder arose two tall forms, one on the right, one on the left.

They lacked definition at first, but they sharpened into forms that looked like human heads and torsos without legs, but the resemblance ended there. Instead of arms, the two forms sprouted a pair of narrow serpentine tentacles on each side of their torsos, and a gaping mouth full of jagged teeth opened in the centers of their abdomens, near the base of their bodies.

Two red eyes opened in each head.

Their high-pitched shrieks shook Calum to his core. Everything above the thing's boulder-like shell began to glow with an eerie green light that illuminated the tunnel.

Axel staggered back, his wide eyes reflecting the green light. "What in the Overlord's name is that?"

Calum's heart pounded. Although he'd never seen one, he'd heard those shrieks and seen that green light before.

"It's a Gronyx."

CHAPTER THIRTY-EIGHT

"Run!" Riley yelled. He wove through the stunned soldiers, some of whom reached for him to no avail, and he disappeared into the darkness down the tunnel.

"Riley, wait!" Calum shouted.

Too late. The Gronyx lashed its tentacles at Magnus and grabbed his ankle before he could swing his sword. He dropped both his torch and his sword as he slid toward the Gronyx, all the while snarling and clawing at the dirt.

"We have to do something!" Calum pointed his sword at it. "Attack!"

Together with Axel and Nicolai, he charged the Gronyx. Tentacles whipped at them, but the trio cut them away as if they were low-hanging branches in the forest. Glowing green liquid oozed from the ends of the severed tentacles, and with each slice the Gronyx shrieked louder.

With a roar, Magnus reached forward, grabbed the tentacle that had coiled around his leg, and severed it with the blade attached to the end of his tail. He got to his feet and darted back to the rest of the group, where he collected his sword again.

The Gronyx recoiled on all four of its stony legs and writhed, screeching all the while.

WIDE-EYED, Commander Anigo stared at the monster.

"Sir, the Wolf got past us. We've already lost at least five men. Possibly six or seven. Do we engage the rest of them?" one of his soldiers asked.

Commander Anigo shook his head. He'd learned his lesson the last time regarding third parties. "No. Order the men to fall back and form a defensive perimeter. Let them fight it. We'll clean up whatever's left."

"THAT WILL NOT STOP it for long." Magnus gripped his sword with two hands. "And I do not know how to kill it."

Before Calum's eyes, each of the Gronyx's eight original tentacles flared with green light and then split into two tentacles each. By the time the process ended, the Gronyx had sixteen new tentacles, and it started to reach toward them again.

"Is that gonna happen any time we cut one off?" Nicolai asked.

Magnus nodded and glanced at Calum. "When I went into the Gronyx's pit at the quarry, I took out several tentacles with the pickax Burtis gave me, but they kept splitting and growing back in pairs. They don't traverse the ground quickly, but their tentacles are more than fast enough.

"I only got out of there alive because it went after the man who fell into the hole before you did. I even whacked one of its heads once, but that just made it mad." Magnus's voice deepened. "And that one was half the size of this one."

Along with the rest of the group, Axel stepped back as the Gronyx approached. "Then what do we do? And what about the soldiers?"

Magnus stole a look back. "They are not moving. Let's focus on this. If we can get past it, then perhaps we can go back the way we came."

"It's filling almost the entire tunnel. I don't think we're gonna get past it," Nicolai said.

"Lilly, try to shoot an arrow at it," Calum said.

She drew back her bow. "Where do you want me to aim?"

"Try to hit one of the heads if you can."

An arrow zipped past Calum's ear and lodged in the left head where the mouth should have been, and more green goo spurted out. The Gronyx's left torso reeled back, shuddered, and then dropped forward, and its eight tentacles draped over the front of its legs.

The right torso lurched around, and its boulder legs adjusted so the left torso was in the back. The right torso lashed its tentacles toward the group.

"Shoot it again!" Calum ducked under one tentacle and jumped over another, but he had to slice one away so it wouldn't hook his ankle. Irradiated green ooze splattered on the dirt next to his foot, and the tentacle retracted.

Lilly released another arrow, but the Gronyx raised its tentacles. The arrow skewered one of them, but the Gronyx kept coming toward them.

"Keep shooting at it!" Calum yelled.

She fired three quick arrows at the Gronyx's other head, but its tentacles intercepted them all. "I can't hit it if those tentacles are in the way."

"Then we have to risk cutting off the tentacles to kill it." Axel whacked Magnus's shoulder with the back of his hand. "You go right, I'll go left. Lilly, stay in the middle and wait for your shot. Calum and Nicolai, don't let it get Lilly. Divide its attention. Whoever has a chance to hit it, do it."

Magnus, Nicolai, and Calum nodded, and they took their positions. Tentacles zipped toward them and smacked Calum's armor, but he fended them off without having to cut any more of them. Axel's plan was working.

"Do you have the shot?" Axel called.

"Not yet," Lilly replied. She took to the air and shifted her position to try to get a better angle, but shook her head. "No shot."

The tentacle Calum had cut a moment earlier glowed bright green and split, just like the original eight had. One of them launched back toward Calum, but the other snaked around behind the Gronyx's right torso. Calum batted the tentacle away with his left forearm and craned his head to see where the other one went.

It curled around the arrow lodged in the left head and ripped it out. Green goo splattered on the dirt, and bright green light flared from the head. Then it began to move—

Toward Axel.

"Axel!" Calum yelled "Watch out!"

Too late.

The Gronyx's body swiveled and the left torso rose up, its tentacles flailing. Six of them latched onto Axel's limbs, torso, and neck, and reeled him toward the left torso's mouth at the base of its body. He screamed and strained against the tentacles.

Do you got any idea what a Gronyx does with its victims? Jidon had asked Calum after the incident at the Gronyx's pit. *It rips its food apart before it feeds.*

No. Calum couldn't let that happen. Not to Axel.

His legs pumped harder than they ever had. He yelled to Nicolai, "Take the right side!"

Axel's sword dropped from his hand, and despite his strong body, the tentacles stretched his limbs to their extremes. His cries reverberated off the tunnel walls, mixing with the Gronyx's wails in a cacophony of horror.

Calum leaped toward the tunnel wall, sprang off of it with his left foot, and soared toward the Gronyx's left torso with his sword cocked over his shoulder. Two tentacles caught Calum by his waist and his leg in midair, but they couldn't stop his momentum.

He swung his red-bladed sword with all of his might and severed the tentacles from Axel's body. Green fluid spurted all over Calum's face, arms, and chest, temporarily blinding him.

Something heavy batted him away from the left torso. His feet hit the ground first, then his body smacked against the tunnel wall. He dropped to the dirt, stunned, but somehow still gripping his sword.

A set of hands yanked him to his feet.

Axel smiled at him. "Wake up, brother. We're not done yet."

Calum wiped green goo from his face and blinked, and his vision sharpened back to normal. He spat more of it out of his mouth, disgusted by its bitter, putrid taste, then he re-gripped his sword and followed Axel to rejoin Magnus, Nicolai, and Lilly, who dodged and smacked tentacles away from themselves.

"We must find a way to kill it," Magnus urged. "We will not last much longer down here."

"It's your turn to try something stupid." Calum sucked in several deep breaths and wiped more green stuff off his face. "I'm taking a break."

"I'm on it." Nicolai raised his sword and started forward.

The tunnel shook with violence again, and the Gronyx stopped its attack. Calum's eyes fixed on the Gronyx, but the rumbling seemed to originate from behind him. Then a chorus of yells sounded from the soldiers.

Calum whirled around. A large gray boulder broke through the ground beneath some of the soldiers, and those who didn't drop into the sinkholes around it scrambled to get away from it.

Commander Anigo dropped halfway into one of the sinkholes, but he clawed his way out and rolled away from the boulder before it opened and began to separate as the first boulder had.

Familiar green light now emanated from both sides of the tunnel.

Shrieks flooded the cavern, not just from the first Gronyx, but also from the second one that now prevented them, Commander Anigo, and his ten remaining soldiers from escaping in either direction.

They were all trapped.

CHAPTER THIRTY-NINE

Terror threatened to overwhelm Commander Anigo as he realized the futility of his situation. With the arrival of the second Gronyx, there was no hope of escape for either him or his soldiers.

Only about a hundred yards separated the two behemoths from each other, with Commander Anigo, his remaining soldiers, and the fugitives in the middle. Worse yet, the Gronyxes had begun to edge forward, gradually tightening the noose around their collective necks.

He shouldn't have even been here in the first place. It wasn't his job to battle grotesque, wretched monsters underground. He'd been trained to do so much more, to usher in a brighter future for all of Kanarah, but especially Solace.

It wasn't *fair*. He'd done nothing to deserve such a horrific fate. He should've been enjoying brunch with his superior officers in the capitol, but instead he was entombed in a dark hellscape aglow with pale green light.

"Commander?" someone called.

Commander Anigo whirled around with his spear raised and glared at the young blond man who had called his name.

"We need to work together on this." He pointed. "Have your men take that one, and we'll fight this one."

Commander Anigo clenched his teeth. He didn't need some fugitive kid telling him how to fight this battle, even if his strategy was sound.

"Commander, look out!" one of his soldiers yelled.

He turned back in time to see a tentacle lash at his head. Commander Anigo ducked and swung his spear at the tentacle, careful to knock it off its trajectory with the spear's shaft rather than risk severing it. He'd seen enough of the fugitives' fight with the first Gronyx to know what not to do.

But apparently, his soldiers hadn't been paying attention. Nearby, one of them hacked a tentacle free from his leg.

"Don't cut the tentacles!" Commander Anigo shouted. *Idiots.* "Aim for its bodies! For the torsos!"

Four of the Gronyx's tentacles ensnared one of the soldiers, one tentacle on each of his limbs, and raised him in the air. Commander Anigo watched as he struggled at first to cut at one of the tentacles to free himself, but the tentacles pulled his limbs taut.

Then they tightened.

The soldier screamed for help and dropped his sword. Another tentacle coiled around the soldier's neck and ceased his screams, and the Gronyx raised him above Commander Anigo's head.

A sickening crack sounded, and red liquid showered down on Commander Anigo. He recoiled with his spear primed to strike, but the Gronyx remained focused on the soldier who now lacked a left arm, which dangled freely in the Gronyx's tentacle.

Another crack. A leg this time, but it belonged to another of his soldiers.

It was ripping them apart.

He stood there, mouth agape. *King's mercy...*

"Attack its torsos and its heads!" Commander Anigo repeated. It was all he could think to do.

By the time he'd rallied them, he realized it was a lost cause. The Gronyx had already killed four of his ten remaining soldiers and mortally injured two others.

Instead of joining the last of his men in the fray, Commander Anigo backed away from the Gronyx with his spear at the ready. He'd come in here to capture or kill the fugitives who'd eluded him for the last few months, but now these tunnels threatened to devour him —literally.

Captain Fulton's death—providence? Certainly not anymore.

Within moments, the Gronyx killed the last of his men, tore his limbs off, and devoured his body in pieces. Commander Anigo's heart pounded as the Gronyx began to advance toward him.

Now he was alone.

Then he bumped into someone, and he whirled around.

CALUM SPUN around to find Commander Anigo facing him with desperate eyes and dread written on his bloodstained face. Behind him, the Gronyx advanced, and no soldiers remained to fight it.

"Don't give up," Calum told him. It was a peculiar thing to say to a commander in the King's army, but what else was Calum supposed to say? The situation was hopeless, but just giving in only meant they'd die quicker.

He shoved Commander Anigo to face the advancing Gronyx, and he stole a look back at the one his group had engaged, but they hadn't killed or even significantly wounded it. Calum had meant for his words to inspire Commander Anigo, but they withered away to nothing in the face of the terrible truth.

They were doomed.

Unless... One idea pierced Calum's mind like Lumen's light shining clear through his body in his dreams. He didn't even know if it would work, but it was truly their last chance.

"Magnus!" Calum shouted as he batted another tentacle away. "You need to use your Dragon Emerald!"

"What?" Magnus stole a furtive glance back at him.

"You need to become a Sobek *now*, or we're all dead!"

"Yeah, do it!" Axel sucked under an errant tentacle swipe. "We need you!"

Magnus dug his hand into the pouch attached to his belt and

removed the Dragon Emerald, now appearing as little more than a black lump of stone in the green light blanketing them.

He held it in his left hand and knocked a trio of tentacles away with the sword in his right. "What if it fails to work?"

"Look." Calum pointed to Commander Anigo, who stood alone facing the Gronyx behind them as it eased toward them. "The soldiers are all but dead, and so are we if you don't try it. If it doesn't work, we're dead anyway!"

Magnus nodded. "Stand back. I do not know what's going to happen."

He sheathed his sword and hurriedly pulled off his breastplate and helmet. Then he loosened the straps of his arm, leg, and tail armor and let them fall from his body as well, leaving only the blade strapped to the tip of his tail.

Within a minute, the Gronyxes would converge on the group's position.

"You guys?" Nicolai held his sword higher. "They're getting *closer*."

"Is one of the requirements that you gotta be totally *naked*, Scales?" Axel shouted more out of frustration than joking. "We're running out of time here!"

Magnus paid him no mind as he worked to shed the rest of his armor from his body.

"Come over here." Calum pulled Axel and Lilly along with him toward the Gronyx that killed the King's soldiers, and Nicolai joined them. They lined up next to Commander Anigo, who eyed them with incredulity. "We'll hold this one off until Magnus can transform."

"That's *if* he can transform," Axel grumbled.

Nicolai turned toward him. "Are you ever *not* skeptical?"

Commander Anigo's gaze jumped between the two of them and then refocused on the Gronyx. He never lowered his spear, and he never said a word.

"*Guys*," Calum said. "Let's try to take this one down quickly in case this doesn't work. Maybe we can find a way to kill it before we have to fight the other one."

"How? The only time we even managed to hurt the thing was when

Lilly put an arrow in one of its heads." Axel dodged an approaching tentacle.

Nicolai nodded. "Then that's what we do. We go for the heads and torsos and avoid cutting the tentacles if we can."

"So it's the same dumb plan as before?" Axel almost shouted, his eyes wild.

"It was working until it didn't," Calum countered. "Look, we have to do something!"

"Watch out for its mouths." Lilly drew back her arrow.

Calum looked at Axel. "Are you in?"

"Of course I'm in!" he shouted. "Even if the plan is stupid, do you really think I'd let you die alone? No. We're all gonna die together, because then it's *fair*."

Calum wasn't about to argue Axel's logic—or lack thereof—so instead, he nudged Commander Anigo, who sharply recoiled and stared at him with shock in his eyes.

"Easy." Calum held up his hand and nodded toward Commander Anigo's spear. "You any good with that thing?"

Commander Anigo's eyes narrowed, and his eyebrows arched down. Something had broken him out of his stupor. "Of course I am."

"I mean can you throw it and hit what you're aiming at?"

Commander Anigo scowled at him. "Yes."

"So aim for one of the heads and throw it. Then draw your sword and help us finish it off."

Commander Anigo's jaw tightened, but he turned toward the Gronyx and cocked his spear over his shoulder. "Fine."

The first Gronyx shrieked at them and charged, but a brilliant golden light flared from behind them and stopped it short. The light washed away most of the eerie green radiated by the Gronyxes, and Calum and the others all whirled around.

With both hands, Magnus pressed the Dragon Emerald against his bare chest. Golden light emanated from its center and streamed in every direction, including at Magnus—*into* Magnus.

The Dragon Emerald's light transferred to him, and his entire body began to glow the same golden color. Then the Dragon Emerald darkened to an even deeper green color than before he'd used it. There, before Calum's eyes, Magnus began to change.

His fingers and arms lengthened, and so did his legs, his torso, and his tail. His arm and leg muscles swelled to nearly twice their previous size.

Black spikes pierced through his scales along his spine. They extended down his tail, which had thickened as well. More spikes pierced through the skin on the top of his head, including a small one on the tip of his reptilian snout.

By the time the golden light faded, Magnus stood six inches taller than his previous seven-foot height and must've added fifty pounds to his already muscular form—maybe more. When Magnus opened his eyes and faced them, Calum wasn't sure he was the same Saurian he'd befriended back at the quarry.

"You take that one. I will handle this one." Magnus crouched down and tucked the Dragon Emerald back into the pouch on his belt, drew his broadsword from its sheath, which now lay on the ground, and started toward the Gronyx on his side.

Calum turned on his heels and pointed his sword at the Gronyx coming from the other direction. "Kill it."

Commander Anigo cocked his spear for a throw and launched it toward the Gronyx. It lodged in the center of one of the beast's heads, accompanied by a spurt of green blood, and Commander Anigo brandished his sword.

Calum grinned. "Nice wor—"

The tunnel swirled before Calum's eyes. The ground whacked his shoulder, then his head, and his body skidded along the tunnel floor toward the Gronyx. He swung his sword to sever the Gronyx's tentacle from his ankle, but he no longer held it. Calum glanced back and saw it lying on the stone floor three feet behind him. Then four feet. Then five.

Lilly shouted his name first, then Nicolai, then Axel. Four more tentacles curled around his wrists, his other ankle, and his waist, and they lifted him into the air. A fifth reached toward his neck, but an arrow pinned it to the ceiling.

"I've got you, Calum!" Nicolai charged toward him, hopped a

tentacle that lashed at his ankles, and flung himself between the two torsos. He somehow found his footing at the base of the torsos and raised his sword.

Pressure swelled in Calum's shoulders and hips and quickly spread to his elbows, wrists, knees, and ankles. He pulled back, trying to resist, but the tentacle in his midsection pulled against his spine and arched his back, stealing the strength from his limbs. He fought them nonetheless, pouring every last bit of himself into the effort, but the tentacles were too strong.

And as usual, he was too weak.

The Gronyx was going to rip him apart.

Then Nicolai's sword cut the tentacles gripping two of Calum's limbs and his waist. A wave of relief spread through Calum's body, and his joints reset as he dangled upside down, suspended by his left leg and his right arm by two other tentacles.

They continued to pull, but Calum quickly grabbed his own wrist with his free hand and pulled back. With two limbs against one tentacle, he managed a stalemate—at least for the time being.

Below him, the Gronyx curled two tentacles around Commander Anigo's spear. Just as Calum shouted for someone to stop it from pulling the spear out, the Gronyx ripped it from its head and dropped it. The spear clanged against the ground, and the torso straightened up.

Then the rejuvenated torso turned toward Nicolai.

Horror seized Calum's chest, and he yelled, "Get off of there, Nicolai!"

Nicolai spun around and hacked at the torso with his sword, but a wall of tentacles stopped his swing. Another tentacle swept behind his legs, and he dropped to his back.

"Axel, help him!" Calum strained and thrashed against the tentacles, but without a weapon, he couldn't get free.

"I'm trying!" Axel shouted back. He carved his way toward the Gronyx, hindered by its tentacles.

Arrows from Lilly's bow peppered the Gronyx but did nothing to stop it from attacking Nicolai.

Commander Anigo wove through and rolled under tentacles, but he couldn't reach Nicolai either.

None of them could.

"Help!" Nicolai cried as the Gronyx's tentacles pulled him toward the right torso's gaping jaws, all while preventing him from swinging his sword.

It pushed Nicolai into its mouth, and its jagged teeth clamped down on his legs.

Nicolai screamed.

All Calum could do was holler. "*Nicolai!*"

One of Lilly's arrows struck the Gronyx's right torso, and it convulsed. Axel ducked under a flailing tentacle and grabbed Nicolai by his arm, and Commander Anigo met him there. Together, they yanked Nicolai free from the Gronyx's mouth, onto the tunnel floor, and then dragged him away.

The lower halves of his legs were gone, and he wasn't moving.

An arrow knifed through the tentacle holding Calum's leg, and he fell upside down toward the hard ground. Before he could hit, the tentacle around his wrist went taught, and his legs swung down underneath him, righting him again. His blood rushed out of his head and back into the rest of his body, leaving him woozy for a second.

But this was his best chance to get free. He dug his gauntleted fingers into the tentacle around his wrist and pried it off, and it finally released him—until a flurry of new tentacles zipped toward him and latched onto his limbs again.

They pulled on his joints as they had before, and he again cried out for help. By now, his strength was all but gone. Nicolai was out of the fight, unable to save him, and Magnus had the other Gronyx to handle on his own.

Axel charged back into the fray but couldn't reach Calum.

Lilly shot more arrows, but they didn't stop the Gronyx from pulling on his limbs.

Commander Anigo ran forward as well, but a barrage of tentacles leveled him.

The tentacles pulled even harder, and though Calum's joints begged for relief, they found none.

Another tentacle coiled around Calum's neck.

He would die soon.

And he would die horribly.

CHAPTER FORTY

A mass of gray-and-brown fur filled Calum's field of vision and landed on the Gronyx's left torso.

Riley.

He chomped down on the torso's neck and thrashed his head back and forth. Glowing green blood and chunks of flesh splattered on the walls around them.

The Gronyx wailed and writhed, but Riley didn't let go.

The tentacles' grip went slack, and Calum hit the ground. They lashed to grab Riley, but Axel's sword severed them from its torso.

Commander Anigo recovered, darted forward, and together with Axel, he hacked at the torso's base. It disconnected altogether and dropped to the tunnel floor with Riley's jaws still locked onto its throat.

The other torso whipped its tentacles wildly—almost frantically. Commander Anigo ducked under them, but they batted Axel clear over Calum's head. He smacked into the tunnel wall with a clank.

"Get up!" Lilly shouted, perhaps to Axel, perhaps to Calum—probably to both of them. She sent another arrow at the Gronyx then zoomed toward Calum and Axel.

Riley darted over to them as well and nudged Axel with his nose until he clamped onto Riley's fur and pulled himself up.

While Commander Anigo bravely distracted the Gronyx, Calum recovered his sword. Axel recovered his, too, all while moaning about his left arm. It hung at a strange angle, and it looked like the impact with the wall had dislocated it, but Calum couldn't tell for sure.

Commander Anigo pulled back, breathing heavily, and regrouped with the rest of them. He glanced between all of them, his bloody face now streaked with glowing green slime as well. "We need a better plan."

"Riley, you're the fastest one," Calum said. "I need you to distract it. Get it to chase you, and try to get behind it if possible. If we can divide its attention, it'll be easier to fight."

Riley rolled his eyes. "Great. I get to be bait."

"Commander," Calum asked, "are you on board with this plan?"

"I am. We killed one of its torsos. Now we just need to kill the other."

Calum turned to Axel, but didn't take his eyes off of the shrieking, flailing beast before them. "Axel, are you alright?"

"My left arm is out, but thank the Overlord I'm right-handed. I can still fight," Axel grimaced, and his left arm hung limp at his side. "For your sakes, I'll have to if we're gonna get out of this."

Calum smirked. Even injured, Axel's confidence never ran dry. "Keep its attention focused on us. Try to distract it from reaching Nicolai again."

Lilly nodded. "Let's finish this."

Riley growled, and they started toward the Gronyx again.

A POWER unlike anything Magnus had ever felt permeated his body. It flowed through his veins, teased his taloned fingertips, and pulsed through his muscles, begging for release. Pleading to be used.

The Gronyx in front of Magnus lashed the full multitude of its tentacles at him. With his sword still in his right hand, Magnus allowed the tentacles to ensnare his limbs, waist, tail, and neck. The Gronyx lifted him off the ground and began to wrench his limbs in opposite directions.

Magnus glared at it and pulled back, using a portion of that newfound strength. The tentacles strained against his resistance but couldn't do him any harm.

Let us see what more I am capable of. Magnus concentrated his strength and jerked his arms and legs. The Gronyx's two torsos lurched forward and smacked into each other.

Amid the Gronyx's pained screeches, the tentacles released their grip, and Magnus landed on his feet. He lunged forward, grabbed all four of the right torso's tentacles in his left hand, and yanked on them so hard that the right torso not only tottered toward him, but the Gronyx actually had to take a rocky step forward in an attempt to right itself.

As the right torso lowered toward him, Magnus released his grip on the tentacles and leaped forward. The right torso's red eyes flickered at him until Magnus's broadsword cleaved clear through its head.

He wrenched the blade out, flinging green blood against the cavern walls, and swung it at the bottom of the torso. It severed from its base in one blow, and a geyser of glowing green blood erupted in its place.

The Gronyx wailed and shrieked again. The left torso's tentacles pummeled him into the tunnel wall, but he rebounded, unfazed, and reengaged the fight.

LILLY'S SCREAM stole every ounce of Calum's focus away from the fight. A tentacle had latched onto her ankle and now pulled her down toward its chomping ravenous mouth, unwilling to stop even though she rained arrows down on it like a thunderstorm.

Calum rushed toward her, but Commander Anigo got there first.

"Cut her free!" Calum shouted.

Axel dodged a pair of stray tentacles and severed the one that had hooked around Lilly's ankle. Commander Anigo caught her when she fell out of the air, and Calum exhaled relief.

"Thanks," she said.

As soon as Commander Anigo set her down, she drew another arrow and shot it at the left torso, then she took to the air again. The arrow embedded just above the fang-ridden mouth in its gut, but it didn't seem to faze the Gronyx.

"I can't get behind it!" Riley called between snarls.

"Axel, let's do a jump," Calum hollered. "Commander, come at it from the left."

Axel shuffled back over to Calum.

Riley darted behind him, barking, trying to steal the Gronyx's attention.

Together, Axel and Calum rolled under the first two tentacles and sliced through two more that came at them, then Axel dropped to the dirt in front of the right torso on his hands and knees.

Calum ran up behind him, planted his right foot on Axel's back, and leaped toward the Gronyx. He sliced his sword down at the left torso's head.

Before Calum's sword could make contact, a wall of tentacles smacked him away as if he weighed nothing, and he skidded to a halt on the tunnel floor. Dirt mixed with glowing ooze in a clump in his mouth, and he spat out the foul taste.

A tentacle coiled around his ankle and lurched him back toward the Gronyx. One swing from Commander Anigo's sword freed Calum, and he jumped to his feet and reentered the fracas.

MAGNUS BATTED four tentacles away in one swing with his left arm. The left torso shrieked and whipped its tentacles at him again. They latched onto his arms and legs, but they couldn't stop him from advancing.

Then, to Magnus's surprise, the monster actually started retreating.

No. Magnus smirked. *You started this. We are going to finish it.*

He plunged his sword into the hard-packed ground, grabbed the Gronyx's front left leg—originally a quarter section of its original boulder shape—and started to twist.

The Gronyx reeled back on its hind legs and released its tentacles' grip on Magnus. It used its tentacles to brace itself against the wall to keep from tipping over, but that was exactly what Magnus wanted.

With one jerk to his left, Magnus ripped off the Gronyx's boulder leg. Glowing green blood sprayed him from the wound, and the Gronyx pitched forward, shrieking like it never had before.

Magnus wrenched his sword from the ground, drew it back, and slammed it down on the monster's left torso. It cleaved all the way through the torso and into the base in another eruption of green blood.

The Gronyx let out a final pitiful wail, then it dropped, dead.

As LILLY DREW her last arrow from her quiver, every regret she'd ever had about leaving home sharpened in her mind.

She'd gotten into so much trouble in just a few months' time, all because she'd made one emotional decision. If there had ever been any doubt in her mind about whether or not she'd been right to leave, it was long gone, now.

She never should have left her home. It was an inescapable truth, and Kanarah, or the Overlord, or life itself had insisted on proving it to her time and time again ever since she'd left.

As Lilly moved to nock her final arrow, a tentacle lashed at her left arm. It caught her by surprise and batted her bow to the ground far below, but she still held that last arrow in her right hand.

She swooped down to retrieve her bow, but another tentacle wrapped around her waist and stopped her momentum. She gritted her teeth and resisted.

She'd already learned that no matter how hard she pulled, whether flying or not, she couldn't escape its grasp. But there were other ways to fight back, especially with an arrow in her possession.

"Lilly!" Calum yelled from somewhere beneath her. She caught sight of him trying to rush to her aid, but a tentacle tripped him. "Axel, Riley, help Lilly!"

A valiant attempt, and one Lilly felt grateful for, but she'd had enough of this mayhem. She had a plan, and she was going to see it through to the end.

Below her, the others moved to try to come to her aid. Axel ducked under one tentacle, but another leveled him with a blow to his face.

Riley leaped toward the tentacle that held Lilly but two others walloped him into the tunnel wall. He let out a miserable whimper and slowly forced himself back up to his feet.

Commander Anigo dueled with a trio of tentacles that kept trying to grab him, but he couldn't get away.

Lilly was on her own. Again.

The Gronyx pulled her toward its gaping mouth. This time, she didn't scream, didn't yell. She just drew her arm back and waited for the right moment.

She couldn't pull away from the Gronyx—it was too strong.

But she *could* push toward it.

She timed her move, pushed against the putrid air in the tunnel, and plunged her last arrow into one of the Gronyx's bitter red eyes.

Green fluid squelched out of its wounded head, and it wailed and slammed Lilly to the ground. The impact hurt—a lot, actually—but her armor kept her from sustaining any serious injuries. At least, she hoped that was the case.

Regardless of her own fate, she inhaled a breath of foul air into her lungs and shouted, "Kill it now!"

Dozens of tentacles flailed in every direction, lashing like glowing green whips as Calum, Axel, and Commander Anigo rushed forward. In a moment of perfect synchronization, they swung their swords with the timed dexterity of lumberjacks felling a mighty tree from three angles. They hacked and hacked at its base, relentless and furious.

The tentacles plowed into all three of them, pulling them in opposite directions up and away from its torso, which teetered forward and backward like a drunkard. They couldn't finish it.

A stone-shattering roar filled the tunnel.

Lilly grinned.

They couldn't finish it, but Magnus could.

The newly minted Sobek soared through the air, his brilliant blue sword clutched in both hands, and felled the right torso in one stunning slash.

The Gronyx released its grip on the other three, and they hit the ground in quick succession. Luminous green ooze splattered everywhere.

After a final moan, the Gronyx lay there, silent as its green light faded away.

Lilly lay on her back and exhaled a relieved breath. She couldn't help but laugh to herself—*at* herself. She definitely should never have left her home.

But if I'd never left, she reasoned, *I never would've gotten to experience all of... this.*

She lay there, staring at the green ooze coating every surface and everyone around her, and she continued to laugh.

As CALUM MADE it to his feet, so did Axel and Commander Anigo. Riley soon joined them, and the sight of the Wolf turned Calum's head toward Lilly.

To Calum's dismay, Axel was already helping her to her feet. He cursed himself for not reacting faster.

The five of them gathered together, their eyes fixed on Magnus and his new massive form.

Calum marveled at the sight. It felt like the first time Magnus had walked into the quarry, escorted by the King's soldiers, all over again. The effect of seeing him was the same: utter shock laced with a hefty dose of fear.

"Is it still you?" he asked.

Magnus's hard gaze softened into a grin, and his deep voice vibrated through Calum's chest. "Of course it is me."

Calum lurched forward and threw his arms around Magnus's midsection, now armored with darker yellow scales that felt rough and angry against Calum's face. But it didn't matter. His friend was alive, and he'd grown stronger—far stronger. Strong enough to save them all.

Soon after, Axel joined them, much to Calum's surprise.

Then, of course, he ruined it.

"Just when I thought you couldn't get any uglier," Axel said, still hugging them both, "you go and do somethin' like this, Scales."

Calum laughed, and even Magnus gave a chuckle. Whether it was out of pity or not, Calum didn't know.

He glanced at Lilly, Riley, and Commander Anigo. Dirt mired with glowing Gronyx blood covered all three of them. He grinned and motioned them over. "You belong with us, over here."

Commander Anigo declined, but Riley and Lilly looked at each other, then they joined their friends.

All except for Nicolai.

CHAPTER FORTY-ONE

Nicolai.

Calum tore free from the group embrace and ran past Commander Anigo to Nicolai.

He still lay on the ground, almost perfectly centered between the two dead Gronyxes. The Gronyx had clipped off his legs beneath his knees, but the wounds, instead of bleeding, had crystallized into a variety of brilliant, shining colors still visible in the Gronyxes' fading light.

Additional crystals had formed in the corners of Nicolai's eyes and mouth, and his breathing rasped against his lungs. Now Calum understood why Gronyx stones were so valuable—and what it cost to create them.

Calum knelt to the ground next to him, sighed, and hung his head. "I'm so sorry, Nicolai."

Nicolai looked up at him with those dark eyes, now glassy. He rasped, "Don't be."

"What's happening to him?" Lilly asked from behind Calum.

"Some kind of poisoning, I guess. When the Gronyx bit off his legs, it must've spread throughout his body." Calum clenched his teeth. "I don't know for sure, but it looks like his entire body will crystallize in time."

"Is there a cure?" Axel bent down next to Nicolai and touched one of the crystals that had formed on his severed legs. It broke off onto the dirt, still shimmering in the waning light, and Axel recoiled.

Calum smacked his hand away. "Don't touch him."

His eyes wide, Axel backed off. "Sorry."

"It's alright." Nicolai's voice scraped against his throat. "It doesn't hurt... much."

Lilly turned to Magnus. "Will your veromine help him?"

Magnus shook his head. "I regret that all the veromine in the world could not save him now."

"Calum." Nicolai's gritty voice pulled his attention back. "I know I don't have long, but I wanted to thank you again for sparing me back in the fields—both times. You believed in me when no one else did. You're —honestly—you're the best friend I've ever had."

Calum managed a half-smile. He felt horrible admitting it, but he owed Nicolai the truth, at least. "I barely know you."

Nicolai smiled, and tiny crystals rolled down his cheeks to the tunnel floor. "But I know *you*. You see the best in people, even when there isn't much worth seeing. Don't lose that."

Calum granted himself a sad chuckle, and Lilly touched his shoulder again. He turned back to glance up at her, and her warm smile eased the pain in his heart.

She gasped, and Calum turned back to find that Nicolai's chest no longer heaved up and down. His eyes had turned to glass—literally— and he'd stopped moving entirely.

You see the best in people, even when there isn't much worth seeing. Don't lose that.

Calum would remember those words as he continued his journey. They would drive him forward just as much as his dreams of Lumen did.

"Your debt to me is more than paid, my friend." Calum leaned over Nicolai and shut his eyelids with his fingers. "You have fulfilled the Law. Be at peace."

Lilly touched Calum's shoulder again, and he stood up and faced her. "He was right, you know."

"About what?"

She smiled. "About you. You truly are amazing, Calum. I don't know you that well either, but you have a genuine heart. That much is apparent."

"Thank you." He gave her hand a squeeze, though he longed for much more.

Maybe in time, he considered. After all, their journey was far from over. Who knew what the future held? *Maybe in time.*

Even in the growing darkness, Calum could see Axel glaring at him. "Are we just gonna hang around here all night and let another one of those things find us, or are we getting outta this death trap?"

"I'm afraid I can't let you do that," a firm voice said. A sword-wielding silhouette stood before the dead Gronyx's body, between them and the path to Trader's Pass, the way out of the tunnel.

Commander Anigo.

HE MUST'VE BEEN crazy to challenge five opponents in the near-darkness of the tunnel, one of whom could fly, and one of whom was the largest, strongest Saurian he'd ever seen, but Commander Anigo had a duty to perform.

He would bring as many of them to justice for their crimes as possible, even if it cost him his life in the process. He would die in the service of his King, as he'd intended for as long as he could remember, and he would receive his due reward from the Overlord in whatever afterlife awaited them.

"Come on, Commander," Calum said, exasperated. "We don't have to do this."

"On the contrary," Commander Anigo said, "we absolutely must."

"You really expect to stop all five of us?" Axel stepped forward. His left arm still hung at his side at an awkward angle.

Commander Anigo shook his head. "I don't. In fact, I expect to die in these tunnels with the rest of my men who perished if I face you in combat."

"I beat you once. I can do it again." Axel raised his sword. "Even with a dislocated arm."

Not likely. Commander Anigo smirked. "Then I'll be happy to kill you first."

"There's no need for this," Calum stepped between them, but he was smart enough to keep his sword up as well. "Commander, you'd be dead if it weren't for us."

"And I may yet die *because* of you."

The Wolf snarled at him, and the Saurian—Magnus—started forward.

"No." Calum shook his head, and Magnus stopped his advance. "You of all people should know the Law of Debt, that when one person saves another—"

"Don't presume to lecture me on the laws of this land, boy." Commander Anigo pointed his sword at Calum. "I've been studying the law since before you were born."

"Then you know you're indebted to us for saving you from death in these tunnels, just as we're indebted to you for your help in defeating these monsters," Calum said.

"That's—" Commander Anigo clenched his teeth and shifted his grip on his sword. The Gronyx's green blood had made his hilt slick in his hands. "That's not how it works."

Calum glanced at Magnus, then he looked back at Commander Anigo. "If that's not how it works, then explain where I've gone wrong?"

Commander Anigo's eyes narrowed. If he capitulated to Calum, he'd live, but he'd have to allow them to go free.

They had violated the King's laws, but the Law of Debt, which the Overlord had personally established millennia ago, superseded the King's laws.

If he refused to uphold the Law of Debt, he'd be violating the oldest and most sacred law there was—the Law he was bound to uphold first and foremost, according to the oath of service he'd sworn upon entering the King's service.

He couldn't win either way. He either forfeited his life and his obedience to the Law of Debt, or he could live and uphold the most sacred of all laws, but they would go free.

"Choose life," Lilly said from behind the others.

It was a compelling recommendation, not just because it came from someone of such beauty, but more so because she had an arrow trained on his face.

Needs, not wants, he reminded himself. He wanted to uphold the King's laws, but he *needed* to uphold the most important Law. *Needs, not wants.*

Commander Anigo exhaled an angry sigh, and he lowered his sword. "Very well."

Magnus huffed. "Wise decision."

Lilly let the tension in her bow slacken, Calum lowered his sword, and the Wolf stopped snarling, but Axel continued to glare at Commander Anigo.

"But I must make two requests of you," Commander Anigo said.

"Name them," Calum said.

"First, I request that you allow me to accompany you to the surface, and then we can part ways."

"Agreed. And the other?" Calum asked.

"I request that once we part ways, and I return to Kanarah City, that you consider me released from this debt, and I shall offer you the same courtesy," Commander Anigo said. "I have sworn an oath to the King, and I must see his mandate through to completion."

Calum glanced at Magnus, who nodded, then Calum turned back to Commander Anigo. "We would rather not have you as an enemy, but if we must agree, then we agree."

"Thank you."

"You should know, we plan to cross Trader's Pass over to Western Kanarah," Magnus said. "The King's soldiers are not a welcome sight west of the Valley of the Tri-Lakes."

"Then you should have little trouble avoiding coming into contact with me," Commander Anigo replied. "Unless you return to Eastern Kanarah, that is. Then I will be forced to continue my pursuit of you."

"Fair enough," Magnus said.

Calum motioned toward the ground. "If someone can find a torch while there's still a little light from the Gronyxes left, see if you can get it lit. Let's grab our belongings and start walking. I don't want to risk running into any more Gronyxes if we can help it."

The Wolf, Riley, nudged his leg, and Calum looked down and took the torch he held in his mouth. Commander Anigo sheathed his sword and pulled a flint from his belt. Like the other soldiers, he'd brought one of his own along.

He approached Calum, but stopped just beyond the tip of Axel's sword. He extended the flint in his hand. "Here. Use this."

"Easy, Axel." Calum pushed Axel's sword aside and took the flint from Commander Anigo. "Thank you."

With the torch lit, Lilly darted around in search of spent arrows to refill her empty quiver, and Riley roamed the tunnel looking for more torches and to identify any leftover sinkholes they might not be able to see in the darkness.

Commander Anigo stood by and watched them all. Despite his orders, he couldn't help but admit that the only reason he was still alive was because of the very people he'd been tasked to capture and bring to justice.

He rightfully had to let them go this time, but if they should happen to return to Eastern Kanarah, he would be there.

And he would be ready for them.

When they finished rounding up what supplies they could, Commander Anigo led them out of the tunnel with Riley and Axel close behind.

FINALLY FREE OF the tunnel's darkness, Calum stretched his sore limbs and sucked in his first breath of fresh air in hours.

On the horizon, the morning sun dawned over the Valley of the Tri-Lakes. In the distance, the waters of two of the Lakes glistened with golden sunlight, one to the north of Trader's Pass and one to the south.

Axel moaned and rubbed his arm. "I think it's dislocated."

Magnus beckoned him over with a wave of his hand and set down the armful of Blood Ore armor he'd carried out of the tunnels. "Let me see it."

A loud pop sounded, followed by a scream almost reminiscent of the Gronyxes' shrieks, and then a slew of curses.

"Another scream like a weak, whiny girl." Magnus shook his head. "And I thought you were supposed to be the strong one."

Axel rubbed his left shoulder and scowled up at Magnus. "A little *warning* would have been nice, *Scales.*"

Magnus shrugged. "You asked me to help you, so I helped you."

Riley just snickered.

"This is where I leave you." Commander Anigo stood facing the five of them with his back to Kanarah City, which amounted to little more than a dark blot against the horizon. "I do not wish you ill will, but I hope that you will remain far away from the scope of my influence."

"I understand." Calum nodded. He gave Commander Anigo a slight nod, then he faced his companions. "Are we ready to go?"

They nodded and turned west.

"Calum?"

He turned back to Commander Anigo.

"Thank you, all of you, for your help in the tunnels," Commander Anigo said. "What you said is true: I'd be dead without you. Regardless of our differences, I am grateful to be alive."

Calum smirked. "You know, if you want, you could come with us."

A long sigh sounded behind him. Axel asked, "Why do you insist on inviting every straggler we find to join us?"

Calum shrugged. "Look, I just figured he needed somewhere to—"

"No, thank you." Commander Anigo held up his hand. "My place is in the King's service. There is much I have left unfinished back in Solace. It is my life's work to see it done."

Calum felt exactly the same way about finding and freeing Lumen. "I understand."

As Commander Anigo turned and walked away, an invisible burden lifted from Calum's shoulders. He couldn't believe his eyes. He was actually here, on Trader's Pass, on his way to the Blood Mountains to uncover the secret to setting Lumen free.

He didn't know what would happen next, but whatever challenge rose to meet them, whatever threatened their lives, he knew they would overcome it together, glowing green blood or otherwise.

Together, Calum, Axel, Magnus, Lilly, and Riley took their first steps along Trader's Pass, their first steps toward their own bright futures and for all of Kanarah.

EPILOGUE

Lumen's eyes opened in the darkness.

He could see them, feel them. Especially the boy.

Especially Calum.

There was something special about him.

A determination, a drive, a hunger.

Those qualities had brought him and his friends much closer now.

Much closer to Lumen, to release.

As the King had proclaimed nearly a thousand years earlier, Lumen would soon be set free.

And when he was set free, he would save Kanarah.

SHAMELESS COMMERCIAL

Magnus set down the book he was reading and looked up at Calum. "This is a truly fascinating work of fiction."

"What's it called?" Calum asked as he took a seat next to Lilly against a large boulder just off Trader's Pass. To his surprise, she didn't shift away but instead fixed her curiosity on Magnus along with Calum.

"It is called *The Ghost Mine*, written by a legendary author known as Ben Wolf. It tells the thrilling story of an energy mine that reopens three years after a horrific accident, but even now, much of what happens there goes terribly awry—often at the cost of the characters' lives."

Calum shook his head. "Oh, that one? Isn't that the one you were reading at Stavian and Reginia's house?"

"The very same," Magnus replied.

"What, did you steal it, Scales?" Axel said with a scoff.

"On the contrary, Reginia offered it to me freely," Magnus said, unfazed by Axel's jab. "It is an excellent story. Though I must confess, the sciences in this book seem more like magic. Perhaps that is why it is called 'science fiction.'"

"Chalk it up to artistic license," Riley muttered from his spot atop the boulder.

"I love a good book," Lilly said. "Mind if I read it when you finish?"

"I just did." Kent handed it to her. "I am starting the next book in the trilogy."

As Lilly accepted the book and looked it over, Magnus pulled two other books out of his pack to show Calum.

"Wow. These look scary," Calum said. "But also awesome."

"Probably not any scarier than those Gronyxes we just faced down," Axel said.

"Perhaps not, but they are worth a read for anyone who enjoys mystery, plenty of horror, combat, and action," Magnus said. "In addition, Reginia was kind enough to lend me another series as well, one much closer to our own story, but set in a different world with vastly different rules and extraordinary magic."

Riley's ears perked up. "Alright... now you've got my attention. If I had opposable thumbs, I might ask to borrow that series from you."

"Perhaps I could read them to you," Magnus offered. "Take look."

"Reginia said she contacted and ordered signed copies of these books from Ben Wolf directly, thanks to some sorcery known as 'email.' And apparently, the books are also available through a worldwide vendor known as 'Amazon.'"

Lilly gave an enthusiastic nod. "I'm gonna start reading now!"

"I wouldn't mind reading the first one of the Blood Mercenaries books if you're willing to share," Calum said. "I'll read it to you, Riley."

Riley smirked. "I'm up for that."

Axel rolled his eyes and turned away from the group. "Let them read their books. I'm more concerned with something else. You—yeah, you, the person reading this—you should write a review of *this* book on Amazon. It'll help Ben Wolf write more stories, and it might keep him from being as poor as we are."

Axel paused for a long moment.

"Seriously, though—why are you still reading this? Go write the review while this story is fresh in your mind," he insisted. "Do it now. And don't forget to read the next book in our series as well so you can watch me save everyone's butts a bunch more times." Axel sighed. "What would these nimrods do without me?"

THIS BOOK IS OVER, BUT THE ADVENTURE DOESN'T STOP HERE!

The story continues in *THE WAY OF ANCIENT POWER*
Book Two of THE CALL OF ANCIENT LIGHT SERIES

Need more books? Check out www.benwolf.com
or email me directly at ben@benwolf.com to place your orders.

If you enjoyed this book, please leave a review on Amazon.com!

ACKNOWLEDGMENTS

I first started this series twelve years ago (in Feb. of 2009) because of a map I saw in a dream, much like Calum did in this story. At the time, I was working in Brooks Brothers as a sales guy, and jotting this story helped me pass the time in an otherwise mindless and miserable job.

Like Calum, I felt I was meant for something more, but I didn't know how to get out of my daily rut. Seven months later, I attended the first writers conference of my life—one that changed my life forever.

Now this book has not only been published, but someone—you—chose to pick it up and read it. So thank YOU for reading.

Thank you to Jesus Christ for changing my life forever.

Second, thanks to my parents for believing in me from an early age and for helping to support my dreams and my growth. I love you both.

Thanks to my all-star beta readers, Daniel Kuhnley, Luke Messa, and Paige Guido, for your excellent feedback and encouragement.

Thank you to Andrew Winch and Davis Bunn, who both critiqued early horrible versions of this book. Your input helped me out so much.

Hannah Sternjakob, you are a genius. The cover is exactly what I'd envisioned (only better). Thank you for your long-suffering patience!

Thanks to all of my readers! Without you, I wouldn't be doing this.

Lastly, thank you especially to my intelligent, beautiful, and ultra-supportive wife, Charis Crowe. Your flexibility with my weird writing schedule makes all the difference in getting my writing done. I love you.

About Ben Wolf

In 7th grade, I saw the movie *Congo*. Then I wrote a parody of it set in Australia that featured killer kangaroos. So began my writing career.

I've spoken at 50+ writers conferences and comic cons nationwide. When not writing, I occasionally choke people in jiu jitsu. I live in the Midwest with my gorgeous wife, our kids, and our cats Marco and Ivy.

Check out my other books on Amazon.com.

Want updates? Sign up for my author email newsletter now!

WWW.SUBSCRIBEPAGE.COM/FANTASY-READERS

Or find me on social media:

facebook.com/1benwolf
instagram.com/1benwolf
amazon.com/author/benwolf